"DEARLY BELOVED, WE ARE GATHERED..."

Dazed, Tallie stood there listening to herself being married to The Icicle. And a very bad-tempered icicle he was, too. He was positively glaring at her. Of course, he did have reason to be a little cross, but it wasn't as if she had meant to hit him on the nose, after all.

Mind you, she thought dejectedly, he seemed always to be furious about something—mainly with her. Toward others, he invariably remained cool, polite and, in a chilly sort of fashion, charming. But not with Tallie... It didn't augur at all well for the future.

Anne Gracie was born in Australia, but spent her youth on the move, living in Malaysia, Greece and different parts of Australia before settling down. Her love of the Regency period began at the age of eleven, when she braved the adult library to borrow a Georgette Heyer novel, firmly convinced she would at any moment be ignominiously ejected and sent back to the children's library in disgrace. She wasn't. Anne lives in Melbourne, in a small wooden house that she will one day renovate.

TALLIE'S KNIGHT

ANNE GRACIE

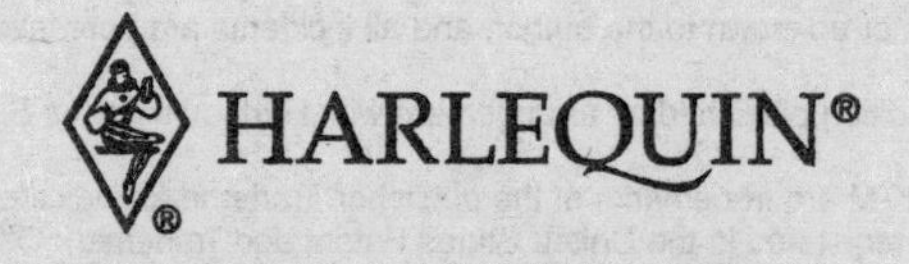

TORONTO • NEW YORK • LONDON
AMSTERDAM • PARIS • SYDNEY • HAMBURG
STOCKHOLM • ATHENS • TOKYO • MILAN • MADRID
PRAGUE • WARSAW • BUDAPEST • AUCKLAND

ISBN 0-373-51137-X

TALLIE'S KNIGHT

This edition published by arrangement with Harlequin Books S.A.

Visit us at www.eHarlequin.com

Printed in U.S.A.

Prologue

Yorkshire, February 1803

'My lord, I...I am sure that Mr Freddie—'

'Mr *Freddie*?' Lord d'Arenville's disapproving voice interrupted the maidservant. She flushed, smoothing her hands nervously down her starched white apron.

'Er...Reverend Winstanley, I mean, sir. He won't keep you waiting long, sir, 'tis just that—'

'There is no need to explain,' Lord d'Arenville coldly informed her. 'I've no doubt Reverend Winstanley will come as soon as he is able. I shall wait.' His hard grey gaze came to rest on a nearby watercolour. It was a clear dismissal. The maid backed hurriedly out of the parlour, turned and almost ran down the corridor.

Magnus, Lord d'Arenville, glanced around the room, observing its inelegant proportions and the worn and shabby furniture. A single poky window allowed an inadequate amount of light into the room. He strolled over to it, looked out and frowned. The window overlooked the graveyard, providing the occupants of the house with a depressing prospect of mortality.

Lord, how unutterably dreary, Magnus thought, seating himself on a worn, uncomfortable settee. Did all vicars live this way? He didn't think so, but he couldn't be certain, not having lived the sort of life that brought him into intimacy with the clergy. Quite the contrary, in fact. And had not his oldest friend, Freddie Winstanley, donned the ecclesiastical dog collar, Magnus would be languishing in blissful ignorance still.

Magnus sighed. Bored, stale and unaccountably restless, he'd decided on the spur of the moment to drive all the way up to Yorkshire to visit Freddie, whom he'd not seen for years. And now, having arrived, he was wondering if he'd done the right thing, calling unannounced at the cramped and shabby vicarage.

A faint giggle interrupted his musings. Magnus frowned and looked around. There was no one in sight. The giggle came again. Magnus frowned. He did not care to be made fun of.

'Who is there?'

'Huwwo, man.' The voice came, slightly muffled, from a slight bulge in the curtains. As he looked, the curtains parted and a mischievous little face peeked out at him.

Magnus blinked. It was a child, a very small child—a female, he decided after a moment. He'd never actually met a child this size before, and though he was wholly unacquainted with infant fashions it seemed to him that the child looked more female than otherwise. It had dark curly hair and big brown pansy eyes. And it was certainly looking at him in that acquisitive way that so many females had.

He glanced towards the doorway, hoping someone would come and fetch the child back to where it belonged.

'Huwwo, man,' the moppet repeated sternly.

Magnus raised an eyebrow. Clearly he was expected to answer. How the devil did one address children anyway?

'How do you do?' he said after a moment.

At that, she smiled, and launched herself towards him in an unsteady rush. Horrified, Magnus froze. Contrary to all his expectations she crossed the room without coming to grief, landing at his knee. Grinning up at him, she clutched his immaculate buckskins in two damp, chubby fists. Magnus flinched. His valet would have a fit. The child's hands were certain to be grubby. And sticky. Magnus might know nothing at all about children, but he was somehow sure about that.

'Up, man.' The moppet held up her arms in clear expectation of being picked up.

Magnus frowned down at her, trusting that his hitherto unchallenged ability to rid himself of unwanted feminine attention would be just as effective on this diminutive specimen.

The moppet frowned back at him.

Magnus allowed his frown to deepen to a glare.

The moppet glared back. 'Up, man,' she repeated, thumping a tiny fist on his knee.

Magnus cast a hunted glance towards the doorway, still quite appallingly empty.

The small sticky fist tugged his arm. 'Up!' she demanded again.

'No, thank you,' said Magnus in his most freezingly polite voice. Lord, would no one come and rescue him?

The big eyes widened and the small rosebud mouth drooped. The lower lip trembled, displaying to Magnus's jaundiced eye all the unmistakable signs of a female about to burst into noisy, black-mailing tears. They certainly started young. No wonder they were so good at it by the time they grew up.

The little face crumpled.

Oh, Lord, thought Magnus despairingly. There was no help for it—he would have to pick her up. Gingerly he reached out, lifting her carefully by the waist until she was at eye-level with him. Her little feet dangled and she regarded him solemnly.

She reached out a pair of chubby, dimpled arms. 'Cudd'w!'

Again, her demand was unmistakable. Cautiously he brought her closer, until suddenly she wrapped her arms around his neck in a strong little grip that surprised him. In seconds she had herself comfortably ensconced on his lap, leaning back against one of his arms, busily ruining his neckcloth. It had only taken him half an hour to achieve its perfection, Magnus told himself wryly.

She chattered to him nonstop in a confiding flow, a mixture of English and incomprehensible gibberish, pausing every now and then to ask what sounded like a question. Magnus found himself replying. Lord, if anyone saw him now, he would never live it down. But he had no choice—he didn't want to see that little face crumple again.

Once she stopped in the middle of what seemed an especially involved tale and looked up at him, scrutinising his face in a most particular fashion. Magnus felt faintly apprehensive, wondering what she might do. She reached up and traced the long, vertical groove in his right cheek with a small, soft finger.

'What's dis?'

He didn't know what to say. A wrinkle? A crease? A long

dimple? No one had ever before had the temerity to refer to it. 'Er...it's my cheek.'

She traced the groove once more, thoughtfully, then took his chin in one hand, turned his head, and traced the matching line down his other cheek. Then carefully, solemnly, she traced both at the same time. She stared at him for a moment, then, smiling, returned to her story, reaching up every now and then to trace a tiny finger down the crease in his cheek.

Gradually her steady chatter dwindled and the curly little head began to nod. Abruptly she yawned and snuggled herself more firmly into the crook of his arms. 'Nigh-nigh,' she murmured, and suddenly he felt the small body relax totally against him.

She was asleep. Sound asleep—right there in his arms.

For a moment Magnus froze, wondering what to do, then slowly he began to breathe again. He knew himself to be a powerful man—both physically and in worldly terms—but never in his life had he been entrusted with the warm weight of a sleeping child. It was an awesome responsibility.

He sat there frozen for some twenty minutes, until a faint commotion sounded in the hall. A pretty young woman glanced in, a harried expression on her face. Freddie's wife. Joan. Jane. Or was it Jenny? Magnus was fairly sure he recognised her from the wedding. She opened her mouth to speak, and then saw the small sleeping figure in his arms.

'Oh, thank heavens!' she exclaimed. 'We've been looking everywhere for her.'

She turned and called to someone in the hallway. 'Martha, run and tell Mr Freddie that we've found her.'

She turned back to Magnus. 'I'm so sorry, Lord d'Arenville. We thought she'd got out into the garden and we've all been outside searching. Has she been a shocking nuisance?'

Magnus bethought himself of his ruined neckcloth and his no longer immaculate buckskins. His arm had a cramp from being unable to move and he had a nasty suspicion that there was a damp spot on his coat from where the little moppet had nuzzled his sleeve as she slept.

'Not at all,' he said slowly. 'It's been a pleasure.'

And, to his great surprise, Magnus realised he meant it.

Chapter One

London, February 1803

'I want you to help me find a wife, Tish.'

'Oh, certainly. Whose wife are you after?' responded Laetitia flippantly, trying to cover her surprise. It was not like her self-sufficient cousin Magnus to ask help of anyone.

His chill grey stare bit into her. 'I meant a bride. I find my own amours, thank you,' said Magnus stiffly.

'A *bride*? You? I don't believe it, Magnus! You've hardly even talked to a respectable female in years—'

'Which is why I require your assistance now. I wish the marriage to take place as soon as possible.'

'As soon as possible? Heavens! You will have the matchmaking mamas in a tizzy!' Laetitia sat back in her chair and regarded her cousin with faintly malicious amusement, elegantly pencilled eyebrows raised in mock surprise. 'The impregnable Lord d'Arenville, on the scramble for a bride?' Her rather hard blue eyes narrowed suddenly. 'May I ask what has brought this on? I mean, seeking a bride is unexceptional enough—you will have to set up your nursery some time soon—but such unseemly haste suggests... There is no...ah...*financial* necessity for this marriage, is there, Magnus?'

Magnus frowned repressively. 'Do not be ridiculous, Tish. No, it is as you have suggested—I have decided to set up my nursery. I want children.'

'Heirs, you mean, Magnus. Sons are what you need. You wouldn't want a string of girls, would you?'

Magnus didn't reply. A string of girls didn't sound at all bad, he thought. Little girls with big clear eyes, ruining his neckcloths while telling him long, incomprehensible stories. But sons would be good, too, he thought, recalling Freddie's sturdy-legged boy, Sam.

The issue of getting an heir was, in fact, the last thing on his mind, even though he was the last of a very distinguished name. Until his journey to Yorkshire it had been a matter of perfect indifference to Magnus if his name and title ended with him. They had, after all, brought him nothing but misery throughout his childhood and youth.

However, far easier to let society believe that d'Arenville required an heir than that a small, sticky moppet had found an unexpected chink in his armour. It was ridiculous, Magnus had told himself a thousand times. He didn't *need* anything. Or anyone. He never had and he never would. He'd learned that lesson very young.

But the chink remained. As did the memory of a sleeping, trustful child in his arms. And a soft little finger curiously tracing a line down his cheek.

It was a pity he'd had to ask Laetitia's assistance. He'd never liked her, and saw her only as often as duty or coincidence demanded. But someone had to introduce him to an eligible girl, damn it! If he wanted children he had to endure the distasteful rigmarole of acquiring a wife, and Laetitia could help expedite the matter with the least fuss and bother.

He returned to the point of issue. 'You will assist me, Tish?'

'What exactly did you have in mind? Almack's? Balls, routs and morning calls?' She laughed. 'I must confess, I cannot imagine you doing the pretty, with all the fond mamas looking on, but it will be worth it, if only for the entertainment.'

He shuddered inwardly at the picture she conjured up, but his face remained impassive and faintly disdainful. 'No, not quite. I thought a house party might do the trick.'

'A house party?' She shuddered delicately. 'I loathe the country at this time of year.'

Magnus shrugged. 'It needn't be for long. A week or so will do.'

'A week!' Laetitia almost shrieked. 'A week to court a bride! Lord, the *ton* will never stop talking about it.'

Magnus clenched his jaw. If there had been any other way he would have walked out then and there. But his cousin was a young, apparently respectable, society matron—exactly what he required. No one else could so easily introduce him to eligible young ladies. And she could help him circumvent the tedium of the dreaded marriage mart—courting under the eyes of hundreds. He shuddered inwardly again. Laetitia might be a shallow featherbrain with a taste for malicious gossip, and he disliked having to ask for her assistance in anything, but she was all he had.

'Will you do it?' he repeated.

Laetitia's delicately painted features took on a calculating look. Magnus was familiar with the expression; he usually encountered it on the faces of less respectable females, though he'd first learnt it from his mother. He relaxed. This aspect of the female of the species was one he knew how to deal with.

'It might be awkward for me to get away—the Season may not have started, but we have numerous engagements...' She glanced meaningfully at the over-mantel mirror, the gilt frame of which bore half a dozen engraved invitations.

'And to organise a house party at Manningham at such short notice...' She sighed. 'Well, it is a great deal of work, and I would have to take on extra help, you know...and George might not like it, for it will be very expens—'

'I will cover all expenses, of course,' Magnus interrupted. 'And I'll make it worth your while, too, Laetitia. Would diamonds make it any easier to forgo your balls and routs for a week or two?'

Laetitia pursed her lips, annoyed at his bluntness but unable to resist the bait. 'What—?'

'Necklace, earrings and bracelet.' His cold grey eyes met hers with cynical indifference. Laetitia bridled at his cool certainty.

'Oh, Magnus, how vulgar you are. As if I would wish to be paid for assisting my dearest cous—'

'Then you don't want the diamonds?'

'No, no, no. I didn't say that. Naturally, if you care to present me with some small token...'

'Good, then it's decided. You invite half a dozen girls—'

'—and their mamas.'

A faint grimace disturbed the cool impassivity of his expression. 'I suppose so. Anyway, you invite them, and I'll choose one.'

Laetitia shuddered delicately. 'So cold-blooded, Magnus. No wonder they call you The Ic—'

His freezing look cut her off in midsentence. He stood up to leave.

'You cannot intend to leave yet, surely?' said Laetitia.

He regarded her in faint puzzlement. 'Why not? It is all decided, is it not?'

'But *which* girls do you want me to invite?' she demanded through her teeth.

Magnus looked at her with blank surprise. He shrugged. 'Damn it, Tish, I don't know. That's your job.' He walked towards the door.

'I don't believe it! You want *me* to choose your bride for you?' she shrieked shrilly.

Faint irritation appeared in his eyes. 'No, I'll choose her from the girls you pick out. Lord, Tish, haven't you got it straight yet? What else have we been talking about for the last fifteen minutes?'

Laetitia stared at him in stupefaction. He was picking out a bride with no more care than he would take to buy a horse. Less, actually. Magnus was very particular about his horseflesh.

'Are... I mean, do you have any special requirements?' she said at last.

Magnus sat down again. He had not really thought past the idea of children, but it was a fair request, he supposed. He thought for a moment. 'She must be sound, of course...with good bloodlines, naturally. Umm...good teeth, reasonably intelligent, but with a placid temperament...and wide enough hips—for childbearing, you know. I think that about covers it.'

Laetitia gritted her teeth. 'We are talking about a lady, are we not? Or are you only after a brood mare?'

Magnus ignored her sarcasm. He shrugged. 'More or less, I suppose. I have little interest in the dam, only the offspring.'

'Do you not even care what she looks like?'

'Not particularly. Although I suppose I'd prefer someone good-looking, at least passably so. But *not* beautiful. A beautiful wife would be too much trouble.' His lips twitched sardonically. 'I've known too many beautiful wives not to realise what a temptation they are—to others.'

His subtle reference was not lost on Laetitia, and to her annoyance she found herself flushing slightly under his ironic gaze. She would have liked to fling his request in his even white teeth. However, a diamond necklace, earrings and a bracelet were not to be looked in the mouth.

Even if Lord d'Arenville's bride was.

'I'll do my best,' she said sourly.

The black knight reached down, caught her around the waist and lifted her onto his gallant charger, up and away, out of reach of the slavering wolves snapping at her heels.

'Begone you vicious curs!' he shouted in a thrillingly deep, manly voice. 'This tender morsel is not for you!' His arms tightened around her, protectively, tenderly, possessively. 'Hold on, my pretty one, I have you safe now,' he murmured in her ear, his warm breath stirring the curls at her nape. 'And now I have you, Tallie, my little love, I'll never let you go.' Clasping her hard against his broad, strong chest, he lowered his mouth to hers...

'Miss? Miss Tallie? Are you all right?'

Tallie jerked out of her reverie with a start. The buttons she had been sorting spilled out over the table and she scrabbled hurriedly to retrieve them. Brooks, her cousin's elderly butler, and Mrs Wilmot, the housekeeper, were bending over her, concerned.

'Oh, yes, yes, perfectly,' Tallie, blushing, hastened to assure them. 'I was in a silly daze—miles away, I'm afraid. Was there something you wanted?'

Brooks proffered a letter on a silver tray. 'A letter, Miss Tallie. From the mistress.'

Tallie smiled. Brooks still behaved as if he were in charge of the grand London mansion, instead of stuck away in the country house belonging to Tallie's cousin Laetitia. Tallie took the letter from the tray and thanked him. Dear Brooks—as if she were the lady of the house, receiving correspondence in the parlour, instead of a poor relation, dreaming foolish dreams over a jar of old buttons. She broke open the wafer and began to read.

'Oh, no!' Tallie closed her eyes as a sudden surge of bitterness rushed through her. She had assumed that with Christmas over, and Laetitia and George returned to Town, she and the children would be left in peace for several months at least.

'What is it, Miss Tallie? Bad news?'

'No, no—or at least nothing tragic, at any rate.' Tallie hastened to reassure the elderly housekeeper. She glanced across at Brooks, and explained.

'Cousin Laetitia writes to say she is holding a house party here. We are to make all the arrangements for the accommodation and entertainment of six or seven young ladies and their mothers, possibly a number of fathers also. Five or six other gentlemen may be invited, too; she is not yet decided. And there is to be a ball at the end of two weeks.' Tallie looked at Brooks and Mrs Wilmot, shook her head in mild disbelief, and took a deep drink of the tea grown cold at her elbow.

Mrs Wilmot had been counting. 'Accommodation and entertainment for up to twenty-five or six of the gentry, and almost twice that number of servants if we just count on a valet or maidservant for each gentleman or lady. Lawks, Miss Tallie, I don't know how we'll ever manage. When is this house party to be, did she say?'

Tallie nodded, a look of dire foreboding in her eyes. 'The guests will start arriving on Tuesday next. Cousin Laetitia will come the day before, to make sure everything is in order.'

'Tuesday next? Tuesday next! Lord, miss, whatever shall we do? Arrangements for sixty or more people to stay, arriving on Tuesday next! We will never manage it! Never.'

Tallie took a deep breath. 'Yes, we will, Mrs Wilmot. We have no choice—you know that. However, my cousin has, for once, considered the extra work it will entail for you both and all the other servants.'

'And for you, Miss Tallie,' added Brooks.

She smiled. She knew he meant well, but it was not a comforting thought that even her cousin's servants regarded her as one of them, even if they did call her Miss Tallie. She continued.

'I am empowered to hire as much extra help as we need, and no expense spared, though I am to keep strict accounts of all expenditure.'

'No expense spar—' In a less dignified person, Brooks's expression would have been likened to a gaping fish.

Tallie attempted to keep a straight face. The prospect of Cousin Laetitia showing enough consideration for her servants to hire extra help was surprising enough, but for her *not* to consider expense would astound any who knew her.

'No, for she says the house party is for her cousin Lord d'Arenville's benefit, and he is to pay for everything, which is why I am to keep accounts.'

'Ahh.' Brooks shut his mouth and looked wise.

'Lord d'Arenville? Lawks, what would he want with a house party full of young ladies—oh, I see.' Mrs Wilmot nodded in sudden comprehension. 'Courting.'

'I beg your pardon?' said Tallie, puzzled.

'He's courting. Lord d'Arenville. One of those young ladies must be his intended, and he wishes some time with her before he pops the question. He'll probably announce it at the ball.'

'Well, well, so that's it. A courting couple in the old house once again.' Brooks's face creased in a sentimental smile.

'Lord, Mr Brooks, you're a born romantic if ever I saw one,' said Mrs Wilmot. 'I can no more see that Lord d'Arenville lost in love's young dream than I can see me flying through the air on one of me own sponge cakes!'

Tallie stifled a giggle at the image conjured up. 'And why is that, Mrs Wilmot?' she asked.

'Why?' Mrs Wilmot turned to Tallie in surprise. 'Oh, yes, you've never met him, have you, dearie? I keep forgetting, you're related to the other side of madam's family. Well, you've not missed out on much—a cold fish if ever I saw one, that Lord d'Arenville. They call him The Icicle, you know. Not a drop of warm blood in his body, if you ask me.'

'But I thought all you females thought him so handsome,' began Brooks. 'He had you all in such a tizz—'

'Handsome is as handsome does, I always say,' said the housekeeper darkly. 'And though he may be as handsome as a statue of one of them Greek gods, he's about as warm and lively as a statue, too!' She shook her head and pursed her lips disapprovingly.

Intrigued though she was, Tallie knew she should not encourage gossip about her cousin's guests. And they had more than enough to do without wasting time in idle speculation. Or even idol speculation, she giggled silently, thinking of the Greek god.

'Well, then,' she said, 'it is fortunate that we need not concern ourselves with Lord d'Arenville except to spend his money and present him with a reckoning. And if we need not worry about expense, the servants may be billeted in the village. I suppose we should begin to make a list of what needs to be done.' She glanced at the clock on the mantel. 'I am expected back in the nursery in half an hour, so we will need to hurry.'

Later that evening, as she walked slowly out of the nursery, leaving her three charges yawning sleepily in their beds, their loving goodnight kisses still damp on her cheeks, Tallie decided she would have to take herself more firmly under control. She could not go on in this fashion.

The degree of resentment she'd felt this morning had shocked her. And it was not Laetitia's thoughtlessness Tallie resented, but the mere fact that she was coming home.

It was very wrong of her to feel like that; Tallie knew it. She ought to feel grateful to Laetitia for the many things she had done for her—giving her a home, letting her look after her children... And it was Laetitia's home, Laetitia's children. Laetitia was entitled to visit whenever she wished.

The problem lay with Tallie. As it always did. With her foolish pretences and silly, childish make-believe. It was getting out of hand, pretending, day after day, that these three adorable children were hers. And that their father, a dashing and romantic if somewhat hazy figure, was away on some splendid adventure, fighting pirates, perhaps, or exploring some mysterious new land. She had dreamed so often of how he would arrive home on his coal-black steed, bringing exotic gifts for her and the children. And when they had put the children to bed he would take her in his arms and kiss her tenderly and tell her she was his pretty one, his love, his little darling...

No. It had to stop. She was no one's pretty one, no one's darling. The children's father was bluff, stodgy George, who drank too much and pinched Tallie's bottom whenever she was forgetful enough to pass within reach. He never came near the children except at Christmas, when he would give them each a shilling or two and pat them on the head. And their mother was Laetitia, beautiful, selfish, charming Laetitia, ornament of the London *ton*.

Tallie Robinson was nothing—a distant cousin with not a penny to her name; a plain, ordinary girl with nothing to recommend her; a girl who ought to be grateful to be given a home in the country and three lovely children to look after.

There would never be a dashing knight or handsome prince, she told herself savagely. The best hope she had was that a kind gentleman farmer might want her. A widower, probably, with children who needed mothering and who would notice her in church. He would look at her plain brown hair and her plain brown eyes and her plain, sensible clothes and decide she would do. He would not mind that her nose was pointy, and marred by a dozen or so freckles—which *no* amount of lemon juice or buttermilk would shift. He would not care that one of her front teeth was slightly crooked, nor that she used to bite her nails to the quick.

Tallie looked down at her hands and smiled with pride at her smooth, elegant nails. That was one defect, at least, she had conquered since she left school. Her kindly gentleman farmer would be proud... Drat it—she was doing it again. Weaving fantasies with the slenderest of threads. Wasting time when there were a thousand and one things to be done to prepare for Cousin Laetitia's house party. Tallie hurried downstairs.

The Russian Prince cracked his whip over the arched necks of his beautiful grey horses, urging them to even greater speed. The curricle swayed dangerously, but the Prince paid no heed—he was in pursuit of the vile kidnappers... No! Lord d'Arenville was not a prince, Tallie told herself sternly. She patted her hair into place and smoothed her hands down her skirts. He was real. And he was here to be with his intended bride. He was *not* to appear in any of her silly fantasies.

But Mrs Wilmot was right—he certainly was handsome. Tallie waited for her cousin to call her forward and introduce her to the guest of honour. He had arrived only minutes before, clad in a caped driving coat and curly brimmed beaver, sweeping up the drive in a smart curricle drawn by two exquisitely matched greys. Tallie knew nothing at all about horses, but even she could tell his equipage and the greys were something out of the ordinary.

She'd watched him alight, springing lightly down from the curricle, tossing the reins to his groom and stepping forward to inspect his sweating horses before turning to greet his hosts. And thus, his priorities, Tallie told herself ironically—horses before people. Definitely *not* a prince.

He was terribly handsome, though. Dark hair, thick and springy, short cropped against a well-shaped head. A cleanly chiselled face, hard in its austerity, a long, straight nose, and firm, unsmiling, finely moulded lips. His jaw was also long, squaring off at the chin in a blunt, uncompromising fashion. He was tall, with long, hard horseman's legs and a spare frame. And once he'd removed his greatcoat she could see that the broad shoulders were not a result of padding, but of well-developed musculature. A sportsman, not a dandy... *A pirate king...* No! A haughty guest of her haughty cousin.

Tallie watched him greet Laetitia—a light bow, a raised brow and a mere touch of lips to hand. No more than politeness dictated. He was not one of her...*cicisbeos*, then. Tallie heaved a sigh of relief. It was not to be one of *those* house parties. Good. She hated it when her cousin used Tallie and the children to cover up what she called her 'little flirtations'.

Laetitia turned to introduce him to those of the staff whose names he might need—the butler, the housekeeper and so on. Tallie watched him, noting the way his heavy-lidded grey eyes flickered indifferently over Brooks and Mrs Wilmot.

'And this is a distant cousin of mine, Miss Thalia Robinson, who resides here and keeps an eye on things for me.' *Insignificant poor relation who hangs on my sleeve, depending on my charity,* said her tone, dismissively.

Tallie smiled and curtsied. The cold grey eyes rested on her for a bare half-second and moved on. Tallie flinched, knowing that in a single glance Lord d'Arenville had noticed the freckles, the pointy nose *and* the crooked tooth, and despised her. He hadn't even glanced at her nice nails. *No gallant knight, he, but a cruel count, coldly plotting the heroine's downfa—* Enough!

Tallie watched his progression into the house with rueful disappointment. Mrs Wilmot was right. The man acted as if he expected the whole world to fall at his feet, while he would not so much as notice if it crumbled to dust right under his long, aristocratic nose! She wondered which of the young ladies was his intended. She had not taken to any of them, but she could not imagine anyone wishing to wed this arrogant Icicle.

'Thalia!' Her cousin sounded annoyed. Tallie hurried inside.

'You called, Cousin Laetitia?' She did not allow herself to look at Lord d'Arenville, although she was very aware of him standing close by.

'I thought I made myself clear!' Her cousin gestured crossly.

Tallie looked upwards and repressed a grin. Three small heads were poking through the railings in complete defiance of the orders which Laetitia had issued to the nursery. Children were neither to be seen nor heard during the house party.

'I'll see to it at once, Cousin.'

'Your children, Tish?' His voice was deep and resonant. In a warmer-natured man it could be very appealing, thought Tallie irrelevantly as she gathered her skirts to run up the stairs.

'Do they not wish to come down?' he added.

Tallie paused and looked at him in surprise. The Icicle was interested in her cousin's children? No, for he seemed wholly engrossed in removing a speck of fluff from his sleeve.

'No, they do not,' said Laetitia quickly. 'It is high time they went to bed, and it is one of Thalia's little duties to see that they do so. Thalia! If you please!'

Tallie ran quickly up the stairs, biting her lip to prevent the retort she knew would escape if she stayed a moment longer. Time they were in bed, indeed! At five o'clock in the afternoon? And *one* of her little duties? Amongst the other hundred or so her cousin daily required of her in exchange for bed and board. She reached the second landing where two little girls and a boy were sitting. Watched by two pairs of eyes, she lifted up the toddler, took the other little girl by the hand and headed for the nursery, the small boy jumping and hopping on ahead.

'Now, Magnus,' said Laetitia, 'Brooks will show you to your room, and you can prepare yourself to meet my other guests in the drawing room at about six. Brooks, have hot water sent to his lordship's room immediately. And...brandy, Magnus? Or would you prefer a cup of tea?'

'A refreshment tray has already been sent up, madam, with hot tea and coffee, sandwiches *and* brandy,' said Brooks. 'And the hot water is awaiting his lordship.'

'Oh, er, good. Well-done, Brooks,' said Laetitia.

'Miss Tallie saw to it all, madam. She does the same for all the guests,' said Brooks, hiding a smile. Just another of her *little duties*. He felt the cold gaze of Lord d'Arenville on him and his face pokered up into its usual butlerish impassivity.

'If you would care to follow me, your lordship. Madam has put you in the Blue Room, as usual.'

'Thalia, you must dine at table this evening. That wretch Jimmy Fairfax has brought two friends with him and we have a shortage of ladies. And did you tell Cook that we must have goose as well as the capons? I have no time to discuss the menu with her so you must check it. And see that the extra guests have beds made up for them. I am utterly exhausted and need to repose myself before dinner. Lord, I hope Magnus is grateful for the efforts I am making on his behalf. I shall be glad when it's all over.'

Tallie mentally agreed. The last ten days had been exhausting and frustrating, and she was counting the hours until the guests departed. Still, she flattered herself that everything was going off quite smoothly.

This was, however, one order she felt unable to carry out. 'I have nothing to wear to dinner, Cousin.'

'Lord, girl, as if anyone will care what you wear. No one will take any notice of you—you are just there to make up the numbers. Any old thing will do.'

'I have only one evening dress, Cousin, the one you gave me several years ago, and as you must know it does not fit me.'

'Then alter it, for heaven's sake! Or wear a shawl or something over it. I cannot be expected to think of everything! Now leave me at once, for if I do not get some peace and quiet I fear I will have the headache by dinnertime.'

'Yes, Cousin,' Tallie murmured between her teeth. It went very much against the grain to submit so tamely to her cousin's rudeness, but poverty had taught her to take a more pragmatic view. In the short term, it was unbearable to be treated in this fashion. On the other hand, Laetitia was rarely here, and for most of the year at Manningham there were just Tallie and the children and servants. In truth, she told herself severely, she had a delightful life. An orphan with not a penny to her name ought to be grateful to have a roof over her head. That she didn't *feel* grateful was, no doubt, a deficiency of character.

Tallie hurried downstairs. She consulted with Cook about the menu, Mrs Wilmot about the arrangements for the unexpected guests and Brooks about the wines for dinner, then hurried back upstairs to see to her dress.

Ten minutes later she was in despair. Laetitia was a smaller woman than she, with a dainty, sylphlike figure. The pale green muslin gown was designed to sweep low across the bosom and shoulders and fall loosely from a high waistline. On Tallie the deeply scooped neckline clung, causing her bosom to bulge embarrassingly. The waist was too tight and her ankles were scandalously revealed. Tallie went to her wardrobe and glanced through it again, desperately hoping that by some magical process an alternative would present itself. Two winter day dresses, two summer day dresses, all rather worn and out of date. She sighed and returned gloomily to the green muslin.

She was no needlewoman, and even if she were she could not make larger that which was too small in the first place. After some experimentation she managed to fill in the neckline with a piece of old lace, so that it covered her decently at least, even if it was still too tight. She tacked a frill along the hem. It looked quite ridiculous, she knew, but at least it covered her ankles.

Finally she draped herself in a large paisley shawl to disguise the tightness of the dress. It would surely suffice to get her through dinner. She glanced at herself in the glass and closed her eyes in momentary mortification. The green colour did bring interesting highlights to her brown hair and eyes, and her curly hair was neat for once, but—she looked a perfect quiz! Still, she told herself bracingly, Laetitia was right. No one would take any notice of her. She was just an extra female—the poor relation—and she would slip away the moment dinner was over. In any case, she didn't like her cousin's guests, so what did it matter what they thought of her? Taking a deep breath, she headed downstairs to check on the arrangements for dinner.

Magnus took another sip of armagnac and wondered how much longer he could endure the girlish flutterings going on around him. His temper was on a knife-edge and he had no one to blame but himself. The house party had been a disaster.

Ten days of the unalleviated company of high-bred young women would have been bad enough—he'd nerved himself for that ordeal. But he should have realised that Laetitia would select a gaggle of young ladies most like herself—spoiled, vain, vapid and silly. Magnus was almost rigid with boredom.

And exasperation—for he'd hoped to observe the young ladies unobtrusively, make a discreet selection and quietly arrange a marriage. Ha! What a joke! His wretched cousin had about as much discretion as a parrot! That had been made plain to Magnus within days, when he'd realised he was being hunted—with all the subtlety of a pack of hounds in full pursuit.

Creamy bosoms were made to heave and quiver under his nose at every opportunity. Well-turned ankles flashed from modest concealment. And every time he entered a room eyelashes batted so feverishly there was almost a draught. He'd been treated to displays of virtuosity on harp, pianoforte and flute, had folios of watercolours thrust under his nose, his expert inspection bashfully solicited. His superior masculine opinion had been sought and deferred to on every topic under the sun and his every reluctant pronouncement greeted with sighs, sycophantic titters and syrupy admiration.

They accosted him morning, noon and night—in the garden, in the drawing room, in the breakfast parlour—even, once, behind the stables, where a man had a right to expect some peace and quiet. But it was no use—eligible misses lurked, apparently, in every corner of the estate.

Yet, despite his overwhelming aversion to the task in hand, Magnus was still determined to select a wife. The house party had convinced him it was best to get the deed over with as soon as possible. Any courtship was bound to be appalling to a man of his solitary tastes, he reasoned, and if he did not choose now, he would only prolong the process. And this collection of girls seemed no different from any others currently on the marriage mart.

The trouble was, Magnus could not imagine any of them as mother to his children. Not one had two thoughts to rub together; each seemed completely devoted to fashion, gossip and male flattery—not necessarily in that order. And, like Laetitia, they despised rural life.

That was a problem. He had somehow assumed his wife would live at d'Arenville with the children. Though why he should expect his wife to live in the country when few women of his acquaintance did so, Magnus could not imagine. His own mother certainly had not. She hadn't been able to bear the country. But then he didn't want a wife like his mother.

Freddie's wife lived, seemingly content, all year round in the wilds of Yorkshire with her husband and children. The children's obvious happiness had made a profound impression on Magnus—his own parents had been virtual strangers who had descended on his home at infrequent intervals, their visits the bane of his youthful existence.

But Freddie's wife truly seemed to love her children. Magnus's own mother had appeared to love Magnus—in company. So Freddie's wife could have been fudging it, but Magnus didn't think so. Freddie's wife also seemed to love Freddie. But Freddie was, Magnus knew, a lovable person.

It was not the same for Magnus. He had clearly been an unlovable child. And was therefore not a lovable man. But he would do everything in his power to ensure his children had the chance to be lovable. And therefore to be loved.

Magnus glanced around the room again. He supposed it was possible that some of these frivolous girls would settle into motherhood, but it was difficult to believe, especially with the example of his cousin before him.

'Oh, it is such a delightfully mild evening,' cried Laetitia. 'Let us stroll on the terrace before dinner. Come Magnus, as my guest of honour, you shall escort the lady of your choice.'

A dozen feminine gazes turned his way. There was an expectant hush. Magnus silently cursed his cousin for trying to force his hand. Clearly she wished the house party concluded so that she could return to Town and the myriad entertainments there. Magnus smiled. He danced to no female's tune.

'Then, as a good guest, I must look to the care of my charming hostess,' he responded lightly. 'Cousin, shall we?' He took her arm, allowing her no choice, and they stepped through the French doors onto the terrace. The other guests followed.

Tallie trailed awkwardly in their wake. She felt most uncomfortable. Several of the young ladies had eyed her gown, whispering and tittering with careless amusement. Their mothers had totally ignored her and two of the gentlemen guests had made improper suggestions. The guests had taken their tone from Laetitia—Tallie was an unconsidered encumbrance, little better than a servant, and in the current mood of thwarted ambition she was a convenient target.

Tallie was angry, but told herself sternly that there was little point in expressing her feelings—they would be gone soon, and she would be left in peace again with the children and Brooks and Mrs Wilmot. It should be simple enough for her to ignore the spite of a few ill-bred aristocrats.

The pale young marquise held her chin high, ignoring the vile insults flung at her by the ignorant canaille, as the tumbrel rolled onwards. She was dressed in rags, her lovely gowns stolen by the prison guards, but her dignity was unimpaired...

Tallie slipped unobtrusively to the edge of the terrace and looked out over the stone balustrade to the closely scythed sweep of lawn and the woods beyond. It was a truly lovely view...

'Aaargh! Get down, you filthy beast!' Laetitia's screeches pierced the air. 'Get it off me, someone! Aaargh!'

Tallie hurried to see what had occurred. She wriggled between some of the gathered guests and let out an exclamation of distress.

Her cousin's small son, Georgie, had obviously escaped from the nursery and gone adventuring with the puppy that Tallie had given him several weeks before. He stood in front of his mother, a ragged bunch of snowdrops held pathetically out towards her. His shoes and nankeen pantaloons were covered in mud, as was the puppy. It was the cause of the trouble—muddy pawprints marred Laetitia's new jonquil silk gown.

Laetitia, unused to dogs, screeched and backed away, hysterically flapping her fan at the pup, who seemed to think it a delightful game. He leaped up, yapping in excitement, attempting to catch the fan in his jaws, liberally spattering the exquisite gown in the process.

Tallie was still attempting to wriggle through the press of guests when Lord d'Arenville grabbed the pup and handed him by the scruff of its neck to the little boy. Tallie reached the child just as his mother's tirade broke over him.

'How *dare* you bring that filthy beast near me, you wicked boy! Do you see what it has done? This gown is *ruined*! Ruined, I tell you!'

The small face whitened in distress. Mutely Georgie offered the wilting bunch of snowdrops. Laetitia dashed them impatiently from his hands.

'Do not try to turn me up sweet, Georgie! See what you have done? *Look* at this dress! Worn for the *first* time today, from the *finest* of London's modistes, and costing the *earth*! Ruined! And why? Because a *wicked boy* brought a filthy animal into a *civilised gathering*! Who gave you permission to leave the nursery? I left the *strictest* orders. You will be punished for such disobedience! And the animal is clearly dangerous! It must be shot *at once*! Someone call for a groom—'

The little boy's face paled further. His small body shook in fright at the venom in his mother's voice. His face puckered in fear and distress and he clutched the puppy tightly to his chest. It whimpered and scrabbled for release.

Magnus watched, tense in a way he hadn't been since he himself was a small boy. He fought the sensation. His eyes darkened with sympathy and remembrance as he observed the frightened child and his puppy. He felt for the boy, but it was not his place to interfere with a mother disciplining her child. And anyway, he supposed it was how it had to be. It was certainly how his own childhood had been.

It would be hard for the boy to lose his beloved pup, but it was probably better for Georgie that he learn to toughen up now, rather than later. Pets were invariably used as hostage to one's good behaviour. Once the boy learnt not to care so much, his life would be easier. Magnus had certainly found it so...although the learning had been very hard... Three pets had died for his disobedience by the time he was eight. The last a liquid-eyed setter bitch by the name of Polly.

Polly, his constant companion and his best friend. But Magnus had taken her out hunting one day instead of finishing his Greek translations and his father had destroyed Polly to teach his son a lesson in responsibility.

Magnus had learned his lesson well.

By the age of eight Magnus had learned not to become attached to pets.

Or to anything else.

'I am sorry for the unfortunate accident, Cousin.' It was the shabby little poor relation. Magnus watched as she interposed her body between the cowering small boy and his infuriated mother, her calm voice a contrast to Laetitia's high-pitched ranting.

'*You* are sorry?' Laetitia continued. 'Yes, I'll make sure of that! The children are in *your* charge, so how was it that this child was allowed to escape from the nursery? I gave strict instructions...'

Magnus leaned back against a large stone urn, folded his arms and coolly observed the scene. He noted the way the dowdy little cousin used her body to shield the child, protecting him from his own mother. It was an interesting manoeuvre—for a poor relation.

The little boy pressed into her skirts, the muddy pup still in his arms. Magnus watched as the girl's hand came to rest unobtrusively on the nape of the child's neck. She stroked him with small, soothing movements. Magnus noticed the little boy relax under her ministrations, saw his shivers die away. After a few moments Georgie leaned trustfully into the curve of her hip, resting his head against her. She held him more fully against her body, all the time keeping her cousin's rage focused on herself. Her words were apologetic, her body subtly defiant.

Fascinating, thought Magnus. Did the girl not realise what she risked by defying her cousin? And all to protect a child who was not even her own.

'The accident was my fault, Cousin,' she said. 'You must not be angry with poor Georgie, here, for he had my permission to be out of the nursery—'

The little boy's start of surprise was not lost on Magnus.

'And I am sorry for the soiling of your gown. However, I cannot allow you to have the puppy destroyed—'

'*You?* You cannot—' spluttered Laetitia.

'No, for the pup belongs neither to Georgie nor to you.'

The child stared up at the girl. Her hand soothed him, and she continued. 'The pup is mine. He...it was a gift from...from the Rector, and I cannot allow you to destroy a gift because of a little high spirits...'

'You cannot *allow*—' Laetitia gasped in indignation.

'Yes, puppies will be puppies, and small boys and puppies seem to attract each other, don't they? Which is why I was so very grateful to Georgie here.' She turned a warm smile on the small boy.

'Grateful?' Laetitia was astounded. Georgie looked puzzled. Magnus was intrigued.

'Yes, very grateful indeed, for I have been too busy lately to exercise the puppy, and so Georgie has taken over that duty for me, have you not, Georgie dear?'

She nodded encouragingly down at him and, bemused, Georgie nodded back.

'Yes, so any damage the puppy has done to your gown you must lay at my door.'

'But—'

The girl was not paying attention. She bent down to the child. 'Now, Georgie, I think you and my puppy have had enough excitement for one night, but would you do one more thing for me, please?'

He nodded.

'Would you please return, er...Rover—'

'Satan,' Georgie corrected her.

Her eyes brimmed with amusement, but she continued with commendable control. 'Yes, of course, Satan. Would you please take, er, Satan, to the kennels and wash the mud off him for me? You see, I am dressed for dinner, and ladies must not go to the kennels in their best gown.'

Her words had the unfortunate effect of drawing all attention to her 'best gown'. There were a few sniggers, which she ignored with a raised chin. Georgie, however, stared at her, stricken.

'What is it, love?' she said.

Guiltily, he extended a grubby finger and pointed at the mud which now streaked her dress, liberally deposited by himself and the squirming puppy in his arms. She glanced down and laughed, a warm peal of unconcern.

'Don't worry about it, my dear, it will brush off when the mud is dry.' She ruffled his hair affectionately and said in a low voice, 'Now for heaven's sake take that wretched pup and get it and yourself cleaned up before any other accidents happen.'

Relieved, the small boy ran off, his puppy clutched to his chest.

'You'll not get off so easily—' began Laetitia, incensed.

'Do you think it is quite safe for you to be out in the night air in a damp and muddy dress, Cousin?' interrupted Tallie solicitously. 'I would not want you to take a chill, and you know you are extremely susceptible...'

With a stamp and a flounce of jonquil silk Laetitia left the terrace, calling petulantly for her maid to be sent to her at once. The guests drifted in after her, and Brooks began to circulate with a silver tray.

Tallie bent down and gathered up Georgie's scattered flowers. She straightened a few bent stems, gathered the shawl more tightly around her shoulders and stepped towards the French doors, then noticed Lord d'Arenville, who had remained on the terrace.

His expression was unreadable, his grey heavy-lidded eyes observing her dispassionately. The hard gaze made her shiver. Horrid man, she thought. Waiting to see if there is any more entertainment to be had. She raised her chin in cool disdain, and marched past him without saying a word.

Chapter Two

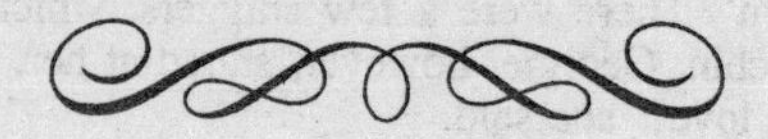

'Well, Magnus, how do you like my candidates? Any take your fancy?'

Tallie froze. Partway into writing the events of the day into her diary, she'd run out of ink. She'd slipped down the servants' stair to the library, secure in the belief that the guests were all in the ballroom, dancing, or playing cards in the nearby anteroom. Concentrating on the tricky task of refilling her inkwell, she hadn't heard her cousin and Lord d'Arenville enter the library. She glanced around, but they were hidden from her view by the heavy velvet curtains pulled partly across the alcove where she was seated.

She stood up to announce her presence, but paused, recalling the shabby dress she wore. If she emerged, she would have to leave by the public route, enduring further sniggers and taunts. She'd had enough of that at dinner. Laetitia, still furious about the way Tallie had confronted her over Georgie and the puppy, had encouraged her guests to bait Tallie even more spitefully than before, and Tallie could endure no more of it.

Lord d'Arenville spoke. 'You know perfectly well, Tish, that my fancy does not run to society virgins. I am seeking a wife, not pursuing a fancy.'

Tallie swallowed, embarrassed. This was a terribly private conversation. No one would thank her for having heard that. Perhaps she should try to slip out through the French doors onto the terrace. She edged quietly towards them. Stealthily she slid the bolt back and turned the handle, but it didn't budge—the catch was stuck.

'Well, dearest coz, which one has the teeth, the hips and the placid temperament you require for the mother of your heirs? They all have impeccable bloodlines, be assured of that.'

Tallie gasped at Laetitia's effrontery and waited for Lord d'Arenville to give her a smart set-down for speaking of his intended bride with such disrespect. It was far too late to declare her presence now, and besides, she was fascinated. She edged back behind the curtains and wrestled half-heartedly with the door catch.

'As far as those requirements are concerned, most of your candidates would do, although Miss Kingsley is too narrow-hipped to be suitable.'

Tallie's jaw dropped. Requirements? Candidates? Those young women out there had been assembled as *candidates*? Miss Kingsley eliminated because of her *hips*? Laetitia hadn't been joking when she'd referred to teeth, hips, placidity and bloodlines!

Tallie was disgusted. What sort of man would choose a wife so coldly and dispassionately? No wonder he was called The Icicle. Mrs Wilmot was right—he was as handsome as a Greek statue but he obviously had a heart of stone to match. Tallie passionately hoped he would select Miss Fyffe-Temple as his bride.

Miss Fyffe-Temple was one of the prettiest of the young lady guests and the sweetest-spoken—in company. In truth she was a nasty-tempered, spiteful little harpy, who took her temper out on the servants, making impossible demands in a shrill voice, and pinching and hitting the younger maids in the most vicious fashion. The below-stairs members of the household had quickly labelled her Miss Foul-Temper, and in Tallie's opinion that made her a perfect wife for the great Lord d'Arenville!

'Actually, I have come to see, on reflection, that my requirements were rather inadequate,' said Lord d'Arenville.

Perhaps she was too hasty in judging him, Tallie thought. She did tend to make snap judgements, and was often forced to own the fault when she was later proved wrong.

'Strong hocks, perhaps, Magnus?' Laetitia had clearly imbibed rather more champagne than was ladylike. 'Do you want to check their withers? Get them to jump over a few logs? Put them at a fence or two? Or ask if they are fond of oats? I believe Miss Carnegie has Scottish blood—she will certainly be fond of oats. The Scots, I believe, live on little else.'

Tallie shoved her fist against her mouth to stop herself from laughing out loud. Heavens! To think she would be in such sympathy with Cousin Laetitia.

'Very funny, Tish,' said Lord d'Arenville dryly. 'I have no interest in the culinary preferences of anyone north of the border, nor do I wish to concern myself with any additional physical characteristics of the young ladies you selected for me.'

Tallie's eyes widened. *Laetitia* had selected the young ladies? Did he simply expect to choose one? Without the bother of courtship? What an insufferable man! To be so puffed up in his own conceit that he need not consider the feelings of any young lady, assuming she would be flattered enough by his offer!

Well, if a spineless ninny was what he wanted, she hoped he would choose The Honourable Miss Aldercott. Already she showed what Tallie considered to be a very sinister preference for gauzy drapery and sonnets about Death and Lost Love. The Honourable Miss Aldercott had fainted five times so far, had had the vapours twice and made recourse to her vinaigrette a dozen times a day. With any luck, thought Tallie viciously, Lord d'Arenville would think The Honourable Miss Aldercott charmingly fragile—then find himself leg-shackled to a clinging, lachrymose watering-pot for the rest of his life!

'So, Magnus, what other criteria do you have for the mother of your heirs?'

'It has occurred to me that most of your candidates are rather spoiled and used to being indulged.'

'Well, naturally they are a little petted, but that is only to be expected...'

'You miss my point, Tish. Most of these young ladies have found it an almost intolerable hardship to come to the country.'

'Well, of course they have, Magnus!' Laetitia snapped acerbically. 'Any woman would. Who in their right mind would moulder away in the country when they could have all the delightful exhilaration of London society? Is that your latest requirement?'

'Yes, actually—it is. I wish the mother of my children to reside with the children, and London is no place for a child.'

'What rubbish!'

'You know it's true, Tish, for you yourself keep your children here in the country all year round.'

'Yes, Magnus, *the children* live here all year round, not me.

And that is the difference. Why, I would go into a decline if I were buried here for an entire year!'

'And the children—do they not miss their mother's care?'

Tallie had to stifle another laugh at that. Laetitia, a doting mother! The children would love her if she would let them. As it was, they tiptoed around on their best behaviour during their mother's visits, hoping to avoid her criticisms and sharp temper and heaving sighs of wistful relief when she left.

'Naturally I spend as much time as I can with my darlings, but I have my needs also, Magnus. And I have responsibilities as George's wife, and *they* take place in London, which is no fault of mine. But you need not think I neglect my children, for I leave them in the best of care.'

'Yes, I've noticed that.' Lord d'Arenville's voice was thoughtful. 'Your sturdy little cousin.'

Sturdy! How dared he? Sturdy? Tallie was mortally insulted. She might not be as sylphlike as Laetitia, but she was *not* sturdy!

'You're wandering off the point, Magnus.'

Sturdy! Insensitive beast!

'Would you say that any of these young ladies would be willing to live for, say, ten years in the country?'

'Ten years?' Laetitia's voice rose to a horrified screech. '*No* sane woman would agree to that! She would die, rather! Why on earth would you wish to immure *anyone* in the country for ten years, anyway?'

There was a short silence. Tallie craned to hear, but there was nothing. Suddenly Laetitia laughed—a hard, cynical laugh.

'Good God, you want a nun, not a wife, don't you?' She laughed again. 'Your father tried that, if you recall, and stuck to it for all of six months, while your mother cuckolded him with every groom, stableboy and tenant farmer in the district. And serve him right, say I. No, you couldn't possibly think that isolating a wife in the country would ensure her fidelity, not after that.' She laughed again. 'And if you have any doubts on the matter, dearest coz, ask George.'

Lord d'Arenville said stiffly, 'My decision is nothing to do with either you or my mother. It is simply that my bride must not mind spending my children's growing years at my country seat with them.'

'Well, I wish you'd told me earlier,' said Laetitia, 'for I

wouldn't have bothered wasting everyone's time with this ridiculous charade. I am very angry with you, Magnus. I should have realised you were not serious about wanting a bride—'

'I am quite serious.'

'Well, you certainly won't find one here who could accept—'

'But I have.'

'You've what?' Laetitia sounded flabbergasted. 'Don't tell me one has agreed to your outrageous terms, Magnus! Oh, I cannot believe it. Who is she? No—do not tell me—let me guess. Lady Helen...no, she is positively addicted to Almack's. And it could not possibly be Miss Blakeney—no one so *à la mode* would agree to be buried in the country for ten years. Oh, I give up Magnus, who is she?'

There was a long pause. Tallie waited with bated breath. Truly, she could imagine no young lady agreeing to such inhuman terms. It was a shame his mother had behaved so shockingly, but not all women were like his mother and Laetitia, and why should an innocent wife be punished for the things they had done?

Ten years in the country indeed! And would Lord d'Arenville confine himself similarly to the restrictions of country life? Tallie almost snorted out loud. Of course he would not! It was only his poor wife who would be shut away from society, breeding his heirs like a good little brood mare.

'Well, Magnus, don't keep me waiting all day,' said Laetitia impatiently. 'Which bride have you chosen?'

Tallie leaned against the doorhandle, eager to hear his answer.

'I have decided to wed—'

Suddenly the catch gave, and Tallie tumbled out into the night, missing his reply. Fearful that her eavesdropping would be discovered, she pushed the door shut and slipped away. A little irritated to be denied the juicy morsel of gossip, she hurried towards the kitchen. Which unfortunate young lady had Lord d'Arenville chosen for his bride? She would find out soon enough, she supposed. Whoever it was, Tallie did not envy her. However, it was nothing to do with her, except that his choice would signal the end of the house party. All the unpleasant guests would return to London, the children would be released from their unnatural curfew and she would return to the peaceful life she had led before. Tallie almost skipped with joy at the prospect.

* * *

When Tallie came down to breakfast the next morning she was surprised to find many of her cousin's guests already arisen. She paused on the threshold, feeling dowdy and unwelcome. Still, she decided, this was her home, and she had every right to her breakfast. Chin held high, she entered the breakfast room.

A sudden hush fell. Tallie ignored it. No doubt they were preparing to make sport of her yet again—the dress she wore was even shabbier than yesterday's. She went to the sideboard and inspected the selection of breakfast dishes, uncomfortably aware of hostile eyes boring into her back. After a moment, the buzz of conversation resumed. From time to time a low-voiced comment reached her ears as she slowly filled her plate.

'...done rather well for herself.'

'...but, my dear, one wonders what precisely she *did* to ensure...'

They were talking of Lord d'Arenville's bride, Tallie thought. He must have announced his betrothal at the ball. That would explain why so many had come down to breakfast. No doubt those who had not been chosen wished to make an early start on the journey back to Town.

'And, of course, poor Tish is utterly furious.'

'Naturally, my dear. Would not you be? After all she's done for her, and now this! The very ingratitude...'

'Trapped, undoubtedly.'

'Oh, undoubtedly!'

Tallie wondered which of the young ladies Lord d'Arenville had chosen. It had to be either Miss Blakeney or Lady Helen Beresford—they were the only two young ladies not at breakfast. That explained why she could sense such an atmosphere of hostility in the room—failed candidates seething with frustration and anger. Tallie tried to close her ears to the vehement mutterings. It would be a relief when Lord d'Arenville, Laetitia and all their horrid friends had gone back to London.

'Thrusting little baggage. A man of honour...no choice.'

'And that dress last evening—positively indecent!'

'No other word for it.'

Tallie began to eat her breakfast, though her appetite had quite vanished. Her cousin's friends were quite unbearable.

'More coffee, Miss Tallie?' murmured Brooks at her ear.

A friendly face at last. 'Oh, yes, please, Brooks.' Tallie beamed up at him and held her cup out for him to refill.

As Brooks poured, Miss Fyffe-Temple, one of Tallie's neighbours, roughly jogged his elbow. Hot coffee boiled over Tallie's hand and arm. She leapt up with a shriek of pain.

'Oh, Miss Tallie!' exclaimed Brooks, horrified.

'How very clumsy of me, to be sure,' purred Miss Fyffe-Temple. 'What a nasty red mark it has made. I do hope it won't leave a scar.'

'Yes, it's quite disgustingly red and ugly. Is it terribly painful?' Miss Carnegie added.

'Oh, how horrid...I think I'm going to faint,' exclaimed The Honourable Miss Aldercott. The others immediately gathered around Miss Aldercott, cooing with pretty concern.

Blinking back tears, Tallie ran from the room and headed for the scullery. She plunged her arm in a pitcher of cold water and breathed a sigh of relief as the pain immediately began to ebb. After a few moments she withdrew it and blew lightly on the reddened skin. It was quite painful, but she didn't think it was too serious a burn. But why had Miss Fyffe-Temple done it? Tallie hadn't missed the gleam of spiteful satisfaction in her eyes as she had made her mocking apology.

'Are you all right, Miss Tallie?' It was Brooks, his kindly old face furrowed with anxiety. 'I am so sorry, my dear.'

'It is not serious, Brooks, truly,' Tallie reassured him. 'It gave me more of a fright, really. It hardly hurts at all.'

'I don't know how it happened. She... My arm just slipped.'

Tallie laid a hand on his arm. 'It's all right; I know whose fault it is, Brooks. The thing I don't understand is why.'

Brooks stared for a moment, then suddenly looked awkward. 'I think you'd best speak to your cousin, miss,' he said. 'She's still abed, but I have no doubt she's expecting you.'

Tallie frowned. 'I shall go up to her, then, as soon as I have put some butter and a piece of gauze over this burn,' she said slowly. Judging from Brooks's expression, something was amiss. She could not think what it was. No doubt her cousin would enlighten her.

'Me?' Tallie's voice squeaked. She stared at her cousin, her jaw dropping in amazement. The effects of her indulgences the night

before had kept Laetitia in bed, and from the sounds of things she was still inebriated. Or demented.

'Me?' repeated Tallie, stunned. 'How can you possibly say such a thing, Cousin? He does not even know my name.'

'Ha!' spat Laetitia, holding her delicate head. 'I'll wager he *knows* you in other ways, you hussy! In the Biblical sense! Why else would he choose a wretched little nobody?'

Tallie gasped, first in shock and then in swelling outrage. It was one thing to be asked to swallow such a Banbury tale—Lord d'Arenville wishing to wed Tallie Robinson, indeed! But to be accused of immorality! She was not entirely sure what knowing 'in the Biblical sense' meant, but she was very certain it was immoral. Tallie was furious. She might be poor. She might be an orphan, shabbily dressed and forced to live on other's generosity. But she was *not* immoral.

'Firstly, let me tell you, Cousin,' Tallie said heatedly, '*no* man has known me in the Biblical sense, and I am shocked that you could even suggest such a thing! Secondly, I cannot help but believe you must have made an error about Lord d'Arenville's intentions. Perhaps you misheard him.'

'I did not,' snapped Laetitia. 'Do you think I would imagine such an appalling thing?'

Tallie gritted her teeth. Imagination indeed! She could imagine no member of the aristocracy, let alone the arrogant Lord d'Arenville, choosing his cousin's poor relation for his bride.

'But I have not exchanged even *one word* with his lordship,' exclaimed Tallie.

'I do not believe—' shrilled Laetitia, holding her head.

'Cousin! I promise you.' Tallie tried to keep her voice calm, despite her frustration. Her cousin was very angry.

'Do not lie, girl! He told me himself he had chosen you.'

A small, cold knot of fear lodged in Tallie's stomach. She had never seen Laetitia this furious before, and she knew her cousin well. There was a hard, ruthless streak in Laetitia. This foolish misunderstanding—the result of too much champagne, no doubt, or perhaps a jest on Lord d'Arenville's part—could have dire consequences for herself.

'Well, either you misheard him, Cousin, or else he is playing a nasty joke on you. Yes, that's it—it must surely be a jest.' People like her cousin's friends were always playing tricks on some poor unfortunate. The joke this time might be on Laetitia, but Tallie was the poor unfortunate.

'Jest?' Laetitia snorted. 'Magnus does not jest—not about marriage.'

'Perhaps you took a little too much champagne, Cousin, and did not realise he was hoaxing you,' Tallie suggested tentatively.

'Nonsense! I know what I heard!' said Laetitia, but her tone belied the words. It was clear that she was starting to entertain doubts. Tallie felt a trickle of relief.

'I will speak to his lordship, shall I, and clear the matter up once and for all?' Tallie rose to her feet. It just had to be some trick Lord d'Arenville was playing on Laetitia. Tallie was not amused. His little joke had already got her scalded by boiling coffee, and now it threatened her position in Laetitia's household. But would His High-and-Mightiness think of that? Not he!

He who had been given everything his heart desired, ever since he was born—it would not occur to him that some people existed on a fine line between survival and destitution. All that stood between Tallie and abject poverty was her cousin's good will, and no careless jest was about to jeopardise that! Lord Look-Down-His-Nose would soon learn that one person at least was not prepared to have her life wrecked for a mere lordly whim!

She found him in the downstairs parlour, idly leafing through a freshly ironed newspaper, lately arrived from London. Fortunately he was alone for a change.

'Lord d'Arenville,' she began, shutting the door firmly behind her. 'I have just been speaking with my cousin Laetitia, and she seems to be under the impression that you...'

He laid the paper courteously aside, stood up and came towards her. Tallie's voice dwindled away. Heavens, but he was so very tall. She'd noticed it earlier, of course, but now, when he was standing so close, looming over her...

'Ah, Miss Robinson. Good morning. Is it not a pleasant day? Will you be seated?'

Miss Robinson? He remembered her name? She could have sworn he hadn't taken a whit of notice of her the day they were introduced. Or since.

'Er, thank you.' Tallie allowed herself to be led to a low divan. He drew up a chair opposite, a look of faint enquiry lifting his dark brows.

'You wished to speak with me?'

To her great discomfort Tallie felt a blush rising. It was one thing to storm out of her cousin's boudoir, declaring she would soon clear up this whole silly mistake, and quite another to confront this immaculate, gravely polite aristocrat with a wholly impossible tale.

'Laetitia seems to be under the impression...?' he prompted.

Tallie felt her blush intensify. The whole thing was too ridiculous. She had to escape. She could not ask this man whether there was any truth in the rumour that he wished to marry her. It was obviously a mistake. She knew she was being cowardly, but she could not imagine this coldly serious creature considering her—even for a jest—as an eligible bride. On the other hand, Tallie would not put it past her cousin to set her up for a humiliating fall. In fact, it would be very like her...

Tallie could just imagine Laetitia entertaining her London friends with the joke... *Imagine, that plain, foolish lump of a girl actually believing that Magnus wanted to marry her! When he has the pick of the* ton *at his fingertips! Oh, my dears, I laughed until the tears ran down my cheeks! But there, 'tis not kind to laugh at one's inferiors...but really, if you could have seen Magnus's face when the girl confronted him, Lord, he thought he was being pursued by a lunatic!* And gales of laughter would follow.

'Er...Cousin Laetitia was under the impression...' Tallie's eye fell on the newspaper '...that the maids might have forgotten to press the paper for you, but I see they have, so I will go at once and tell her that everything is...organised.' She stood up to leave. Lord d'Arenville rose also.

Heavens! He was looming again, standing so close she could just smell the faint tang of a masculine cologne. Tallie took a step backwards and stumbled against the divan. A strong hand shot out and caught her by the arm, holding her until she steadied, then releasing her.

'Thank you... So clumsy...' she muttered, flustered, and annoyed with herself for being so.

'Stay a moment, Miss Robinson. I wish to speak to you.' His hand touched her arm again, a light touch this time, not the firm, warm grip of before.

Tallie looked up, puzzled. A faint warning bell sounded in her mind as she saw the purposeful look in his cold grey eyes, but she quashed it immediately. No doubt he had some complaint about a servant, or a message he wished her to carry to her cousin. Outwardly calm, she allowed herself to be seated a second time, folded her hands demurely in her lap and waited.

Magnus noted the quiet way she folded her hands. It seemed to him a pleasantly womanly gesture. Her whole demeanour pleased him. Clearly Laetitia had told her of his decision, and, whilst he wished she had not, this girl's reactions bore out the soundness of his choice. She was neither filled with vulgar excitement nor coy flutterings. Yes, she would do nicely. He took a deep breath, surprised at how unexpectedly nervous he suddenly felt.

'You said you had spoken with Laetitia?'

The cold knot in the pit of Tallie's stomach grew. Wordlessly she nodded.

'Yes, I should have expected she could not keep it to herself.' Without waiting for her reply, Lord d'Arenville began to explain. 'It would be best if the wedding took place almost immediately—it takes three weeks for the banns to be called. We would be married from this house and my cousin's husband George would give you away. I would prefer a small affair, just my immediate family—Laetitia and her husband—and of course any friends or relations you wish to invite...'

It could not be true. She was not sitting here listening to this cold, proud man elaborate on the arrangements for his wedding. *Her* wedding! His wedding to Tallie Robinson! A girl to whom he had scarcely spoken two words.

But his cool, indifferent demeanour, his very seriousness convinced her. It was not a joke, not a malicious trick to make sport of the poor relation.

But he hadn't even *asked* her if she wanted to marry him!

After a time, Tallie's shock wore off, and she realised she was furious. And utterly mortified. She had known the likelihood of her ever marrying was slim. Living in the country as Laetitia's unpaid governess, she came into contact with few eligible men, and with neither looks nor fortune to recommend her, her prospects were few and far between. But it was one thing to face the prospect of a lonely and loveless future, and another to be so little regarded that she did not even merit the appearance of a courtship. Were her feelings and desires of so little significance to him?

Tallie stared down at her knees, flushed and fuming, biting her lip to prevent her rage from spilling out. Her hands shook, itching to slap the smug condescension off his face. She clenched them into fists, dwelling on how pleasant it would be to box his arrogant ears! She took in very little of what he was saying!

Lord d'Arenville rose from his seat and paced up and down before her, explaining the arrangements. He noted his bride's delicate blush, her modestly bowed head, and congratulated himself again on the excellent choice he had made. No pampered miss, this. She sat there, meekly listening to his plans for her future. Quiet, submissive, delightful!

How could he ever have been so foolish as to consider a sophisticated woman of the *ton* as the mother of his children? Laetitia's candidates had been self-centred, selfish, and far too sure of themselves. Much better to have chosen this sweetly shy girl with her modest, downcast eyes. Thalia Robinson would be grateful for his offer—she had no worldly ambition, no highly strung temperament.

His eyes ran over her figure. It was difficult to tell in that frightful dress she wore, but she seemed sturdy—certainly robust enough to survive the rigours of childbirth. And this girl, he believed, had the capacity to love, and he needed that—for his children. He recalled the tender way her hands had caressed young Georgie. He wanted that for his child...yes, for his child...

Her hands were trembling, he realised. Magnus watched approvingly as she clenched her fingers tightly together in an effort to control her emotions. Excellent. Self-control was a good thing in a wife.

He gentled his voice. Doubtless such disparity in their respective stations in life made her a little nervous, a little eager to oblige. The thought did not displease Magnus. He intended to treat her kindly—her nervousness would pass with time and she would no doubt be grateful for his forbearance. It would be a start... She would find him a good husband, he hoped. He would look after her, protect her, take care of all her needs. He continued to pace the floor, describing d'Arenville, the family seat, and how much she would like living there.

Tallie fumed silently, letting his words wash over her. So *she* was to be his quiet, compliant little brood mare, was she? The wife he intended to keep immured in his beastly d'Arenville for ten years or more!

In a pig's eye she was!

The nerve, the arrogance, the presumption of the man! He must have decided a plain, poor woman would give him the least trouble, a woman without prospects but with the hips and teeth and bloodlines to bear his heirs! A *sturdy* woman!

She longed to leap up, to fling his proposal of mar... No— Tallie Robinson, poor relation, did not merit a *proposal,* for he had not even waited for her reply. He'd presented his prospective brood mare with an *assumption* of marriage!

Well, whichever it was, she would fling it in his teeth! That would bring a shocked look to that insufferably complacent face. And how she would enjoy snapping her fingers under that long, proud nose! She would wait until he had finished describing the wonderful treats that marriage to him would bring her! What was he talking about now? The view of the lake from the summerhouse at sunset? Hah!

I'm sooo sorry, Lord d'Arenville, she would tell him, *but even the delightful prospect of viewing the d'Arenville duck pond at dawn cannot tempt me to marry you. I would much prefer to remain unwed. Sooo sorry to disappoint you.* And she would sail out of the room, head held high, leaving him stunned, furious, gnashing his teeth with chagrin.

No, she decided. Too tame, too straightforward. He deserved a taste of his own medicine. He hadn't even bothered to speak to *her*! He'd merely informed Laetitia, no doubt offering to take a poor relation off her hands. Tallie had been scalded and abused and accused of outright immorality. And all because of his arrogance. He needed to be taken down a peg or two! Or three!

Tallie smiled to herself, planning her revenge—she'd keep him guessing. A man of his pride and consequence would loathe being kept waiting. Especially by a little nobody from nowhere! A *sturdy* little nobody at that!

Laetitia's guests obviously knew of Lord d'Arenville's choice. They would be waiting for the announcement. And Laetitia—what would it do to her pride to have the despised poor relation keeping the head of the family dangling?

The thought filled Tallie with glee—she would let them all wait...and wait...and wait. And they would marvel at her temerity in making her future husband wait, for of course it would never occur to any of *them* that she could be so foolish as to refuse such a prize!

A prize indeed, Tallie thought scornfully, glancing up at him from under her lashes. As if a handsome face and figure and a wealthy purse were everything!

Yes, she would make him, and everyone else, wait. And then, just when everyone was starting to wonder how much longer Lord d'Arenville's temper would stand it, Tallie would carelessly decline his offer. *That* would serve him right! How his pride would suffer—the great Lord d'Arenville, prize of the marriage mart, courted and pursued by every matchmaking mama in the country, rejected by the plain and insignificant poor relation!

'The banns would be called immediately and the wedding set for three weeks from now. Would that be enough time for you to organise your bride clothes?' said Lord d'Arenville.

Tallie blinked up at him in mocking surprise. Was that a *question* he was asking? Something he *didn't* know? An arrangement he hadn't made? Something for *her* to comment on? Amazing.

She stood up. 'Lord d'Arenville. I thank you for your very...surprising...offer of marriage. May I consider my reply?' Without waiting for his response, Tallie hurried on, 'Thank you. I will let you know my answer as soon as is convenient.'

Magnus's jaw dropped.

She walked to the door, opened it, paused, turned back to face him and smiled sweetly. 'Until then, may I suggest you make no irrevocable arrangements?'

Chapter Three

'Well, what did he say? It was a hum, was it not?' Laetitia dragged Tallie into a nearby anteroom.

'No, I am afraid it was not,' said Tallie reluctantly. 'You were perfectly correct, Cousin, he thought to marry me.'

Laetitia caught the tense Tallie used and pounced eagerly. 'But he has changed his mind?'

Tallie knew she had to choose her words carefully, so as not to exacerbate her cousin's volatile temper any further. She was skating on very thin ice as it was. 'No, not exactly.'

'I knew it!' Laetitia stamped her foot. 'He is such a selfish wretch! How could he put me in *such* a position? Each girl out there was in daily expectation of being made an offer!' She glared at Tallie. 'Each one a diamond of the first water, an heiress or a duke's relative—and he chooses *you*!'

Tallie nodded, ignoring the insult. She understood how foolish her cousin felt. She even felt some sympathy for her. Lord d'Arenville was an arrogant, selfish, thoughtless boor.

'It is all right, Cousin,' she said soothingly. 'I intend to refuse him.'

Laetitia froze. She stared, stupefied. Her face went white beneath the rouge. 'What did you say?' she whispered.

'I am going to refuse him.' Tallie smiled reassuringly.

'Refuse *Magnus*?'

Tallie nodded. 'Yes.'

'*You*—to refuse my cousin Magnus? Lord d'Arenville?'

Tallie nodded again. 'Absolutely. I have no wish to marry him, so there is nothing for you to be upset—'

'Of all the brazen effrontery! You arrogant little bitch!'

Tallie took a step backwards, unnerved by the fury she saw in her cousin's face.

'Who do you think *you* are to refuse *my cousin Magnus*? You—a complete nonentity! A mere *Robinson*! Why, he is so far above the likes of you that he is the sun to your, your...' Laetitia waved her hand in frustration, unable to find a suitable comparison to convey to Tallie just how far beneath him she was. 'How *dare* you think to humiliate me in this fashion?'

'But, Cousin, how does my refusing Lord d'Arenville humiliate you?' interrupted Tallie, confused by her cousin's abrupt volte-face. 'I can see how choosing me instead of your—'

'Do not for one minute dare to gloat, you insolent hussy!'

'I am *not* gloating,' said Tallie indignantly. 'But I don't understand. Surely if I refuse him it saves you the embarrassment of people knowing he preferred me to your friends? We can say that your guests misunderstood.'

Laetitia threw up her hands. 'She even has the brass to boast of her conquest!' she muttered. 'Mortifying enough that my cousin chooses a shabby little nobody over my friends, but for the nobody to *refuse* him! No. No! It is too much!'

She turned to face Tallie, hands on hips. 'Little did I think when I accepted you into my household that it would come to this. You will pack your bags and be out of here within the hour. John Coachman will take you back to the village where you lived before you insinuated yourself into my home.' Laetitia's voice was low, furious and vengeful, her expression implacable.

Tallie stared at her, shocked. There was no hysteria in her cousin's manner now. 'You...you cannot mean it, surely, Cousin?'

Laetitia sniffed and turned her face away.

Tallie tried again. 'Please, Cousin, reconsider. There is nothing for me in the village. The school closed down when Miss Fisher died. And...you know I have no money.'

'You should have considered that before you set your cap at my cousin.'

'I did *not* set my cap at him. I never even spoke to him! It was Lord d'Arenville who—'

'I am not interested in your excuses. You have one hour.' Laetitia was adamant.

Tallie's mouth was dry. 'You cannot mean it, surely, Cousin?' she began. 'I have nowhere to go, no one to turn to.'

'And whose fault is that, pray? Had I known before what an ungrateful, scheming jade you were, I would never have taken you into my home. The subject is closed. One hour.' Laetitia swept towards the door.

'Cousin!' called Tallie. Laetitia paused and glanced disdainfully back. Tallie swallowed. She had been about to beg, but she could see from her cousin's expression that her cousin was hoping for just that. No, she would not beg. In her current mood Laetitia would enjoy seeing her grovel, and it would do no good; Tallie could see that now.

'Will you write me a letter of recommendation so that I may at least seek work as a governess?'

'You have a nerve!' spat Laetitia. 'No, I will not!'

Magnus strode through the damp grass, snapping his whip angrily against his booted leg. He'd planned to go for a long ride, but had found himself too impatient to wait for a groom to saddle his horse so he'd gone for a walk instead. The gardens were looking quite pretty for the time of year. He stopped and stared at a clump of snowdrops, their heads nodding gently in the faint breeze.

He recalled the way she'd sat there, listening to his words with downcast eyes, all soft and submissive, her pale nape exposed, vulnerable and appealing. Her hair was not plain brown after all, but a soft honey colour, with a tendency to curl. And when she'd looked up at him at the end he'd realised that she had rather pretty eyes, a kind of deep amber, with long dark lashes. And her skin looked smooth and soft.

Yes, he'd been pleased with his choice. Right up until the moment she'd spoken and revealed that flash of...temper? Pique?

Magnus lashed at the nodding snowdrops with his whip, sending them flying. He stared unseeing at the carnage.

The chit was playing games with him! *Make no irrevocable arrangements.* There'd been a malicious kind of pleasure in the way she'd said it, sweet smile notwithstanding. He strode on, frowning.

For almost the whole of the house party the girl had been quiet, docile and obedient. He was convinced it was her usual state—it must be—how else had she survived living with Laetitia? And she lived here with the children all year round without complaint.

No. He must have imagined her anger. He'd taken her by surprise, that was all. He should have given her a little more warning of his intentions. And perhaps he'd been a little clumsy—he had never before offered marriage, and his unexpected nervousness had thrown him a little off balance.

He should have made a flowery speech and then a formal offer, instead of rushing into his plans. Females set store by that kind of thing. She was quite right to put him off for a time. It was what every young girl was schooled to do, pretending to think it over, as a true lady should.

His mouth twitched as he remembered the way she'd held her chin so high. For all the world as if she might refuse. Cheeky little miss! The small flash of spirit did not displease him. A spirited dam usually threw spirited foals, and he wouldn't want his children to be dull. Not at all. And he'd seen the mettle in her when she'd flown to little Georgie's side, like a young lioness defending her cub.

And spirited defiance was permissible, even desirable in the defence of children. It was a little disconcerting for it to be directed against himself, perhaps, but he was *not* displeased, he told himself again.

So why could he not shake the feeling that he'd reached to pluck a daisy and had grasped a nettle instead? He savagely beheaded another clump of his cousin's flowers and strode on, indifferent to the damage the wet grass was doing to the shine on his boots.

'Magnus, what on earth are you doing to my garden?'

Laetitia's voice jerked Magnus out of his reverie. He glanced back the way he'd come and flinched when he realised the havoc his whip had wrought.

'Sorry, Tish. I didn't realise—'

'Oh, never mind that. I need to talk to you at once, but do come away from that wet grass; it will ruin my slippers. Here, into the summerhouse, where we can be quite private.'

Laetitia settled herself on a bench and regarded her cousin severely. 'How *could* you, Magnus? In front of all my guests! I could just kill you! You have been extremely foolish, but I think we can pass it off as a jest—not in the best taste, of course, but a jest all the same. In any case, I have got rid of the girl—for which, I may add, you owe me your undying gratitude. Although, knowing you, you will be odiously indifferent as you always—'

Magnus cut to the heart of the rambling speech. 'What do you mean, ''got rid of the girl''? You cannot mean Miss Robinson, surely?'

'Miss Robinson indeed!' Laetitia sniffed. 'She is lucky I even acknowledged her as cousin. Well, that is all at an end now. She will be gone within the hour!'

'Gone? Where to?'

'The village she grew up in. I forget its name.'

Magnus frowned. 'What? Is there some family emergency? I understood she was an orphan.'

'Oh, she is. Not a living soul left, except for me, and that's at an end after her base ingratitude and presumption.'

'Then why is she going to this village?'

Laetitia wrinkled her nose. 'I believe she spent virtually all her life in some stuffy little school there. Her father was in the diplomatic service, you know, and travelled a great deal.'

Poor little girl, thought Magnus. He knew what it was like to be sent away, unwanted, at a young age. 'And she wishes to visit this school? I suppose she must have friends there whom she would wish to ask to her wedding. I did not realise.'

'Magnus, what is *wrong* with you? What does it *matter* where the wretched girl goes?'

'Tish, of course it matters. Do you not realise I asked Miss Robinson to be my bride?'

'Of course I do, and it will be a long time before I will forgive you for making such a fool of me, Magnus! But that wretched little nobody plans to make a fool of us both, and *that* I will not allow!'

Magnus frowned. The uneasy feeling he'd had ever since he'd spoken to Miss Robinson intensified. His whip tapped a sharp and fast tattoo against his boot. 'What do you mean, ''a fool of us both''?'

'She plans to refuse you!'

'*What?*' The instant surge of temper caught Magnus unaware. He reined it in. 'How can you know such a thing, Tish?'

'She told me to my head, not fifteen minutes ago. *Boasted* of it!' Laetitia noted his stupefaction, nodded smugly and laid a compelling hand on his arm. 'You see now why she must be got away from here at once. I will not have a *Robinson* crow to the world that my cousin, Lord d'Arenville, was not good enough for her!'

'Are you sure?' Magnus was flabbergasted. He had not expected any girl to refuse his offer...but a penniless orphan? Boasting? If it was true, it was more than a slap in the face.

'She actually said so? In so many words?'

'Yes, Magnus, in just so many words. First she *gloated* of her success in cutting all my friends out to snare you, and then she *boasted* of how foolish we would all look when she refused you. The ungrateful trollop! I would have her *drowned* if I could!'

Magnus stood up and took a few jerky paces back and forth across the small summerhouse, his whip slapping hard and fast against his boot. 'I...I must consider this. Until I speak to you again, do nothing,' he said, and stalked off into the garden, destroying the herbaceous border as he passed.

No, no, dearest Tallie, you cannot leave us...it was a foolish misunderstanding... What would we do without you? What would the children do? And George and I—oh, please do not let my wretched cousin Magnus come between us—he is nothing but a cold, proud Icicle! You are family, dearest Tallie, and you belong here! Oh, do not leave us, we need you too much...

'I...I've been sent up to make sure you're packed, miss.' The maidservant hovered uncomfortably, wringing her hands in distress. 'And John Coachman has been told to ready himself and the horses for a long journey... I'm that sorry, Miss.'

'It's all right, Lucy,' said Tallie shakily. Reality crashed around her. Laetitia had not changed her mind. Tallie truly was being thrown out of her cousin's house.

She got off the bed where she'd been huddled and tried to pull herself together, surreptitiously wiping her eyes. 'There's a bag on top of that wardrobe—if you could put my clothing in that...I...I must see to other matters.' She rushed out, her brimming eyes averted from the maid's sympathetic gaze.

Moments later she slipped out of the side door, across the south lawn and into the garden maze. Tallie knew the convoluted paths by heart, and unerringly made her way towards the centre. It was a favourite spot. No one could see over the high, clipped hedges, and if anyone entered it she would have plenty of warning. She reached the heart of the maze, hurled herself down on the wrought-iron seat and burst into tears.

She had lost everything—her home, the children. She was about to become a pauper. She'd always been one, she supposed, but now she would truly be destitute. Homeless. Taken out and dumped like an unwanted cat.

She sobbed until there were no more tears, until her sobs became hard, dry lumps stuck in her chest, shuddering silently out of her with every breath she drew. Eventually they subsided, only coming every minute or so, in an echo of the distress she could bear no more of.

What would she do? This very night, unless some miracle intervened, she would find herself deposited in the village square. Where would she go? Where would she sleep? Unconsciously her hand crept to her mouth and she began to nibble at her nails. No one in the village would remember her. The vicar? No, she recalled—he'd died shortly after she'd left. A churchgoer might recall her face amongst the dozens of schoolgirls who'd filed dutifully into St Stephen's each Sunday, but it was unlikely. It was two years ago—vague recognition was the best she could expect from anyone in the village. And no one would be likely to take her in.

There was not a soul in the world she could turn to.

The sharp, clean scent of the close-trimmed cypress hedges was fresh in the damp, cool air. Tallie drew her knees up against her chest and hugged them to her. In the distance she could hear the haunting cry of a curlew. It sounded as lost and alone as she felt.

She'd been happy at Laetitia's, but her happiness had been founded on a lie. She had deluded herself that she was part of a family—the family she had always yearned for. In fact she was little better than a servant. Worse—a servant was paid, at least. If Tallie had been paid she would have had the wherewithal to pay for a night's lodging or two. As it was, she had nothing.

Enough of self-pity, she decided at last. There was a way out of this mess. It was the only possible solution. She knew it, had known it all along; she'd just been unable to face the thought until she'd explored every other option. But there were no other options. She would have to marry Lord d'Arenville.

Lord d'Arenville. Cold-eyed, cold-voiced, handsome Lord

d'Arenville. A cold proud Icicle, who simply wanted a brood mare for his heirs. Not a wife. Not a loving companion. A vessel for his children. A *sturdy* vessel! Tallie's mouth quivered and she bit down hard on her nails to stop herself weeping again.

There would be no love for Tallie now—the love she'd dreamed of all her life. But there would be security. And with the thought of sleeping in the village churchyard that night, security was suddenly more important than love—or, if not more important, certainly of more immediate significance.

No, there would be no Prince Charming for Tallie, no Black Knight galloping to her rescue, not even a dear, kind gentleman who was no one in particular. Nobody for Tallie to love, nobody who would love her in return. There was only Lord d'Arenville. Was it possible to love a statue? An Icicle?

Oh, there would be children, God willing, but children were different. You couldn't help but love children. And they couldn't help but love you back. Children were like puppies, loving, mischievous and endlessly thirsting for love.

Tallie knew. She'd thirsted all her life, ever since she'd turned six and had been sent away to school.

That was one thing she'd have to make clear to Lord d'Arenville from the start. She wouldn't allow him to send *her* children away to school. Not until they were quite old—fourteen, fifteen, something like that. And she would write to them *every* week, and send them special treats sometimes to share with their chums. And they would come home for every holiday and term break. And bring any of their schoolfriends who couldn't go to their own families. None of *her* children's friends would spend Christmas after Christmas alone in an empty school, with no one but an elderly headmistress to keep her company.

Her children would know they were *loved*, know they were *wanted*, know that their mother, at least, cared about them.

And the love of her children would have to be enough for her, she decided. It was only the lucky ones, the golden ones of this world, who were loved for themselves, after all. Who found a partner to share secret dreams and foolish ideas with. Who found a man to cherish them. *Cherish.* Such a beautiful, magical word.

Tallie took a long, shaky breath, a sob catching in her throat as she did so. Such dreams were for silly girls. She scrubbed at her swollen eyes with a handkerchief. It was time to put her dreams and her girlhood away.

It was time to go to Lord d'Arenville and tell him she would marry him.

It was a chilly, withdrawn and much chagrined Lord d'Arenville who returned from the garden half an hour after he'd spoken with Laetitia. The house party had been an unmitigated disaster. And now his ego was severely dented by the news that a penniless girl could not bear the thought of marrying him. Part of him concurred with his cousin that he would like to drown Miss Thalia Robinson. Or strangle her slowly, taking her soft, creamy throat between his bare hands... But an innate sense of fair play told him it would be a gross miscarriage of justice if he allowed his cousin to turn Thalia Robinson out on the streets merely because she didn't wish to wed him.

And he had been uncannily disturbed by the sound of someone weeping in the maze. Weeping as if their heart would break. Magnus *hated* it when women wept!

He'd taken a few steps into the maze and hovered there for some time, clenching and unclenching his fists, listening helplessly. Not knowing what to do. Knowing who it was, sobbing so piteously. Thalia Robinson.

He had told himself she'd brought it on herself, boasting to Laetitia of how she would spurn his offer. He'd told himself she deserved to be miserable, that the girl must be a cold-hearted little bitch. He'd made her an honourable offer—there was no need for her to publicly humiliate him. He, who had long been regarded as the finest prize on the marriage mart, hunted by matchmaking mamas and their daughters alike! Most girls would have been grateful for an offer from him, but not Miss Thalia Robinson. No. She planned to humiliate him—and so she was reaping what she had sown. Her regrets had come too late.

Magnus had told himself all these things, but they hadn't helped—he just couldn't bear the sound of a woman sobbing.

The part of him that didn't want to strangle her had wanted to go into the maze and speak to her—and what a stupid idea that would have been! As if women ever made any sense when they were weeping. And as if he would know what to do anyway. He'd always managed to stop them crying by giving them some bauble or other, but then all the women he'd ever known had cried *at* him, not taken themselves into the middle of a maze on a damned cold day and sobbed their little hearts out in absolute solitude.

Magnus was sure he wouldn't know how to deal with someone who wept like that.

'Tish, I intend to withdraw my offer. She cannot refuse me if there is no offer, so you need not worry about any insult to the family pride. No one will know of it. I will speak to the girl before any irrevoc—' He faltered for a moment, recalling those cheeky last words: *make no irrevocable arrangements*. Thalia Robinson had not realised she was sounding her own doom. 'Before any irrevocable steps have been taken. Have her sent to me at once, if you please.'

'But, Magnus—'

'At once, Tish.'

'Oh, very well. But it will make no diff—'

But Magnus had left. Laetitia pulled the bell cord to summon Brooks.

Magnus decided to receive Miss Robinson in the library. He would speak kindly to her, show her he bore her no grudge for her poor judgement. She would have no idea that she had, somehow, got under his skin. He would be casual, relaxed, indifferent. He would not receive her in formal dress, as a gentleman would normally do when receiving a lady's answer to his proposal of marriage. His offhand manner would be conveyed by the silent message of his riding buckskins. It would appear to be a spur of the moment chat, the outcome of which held only lukewarm interest for him.

His brow furrowed as he tried to recall every detail of their previous conversation. A cold smile grew on his face as he realised he had not actually *asked* her to marry him. Not in so many words. He had spoken of an intention to organise a ceremony. Had used the conditional tense. Thank heavens. He might be able to fudge it. He would make Miss Robinson understand she was mistaken, that he'd made her no actual offer.

It was not an honourable solution, but it should smooth things over with Laetitia—enough to stop her throwing the wretched girl into the streets. And then he would get the hell out of this appalling house party and never have to set eyes on the blasted girl or his blasted cousin ever again!

He leant against a high, leather-covered writing desk, one leg crossed casually over the other, awaiting her entrance with an expression of bored indifference on his face. The whip snapped fast and furious against the glossy leather of his boot.

'Lord d'Arenville?'

She'd entered the room so silently that Magnus was caught unaware. He stared, mesmerised, at the red-rimmed eyes which failed to meet his, the drooping mouth and the woebegone little face, and it was as if he could hear every choking sob again. With an effort, he gathered himself and began to speak, feeling dishonest and uncomfortable as he did so.

'Miss Robinson, I gather from my cousin that you are under the mistaken impression that I off—'

'Lord d'Arenville, I accept your offer of marriage,' she said at the same time.

There was a long, tense moment of silence in the room.

What happens now? wondered Magnus. In all honour, he could not continue with his reluctant pretence that he had made no offer. There was no need—she had accepted him. So that was it. An offer had been made and was accepted. The rest was inevitable. Irrevocable. Ironic, that. *She* could call the wedding off, but there was no question that he could do the same. Lord d'Arenville was to wed Miss Thalia Robinson. Thalia Robinson, who looked more like a martyr going to the stake than a blushing bride.

The realisation was like a kick in the teeth. Until this moment he'd half believed that Laetitia was mistaken in saying the girl was going to refuse him. But this miserably bleak acceptance of his offer had convinced him as a thousand explanations could not.

It could not be said that Thalia Robinson actually *preferred* poverty to himself, but it would be clear to a blind man that it was a damned close race. The girl might be going to her execution, the face she was wearing. Magnus stared at the downcast face, the red-tipped nose, the resolute chin and the trembling lips and felt his anger rising. It had clearly taken a great deal of anguish and resolution for her to decide between abject poverty—or marriage to Lord d'Arenville.

Starvation and misery—or Lord d'Arenville!

The gutter—or Lord d'Arenville!

And finally, by a nose, or a whisker, or a hair's breadth, Lord d'Arenville had won. Lucky Lord d'Arenville!

Lord d'Arenville was furious. He could not trust himself to speak another word to her. He bowed stiffly, turned and stalked out of the room. Tallie watched him leave, blinking in surprise.

'Magnus, what—?' Laetitia was standing in the hallway, speaking to the vicar. Her voice died as she saw the look on his face.

'You may wish me happy!' he snapped.

'What?'

'She has accepted me.' He broke his whip in half and flung the pieces into a corner.

'Oh, Magnus, how dreadf—'

'I am *ecstatic*!' he snarled. 'The wedding will be in three weeks' time. Make all the arrangements. Spare no expense.' He laughed, a harsh, dry laugh. '*Nothing* is too good for my bride!' He noticed the vicar, standing there, jaw agape and added, 'You, there—Parson. Call the banns, if you please. I will return in three weeks for the ceremony.'

He stormed out of the door and headed for the stables. Laetitia trailed after him, pleading with him to slow down, to explain, but to no avail. Lord d'Arenville mounted his horse, and with no warning, no preparations and no baggage, set off for d'Arenville Hall, a good two days' journey away.

Chapter Four

'Blast and bother!' Tallie glared at her reflection. She'd brought a mirror up from one of the salons and propped it against the wall. It told her what she had already suspected—that she was the worst seamstress in the world and that her wedding dress looked like a dog's breakfast.

She tugged at the recalcitrant sleeves, pulling them this way and that in an effort to make them appear balanced. It was hopeless. One sleeve puffed beautifully whilst the other, which *should* have been an exact twin, sagged and drooped. She'd put the sleeve in and taken it out a half-dozen times and still it looked uneven—and slightly grubby from all the handling.

Tallie had no idea what arrangements had been made for her wedding. She'd tried several times to speak to her cousin, but Laetitia was still furious and had ordered Tallie to keep out of her sight or she would not be answerable for the consequences.

No one, not the servants, Laetitia nor Lord d'Arenville, had seemed to recall that the bride had not a penny to her name. Hopefully someone would remember the bride needed a suitable gown, but as the dreaded day grew closer Tallie decided she had better make alternative arrangements—just in case.

The attics contained dozens of trunks and bandboxes, filled with old dresses and ballgowns, relegated there over the years. She and the children had rummaged through them frequently, searching for dress-up materials. Tallie had found a lovely pale amber silk ballgown, hopelessly outmoded, with wide panniers and yards of ruching, but with enough good material left, when it was unpicked, to make a wedding frock. Using one of her old dresses as a pattern, she had cut and sewn it laboriously, wishing she had been more diligent in Miss Fisher's sewing class.

In another trunk she had found an almost new pair of blue kid slippers, which only pinched her feet a little, and a stained pair of long white satin gloves. The stains were impossible to remove, so she'd dipped the gloves in coffee until they almost exactly matched the amber silk.

She smiled at her reflection and pirouetted several times. It was not so bad after all. Oh, the neckline was a trifle crooked, to be sure, but Tallie was convinced only the most critical would notice it. And if the gathers she had made at the back were slightly uneven, what did that signify? It was only obvious when she was motionless, so she would be sure to keep moving, and if she had to stand still for any reason she would keep her back to a wall.

She examined her reflection in the mirror again as she tugged on the long satin gloves. She had never worn anything so fine in her life. She frowned at the sleeves... A shawl! she realised in a sudden flash of brilliance. Laetitia's spangled gauze scarf would hide the sleeves! It was not precisely a bridal mode, but perhaps observers would think it a new fashion. After all, she was wedding a man well-known for his elegance. Tallie's mouth grew dry as she stared at her reflection.

She was not just wedding a man...she was wedding The Icicle. Tomorrow morning. And afterwards he would take her away from the children she loved so much—the only living creatures in the world who loved her. Tomorrow she would belong only to him, swear before God and witnesses to love, honour and obey him. A man she barely knew and certainly didn't like. A cold man, who was famed for caring nothing for the feelings of others. Who wanted a wife he need not dance attendance on, a wife he could get with child and then abandon in rural fastness while he enjoyed himself in London, awaiting the birth of his heir...

Tallie shivered. What did it mean, *get with child*? She knew women bore children, of course, but how it came about she had no idea. She'd lived virtually her entire life in Miss Fisher's Seminary for the Daughters of Gentlemen, and the subject had certainly never been on that prim spinster's curriculum.

It had, however, been a subject of much speculation and whispering in the dormitories. But none of the various theories put forward by the Daughters of Gentlemen had convinced Tallie that any of her schoolfellows were more enlightened than she on the subject. Some had insisted that women carried a baby around in their stomach, for instance. Well, if that was so—how did they get the baby out? Cut it out? Vomit it?

In any case, how did a baby get in there in the first place? The man planted a seed in the woman? *A seed?* Babies didn't grow from seeds! They did, Amanda Forrest had said. Her mother had told her so. Well, how did they plant the seed—swallow it? Tallie suspected it was an old wives' tale—like that which said if you swallowed pumpkin seeds, pumpkin vines would grow out of your ears. Tallie had proven *that* one wrong by eating more than twenty pumpkin seeds—no hint of a vine had appeared from her ears, though she'd been a little anxious for a week or two!

No, Amanda hadn't been sure how the seed was planted, but it was much the same as animals did, she believed. Tallie had scoffed at that one—animals planting seeds? Ridiculous.

One girl, Emmaline Pearce, had spoken ghoulishly of wedding nights and blood and screaming, but everyone had known Emmaline Pearce was a shockingly untruthful girl who made up all sorts of deliciously scary tales. Miss Fisher had forever been punishing her for it.

Get with child. Surely she had the right to be told how it was done. Had her mother lived, she could have explained, but all Tallie's mother had left her was a few letters. And possibly— But there was no time to think on that... She had a wedding night to worry about first.

Tallie decided to ask Mrs Wilmot. She sought her out in the linen room and, with much beating around the bush, blurted out her question.

'Lord love you, Miss Tallie.' The housekeeper blushed. 'I'm not the one you should ask about such matters. I've never been wed, my dear.'

'But—'

'All housekeepers are called Missus, dearie, whether they're wed or not. But Wilmot is my maiden name.' She patted Tallie on the hand. 'You go ask your cousin, miss. She'll set you right.' The kindness shone so warmly from the elderly housekeeper's face that Tallie didn't have the heart to explain how very hostile Laetitia was.

Then she thought of the scullery maid, Maud, who was, according to rumour, *no better than she ought to be*. Surely Maud would know. But when Tallie asked her, Maud shrieked with laughter, tossed her apron over her face and ran from the room giggling, leaving Tallie red to the ears.

Finally she decided to approach her cousin about it.

Laetitia took one look at Tallie's blushing embarrassment, and snapped impatiently, 'Oh, God deliver me from puling virgins! Don't look so mealy-mouthed, girl—I'll tell you all you need to know about your wedding night.' She pulled Tallie down beside her and whispered detailed instructions in her ear. After a moment she sat back and pushed Tallie away.

Horrified, but too mortified to ask questions, Tallie turned to leave, but as she reached the door Laetitia hissed after her, 'Be sure you do not disgrace my cousin or your family. Remember, a lady endures it *in silence—without moving or flinching*. Do you hear me, girl?' She turned back to her mirror, a knowing smile on her face.

They were the last words Laetitia spoke to her, and the more she thought about them, the more nervous Tallie became. *Endure it?* What was *it*? Endurance sounded most unpleasant... And in *silence*? Why would she wish to cry out? Or flinch... It sounded painful. She thought briefly of Emmaline Pearce, then shook her head.

'Miss, miss, he's arrived!' Lucy, the maid, put her head around the door, her face lit with excitement. 'Your betrothed, miss—Lord d'Arenville—he's here!'

Tallie's heart seemed to stop for a moment, and then began to beat in double time. He was here. She would be able to speak to him, then—about Italy—before the wedding. It was what she had been hoping for. In the three weeks since he had galloped off so intemperately, she'd kicked herself often for not having sorted out everything to her satisfaction. She had to speak with him, get the whole thing settled before the wedding, for afterwards there would be little likelihood of him agreeing to the demands of a woman who'd sworn in church to obey him.

'I must see him at once.' Tallie started towards the door.

'Oh, miss, miss, you can't! It's bad luck, no matter how eager you are to see your handsome gentleman again!' Lucy beamed in fond indulgence. The entire household had reacted to the news of Tallie's wedding as if it was a fairy tale come true for her, and Tallie found she didn't have the heart to disillusion them.

'Bad luck? Why?'

Lucy gestured to Tallie's gown. 'For the groom to see the bride in her wedding dress, a'course.' She looked more closely at the wedding dress, and, frowning, reached out to tug one sleeve into place. 'Are you sure this—?'

'Oh, never mind that,' said Tallie. 'I'll change my dress, Lucy, since you say it's so important, but will you please take a message to Lord d'Arenville and tell him I must speak to him as soon as possible? In private.'

Realising she was to be Cupid's Messenger, Lucy beamed and said dramatically, 'Of course I will, Miss Tallie. I'll go straight away, and before you know it you'll be reunited once more with Your Beloved.' She sailed from the room.

Tallie giggled. Her Beloved? She giggled again, trying to imagine The Icicle involved in anything so human as a romantic assignation. It was simply not possible.

Having told the irritatingly coy maidservant he would meet Miss Robinson in the summerhouse in twenty minutes, Magnus found himself wondering why the girl wanted to speak to him so urgently. Something to do with her wedding finery, no doubt. He allowed himself a faint, cynical smile and felt in his pocket for the long oblong package. He was well ahead of her.

Magnus had ridden away from his last interview with his bride-to-be in a white-hot rage. He was still angry, but his rage had cooled to an icy implacability. Thalia Robinson would have to learn her place. If she wanted to be treated as a bride would wish to be treated she had better tread very lightly around him until she'd earned his forgiveness. He frowned and felt the package. He must make his motives for this gift very clear to her. He would not wish her to misunderstand him.

It had occurred to him a week before that she would very likely not possess any adequate jewellery. It was unthinkable that his bride wear cheap or shoddy jewellery at her wedding, so Magnus had looked through his late mother's jewel case until he had found a very pretty rope of matched pearls, earrings, and a bracelet—just right for a young bride. Simple enough to look modest and maidenly, yet the rope was very long and the pearls priceless. They were the perfect betrothal gift—and would be bound to go with whatever she had decided to wear.

From the little he had seen of her clothing, Miss Robinson preferred an odd style of garment, but Laetitia's taste was exquisite, and she would have ensured that his bride would not wear anything outrageous. And after they were married he'd supervise her wardrobe himself. The rest of his mother's jewels he would present to her as and when she deserved it.

'Lord d'Arenville?'

Magnus rose and turned quickly. He bowed slightly. 'Miss Robinson.' His eyes were cold, his patrician features impassive.

Tallie closed the door to the summerhouse behind her. Her heart was pounding as if she had been running and her hands felt clammy. She curtsied automatically, trying not to stare. Gracious, she'd forgotten how very handsome he was. It made it so much harder to remember how cold he was.

'I was under the impression that you wished to converse with me, but perhaps you merely wished to see for yourself that I had returned.' His tone was blighting.

'Oh, no,' Tallie responded instantly. 'I believed Lucy when she told me you'd arrived. Lucy is a very truthful girl.'

He missed her irony. 'Lucy?'

'The maid.' Tallie seated herself on a bench beside a wall.

Lord d'Arenville folded his arms, leaned against the wall and regarded her sardonically. He was looming again, Tallie thought resentfully, and obviously had no intention of making this any easier.

'I wished to see you in private because there are things we need to have clear before the wedding,' she said in a rush.

Have clear? His eyes narrowed. 'Are there indeed?'

'Yes. You left so suddenly I had no chance to talk to you about them.'

'Well, I am here now,' Magnus drawled.

'Th...they are very important to me, and I could not agree to marry you unless we do so.'

'I was under the impression that you had already agreed to marry me, madam,' he said silkily.

'Well, I did, yes, but we had not finished our discussion when you rushed out, and I only discovered later that you had gone to d'Arn...d'Anvil...' She stumbled over the word in her nervousness.

'D'Arenville Hall, madam. You had best learn the name, as it will be your home for the rest of your life.'

This veiled allusion to the rural imprisonment he planned for her threw Tallie into a temper. He did not know she had overheard him in the library that night, telling his cousin his plans for a bride and an heir. She recognised his threat.

'It is *not* my home yet.' Tallie bared her teeth in what she hoped would look like a smile. 'And there are issues to resolve before I agree to make it so—several conditions, in fact.'

Conditions! Magnus was outraged. The chit was trying to blackmail him. Threatening to jilt him unless he agreed to her demands. The day before the wedding, when guests would be arriving at any moment. By God she had a cheek!

With difficulty he held onto his temper, kept his face impassive. He would wait until he had heard her 'conditions'—then he'd show her who was master here! He'd march her to the church and marry her out of hand, and then set about teaching Miss Thalia Robinson a lesson she'd never forget! Gritting his teeth, he coolly inclined his head, inviting her to continue.

Tallie regarded him nervously. He was leaning casually against the wall, seemingly relaxed and at ease, but his jaw was clenched tight, and there was a most disturbing look in his eyes. She should not have spoken of conditions, should have put it more tactfully. He was annoyed. Still, this was her only opportunity to ensure that not all her dreams ended in the dust. A betrothed female still had some power—a wife had none.

'There are a number of cond—matters that we need to agree on. The first concerns children.'

He stared at her and his frown darkened. 'Go on.'

'I...I know you want children...but I must tell you that I will not...' Tallie gulped at the black look on his face, but forced herself to continue. 'I will *not* allow you to send them away to school.'

Magnus blinked. Her statement had taken him unawares. He'd thought she was going to refuse to bear his children, refuse to share his bed. Not send them to school? Did she think it a threat? 'And why should our children not be sent to school? Do you wish them to grow up ignorant and uneducated?'

'Of course not,' she flashed indignantly. 'They shall be taught at home, of course, by the very best and kindest governesses and tutors. I am not saying they shall *never* go to school, only *not* when they are still babies. When they are eleven or twelve, perhaps, but no younger than that.'

Magnus opened his mouth to agree to this extraordinary request, but was cut off.

'No, you need not argue—I am absolutely adamant on this point. I won't have my children sent off to be reared by strangers. Not until they are old enough. And *I* will decide when that is.'

She clenched her fists and glared at him defiantly, a mulish set to her jaw, and continued, 'Oh, you need not think I wish to tie them to my apron strings—I value strength and independence, and will nourish these qualities in my children—but you can have no idea the damage it does to very young children to be away from all that is familiar and those who love them, and I will *not* have my children feeling unloved and unwanted.' Her voice quavered with emotion and she stopped to catch her breath.

Magnus stared. He recalled the devastating loneliness he had first felt when sent off to school himself at the age of six. A lump in his chest made it difficult to breathe. 'I accept,' he said coldly.

Tallie blinked in surprise and relaxed slightly. The first hurdle had been unexpectedly easy. No argument at all. She supposed he didn't particularly care what happened to the children, as long as he had an heir. The next would be a little more difficult, for she could not let on she had overheard his infamous plan to immure her at d'Arenville Hall for ten years.

'You said I would be living at d'Arenville Hall for the rest of my life...'

He nodded curtly.

'Well, I wish to come up to London for a short visit once a year—no more than two or three weeks,' she added hurriedly. The black frown was back again. 'I realise you'd prefer me to stay at d'Arenville Hall, and for the most part I will, but I have never been to London and would very much like to visit it.'

He said nothing. He was going to refuse; Tallie could sense it. She hurried on, 'Your children's mother should not be totally ignorant of the world they will move in.'

Magnus was puzzled. On the contrary, he expected his children's mother to learn the ways of the polite world as soon as possible. Why would he wish her ignorant? He didn't see her point. It had something to do with visiting London. For a few weeks only. Was she trying to tell him she didn't wish to go out in society? The chit made no sense. Well, he would not take no for an answer on this one—he had every intention of taking her to London immediately, to order her new clothing, introduce her to society and teach her how his Countess should conduct herself. And the sooner Miss Thalia Robinson accepted that, the better. He did not want society to think the mother of his children was an obscure, ignorant rag-bag. He knew full well the gossip that had already arisen about his bride as a result of the house party.

'If you lock me away, people will gossip, and I would not want my children to discover that people think their mother is strange or odd or even mad,' concluded Tallie desperately.

Lock her away? Did the silly chit think he had a dungeon at d'Arenville Hall? Her eyes were fixed anxiously on his face. She looked rather appealing. Magnus frowned. 'I have every intention of taking you to London. I have no desire to have my wife thought an eccentric social recluse, madam, and the sooner you realise that the better.'

Tallie was amazed. Somewhere along the line he must have changed his mind about keeping her at d'Arenville Hall for ten years—or perhaps he planned to change his mind back again after the wedding. 'Do I have your word on it, sir?'

Magnus stiffened. He was not accustomed to having his word questioned. By anyone. And certainly not by an ill-dressed poor relation attempting to blackmail him.

'You do, madam,' he grated.

'Good.' Tallie smiled triumphantly. His anger at her question had confirmed her suspicions. He *had* planned to change his mind, but she'd been too clever for him. She'd gained his agreement to the most important things—now there was just the matter of the bride trip. It would be the most difficult, she knew. 'Now, my next request you may find a little unusual...and possibly a trifle expensive,' she said.

Magnus mentally braced himself. The last two 'requests' had, as he'd expected, been mere bagatelles, intended to soften him up. This one would be the cruncher.

'I have always wished to travel,' Tallie began, 'and I was hoping that you would agree that on the honey...on my bride trip we could visit some of the places I have always dreamed of seeing.' She clasped her hands in unconscious supplication. 'On the Continent.'

Magnus relaxed. So that was it. The girl wished to go to Paris. Not surprising. Every woman he'd ever known preferred French gowns, French hats and French perfumes. And the war was over... He shrugged mentally. It would be no hardship to take her to Paris and purchase her new wardrobe there. It might even be a good thing—allow her to acquire a touch of town bronze in Parisian society before she made her entrance in London.

He shrugged indifferently. 'All right. If you wish to brave the Channel crossing, we shall.'

Tallie was incredulous. 'You do not mind?'

Magnus shrugged again. 'Not at all.' He wondered what her final request would be. He shifted, and felt the bump of the jewel case in his pocket.

'The trip will take some time,' said Tallie. 'You may not care for the inconvenience. You are sure?'

The chit was questioning his word again, damn her! 'You have my word on it, Miss Robinson,' he snapped.

Tallie beamed. 'Then may I prepare an itinerary?'

Magnus inclined his head.

'I can speak several languages, you know,' she said confidingly. 'French, of course, and Italian, but also German and a little Dutch, for there was a girl from the Low Countries at school, and she taught me some Dutch and some Flemish, too.'

'What the devil are you talking about? You won't need all those languages in Paris.'

Tallie laughed. 'Not in Paris—for Italy—and elsewhere, of course. I won't need an interpreter in Paris. I told you—I speak French fluently. And Italian.'

'Do you mean to tell me you wish to travel to *Italy*?'

Tallie nodded. 'Yes...and Germany, Switzerland, and perhaps we can visit the Low Countries on our way back to England.' *Anywhere, as long as we go to Italy, where poor Mama died. And then, perhaps, I will be able to find out—for certain—if...*

'That is The Grand Tour,' said Magnus, in a forbidding tone.

'Yes. I have wanted to take it for years.'

'Quite impossible! And too dangerous—Europe is still at sixes and sevens because of the war.'

'Nonsense. It is perfectly safe since the Peace Treaty was signed at Amiens,' retorted Tallie triumphantly. 'Several of my cousin's acquaintances departed for Paris even before it was signed, and they are all surviving nicely.'

Magnus glared at her. Ladies were supposed to know nothing of political matters. She ought not to question his judgement.

'And if it is so terribly dangerous, why did you agree to take me to Paris?' she added.

'Paris is one thing—The Grand Tour another. Ladies do not take The Grand Tour,' he stated coldly.

'They do,' Tallie contradicted him. 'I know of several.'

Magnus stared down his nose at her. 'Perhaps you are speaking of females,' he said. 'I was referring to *ladies*.'

'Well, so was I!' retorted Tallie. 'Lady Mary Wortley Montagu, Lady Fetherstonhaugh, and...and Mrs Ann Radcliffe, who embarked on The Grand Tour with her husband, in the very year that Robespierre was guillotined—the same year her *Mysteries of Udolfo* was published, I believe.'

Magnus was exasperated. 'That damned silly book—'

'It is not a silly book! It is utterly thrilling, as anyone who did not have ice-water in his veins—'

'We are not speaking of Lady Mary Montagu or Lady Fetherstonhaugh or Mrs Radcliffe. We are speaking of *my wife*.'

'I am not your wife yet!' Tallie interrupted him. 'And you gave your word!'

'I gave my word to take you to Paris, but no further.'

'I never mentioned Paris, and neither did you,' argued Tallie. 'Not until *after* you gave your word.'

Magnus thought back. Damn it—the chit was right!

'The rigours and difficulties of The Grand Tour make it too exhausting and dangerous for females to attempt.' His voice brooked no argument.

'Nonsense. I have read *Letters From Italy*, and—'

'Hah!' Magnus snorted. 'Anne Miller's book was written thirty years ago and more.'

Tallie bridled. 'I know, for my mother read it on *her* Grand Tour, when she married my father. And it was *much* more dangerous in those days. Now that The Terror is over, all of England is flocking to the continent. People of the utmost respectability.' Her eyes dared him to contradict her.

There was a short silence. 'It will be extremely uncomfortable.

You will be miserable with the appalling accommodation,' stated Magnus. 'I know because I have travelled on the Continent. You cannot imagine the state of the roads—if roads they can be held to be. And as for the wretched inns—if inn you can find—on several occasions I had to sleep in a barn! With the animals!'

Tallie shrugged, unconcerned. 'It does not seem to have done you any harm. And if it is me you are concerned about, then let me remind you that I have spent most of my life in a seminary for young ladies—'

Despite his anger, Magnus's lips twitched. 'Are you suggesting that a seminary for young ladies is worse than a barn full of animals?'

Tallie laughed. 'Well, there were a couple of absolute cow—' She blushed, and caught herself up. 'No, of course not, but it was a very Spartan place, and I am tougher than I look.' She fixed him with her most determined expression. A few weeks ago he'd called her *sturdy*. Now, to save himself inconvenience, he was pretending she was too delicate. Lord d'Arenville would find he could not have it both ways. 'And anyway, you *promised*.'

Magnus swore under his breath. He was trapped and he knew it. The wretched girl was not going to give in on this—he could tell from her mulish expression. And he had promised, even if he hadn't meant what she said he'd meant. But he was damned if he was going to give in tamely. He cast around for a way out and had a sudden thought.

'Travel is very dangerous for ladies who are *in a delicate state*,' he stated. Let her try to refute that one.

Tallie looked puzzled. 'But I just told you I was stronger than I look. I am not the slightest bit delicate.'

He stared down into her innocent face and cursed silently. 'But you may be *in a delicate state* soon after your wedding,' he said. 'And many ladies become quite ill.'

'But why, when I am strong now? A little thing like a wedding isn't going to weaken me...' Suddenly Tallie paled, realising what he meant. He was talking about *it*. And he expected her to be *ill* after she had *endured it*. It was worse, then, than she had thought. It was not just that she must not move or cry out while she endured it, she could be sick for some time afterwards. Gracious—it must be very dreadful.

'If I were *in a delicate state*, and I am ill, would it last long, do you think?' she whispered.

Magnus was torn between concern at her sudden extreme pallor and embarrassment at discussing pregnancy with such an innocent. At least she *was* an innocent, he thought, and she should be discussing pregnancy with Laetitia, not her prospective bridegroom. But he had clearly frightened her by raising the question and was obligated to respond. 'I am not sure but...I, er...I believe many women feel ill for the first few months.'

Months! It must be appalling, Tallie thought. No wonder people did not inform girls about such things—they would never agree to marry. But surely it got better, otherwise why would women wish their daughters to be married?

'And after that?'

'After that, I believe they usually feel quite well until they are brought to bed.' Magnus drew out a handkerchief to wipe his brow. His betrothed was clearly shaken. Obviously it had not occurred to her that she might begin breeding while she was on the Continent. Strike while the iron is hot, he decided.

'So we are agreed—if you find yourself *in a delicate condition* the Tour will be called off and we will return to England at once.'

Tallie chewed her lip. She was strong. Her mother had managed it. So could she. And if she really was ill, she supposed there would be no point in travelling.

'Very well,' she agreed grudgingly.

Magnus refrained from rubbing his hands in triumph. He had every intention of getting her with child before there was any question of travelling beyond Paris. He would take her to Paris, show her the sights, purchase gowns and hats and perfumes and all manner of feminine fripperies, then whisk her home to d'Arenville Hall to await the birth of their child.

Their child. He could not wait. But first he had to get the wedding over with.

'And what is your next ''condition'', may I ask?' he said.

'Next condition? There are none. You have agreed to everything, more or less.' Tallie was still worrying about the wedding night.

Magnus was stunned, and vaguely suspicious. He'd been certain that she was building up to something truly outrageous.

Tallie stood up to leave. 'Thank you for agreeing to speak to me. You have relieved my mind...about some things.' *And frightened me to pieces about others.* She opened the door.

Magnus recalled the jewel case in his pocket. 'Miss Robinson, a moment longer, if you please.'

'Yes?' She turned back and looked at him, wide-eyed and pale.

'You may wish to wear these at your wedding. They belonged to my mother.' He held out the box.

Tallie opened it. 'Pearls, how pretty,' she said dully. 'Thank you very much. I shall wear them tomorrow, since you ask.'

She shut the box and left the summerhouse. Magnus stood watching her cross the lawn and enter the house, frowning. He'd never had a woman accept jewellery in quite that manner. There'd been no squeals of joy, no excited hugs or kisses, no play-acting and flirtation. Not that he wanted that sort of response from the woman he would take to wife, Magnus told himself. Not at all.

He should be happy to discover his intended bride wasn't greedy or grasping. He *was* happy. Her cool acceptance was well-bred and ladylike... It was, in fact, exactly how his mother had accepted jewels from his father.

And why did that thought annoy him so much?

Nonsense! He was *not* annoyed. There was no reason to be annoyed. She'd answered him perfectly politely.

Too politely.

She'd accepted his gift of priceless pearls like a child accepting an apple, with polite, mechanical thanks, quite as if she was thinking about something else.

Damn it all, but this girl was an enigma to him. Magnus didn't like enigmas. And he was *very* annoyed.

Chapter Five

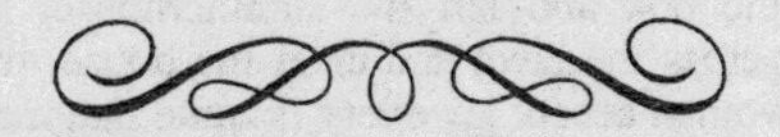

Old Mr Penworthy, the organist, plays the opening chord, so softly that at first the congregation is barely aware of it. Gradually the music swells, filling the ancient and beautiful church with a glorious torrent of sound. The bride has arrived.

The pews are crowded to bursting point, mostly with friends of the bride, well-wishers from the village and from much farther afield. There are foreign dignitaries, resplendent in silk hats, glittering with medals and imperial orders—men who knew the bride's father abroad, who come to her wedding representing princes, dukes—even an emperor.

Outside in the churchyard, tall, handsome men watch from a distance, loitering palely, some gnashing their teeth, others silent and crushed with despair—their hopes and hearts dashed for ever by the bride's acceptance of another.

In the lane beyond the churchyard wall sit two elegant carriages. Rumour has it each carriage contains an aristocratic lady, each one an heiress and a diamond of the first water. Screened from the stares of the vulgar by delicate black netting, the ladies weep. Their beauty, their riches and their rank serve them naught, for the groom has chosen his bride, and she is no famous beauty, nor even rich or aristocratic. But she offers him a prize he values beyond earthly riches—her heart. And he gives her his in return.

The first chord draws to a close and the bride steps into the centre aisle. The congregation turns to look and a sigh whispers around the church. From where she stands, the bride can hear only fragments of what they say... 'Lovely gown...' 'A beautiful bride...'

The music swells again and she begins her slow walk down the aisle. Her beloved awaits her. His eyes feast on her. He makes a small move towards her, as if he cannot wait for her to reach him but must rush up the aisle and take her in his arms. She almost weeps with joy at his loving impatience; she, too, wants to run down the aisle towards him and fling herself into his arms. Instead she walks in proud and happy dignity, her head held high, feeling, as she always does when he looks at her, beautiful.

Mr Penworthy times it perfectly; as she reaches the altar, the music soars to its final crescendo. The last notes echo around the ancient oaken rafters and her beloved takes her hand in his, murmuring, 'Tallie, my own true love, you make me the happiest man on earth.' He lifts her gloved hand to his mouth, and...

'Ouch! Bloody h—what the dev—er, deuce do you think you're doing?' exclaimed Lord d'Arenville angrily, one hand clamped over his nose—the nose that Tallie's gloved hand had forcibly collided with. His eyes were watering from the impact. He blinked down at her, then took her hand, which still hovered dangerously close to his face. A faint cloud of aromatic brown dust rose from her glove.

He stared down at her hands, raised one cautiously to his nose and tentatively sniffed. 'Good God! They reek of coffee!'

Tallie didn't respond. She just stared up at him, the last remnants of her dream shattering around her feet. For one heart-stopping moment, when he had lifted her hand to his face again, she'd thought he was going to kiss it. But it was not to be. The Icicle was incapable of a romantic gesture like that. He was merely inspecting her gloves.

His grip on her hand tightened and he thrust it down between them. He nodded at the vicar. The vicar stood staring at Tallie, bemused.

'Get on with it, man,' said Lord d'Arenville curtly.

'Er, of course,' the vicar muttered, then announced in ringing, mellifluous tones, 'Dearly beloved, we are gathered...'

Dazed, Tallie stood there, listening to herself being married to The Icicle. And a very bad-tempered Icicle he was, too. He was positively glaring at her. Of course, he did have reason to be a little cross, but it wasn't as if she had meant to hit him on the nose, after all.

Mind you, she thought dejectedly, he seemed always to be furious about something—mainly with her. Towards others he invariably remained cool, polite and, in a chilly sort of fashion, charming. But not with Tallie... It didn't augur at all well for the future.

Still, Tallie rallied her spirits, this was her wedding day, and she'd made up her mind to enjoy every moment of it. She began to mentally tick off her blessings: the weather was almost sunny, and the wind not too cold at all. And her frock had turned out quite well—the lovely amber material was absolutely perfect for her colouring, and she was sure no one would notice the one or two little mistakes she'd made. The music had been absolutely glorious—Mr Penworthy had truly outdone himself—and her cousin's husband George had escorted her down the aisle looking every inch a gentleman. He wasn't even very drunk, as far as she could tell.

And if she wasn't the most ecstatic bride in the world, she was determined no one else would notice. All brides were happy and joyful—she didn't want her friends and relations upset by her own misgivings. That was why she'd invoked her fantasy—it was one of her favourites—and because of it she'd been able to act like a radiant bride should. She hoped everyone had been taken in by her performance—she didn't want to disappoint them.

She wondered where they were sitting—she'd been too involved in her fantasy to notice. She turned her head to take a quick glance at the pews behind her, searching for Brooks, Mrs Wilmot and the children...

'Thalia!' Lord d'Arenville's hand jerked her back to face the altar.

Tallie blinked at it for a moment. She felt dizzy, bereft, disorientated. She looked helplessly up at Lord d'Arenville. He stared back, his brow furrowed, his cold grey eyes intense. One hand held hers. His other arm slid around her and tightened around her waist. For a moment it seemed to Tallie that he could see into her very soul. She quivered under the hard gaze and closed her eyes—the intrusion was too painful. For a moment or two she was aware of nothing but the cold chill of the church and the pressure of his arm supporting her. His arm felt warm, but the grey eyes watching her looked angry. In the distance she could hear the vicar mumbling something. She closed her eyes harder, wishing with all her heart she could invoke her fantasy back to deal with this. She heard the vicar mumbling again. Lord d'Arenville gave her a little squeeze and Tallie opened her eyes.

'Do you, Thalia Louise Robinson take this man...?' intoned the vicar forcefully, his manner conveying to Tallie that he was repeating the question, and not for the first time.

Embarrassed, Tallie mumbled, 'I do,' and hurriedly repeated after him the words about loving, honouring and obeying Lord d'Arenville. She shivered.

She was bound for life to Magnus Philip Audley St Clair, Seventh Earl of d'Arenville. A surge of deepest misery washed over her. Her wedding was so very different from what she had hoped for, dreamed of. And she didn't mean all that nonsense about rejected suitors and important guests and beautiful gowns—that silliness had nothing to do with her true dreams.

All she truly wanted was to be loved.

The other had been mere play-acting, an attempt to distract herself, to get through the day with some semblance of good spirits in order not to disappoint her friends. But there hadn't been much point...

Dully, she felt her glove being tugged off.

'With this ring I thee wed, with my body I thee worship...' His voice was deep, harsh.

The ring was cold as it slid onto her finger.

She was married.

Tallie glanced up at her husband. He was staring down at her small hand, still resting in his large one. She followed his gaze and saw the faint brown stains on her fingers from the dye she had used on her gloves and lace. And at the end of each grubby hand was a chewed and ugly fingernail. That was what her new husband was staring at—her dirty hands and horrible bitten nails.

He put back her veil and kissed her, a hard, brief pressure on her mouth, then straightened, having done his duty. A lump rose in her throat and she bit her lip to stop it trembling. Such a cold, hollow sham of a wedding.

It was her own fault, she knew. She had stupidly allowed herself to dream of how it would be, and so of course she was disappointed. She invariably was. Life was always a disappointment when compared with her dreams. So the dreaming would have to stop...

But, oh, she'd never felt so miserable or alone in her life. Tallie felt a tear roll down her cheek, then another. She surreptitiously wiped them away. She straightened, preparing herself for the walk back down the aisle. She looked at the sparse, silent congregation and cast a quick glance up at the grim face of her new husband.

A straggle of the poorer villagers were watching from the very back of the church—come, possibly, with the expectation of largesse from the rich and happy groom. Tallie sighed. The villagers were, like everyone else, doomed to disappointment in her wedding, for the veriest blind man could see that her groom was not happy. There would be no largesse.

Magnus was indeed not happy. He was furious. Had been from the moment his cousin Laetitia, swooning artistically, had claimed she could not move another step that morning, that her head was positively shattered and the pain simply too, too much for a lady to bear. She had collapsed onto a Grecian sofa, reviving sufficiently to forbid that the children be taken to the church, claiming they were sickening for something, a mother always knew. It would be the basest cruelty to tear her beloved ones away from their mama when she was in such agony. A frail wisp of lace had been delicately brandished and applied to dry eyes. A battalion of small crystal bottles had been hastily arranged on a small table nearby—smelling salts, a vinaigrette, cologne water, feathers to burn...

Magnus had been helpless in the face of this determined barrage of feminine sensibility. The children had looked perfectly healthy to him. Nor had he missed their disappointed little faces when they'd come downstairs dressed in their best and their mother's decision had been announced.

Then Laetitia had insisted that she could not possibly spare Mrs Wilmot—no one's hands were as gentle and healing when it came to the headache. And, of course, Brooks would have to remain at the house—someone had to run the household while its mistress was indisposed.

Magnus had seen that Brooks and Mrs Wilmot had also been crushed with disappointment. They too had been dressed in their Sunday best—Mrs Wilmot in a large flowered hat, with a bunch of violets pinned to her bosom. For a moment he'd half expected her to argue with Laetitia. But they were elderly servants, entirely dependent on Laetitia's good will and with an uncertain old age facing them. Like the children, they had had no choice but to obey.

Magnus had fumed impotently. He could not veto the orders of a woman in her own house, particularly when those orders concerned her own children and servants.

But when Laetitia had claimed, in a failing thread of a voice, that she could not do without the comfort of her husband's presence in this, her hour of infirmity, Magnus had intervened. He had practically frogmarched George into the carriage, turning a deaf ear to Laetitia's wailing and George's blustering. The short trip to church had been accomplished in a mood of grim silence.

Alighting from the carriage, Magnus had looked around, frowning. There had been suspiciously few carriages. He'd told Laetitia to arrange a small wedding—meaning he didn't want a huge noisy crowd. But this...

He'd entered the church in a mood of black foreboding. His suspicions had been confirmed. The only people seated had been the two or three people he'd invited himself—none of them particularly close.

Not that he had many close friends—he would have liked Freddie to stand up with him, but Freddie had sent word that there was an outbreak of typhus in the village and he could not leave his wife and children, nor his parish, at such a time. Nor would he wish to risk conveying the disease to Magnus and his new bride.

So the only people seated in the church had been a couple of chaps from his club, a fellow he'd known at Oxford, who lived locally, and Magnus's valet, his groom and his tiger. A congregation of six—three of them servants and all male.

Magnus had cursed long and silently. Better to have no one at all than to humiliate his little bride with such a poor showing. For himself, he cared not a jot—marriage was a business transaction, and required the bare minimum of fuss. He was acquiring a wife who, with God's blessing, would give him children, and she was acquiring wealth, a title, and security for her lifetime.

But women set great store in weddings.

The bigger the better. With hordes of people. Expensive gowns and jewels. Flowers. Champagne. Happy throngs of celebrating guests! That was what women liked—he was sure of it. And little Thalia Robinson would be no exception; he was sure of that, too.

So where the hell was everyone?

And what the hell was he going to do?

What the devil had Laetitia been up to? He'd *told* her to organise everything, damn it! And it wasn't as if she'd indicated it would be any sort of imposition—far from it.

Women *liked* organising these affairs—look at how Laetitia had jumped at arranging that blasted house party with all those simpering debutantes. She'd organised that at a moment's notice. She'd had weeks to arrange his wedding. Three whole weeks. And a day or two to spare. He'd given her *carte blanche* with the arrangements. And the costs. And had sent her a stunning emerald necklace.

So where were all the happy blasted guests?

The organist had played the opening chords and Magnus had turned to see Miss Thalia Robinson, his bride, standing at the entrance of the church. Smiling blissfully. Beatifically. For a moment he'd frozen, staring, riveted by her smile—dazzling, even from behind the lace veil she was wearing. Her smile had driven every angry thought from his head. Every thought.

She had looked radiant. Beautiful. And utterly happy.

Was this the same girl he'd overheard sobbing? Alone and forlorn on a cold afternoon in her cousin's garden maze. Sobbing as if her heart would break—because Lord d'Arenville had offered her marriage.

The girl who, with reddened eyes and blotchy skin, had accepted his offer in a bleak little voice laced with defeat?

The girl who'd cold-bloodedly laid down her set of conditions only days before the wedding?

But today she was smiling...

Music had filled the church, soaring up amongst the blackened oak rafters as she had stepped out onto the strip of red matting which ran down the centre of the aisle. Her movement had jolted him out of his daze, and as he had watched her walking slowly towards him, floating proudly to the music, he'd gradually become aware of what she was wearing. And his frown had slowly returned.

Magnus was no great follower of feminine fashions, but he knew when something looked right. Or, in this case, when it looked wrong. Though exactly what it was he hadn't quite been able to put his finger on. The pale shimmering amber colour was not particularly fashionable, but it suited her. The fabric seemed rather too stiff for the soft, gauzy look which was so *à la mode* today, but that was not the problem...

His eyes had been drawn to the neckline, and for a moment he hadn't believed his eyes. It was *crooked.* Distinctly crooked. And so, now he had come to notice it, were her sleeves—or at least one of them was. And the gown hung all wrong. She had a nice little figure, he had realised suddenly, but this gown was utterly atrocious.

His temper had grown. How the devil had Laetitia allowed Thalia Robinson to go to her wedding dressed in a gown like that? Women always strove to look their best, but the most important time of all, the day when every woman expected to look beautiful, was on her wedding day. It was another thing Magnus understood about women. Which was why he'd specifically told his cousin to spare no expense in fitting out his bride. So why was she not wearing the finest gown a London modiste could provide? Good God, she looked for all the world as if her gown had been made by some half-wit in the village!

The closer his bride had come, the more he had noticed. Stains on the gloves, inadequately removed. A darn in the lace of her veil. A crooked hem. Uneven stitching...the list had grown.

And through it all Thalia Robinson had smiled, as if this truly was the happiest day of her life. As if she was not dressed in a frightful travesty of a wedding dress. As if the church was not virtually empty of well-wishers. As if Magnus was the man she loved...

He'd stared, angry, bemused, dazzled...

And then she'd cracked him on the nose so hard that tears had come into his eye and he'd been embarrassed, and growled out something which had caused the smile to drop from her face and the joy to seep out of her body. He'd watched it happen before his very eyes—one moment she had been joyous and radiant, the next miserable.

So then Magnus had really been furious. With himself.

He'd tried to keep her from noticing how few people there were in the church. He was sure she hadn't yet seen who was or wasn't there—her eyes hadn't left his on her proud, triumphal march down the aisle; she'd been smiling at him and only him.

But he hadn't succeeded. He knew to the second the moment she had realised there was no one on her side of the church. That no one had come to see Thalia Robinson married. The small gloved hand lying so limply in his had suddenly gripped him, tightening convulsively around his fingers. She had made no other sign, had stood straight and slender, looking ahead at the stained glass window above the altar, but Magnus had felt her trembling. Beneath the darned veil he had seen her biting her lip, struggling to maintain her composure. He had slid his arm around her, and unknowingly she had clutched onto him, tighter than ever, hanging onto his hand as if it was all she had to hold her up.

That pathetic, wounded look she'd given him had pierced him to the core. He would never forget it.

She had expected well-wishers—the children, the housekeeper and the butler at least. And was reeling under the cruel impact of the empty pews. And Magnus had been able to do nothing about it. Except become even more furious.

Then he'd tugged off her glove—her attention had been elsewhere at the time—and slipped his ring on her finger. She'd repeated her vows in a wooden little voice, and as he'd listened he had stared down at his ring, gleaming on the small, stained paw with the childishly chewed nails. And had wondered what the hell he was doing, marrying this little orphaned stranger, so very much out of her depth in his cynical, sophisticated world.

And so very innocent and vulnerable and alone.

The coach swayed and bounded along the road at a breakneck pace. Tallie had been proudly informed by Lord d'Arenville's coachman that the vehicle was the latest design, built for speedy modern travel and sprung to ensure the smoothest ride. She hung onto the travelling straps like grim death, wedged into the corner of the coach as tightly as she could to prevent herself being thrown off the seat again. Tallie was feeling rather queasy. She had travelled very little in her adult life—only from Miss Fisher's seminary to her cousin's house. If this was what travelling entailed... And this was England, where the roads were said to be the best in the world...

Her mother must have been stronger than she'd realised. Lord d'Arenville had not exaggerated when he had said that travel was difficult for a lady to endure— But of course! That was it! The realisation hit Tallie like a bolt of lightning. That was the reason for this dreadful journey—undertaken in such a rush and at the last minute! Departing in the late afternoon, when nobody ever travelled in the dark unless they could help it! Pretending he had quarrelled with Laetitia and would stay not a moment longer in her house. Bundling Tallie into his coach on her wedding day, tossing her embarrassingly small bundle of belongings after her and riding off on his own horse as if the hounds of hell were in pursuit. What nonsense!

As if Lord d'Arenville—The Icicle—ever dashed about the country in a rage. The man was a positive by-word for cold self-control. He must be trying to frighten her, to get her to change her mind about foreign travel. The day before, he'd made no secret of his opposition to it. Hah! Lord d'Arenville would find his bride was not so simple—she was awake to his dastardly machinations! She *would* have her Grand Tour. He'd *promised*!

Tallie sat up, her queasiness forgotten in the light of her discovery. For some reason she felt immensely cheered. She'd had some slight suspicion that she'd been, in some unknown way, the cause of his quarrel with her cousin.

The moment they had arrived back from the church he'd sent her upstairs with a maid to refresh herself while he spoke to Laetitia. Tallie, annoyed to be dismissed like a child, had crept back down the stairs to listen at the door, but had heard frustratingly few actual words—only the sound of their voices. His voice had been icy-cold, cutting, as if flaying her cousin with sarcasm, but Tallie could not see why *he* should have been so cross.

She had a right to be upset—a tearful Mrs Wilmot had explained how Laetitia had prevented herself, Brooks and the children from coming to the wedding. But *he* would care little about that; he'd wanted a small wedding—she'd heard him say so. And look at how few people he'd invited!

Pressing an ear to the thick wooden door panel, Tallie had been sure she'd heard something about a dress. Her dress? She'd pressed her ear harder to the door. But then he had said something about a village half-wit, so that couldn't be it. And Laetitia had denied any responsibility for it and burst into noisy tears. It had all been very peculiar, and Tallie had been most intrigued, but then she'd heard his footsteps coming towards the door and she'd fled up the stairs.

So, it was all a hum—Tallie was convinced of it. And she was going to teach her husband a lesson about attempting to trick women out of their promised rights. She pulled open the shutters which covered the coach window. The sound of the pounding hooves and the creaking springs was almost deafening. Holding the leather straps tightly, Tallie knelt on her seat and peered out of the window.

It was very dark. Clouds moved across the sky, obscuring the moonlight intermittently. Wind whipped at her hair, tiny pellets of rain stung her cheeks and dark shadows whooshed past the window at an incredible rate. Goodness knew how fast they were travelling—Tallie had heard some gentlemen kept teams of horses that could travel at twelve, even fifteen miles an hour. The speed was a little scary, but also very exciting.

Tallie took several deep breaths. The fresh night air was most exhilarating, and she felt a thrill of naughtiness as she breathed it in—Miss Fisher had maintained the night air contained evil humours. Her pupils had been strictly forbidden to breathe it. Tallie wound the straps around her wrists more securely and leaned farther out, inhaling blissfully. Her husband was out there somewhere ahead, riding his own horse—not for him a stuffy ride in a horrid jolting coach. The coach lanterns provided some light, by which she could see the outline of the two rear horses, but there was no sign of Lord d'Arenville. He was probably a long way ahead of them.

'What the devil do you think you're doing?' a voice suddenly roared in her ear, giving Tallie such a fright that she almost let go of her straps.

She turned her head and saw her husband had come up close beside the carriage, so close she could almost reach out and touch him. Her mouth dropped open. She stared, wide-eyed, suddenly oblivious of the lurching of the coach. This was her husband? This creature of speed and power, shadows and moonlight—this was The Icicle?

He rode as if born to the saddle. Tallie had heard the expression before but had never been able to imagine it. She stared, half fearfully, at the superb black beast beneath him, gleaming with sweat in the moonlight. She noted its strong arched neck, the powerful hindquarters, the steam coming from its nostrils, the slight flecks of foam at its mouth. It seemed enormous, and very fierce, its hooves pounding through the night. And yet her husband dominated this huge, powerful beast effortlessly. Tallie had never ridden a horse—it had not been on Miss Fisher's curriculum...but ancient myths and legends had.

Suddenly Tallie knew exactly what a centaur looked like.

She had always imagined them to be rather ridiculous creatures—but this... He was...magnificent.

She stared at horse and man, pounding along in the intermittent darkness, now a mysterious black creature of the night, now a gleaming silver knight, kissed by moonlight. He rode bare-headed, and wet locks of dark hair clung romantically to his brow. How he could ride his horse so perilously close to a racing, bouncing carriage was more than Tallie could understand—it looked frightfully dangerous.

And then she suddenly remembered—he was probably trying to scare her. She turned a blinding smile on him, freed one hand and waved.

He moved even closer. 'Is something wrong?' he shouted.

Hah! thought Tallie. You hope in vain, my lord. 'Not...in the least,' she shrieked back at him, her hair whipping about her face. 'In fact...it is monstr—' The coach lurched and she nearly fell off her seat again.

'What did you say?' he yelled. 'Are you all right?'

Tallie plastered her smile back in place. 'I am per—perfectly well, my lord,' she shouted as she jounced around on the leather cushions. 'This tr—trip is...most delightful! I am having—' She hauled herself back from the edge of the seat again and clamped her fingers onto the window frame. 'I am having...a won—wonderful time. It...is monstrous exciting!' She directed the biggest smile she could muster out into the darkness. That should do it, she thought.

'We'll stop in an hour or so.' Lord d'Arenville rode even closer to her window. 'You can rest and recover yourself then. We shall sleep the night at an inn.' He galloped off into the darkness.

Sleep the night! Tallie gulped. She had forgotten—it was her wedding night. And at some time tonight, in some unknown inn, Lord d'Arenville would *know* her, and she would become, in truth, his wife. Her mouth was suddenly dry.

Chapter Six

The inn was small and ancient, with exposed black beams and a sagging roof. Lamps spilled warm puddles of golden light across the wet cobblestones. The coach stood in the courtyard, the horses weary, their breath smoky against the shadows.

The rain had intensified in the last hour. Lord d'Arenville waited to hand Tallie down. She emerged stiffly and stumbled as she landed on the wet and slippery cobbles, but a cold, strong hand caught her and she was safe. Her husband pulled her hard against his body and allowed his greatcoat to drop over her, shielding her from the rain.

The sensation was overwhelming. His body radiated warmth and strength and power. And an odour—not at all unpleasant, she decided—of horse, damp wool, leather and fresh male sweat. Tallie allowed her body to lean against his, knowing her behaviour was indecorous and that there were grooms and other people watching. She was too cold to argue, too tired to pull away—and in any case his arm was wrapped around her like a warm steel band, and she could not have moved away if she'd tried. She had never been so close to a man before and was entirely taken up with the sensations it produced in her. Odd, fluttery sensations. And a sort of breathlessness.

Nerves, she decided. Bridal nerves...

'Landlord!' Lord d'Arenville shouted, hustling her inside. 'A private parlour, and refreshments for my wife!' He handed her over to the care of a large clucking woman, the landlord's wife.

She ushered Tallie to a small, cosy sitting room with a fire crackling in the grate.

Shivering with cold, Tallie stood as close to the fire as she dared. Lord d'Arenville's coach contained several warm fur rugs, which she had used, but they hadn't prevented a chill from seeping into her bones, a chill she knew stemmed as much from nerves as from cold.

Tallie looked around her. The inn might be old, but it was clean and warm. There was a knock on the door and the landlord's wife bustled back in, bobbed an awkward curtsy and set down a tray containing a large steaming jug, some cut lemons, a small brown pot and several pewter mugs. An enticing aroma of wine, spices and citrus fruit came from the jug.

''Ere you are, milady. 'Is lordship bespoke some mulled wine, and says you're to take some immediate and not to wait for 'im to arrive. 'E's seeing to the 'orses, makin' all right and tight.' She chuckled. 'There be no need to worry. Our Jem reckons it's Christmas—such prime bits o' blood 'is lordship's 'orses are.'

She poured some steaming liquid into a mug and handed it to Tallie, beaming. 'Drink it down now, milady. It'll warm your blood proper.'

It was very strange, Tallie thought, to be addressed as milady, but she supposed she would become accustomed to it. She took a cautious sip of the steaming drink, then smiled at the hovering woman. 'It's very good,' she said softly, and sipped again.

The woman beamed. 'Good of you to say so, milady, but there's more lemons if you want them, and honey, too, if it be too sour for you.'

'No, no, it's very good just as it is,' Tallie assured her, taking a large swallow of the hot drink and feeling the tangy warmth of it curl around her empty insides. 'Thank you.'

The landlord's wife seemed to swell with delight. 'A pleasure to be serving such a kind-spoken lady. The Quality ain't so easy to please in general. Now, I'll be off to the kitchen, milady, but I'll be back in a trice with dinner for 'is lordship and yourself. I've got a couple o' fat hens a-roasting, and a stewed pig's ear and faggots, as tender and sweet as you could wish for. And mutton pie, if 'is lordship fancies it.' She frowned and hesitated. 'I—er—I didn't 'ave much warning of your arrival, milady, so I'm afraid I ain't got no jellies or...or delicacies what a lady might—'

'Please don't worry, Mrs...?' Tallie reached for the jug, refilled her mug, added honey, and sat on a plush-covered chair.

'Mrs Farrow, milady. Farrow, my 'usband, be the landlor—'

'Mrs Farrow, you must not worry about any lack of ladylike delicacies. I am hungry enough to eat whatever you can provide, and I am sure Lord d'Arenville is too. And if he is not,' Tallie added, with a gleam of mischief, 'he has only himself to blame, does he not?' She took another mouthful of mulled wine. 'He did not, after all, give you sufficient notice of his arrival.'

The landlord's wife, appalled at being implicated in any criticism of a lord, uttered a series of embarrassed disclaimers and hurriedly curtsied herself out.

Tallie reached forward and refilled her mug. She sat back in her chair, snuggling against the warm plush, remembering Miss Fisher's high, adenoidal voice—'A lady never allows her spine to contact the back of a chair.' She took another sip of mulled wine. It really was a most deliciously warming and relaxing concoction. She had tasted wine before, and had found it rather nasty, but this—the lemons, honey and cinnamon—made such a delightful difference.

She kicked off her slippers and tucked her stockinged feet under her—another of Miss Fisher's solecisms—and basked in the warmth provided by the fire and the mulled wine. The scent of roasting meat tantalised her tastebuds. She leaned her head on the back of the chair. So nice not to be bouncing and jolting around... Such an interesting journey... She closed her eyes...

The dashing highwayman thundered along the road in daredevil pursuit of the runaway coach. The coach lurched and swayed perilously, but the kidnapped princess remained calm, knowing her beloved was riding ventre à terre *to rescue her.*

Desperately she battered at the shutters which the evil Count had nailed over the coach windows, but they were too strong for her. Then, suddenly, crash! With a splintering of wood the shutters were wrenched away from without. Laughing with joy, the lost princess leaned out, her long dark tresses tossing romantically in the wind.

'Beloved,' he called in his deep and manly voice. 'I am here. Hold out your arms.' Smiling into the darkness, the princess trustfully held out her arms. Hooves pounded, wind whipped at her hair, and then out of the inky depths of the night rode the high-

wayman, moving as one with his magnificent jet-black steed. He rode perilously close to the razor-sharp wheels of the coach. The treacherous coachman turned his gun and fired. She gasped, filled with horror.

But the highwayman's gleaming white teeth glinted in the moonlight and she heard his soft laugh. Suddenly she was seized in a strong, secure grip and lifted by powerful arms onto the back of his gallant steed. 'Cold, my little love?' he murmured, his breath warm against her ear, and he wrapped his black velvet cloak around her shivering body and drew her close.

His strength supported her and his body warmed her, smelling of leather, wet wool and fresh male sweat. 'You belong to me now, Tallie, my dearest one,' he said, 'and I belong to you.' And, holding her safe against his heart, he galloped into the night...

Magnus, stripping a sodden pair of leather gloves from his hands, had to duck his head under the low, smoke-stained portal as he entered the private parlour. His riding buckskins and his high leather boots were spattered with mud.

He straightened, sniffing appreciatively. 'Ahh, mulled—' He stopped, seeing his bride of ten hours curled up in a chair like a kitten, her slippers kicked carelessly off, sound asleep. He stood looking down at her. Her hair tumbled about her shoulders; damp wispy curls clung to her pale forehead and clustered around her neck. Long dark lashes fanned her cheeks, which were flushed from the heat of the fire. Or maybe not, he thought wryly, as he bent down and removed the pewter mug which dangled precariously from one hand.

He put a hand on her shoulder. 'Thalia,' he said, then, 'Thalia,' more loudly. She didn't stir. He decided to let her sleep until dinner arrived.

He poured himself a mug of mulled wine and drained it quickly, shuddering pleasurably as the warm spicy liquid flowed down his throat. He poured himself another, then set it down pensively, his eyes on the sleeping girl. She looked exhausted. Magnus watched the gentle rise and fall of her chest and regretted the rough haste of the journey. He should not have inflicted such a long trip on his gently bred bride, especially on her wedding day. Not that little Thalia Robins—no, Thalia St Clair she was now—was particularly gently bred.

He shook his head, recalling the way the little hoyden had hung out the window of the coach, pert little nose in the air, her hair whipping around her face, her eyes huge and dark in the pallor of her face. Her skin had been damp with rain, glowing softly in the moonlight as she had shrieked some nonsense about how much she was enjoying the journey. Monstrous exciting, indeed! His lips twitched. She'd looked frightened half out of her wits.

Magnus sipped the mulled wine and watched his bride sleep. He noticed the faint sprinkling of freckles over the bridge of her tip-tilted nose. Freckles were generally held to be a flaw, but hers were oddly appealing. It was almost impossible to believe that he'd married this little scrap of humanity. He didn't feel married. And he had so little in common with her. His wife. His new Countess. His impulsive choice of her was most unlike him.

He would have to train her, he supposed, train her until she resembled the wives... He frowned, considering the way he'd become acquainted with most of those wives... No, he didn't want her to be a typical society wife at all. He'd be damned if he'd let her cuckold him. This Lady d'Arenville would not stray from her marital bed; he'd make sure of that!

He took another sip of wine and pulled a face. It was almost cold. He leant over towards the fireplace and pushed the blackened poker into the coals. Thalia, he pondered, watching the flames flicker and dance. Peculiar name. It didn't suit her at all. He wouldn't saddle a child of his with a name like that...a child of his... With any luck she could conceive this very night...

The poker soon began to glow red-hot, and he pulled it out, shook the ash from it, then plunged it into the jug of spiced wine. It sizzled briefly, and aromatic steam filled the air. He tossed the poker back onto the hearth, poured the heated mixture back into his mug and drank deeply.

The innkeeper, Farrow, entered with a tray of steaming dishes. Magnus silently indicated his sleeping wife. Farrow and several creeping minions set out cutlery, glasses and dishes with muted clatters and clinks, Farrow issuing instructions in a hoarse whisper that could probably be heard in the next room. The new Lady d'Arenville slept on, serenely oblivious.

When the innkeeper had left, Magnus touched her shoulder. 'Thalia, our dinner has arrived.' She didn't move. He shook her gently and she stirred, but did not awaken. He stood for a moment, oddly unsure of himself. She probably was hungry—there had been no proper wedding breakfast after all—she had eaten nothing for hours. But women seemed to eat almost nothing anyway, and she did seem to be very tired. Perhaps it would be better to let her sleep through dinner and then wake her when it was time to go up to bed.

Yes, that was the better plan. He would wake her then, for he had every intention of consummating his marriage tonight. The sooner he got her with child the sooner she would forget about this Grand Tour nonsense.

Magnus twirled a glass of port in his hand, admiring the flickering flames of the fire through its ruby glow and berating himself for his uncharacteristic state of indecision. After a hearty dinner and several glasses of good claret he was now perfectly ready to undertake his duties as a bridegroom. But she was still asleep. Frowning, he set his glass down and walked towards his wife. He shook her shoulder again. She did not move, did not so much as flicker an eyelid. He bent over, slid his hands under her and lifted. She stirred, muttered, and snuggled her cheek against his chest. Her arms and legs dangled bonelessly. Curse the girl—she slept like the dead.

Grunting slightly, he managed to open the door. He carried her up the narrow steps, taking care not to bump her against the walls—although why he should bother he did not know. Very likely a stampede of elephants would not wake her. He had bespoken only one private bedchamber—it was a small inn, after all. The bedclothes were turned back, and with a sigh of relief he laid her on the bed and regarded her with a jaundiced eye.

His bride was dead to the world. Magnus glared at her, aggrieved. He had not particularly looked forward to his wedding night—he'd never taken a virgin before, had restricted his carnal dealings to experienced women of the world, and the thought of causing pain instead of giving pleasure had caused him to view the coming night with a certain amount of trepidation. But now, having steeled himself to do the deed, his bride was proving most uncooperative.

Furthermore, having departed on his honeymoon in a state of pique, he had failed to provide her with a maidservant. He probably ought to call for the landlord's wife to undress her. And so he would—damn it—if he wanted all and sundry to know how he'd passed his wedding night. No, he had the choice—leave her to sleep in her clothes and emerge as an even more bedraggled bride in the morning, or prepare her for bed himself.

Swearing under his breath, Magnus undid the buttons of her shabby pelisse. He slipped it off and hung it on a hook. He had to grope for the fastenings of her dress, and called down a silent curse on dressmakers when he finally discovered them under her arms. He slipped the dress off her shoulders and tugged it down over her hips, then hung it on the same hook.

Feeling cross and impatient, Magnus turned back to his bride and froze, staring. She lay on his bed, soft and sweet and vulnerable. Her hair was tumbled in an unruly mass, spread out against the white sheets, glinting gold and brown and cinnamon, like strands of honey. Her skin glowed golden-rose in the flickering candlelight.

Magnus's mouth dried as he gazed at her sleeping form. This was his wife, he told himself...but he felt like a thief in the night, standing over her, gazing like this, with her all innocent and unknowing.

But he could not stop himself staring...at the rosy arms flung out high on the pillows, at her long, smooth legs, gently parted and disappearing beneath her petticoat, her breasts rising creamy and rounded from the neck of her chemise...

He reached for the tapes which fastened her petticoat and noticed wryly that his hands were shaking. He wrestled for a moment with the knots, then, losing patience, took out his knife. He cut the remaining tapes and, holding his breath, gently eased the petticoat from her body.

Bloody hell, he thought, staring at her legs, at her thighs hidden beneath the uneven hem of her chemise. His heart was pounding. The chemise was a simple affair, sleeveless, with an adjustable drawstring neckline. It strained across her chest and hips, as if made for a smaller person. Idly his fingers reached out and pulled lightly at one of the ends of the small bow which fastened the drawstring. The bow fell apart and the neckline loosened under his gaze.

By all that was decent he ought to leave her to sleep in her chemise at least. She was a virgin, modest and maidenly. A gentleman should show proper respect for his wife, only raising the hem of her nightgown during their conjugal meetings. It was what he'd expected, planned to do, after all. And she was asleep. Only a cad would bare her naked to his eyes like this on her wedding night. Without her knowledge or consent. Yes, in all decency he should allow her to sleep in her chemise, not stand here staring at his wife as if she were a twopenny peepshow...

She stirred, rolling her face to one side, and flung an arm over her head. Her movement sent the drawstring neckline gaping even wider. Magnus held his breath. Was she about to waken? Candlelight danced over the creamy expanse of skin.

Without further thought Magnus cut through the tapes fastening her chemise and with bated breath tugged the garment down. Her breasts spilled out, creamy and lush, and under his fascinated stare two rosy nipples lifted and hardened in the cold night air. He tugged it further, over her hips and down her legs. Dry-mouthed and aching with desire, he examined the rest of her, her slender waist, her appealingly curved little belly, the flaring hips and the gold-brown triangle of curls at the apex of her rounded, satiny thighs.

Bloody hell, thought Magnus again, dazedly. She was beautiful. Under all those appalling garments she wore, she was beautiful. Soft, lovely and utterly desirable. And she was his wife.

And, the devil confound it, she was absolutely sound asleep, and there was no way in the world that he could avail himself of her beautiful body. He groaned, feeling the painful intensity of his arousal, knowing he would have to wait.

He bent over her, inhaling the scent of her body, and closed his eyes for a moment, savouring it. She smelled unique, in his experience. Most women he knew drowned themselves in strong perfumes. Not his bride. She smelled of soap and nothing else—just herself. Of innocence. She was his lawful wife, wedded to him in the eyes of God and society, he told himself.

Magnus took a deep breath. 'Thalia,' he said urgently, in a loud voice. She did not stir. He cupped her shoulders in moist palms and shook her. The creamy breasts bounced and quivered. Magnus moaned as he watched. But she did not awaken. Instead, she wriggled a little—causing his tongue to cleave to the roof of his mouth—then turned on her side, cuddling into the pillows, curling up her legs and presenting him with a view of a delectable peachy backside. His arousal was rock-hard, and aching like the very devil.

It was no good, he thought frustratedly, Thalia Robinson could sleep through an earthquake. He lifted the bedclothes over her and watched sourly as she snuggled into their warmth. Thalia—God how he disliked that name. It hadn't suited the ill-clad little urchin he'd married and it certainly didn't suit the siren he'd discovered under the dreadful clothes. Perhaps he'd call her by her second name—what was it? Lucy? Louise? He grimaced. No, that didn't suit her either.

Forcing himself to turn away from the temptation in his bed, Magnus bent to pick up the undergarments he'd dropped. He started to hang them on the hook behind the door, then paused, truly noticing them for the first time. Holding them in a clenched fist, he moved closer to the branch of candles burning near the bedside. A surge of anger rippled through him.

The stockings were darned in several places. Both chemise and petticoat contained numerous patches and inserts of different material. Though spotlessly clean, and soft with many washings, they were made of coarse linen, old and well-worn. Not a scrap of lace or a frill enlivened either garment. And these were the delicate ladies unmentionables that Lord d'Arenville's bride had worn on her wedding day! Could Laetitia not even have seen to that? He bunched the offending garments in his fist and hurled them at the far wall.

He stormed towards the door, then paused. He glanced back at the underclothes in the corner. He'd rendered them unusable, cutting through the tapes like that. What would she think when she awoke? Cursing under his breath, he scooped them off the floor and stuffed them into his pocket.

He left the room, slamming the door behind him, and stomped downstairs, his high boots echoing on the wooden steps. Rousing the innkeeper, he called for a bottle of the best brandy and retired to the private parlour to brood on his inexplicable marriage and the debacle of his wedding night.

'Oh, I am utterly ravenous this morning,' exclaimed Tallie, reaching for a slice of fresh crusty bread and buttering it lavishly. She took a mouthful of coffee and closed her eyes, savouring it, then bit into the bread with evident relish.

Magnus watched her sourly. His head ached from the brandy. The fire in the small parlour had smoked, and the landlord's excuses about the unreliability of chimneys when the wind blew from the northwest had not impressed him a bit.

'Can I not tempt you to a slice of this excellent bread and butter, my lord?' said Tallie. She glanced at the tankard by his elbow doubtfully. 'I cannot think it healthful for you to break your fast with nothing but ale.'

Magnus snorted and raised the tankard to his lips.

Tallie glanced guiltily at the empty platter on her left. 'I am sure Mrs Farrow would be delighted to cook more bacon and eggs—I did not mean to consume it all—it was just that I found myself so extremely hungry when I awoke.'

Magnus closed his eyes for a moment, unable to endure even the thought of greasy eggs and bacon.

Tallie reached for the pot of honey. She dipped in a spoon and wound it deftly, then drizzled honey all over her bread and butter. The sight recalled to Magnus the look of her hair on the pillow, gleaming in the candlelight. He glowered silently.

'Mrs Farrow says there is cold pork, fowl, or some mutton pie still remaining from last night's dinner, if you should prefer that—I know many gentlemen prefer meat at breakfast,' persisted Tallie.

Magnus rolled his eyes and took another mouthful of dark, bitter ale.

'I must say,' she continued, 'dinner last night sounded quite delicious. Why did you not awaken me? I was extremely hungry, you know. It was most unkind of you to forget me!' she finished indignantly, licking honey off her fingers.

Forget her? Magnus stared at her in stupefaction. He opened his mouth to respond, but she hadn't finished.

'I would very much have preferred to be woken. So in the future, if you please, remember to do so, should I happen to take a little nap before dinner.' Tallie smiled to soften the impact of her demand, resolving to be more tactful with him, especially in the morning. He seemed to be one of those people whose tempers did not appreciate conversation in the morning.

It occurred to her that he might not have slept very well last night. 'Did you not sleep well, my lord?' She smiled sympathetically at him. 'Some people do not sleep soundly, I believe, if they are in a strange bed. I do not myself. I remember when I first came to my cousin's house it was days before I could accustom myself to the new bed. Was your bed not sufficiently comfortable, my lord?'

Magnus could barely speak. Indignation and outrage choked him. He searched his mind for something sufficiently pithy and cutting to say. A drop of honey quivered on the corner of her mouth and the sight of it distracted him considerably.

She continued. 'Mine was quite comfortable, although I woke up a little cold.' She blushed, and did not meet his eyes. 'I gather Mrs Farrow put me to bed. I must thank her, though I don't understand how she could have missed my nightgown—it was on the top of my valise. And she must have taken my—er—some things to wash, because I could not find them anywhere.'

Magnus's ears turned slightly pink. He walked over to the fire and kicked some of the burning logs with his boot. Smoke gushed into the room.

'My lord—'

'Oh, for God's sake let us have done with all this "my lord" nonsense!' Magnus exclaimed. 'You are my wife. You may call me Magnus and I will call you Thalia. Agreed?'

Tallie wrinkled her nose. 'I would prefer not to be called Thalia.'

'What else should I call you? Lady d'Arenville, perhaps?'

'Good gracious, no,' she said, vigorously scrubbing the honey off her lips with a napkin. 'I should never remember to answer to that.'

Magnus frowned. 'Never remember to answer to your title?' He was stunned. He'd expected the title to be the very first thing his wife would learn to use. That and his wealth.

Tallie perceived she had mortally offended him and smiled placatingly. 'I suppose it is all still so new to me. I cannot seem to think of myself as a countess yet.' She smiled brilliantly, with false confidence. 'I am sure I shall soon grow accustomed to it.'

'But in the meantime I am not to address you as Thalia. You would prefer Miss Robinson, perhaps?' he finished acidly.

'Of course not. It is just that I have always disliked the name Thalia.'

'Well, there we are agreed—it is an appalling name to inflict on someone.'

Tallie suddenly found herself annoyed. It was one thing for her not to like her own name; it was quite another to have him criticising it with such enthusiasm. 'Well, at least I am not called Euphrosyne or Aglaia!' she snapped.

Magnus blinked. 'Why on earth should you be?'

'Euphrosyne and Aglaia were Graces.'

'Good for them. But I don't see—'

'And Thalia was a Grace, too.'

'Grace is a perfectly unexceptionable name.' He shrugged. 'I have no objection to calling you Grace.'

'But I don't wish you to call me Grace!'

'Well, what the devil do you want me to call you? Euphro-what or Agalia?'

Tallie's lips twitched. 'Thalia, Euphro*syne* and Agl*aia* were the three Graces—the daughters of Zeus and servants to the other deities,' she explained severely. 'My mother thought it romantic to name me after one of them.'

'Romantic! She must have been a hen-wit,' he said frankly. 'I suppose she wanted more daughters to complete the set. You must thank your lucky stars you were born first.'

Tallie giggled.

He smiled down at her, feeling more in charity with her. 'So, if you do not wish me to call you Thalia, what is my alternative—Lucy?' he said, pleased with himself for recalling her second name.

Tallie pulled another face and shook her head. 'No, I don't like *Louise* either.' She hesitated. 'My friends from school and my cousin's children call me Tallie, so you could call me that—if you wish it.'

'Tallie...Tallie,' he said thoughtfully, then nodded. 'Yes, it suits you. So, you shall call me Magnus and I call you Tallie—agreed?'

'Agreed, my lor—Magnus.' She found her hand enveloped in his and looked up at him, smiling shyly.

He looked down into her shining amber eyes and his hand tightened its grip. 'Come then, Tallie, for we depart within the half-hour.'

'Where to, my lor—Magnus?' she asked breathlessly.

He couldn't help but smile at her excitement. 'Paris!'

Chapter Seven

'What is that most uncommon smell, my lor—Magnus?' Tallie called from the window of the coach.

They had come to a steep hill. The horses slowed to a walk, and, for the first time in several hours, Magnus was close enough for conversation.

Magnus frowned, inhaled and shook his head. 'I smell nothing untoward.'

'Oh, you must,' she said, sniffing the air vigorously. 'It is...it is... Oh, I cannot explain it, for I have smelled nothing like it before...' She sniffed again. 'It is a little...tart, but vastly refreshing.'

Magnus inhaled and shook his head again. 'I can smell nothing—the wretched sea drowns all other smells.'

'The sea?' Tallie exclaimed. 'It is the sea I can smell? Oh, how very exciting. I have never seen the sea and have always longed to do so.' She bounced up on the carriage seat and craned her neck as far as she could out of the window.

Magnus regarded her thoughtfully for a moment.

She turned her head. 'Pray tell me, my lor—I mean Magnus, in which direction is the sea?'

'You cannot see it yet,' he said, 'but once we are over this hill you should be able to catch a glimpse of it.'

Tallie's eyes avidly scanned the approaching horizon. Sure enough, within a few moments she saw a sparkling blue line stretching between the dip of green hills. 'Ohhh,' she breathed.

She fastened her gaze on the horizon for the next forty minutes, catching tantalising glimpses of blue and silver, until the coach breached the final crest and the English Channel lay spread out before her in an endless gleaming expanse.

'Ohhhhh.'

Amused by her naive enthralment, Magnus signalled the coach driver to stop. He himself dismounted and opened Tallie's door.

'Come,' he said, holding out a hand. 'Alight for a moment or two and gaze your fill.'

Eyes shining, she hastened to do his bidding, almost tumbling into the road as she did so. She hurried up a small rise and stood there, drinking in the incredible sight.

'It is not the true sea, you understand. This is just the Channel.'

She turned to stare at him in amazement. 'Truly? But it is enormous. I cannot see to the other side at all.'

He shrugged. 'Nevertheless...'

She turned back and gazed in silence for several minutes, her hands clasped to her bosom. 'The English Channel...' she breathed reverently. 'It *is* so much bigger than the maps would have you believe... And just over there is Europe.' She clapped her hands. 'Oh, I cannot wait! Come! Let us delay no further.'

She hurried back to the coach and scrambled back up the let-down steps, oblivious of the groom waiting to assist her.

Magnus sighed and made a mental note to find someone to teach his wife how a lady should step into and descend from a carriage.

The town of Dover was not particularly prepossessing, in Magnus's opinion, consisting, as it did, largely of cheap, unsavoury taverns and inns kept by retired rum-soaked sailors for the benefit and entertainment of other rum-soaked sailors. There were but two decent hostelries in which a gentleman could safely repose his bride—the Ship Inn and the King's Head. The Ship Inn being the more fashionable of the two, it was there that Magnus naturally made his way.

To his annoyance, however, the inn was full. The landlord explained. It seemed there had been no wind, not even a breeze for days. The Channel lay smooth and glassy and the boats' sails limp, and so the inn—the whole town, in fact—was crowded with people waiting to leave for France. The landlord was extremely apologetic, but every single room was taken.

'Check again,' said Lord d'Arenville, laying several shining coins on the counter. The landlord regretfully shook his head. Lord d'Arenville added several more to the pile.

Lord d'Arenville's name was not unknown. Nor was it The Ship's practice to turn away titled gentlemen. The landlord hesitated a moment, then leaned forward. 'All I can offer your lordship is accommodation to share, I'm afraid—for a small consideration, of course. There are several young gentlemen who would be pleased to accommodate your lordship for a reduction in their tariff, and your lady wife would, I am sure, be welcome to sleep with Mrs Entwhistle, an elderly widow of the utmost respectability.' His fingers crept towards the money.

'Share?' exclaimed Lord d'Arenville, outraged, sweeping up the coins. His wife to share with some old woman—a cit, no doubt! The notion was preposterous. His countess did not share her bed with strange old women! She shared it with him—or she would as soon as he could manage it. He had waited quite long enough as it was.

The memory of her naked softness had stayed with him the whole day, and each sight of her, each movement, had caused him the sort of discomfort he had not had to endure since he was a green youth. It was a ridiculous situation for a man of his age and experience, and he was determined to remedy it immediately—all he needed was a bed and his bride.

The landlord spread his hands in a gesture of helplessness and shrugged. ''Tis all I can offer you, my lord. Without the wind, the ships can't leave, and until they do we must all make the best of things.'

'Well, then,' said Lord d'Arenville coldly, 'be so good as to recommend some respectable private accommodation where my wife and I can stay.'

The landlord shook his head. 'Nothing left, I'm afraid, my lord. The ships have been stuck here for six days already, and the whole town is full up—as tight as a tick, if you'll forgive the expression.' He paused, then added doubtfully, 'You might find something in one of the taverns near the waterfront, but I'd not wish a lady there, myself.'

'Quite!' said Lord d'Arenville crisply. He pondered the situation. It was far too late to retrace their steps and find some other town. His bride was waiting in the carriage, tired and no doubt hungry, though she had not complained. Repressing his frustration, he accepted the landlord's terms, hiding his chagrin behind an icy demeanour.

Mrs Entwhistle was, as Magnus had feared, a cit. A wealthy widow, she currently owned several large woollen mills and manufactories—a fact of which she did not hesitate to inform them, much to his disgust. She spoke with an assumed air of 'refainment,' which intensified when she found the exalted company in which she was to mix. She was also garrulous to the point of strangulation. Magnus was in her company no more than ten minutes before he had formed an understanding of why all three of her husbands had died young—seeking the peace and quiet of the grave. She was, however, intensely respectable, and only too delighted to share her chamber with a youthful countess, so Magnus was able to leave his bride to dine on a tray in the woman's chamber with no doubts about her safety.

He himself passed a most frustrating night. It took him hours to get to sleep, images of his naked wife being the chief cause. Then, when he finally fell into a fitful sleep, the young blades with whom he shared the room stumbled in, foxed to the eyeballs and talking at the tops of their voices. He bore it as long as he could, then sat up in bed.

'If you young gentlemen do not put yourselves to bed with the utmost speed—and silence—I will be forced to get out of this bed,' he said, in a voice which froze the young men in their tracks. 'I do not believe you would enjoy the consequences.'

After that, the only noise in the room was furtive breathing.

Magnus lay wide awake, wondering what malignant twist of fate had caused him to end up sharing a room with three drunken sots while his wife was curled up in bed with a vulgar old woman. He had never been so uncomfortable—nor so frustrated—in his life. Except for his wedding night.

Nothing had gone right for him since he'd offered for the girl, he thought sourly. Why had he ever been so foolish as to consider marriage? It was all Freddie's fault...

One of the young blades started to snore. Magnus turned over in bed, attempting to block out the sound. A second set of snores joined the first, then a third, making a loud and inharmonious din. Magnus pulled the pillow over his head.

Lord d'Arenville was far from his best when he entered the inn's crowded public dining room to join his bride for breakfast. He had passed a most indifferent night—again—and even the expedience of tossing the noisiest of his companions out of bed had failed to quell the vile nocturnal sounds.

Further, he'd had to shave and dress himself without his valet. Again. He was forced to acknowledge he missed the man's skills—Magnus had detected a hair on his coat when it had been returned to him, his cravats were insufficiently starched and, worst of all, the inn's bootblack had left a thumb-print on his hessians!

'Good morning, my lord.' Tallie greeted him with a sunny smile. 'Did you sleep better last night?'

Magnus gave her a baleful glance and sat down. He ordered kidneys, bacon and a tankard of ale. His wife applied herself vigorously to a plate of kippers.

'I gather you slept well. Again,' he added, noting her bright-eyed demeanour and her clear, smooth skin.

She shook her head, glanced furtively around the room, then leaned forward and whispered, 'No, not at all, for—you will not credit it—Mrs Entwhistle *snores*!'

Magnus let out a surprised snort of laughter.

'Oh, but it is perfectly true,' Tallie whispered, and rolled her eyes. 'It was dreadfully loud.' She glanced around the room again and added, her eyes brimming with mischief, 'It seems she cannot bear to be silent—even in sleep!'

Despite his bad mood, Magnus found himself smiling back at her. 'So, too, did my companions.'

'Oh, then you understand. I do so dislike the sound. And it goes on and on, doesn't it? Until you feel as though you wish to smother the person who is doing it.' She took another forkful of kipper and chewed it meditatively, regarding him with a speculative expression. 'Do you—? I mean...no.'

'Do I what?' said Magnus.

She blushed. 'I have forgot what I was going to say. Er, do you think the wind will be in the right quarter today, my lor—Magnus? For the packet to depart, I mean. It is beautifully sunny, at any rate. If we cannot depart today, do you think we might walk up to the Western Heights? I have heard that the view is most spectacular and the walk very invigorating.'

Magnus frowned. What had she been about to ask him? Something that caused her to blush. Had she been going to ask him whether he snored? He opened his mouth to reassure her...then shut it, disconcerted. He had no idea whether he snored or not.

Certainly no one had ever told him he did—but then he rarely slept with the women he'd been involved with. Pleasured them, yes, and gained his own pleasure. But he generally departed their beds after the event and returned to his own. He was fastidious in that.

Perhaps he did snore. Would his bride wish to smother *him* in his sleep? It was a most unsettling notion. Magnus finished his breakfast in silence.

After breakfast he accompanied Tallie in an exploration of the town and the waterfront, which, to his surprise, she seemed to find fascinating, despite the smells. They climbed the Western Heights, where his wife waxed rapturous about the view. And that, as far as Lord d'Arenville was concerned, was the sum total of entertainment to be found in the dreary little town of Dover.

But the more time he spent in his wife's company the more his thwarted desire grew. She was such a contrast to the bored, world-weary women he knew. She seemed to find unselfconscious pleasure in the smallest things, and he could not help but wonder if she would react with equal delight to the pleasures he planned to introduce her to—as soon as he found the privacy in which to do so. In the meantime, the mere sight of her pressing a shell to her ear to listen to the sea, or clambering over a stile, or running down a hill shrieking with glee was enough to have him almost moan aloud. He attempted to control his response to her, but the very impossibility of it unsettled him and made him, on reflection, furious.

He had never expected to *desire* his wife. He felt it was both unseemly and foolish for a man to do so... He had seen other men in thrall to the charms of their wives—his father, for one—and Magnus had observed that it gave the wife an unwholesome influence over their husband. No woman had ever possessed the slightest control over Magnus, and nothing was going to change that. No, this unaccountable penchant he had for his wife was merely a whim of the moment, a result of a recent lack of female companionship. It would pass as soon as the marriage was consummated—if it ever was!

Damn it! He had never been so desirous of coupling with a woman and so utterly unable to find an opportunity to do so. With any other woman he would have dealt with the matter by hiring a room at some low tavern, or, if the worst came to the worst, there had always been the coach. But Tallie was both a virgin and his wife. He owed it to her to carry out the deed in an atmosphere of respectability, at least.

Lord d'Arenville prayed for wind.

The Channel remained smooth and still.

Her husband might have been acting like a bear with a sore head, but Tallie did not repine. He was clearly a difficult man to please, but she had known that from the start. In fact, marriage to Lord d'Arenville was turning out vastly better than she had expected. Despite his general air of bad temper, she had discovered several unexpected aspects of his character which she found rather endearing—unexpected flashes of kindness, for instance, like stopping the coach so she could look at the sea. She had half expected him to laugh at her ignorance—but he hadn't. And he'd made no demur about escorting her along the waterfront—a place she had seen perfectly well he disliked, wrinkling his long, patrician nose as he steered her around a puddle of fish guts or a basket of live crabs.

Yes, Tallie thought, it felt wonderful to be strolling about the town on the arm of such a handsome gentleman—it was still almost impossible to believe such a magnificent-looking man was actually her husband. The feeling of warmth that glowed within her as she laid her hand on his arm, the occasional bumping of their bodies as they walked—it was most agreeable. And when he smiled, as he had once or twice, and those long, harsh lines down his cheeks deepened, and his sea-grey eyes gleamed, she would look at him and feel her breath catch in her throat...

She could not help but enjoy all sorts of little things he did. Like the way he placed himself protectively between her and the roadway as they walked. And helped her over stiles as if she were some sort of fragile, helpless creature, which heaven knew she wasn't, but still...it was nice to be thought so, at times. And even nicer to reflect that perhaps he didn't think of her as sturdy any more...

Of course, it was probably only good manners. No doubt he would do exactly the same for Mrs Entwhistle—if she ever stopped talking, that was. He had beautiful manners—when he chose to employ them.

Tallie sighed. There were times when she felt as though she and her new husband could come to some understanding, when she felt that she could find some degree of happiness with him after all. But then, for no reason she could see, he would suddenly turn back into The Icicle, and any attempt of hers to thaw him out only seemed to make him snappish as a wolf.

Then Tallie would recall she was not a beloved bride on her honeymoon, but an inconvenient necessity who was putting him to a great deal of trouble instead of quietly retiring to d'Arenville Hall to bear his heirs. Well, she would go into rural seclusion—eventually—but she had made up her mind to enjoy every moment of her bride trip, and enjoy it she would!

So, she told herself, rallying, Dover was a fascinating place, and she had much better things to do than fret herself to flinders over her husband's disposition. There was nothing she could do about that, after all. She was foolish to wish for anything more—she was nothing but a brood mare to him—he had said as much to her cousin, that night in the library. And, though he'd had enough of exploring the town, she had not.

Each morning Tallie slipped away from the Ship Inn to visit the waterfront, secure in her husband's belief that she was with Mrs Entwhistle. He himself could not bear the woman's inane chatter without coldly excusing himself after a few moments, and so Tallie used his ill-concealed antipathy to her own advantage.

She was intensely curious about every aspect of marine life. She marvelled at the way gnarled and twisted fishermen's hands could knot fine and delicate nets. She learned to identify brigantines, sloops and schooners, and was most excited to have the Revenue cutters pointed out to her. The fishermen filled her head with thrilling tales of smugglers, shipwrecks and storms.

One morning a friendly seaman even offered to row her out and show her over one of the ships. Delighted, Tallie accepted, and was deeply impressed to discover the ingenious manner in which its interior was fitted out. The seaman was rowing her back to shore when she noticed the irate figure of her husband awaiting her. His arms were folded, his legs braced, and his head was thrown back in a manner which told her he was not pleased.

When their little boat reached the shore, he hauled her grimly ashore. 'What the *deuce* do you think you are doing, madam?' he said as he escorted her away from the waterfront in such a rush that she would have slipped on the wet cobblestones had he not been clasping her arm so tightly.

'Exploring that big ship out there,' she panted. 'It was really most interest—'

'How dare you leave the inn unescorted?' he raged in an undertone, propelling her onwards at a great rate. 'Have you *no* idea of how to behave? No idea of the sort of villains and ruffians who frequent places of this sort?'

Villains and ruffians indeed, thought Tallie crossly. As if she did not know very well how to tell whether a person was trustworthy or not. And, since he was so obviously bored by her fascination with things nautical, what alternative did she have but to go by herself? She was now a married woman, after all, and had much more licence than an unwed girl to go where she pleased. It was just that he had these stuffy ideas about her behaving more 'suitably', more like a countess. Well, it was not possible to go from being an unwanted poor relation to feeling like a countess in a few days. Particularly when he kept reminding her of her unsuitability!

'Oh, pooh!' she retorted. 'They are most of them very nice.' She smiled and waved at an old woman who sat smoking a pipe outside a tavern, knowing it would annoy her husband. 'Hello, Nell!'

The woman took the pipe out of her mouth and raised it in a salute, baring blackened stumps in a wide grin. 'Ar, Miz Tallie.'

Magnus swore and lengthened his stride, forcing Tallie to hop and skip to keep up with him. He stormed up the stairs of the Ship Inn and flung open the door to Tallie's chamber.

'Oh, there you are, my dears—' began Mrs Entwhistle. Magnus bowed, slammed the door, and strode off along the corridor and up the next flight of stairs to his own room, dragging Tallie with him. He threw open the door to his own room and was about to usher Tallie in when he halted abruptly, swearing. Tallie peered around her husband's body. A half-dozen young sprigs of fashion were sprawled about, smoking, drinking and playing cards.

'Come in, d'Arenville, ol' chap,' called one young fellow, flushed with drink. 'An' bring that pretty li'l filly with you.'

Magnus seemed to harden with icy rage. 'You refer, sir, to my wife!' he said in a soft, savage tone. It quite quelled the young gentlemen, Tallie thought. He pushed her away from the door and shut it. Towing her behind him, Magnus stalked downstairs and coldly summoned the landlord.

'Kindly direct me to a private room immediately—one in which I can speak to my wife without interruption.'

'Regrettably,' said the landlord, 'not a one is to be had, my lord. People are even sleeping in the public rooms tonight.'

The reply fanned Magnus's temper to flames. 'Then summon my carriage!' he snapped.

The carriage was duly brought round, and no sooner were they seated and the driver directed to 'Drive, damn it!' than Magnus began a tirade which blistered Tallie's ears.

He began with her iniquity in sneaking out of the inn behind his back and her perfidy in using a garrulous bloody cit as a smokescreen! He condemned her lack of decorum in venturing out alone and unescorted in such a filthy little town. He was scathing about her foolhardiness in entering into conversations with the most unsuitable people—villainous cut-throats, verminous old women dressed in rags, smoking God knows what in evil-smelling pipes!

Tallie sat, her hands folded submissively in her lap, listening with downcast eyes to all he had to say.

'...and as for the utter folly of venturing aboard a strange ship in the company of...of some tattooed ruffian with gold rings in his ears—why, anything may have befallen you! You could have been kidnapped—or worse. A villain like that would slit your throat as soon as look at you!'

Tallie looked up at this. 'Oh, no, my lord, Jack may look a little rough, but truly he is a decent fellow under all those tattoos. His wife in Jamaica gave him the earring—'

Magnus rolled his eyes and ground his teeth. 'He could have stolen you away on that boat—'

'Ship. A boat is much small—'

'Will you *listen* to me, you foolish chit?' Magnus slammed his fist onto the leather squabs. 'He could have drugged you, stolen you away and sold you as a white slave in some foreign port!'

Tallie stared at him. She had heard of white slaves, of course. The girls had talked of such things after dark in the dormitory. But she had been in no such danger. Everyone on the waterfront had known where she had gone. 'But how could he, my lord—?' she began.

'Quite easi—'

'For there is no wind to enable the ship to sail away,' she finished. 'That is why we are not yet in France. Have you forgot?'

Magnus glared at her, stumped for a response.

The coach rattled onwards. Tallie glanced out of the window. They were well out of town by now, green hedges and trees whipping past in a blur. It was remarkable how accustomed she had become to the speed of coach travel. For a girl who'd never been anywhere, she was fast becoming a seasoned traveller.

She looked back at her husband. He was staring out of the window, a black frown on his face. He obviously still hadn't got over his crotchets. She sighed. One would expect such a handsome man to have a more agreeable temperament, but the least little thing seemed to set him off. Still, anyone who had been reared in Miss Fisher's Seminary for the Daughters of Gentlemen knew all about bad tempers. She sighed again.

The sound made Magnus turn to look at her. She cocked her head and smiled enquiringly at him.

It was the smile that did it, Magnus told himself later. Quite obviously she *still* had no idea of the imprudence of her actions, of the danger she'd been in. Her countenance showed not the slightest sign of contrition. His temper, held rigidly in check, burst its bounds again.

'And what if that damned filthy ruffian had decided to ravish you out there on that boat?' he snarled. 'What then, eh? You could have done *nothing*! Nothing to save yourself! Did you think of that, madam, eh? No, I am very sure you did not. You did not think of anything at all, did you?'

'Oh, he would have done nothing of the sort,' retorted Tallie crossly. 'And if he had—' she glared at him defiantly '—I know very well how to deal with such matters.'

'What?'

'Well—' she began, but her words froze in her throat as Magnus launched himself at her, lunging across the carriage to grab her arms. In seconds he had her hands pinioned behind her back and she was thrust back along the wide seat of the coach, legs flailing, his muscular body pressed heavily on top of hers. She stared up at him, struggling, her eyes wide with surprise.

'What if he'd had you like this?' Magnus growled. 'Your body vulnerable under his. Accessible to his every desire.' He pressed himself against her, his eyes devouring her face.

Tallie felt something hard pressing into her stomach. She tried to wriggle away. Her husband's face loomed dark and angry over hers, his flinty grey eyes boring into her. She could feel his breath warm on her skin. Ignoring her struggles with ease, he gathered both her wrists into one hand, leaving the other free.

'And what if he had wanted to do this to you? What would you have done then, eh?' His hand moved slowly over her breast, stroking and squeezing.

Tallie gasped in amazement. What on earth was he doing? To take such liberties with her person... She knew about men taking liberties with a girl's person from Miss Fisher—she had just never known what exactly 'liberties' were. And she knew very well what the correct response for a genteel young lady was in this situation—she just wasn't sure she wanted to make it—just yet. These liberties felt remarkably pleasant, and she didn't want to stop him...yet.

The big warm hand exploring her breast caused all sorts of wondrous shivery responses in her body. Particularly when he touched her...like that. Ohhh! Like ripples in a pond, the feelings started from her chest and shimmered deliciously outward. And downward. She lay there, entranced, staring up at her husband's dark visage, lost in the sensations his caresses were producing.

'And what if he'd done this?' muttered her husband thickly, and pressed his mouth hard over hers.

Tallie closed her eyes. Her husband's mouth crushed hers for a moment, then softened. His lips explored hers slowly, gently, and she gave herself up to the sensations. His mouth was so tender and warm as it moved caressingly over hers. And he wasn't merely pressing his lips against hers; he seemed to be nibbling and sucking and...licking. She shivered pleasurably and pressed closer to him.

Even his body pressing so heavily on top of hers felt interestingly... Gracious! His tongue was pushing between her lips! Running along between her teeth and her lips...very peculiar...yet...utterly...thrilling. Sensation vibrated through her body from his, and she felt her body softening and melting with the pleasure of it...and yet an odd sort of tension seemed to be rising within her.

His tongue plunged again into her mouth, sweeping in slow, sensual arcs, stroking the roof of her mouth, curling around her own tongue. Tallie shuddered rapturously as wondrous sensations flooded her. His powerful thighs imprisoned her, and he pressed against her, in deliberate, rhythmic movements, his body moving in time with his tongue. Tallie felt languid, thrilled and apprehensive—all at the same time.

His hand had left her breasts, she realised suddenly. It was sliding up her legs, over her stockings... It was past her knee and touching bare flesh! The hand moved higher and she tried to wriggle away from it, at the same time straining to press herself more closely against him. He moaned, caressing her eyelids with his mouth and tongue, nuzzling her throat and stroking the skin of her thighs with warm, strong fingers. Tallie's legs quivered in response, then fell apart, trembling. His hand moved higher, circling, stroking, pressing.

Suddenly the coach lurched, and Tallie abruptly became aware of what she was doing. And where his hands were! She stiffened in shock. These were indeed liberties! And Tallie knew her duty.

'Ohhhh,' she gasped loudly, and collapsed dramatically back against the seat cushions, her body loose and boneless.

'Tallie? What is it?' Magnus pulled his mouth from hers and blinked dazedly down at his bride. Oh, Lord! He'd let himself get carried away. The slightest touch of his lips to hers and the passion he'd tried so hard to repress had flared uncontrollably. Lord help him, he'd been about to ravish his innocent virgin bride in a carriage in the middle of the countryside! And frightened her half to death by the look of things!

'Tallie, are you all right?' He picked up one hand and began to chafe it frenziedly. He patted her cheeks and took her chin in his hand, searching in vain for signs of animation. Her head lolled in his hands. Oh, Lord, what if she were ill?

Thoroughly alarmed, Magnus sat up and ran his hands through his hair, wondering what the devil one did with swooning females. A vinaigrette, that was what he needed. He searched every cranny of the coach, as if one would magically be found to contain a bottle of smelling salts, but no.

What else? Burnt feathers? He'd seen women revived when

burnt feathers were held under their noses—but he had no feathers to burn. What else? he thought in desperation. Cold water? Yes, there was bound to be some lying around outside—a stream or a pond or even a puddle. He shouted at the coachman to stop the coach, and as it slowed he flung open the door.

A noise from his beloved bride halted him in his tracks. He could not believe his ears. The sound came again. Magnus turned in dark suspicion and looked at her. Sure enough, her body was convulsed—in not quite silent giggles.

'You little witch!' Magnus exclaimed wrathfully. 'You were faking it!'

Tallie sat up, groping for her reticule to find a handkerchief to wipe her streaming eyes.

Magnus stared, outraged, incredulous! She was laughing? At *him*? He had been lost in the heights of passion...and she'd faked a swoon...and was *laughing*! He opened his mouth to deliver a blistering tirade to end all blistering tirades.

'You see, my lord, I was in no danger.' Her voice was a little shaky, but she seemed in full control of her faculties.

No danger? Magnus's eyes narrowed into glacial slits. 'Danger of what?' Right now the little baggage was in danger of being throttled! By her brand-new husband!

'From that sailor, of course,' Tallie responded as brightly as she could, given the fact that her body still trembled with the aftermath of his passion. She had reacted automatically, feigning the swoon, but all the time she had lain there with her eyes closed she had been reliving his caresses. She'd felt like bursting into tears when he had sat up, releasing her from his embrace, and begun chafing her hands. She'd been shaken, in turmoil, wondering what to do, but then laughter had bubbled up from nowhere, and she'd let it come...

She continued, 'If he had done what you said he might—what you did to me just now—I would have pretended to swoon, just like I did. Then, while he was wondering what to do, I would have escaped.'

She smiled triumphantly at him and straightened her skirts, hoping he would not notice her trembling hands. She had never known a kiss could be like that, but she could never let him see how strongly it had affected her. She did not wish to disgust him, after all.

She felt quite proud of herself, of her apparent self-possession, as she said, 'Now, shall we return to town?'

He was still looking murderous, so she said earnestly, 'You really have no need to worry about my safety, my lord, for truly there is no need, as you saw. I learned how to deal with unwanted liberties when I was at school, you know. Miss Fisher considered it very important.' She added confidingly, 'Of course, this is the first time I have ever actually *needed* to do so, but I think it worked splendidly, don't you agree?'

'Splendidly.' Lord d'Arenville glared balefully at his bride of only a few days. *Unwanted liberties?* Hell and the devil roast it, but he'd teach her to want those liberties from him—if he died in the attempt!

Chapter Eight

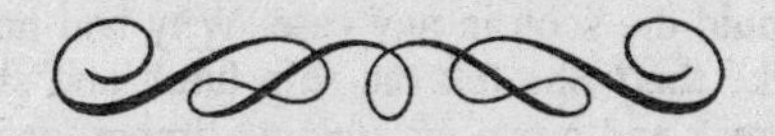

The handsome pirate bent over her, and a lock of crisp dark hair fell over his brow. His sea-grey eyes darkened with passion as he lowered his mouth to hers...

'Ohhhh,' Tallie moaned.

...his arms drew her closer and she felt as if there was no other place on earth she wished to be. He smiled, the long, vertical grooves in his cheeks deepening, and kissed her again.

Tallie groaned.

'Fear not, my love,' the pirate murmured. 'No one can catch us. No one will ever take you away from me. For the wind is blowing swift and strong...'

Tallie moaned again. It wasn't fair. She loved the sea.

'...and my ship is fleet and sure...'

'Ohhhh!' Tallie whimpered. She loved ships, too.

'...and she rides the waves like a dolphin...up and down.'

'Oh, no, no—no more...' Tallie muttered woefully. She was betrayed—by the ship, by the sea!

'Here, take this.' Lord d'Arenville's eyes were sea-dark with concern as he leaned over her. He held out a basin and Tallie clutched it gratefully, closing her eyes again to shut out the sight of the lantern swinging with the motion of the ship.

She bent over the basin for a long, painful interval, then felt it removed from her grasp. A cool, damp cloth gently wiped her mouth and she felt hands tucking the blanket more securely around her shivering body. Warm, strong arms gathered her close and she sighed in relief. She felt herself lifted up and her eyes flew open again in alarm.

'It's all right. I'm taking you up on deck,' Magnus murmured as she clutched his neck in distress.

'No, no.'

'Trust me, you will feel better in the fresh air,' he said, and carried her out of the small, gloomy cabin.

Tallie was certain she would die if she had to go up to the pitching, rolling deck, but she was too miserable and exhausted to argue. She would die soon in any case. Why had no one told her sailing was like this? She felt the ship lurch and shudder, heard the frightful creak and groan of straining timber, and clutched her husband tighter, finding comfort in his warmth and strength. And courage. For he seemed not the least distressed by this dreadful storm which would surely kill them all.

On deck the wind was brisk and cold. Magnus carried her over to the railings and found a place to sit, still holding her in his arms. Splashes of sea spray cooled her clammy skin. Magnus wiped it with his handkerchief. Wind whipped at her hair and tugged at her skirts. He smoothed her hair back and tucked the blanket more securely around her.

'Feeling better?' he said after a while.

Tallie shivered and leaned against his chest. She did feel a little better. The fresh sea air was helping her head to clear—if not her stomach, which was aching dreadfully from all that she had lost from it. She would never eat kippers again.

'It's perfect weather for sailing,' he said.

She stared at him incredulously. Perfect weather? Surely it was a storm! Those white-capped waves were enormous, and the way they dipped and swelled and crashed against the sides of the ship was terrifying.

'According to the captain, this wind will have us in France in under five hours,' he continued. He glanced down at her and smiled slightly. 'That's a little under two hours from now.'

'Two hours,' Tallie groaned.

He laughed—rather heartlessly, Tallie thought.

'Here, this will help settle your stomach.' He pulled out a flat silver flask, unscrewed the top and held it to her lips.

'No,' she muttered, turning her lips away. She couldn't bear to eat or drink anything, knowing she would only lose it in a few minutes.

'Trust me.' He grasped her chin in his hand and tipped what seemed like half the contents of the flask down her throat.

Tallie shuddered as it burnt its way down her throat, then coughed as it hit the pit of her empty stomach, depriving her of all ability to breathe for a moment or two. 'What—?' she spluttered indignantly.

'Brandy.'

She subsided, gasping against his chest, and closed her eyes, waiting to die, but after a few minutes she found a warmth stealing into her body which seemed to banish the dreadful queasiness. Wearily she laid her face against his throat, taking comfort in the scent of his cologne water and his skin. She felt the faint prickle of whiskers against her cheek and rubbed against them, enjoying the sensation.

He had been so very kind to her, she thought drowsily. The last thing she would have expected of Lord d'Arenville was that he would prove so gentle and sympathetic in the sickroom. He was such a fastidious person. She would have expected him to be revolted by her illness...gentlemen were, she'd understood.

But instead he had cared for her with a quiet competence that, now she thought about it, made her almost want to weep... She could not remember when anyone had cared whether Tallie Robinson was well or ill, if she lived or died. And now, this—this so-called Icicle had tended to her needs with a careful tenderness that nearly broke her heart. It was wicked for people to call him The Icicle. He wasn't at all. He was...

'You're so kind,' she mumbled into his skin, feeling tears prickling, hot against her eyelids.

Kind? Had she said he was *kind*? Magnus was stunned. He must have misheard her. No one had ever called him kind before. Any one of his acquaintances would laugh at the notion. He shifted his hold on her slightly, tucking her more securely into the curve of his body, savouring the relaxed weight of her, the feel of her soft cheek against his skin. Errant tendrils of her hair tickled his chin, and he inhaled the scent of it, soap and sea and the faint sour remnants of her recent illness.

Poor little mite. Her seasickness had come as such a shock to her. A blind man would have seen how thrilled she'd been when they had finally embarked, her eyes sparkling with excitement. And not a half hour later she had been drooping, green and wan, over a basin, retching her little heart out, a picture of misery.

And she thought him kind... It wasn't kindness that caused him to look after her, he reflected ruefully. He'd had no choice—there was no one else... And besides, she belonged to him now. He had a duty to her. He was her husband.

He felt her body relax against him, felt her breathing slow to an even rhythm. She was asleep. In his arms. His wife.

Magnus watched the waves, enjoying the brisk salt spray which blew occasionally against his face. He pulled the blanket up to protect her from the wet. It had been nothing like he'd expected, this business of marriage. Lord, what a simpleton he'd been, thinking to get himself a wife in order to get children. He'd thought about the children only; he'd barely considered the wife, except to find a healthy woman who would disturb his life as little as possible. He laughed silently. What a gudgeon, to think a woman would not disturb his life.

Perhaps if he'd married one of Laetitia's candidates... Ironic to think he'd picked Tallie because she'd have so few expectations. She was simply bursting with expectations; that was the trouble. She had a thirst for life that amazed him.

If he'd chosen one of Laetitia's girls he'd have had a conventional bride trip—to Brighton or Bath, perhaps, or even to his country home. Then a season in London, by which time she'd have been pregnant and would have retired gracefully to the country to give birth. And when she'd been ill she would have had her mama and a dozen attendants to care for her. And after the birth she would have returned to London and they would have resumed their separate lives in the normal civilised fashion of the *ton*.

But instead of a cool sophisticate who understood her duty he'd chosen this naive little creature, who'd thrown his life into chaos. He'd not realised just how alone in the world she was— Lord, she didn't even have a maid. He hadn't even arranged to get one for her—he'd just assumed one of Laetitia's maids would accompany her. His cousin had refused, of course.

And so, because of Laetitia's spite and his own lack of forethought, he'd had to be maid, groom, sickroom attendant and protector to his wife. Everything except husband. And because of crowded inns, stinking waterfronts, vulgar cits—not to mention his delayed wedding night—he'd been bad-tempered and unpleasant a good deal of the time.

And yet she called him kind...

He wasn't, of course. Magnus knew that. Along with the knowledge of his duty to his lineage, his lands, and his family name, his father had drummed into him a rigid sense of responsibility for those who were dependent on him. And there was no doubt in Magnus's mind that his bride was more dependent on him than anyone had ever been in his life. *Kind?* She just didn't understand *noblesse oblige*.

But he did enjoy the warm weight of her in his arms.

By the time they reached Calais, she had almost fully recovered from her seasickness. 'France!' she announced in relief as they headed towards the customs house.

The French officials examined their passports with an insulting attitude of suspicion and searched their baggage with greedy hands. One turned to examine Tallie's clothing—while she was wearing it—and Magnus stepped forward with a warning growl. There was a short muttered exchange, gold passed from English to French hands, and they were allowed to leave. John Black, Magnus's coachman and general factotum, remained behind to supervise the luggage.

With every step on firm, dry land, Tallie gathered animation. Her eyes darted everywhere, drinking in the sights and sounds and smells of her first foreign country. A foreign country, moreover, which only a short time ago had experienced bloodthirsty revolution and war—and murdered almost all of its aristocrats. She was now an aristocrat by marriage. Tallie pressed close to her husband, thrilled by the sense of danger, secure in his presence.

And what sights there were too, for almost every man had savage black whiskers and gold earrings, and wore a cocked hat with a red, white and blue cockade pinned to it—the *tricolore*. Some grenadiers marched past, looking very daunting and military, with prodigious moustaches and an erect, menacing gait.

The girls, *grisettes*, were very smartly dressed too, adorned with sparkling crosses, necklaces, earrings—all kinds of glittering decoration—and pretty starched white caps close upon their heads.

The sounds of French surrounded them, and Tallie frowned as she listened. These people spoke very differently from Mademoiselle, who had taught French at Miss Fisher's, and Tallie could only understand a word here and there.

She was surprised at how cheerful and friendly people seemed, but the Peace of Amiens had been signed almost a year before and things had obviously settled. She had half expected them to be rude, or hostile, but nothing could have been farther from the truth—particularly when the landlord bustled out of the Lion d'Argent, bowing and smiling, welcoming *Milord Anglais et la belle milady* with genuine pleasure.

'I...I do not think I am very hungry,' said Tallie as they entered the private dining parlour. Her stomach had settled a good deal, but it was still feeling a little peculiar.

Magnus frowned. 'You will feel more the thing with some good hot food inside you.' He summoned a thin, lugubrious *garçon* and ordered coffee, eggs, steak and ale for both of them. The *garçon* gave a Gallic shrug and pointed out that they were not in England now, and decent Frenchmen did not drink ale. Magnus gave an English shrug in response and said nothing.

Tallie waited until the *garçon* left. 'I have no wish for food, thank you. I am not at all hungry.'

'Nonsense,' Magnus said bracingly. 'You will eat, and that's the end of it.'

The *garçon* returned in a few moments and placed a plate of poached eggs in front of her. Magnus addressed himself to a large, rare steak. Tallie glared at him mutinously and pushed her eggs away. How could she have thought her husband was kind? She was very sure she had not a trace of her insides left. No man with an ounce of sensitivity would expect her to eat runny eggs—or watch him devour a greasy steak—when she was still feeling so delicate. She averted her eyes from the disgusting sight and stared out of the window, where two men dressed in ragged finery played republican tunes on an organ and tambourine.

Magnus signalled to the *garçon*. A moment later he brought in a large cup of steaming, fragrant coffee and a dish of rolls and placed them on the table. Tallie watched Magnus break open the rolls. Wisps of steam escaped as the golden crust broke. The scent was heavenly. He buttered a piece with pale butter and, before she knew what he was about, popped it in her mouth. Reluctantly she chewed and swallowed. It was delicious.

Clearly he was not going to allow her to refuse to eat. Grudgingly she reached out, buttered the next piece herself and ate it cautiously. Next she took a sip of coffee. It was wonderful—hot and strong, milky and sweet. She drained the cup, then looked up to see her husband watching her, a faintly quizzical look on his face. As their eyes met, the long grooves down his cheeks deepened and the grey eyes almost twinkled.

Wryly she smiled, feeling a little foolish. 'Very well, it is delicious. I do feel better.'

He nodded. 'Food is the best thing after a bout of seasickness. Will you have the eggs now?'

Tallie glanced at the orange yolks and shuddered. 'No, I thank you. I will be content with these rolls and some more of this lovely coffee. It is different from English coffee, is it not? And then I would like to wash and to change my clothes.'

'Make haste, then, for we do not stay the night here,' said Magnus. Tallie looked up in surprise.

'We made good time in the ship,' he said, 'but it will not be long before this town is as crowded as Dover was. I have every intention of beginning the journey to Paris as soon as possible and avoid the inconvenience of over-full inns.' He added, 'We shall stop in Boulogne, which is some hours' travel from here. I understand there are several decent inns where we can repose ourselves for the night.'

Tallie nodded and wiped her mouth with a napkin. 'Very well. I shall postpone my bath until just before I retire for the night.'

Magnus met her eyes in an oddly searing glance for a moment, then stared at his plate, 'John Black is, at this minute, arranging transportation with the postmaster. We shall depart as soon as he has hired a post-chaise and four.'

The trip along the post-road from Calais to Boulogne delighted Tallie, the faint aroma of onions that lingered in the hired vehicle notwithstanding. 'One would think that farms would be farms and fields the same the world over, but it is not so at all, is it?' she commented to Magnus. 'Even the people in France look different.'

He nodded, never having given the matter any thought. He'd decided not to ride, the horses for hire being decidedly inferior in his opinion, so he was sprawled lazily in the corner of the chaise, observing his bride's fascination with the passing scenery. Her ability to be pleased by the smallest things struck him again, and it occurred to him that, had he wed one of Laetitia's collection, he would, no doubt, be having to exert himself to entertain her. Tallie was young, he realised, but she had never yet bored him as Laetitia's friends had.

The late afternoon sun was sparkling on the Channel when they reached Boulogne. They found the inn the landlord of the Lion d'Argent had recommended. Magnus engaged a suite of rooms, bespoke an early supper, then went for a stroll while a *bonne* ushered Tallie up to a large chamber and then went to arrange for her bath to be drawn.

Tallie explored. Her chamber was spacious, with a small dressing room attached. It was comfortable, rather than elegant, and contained an enormous bed with a heavenly feather mattress. On top of the bed were several quite peculiar pillows—long, round and narrow—more like bolsters than pillows. She wondered if Magnus's bed had proper pillows and decided, if it did, she would borrow one of his.

Connecting doors led to a private parlour and a narrow balcony overlooked the sea. Tallie passed several enjoyable minutes observing the scenery until the *bonne* returned with a pile of soft towels. Behind her trooped footmen, carrying an enamelled hip bath and numerous buckets of steaming hot water.

Tallie bounced into the wonderfully soft bed and snuggled down under the thick down quilt that the inn provided instead of blankets. It was very light, and quite insubstantial compared with the thick woollen bedclothes she was used to, but it seemed warm enough.

Her first day in France. It had been very exciting, for Magnus had taken her for a stroll through the town before they had sat down to an utterly delicious supper. She had heard about French cooking, and now she knew! Even quite ordinary vegetables took on a new splendour in the hands of a French cook, with delectable subtle sauces and interesting combinations. And the variety of dishes...wonderful. Tallie sighed in pleasure and leaned over to blow out her bedside candle. Before she could do so, however, she heard a knock on the door. She sat up in bed, clutching the down quilt to her chest.

'Who...? Er...*qui est-ce*—?' she called hesitantly.

'It is I,' said the deep voice of her husband.

'C...come in.'

Magnus entered, shutting and locking the door behind him. Tallie pulled the quilt more tightly around her.

'Was there something you wanted, my lor—er, Magnus?'

He looked down at her enigmatically for a moment. 'This is my room, too.'

Tallie blinked. 'But there's only one bed.'

He smiled slowly. 'I know.'

'But...'

'We are married, Tallie. Married couples share a bed.'

Tallie's mouth opened in surprise. It wasn't true. Her cousin Laetitia had her own bed, and most of her married visitors had separate chambers, too—Tallie knew because she'd been the one who had usually arranged the accommodation for guests. The only time they ever shared a bedchamber was when there were too many people for separate ones... Maybe this inn was crowded too.

'Oh,' she said, and swallowed.

'I'll disrobe in here, shall I?' Magnus entered the small dressing room, pulling the door after him.

Tallie sat in the bed, wondering what to do. There was a look in his eye that she had seen before—in the coach in Dover, when he had kissed her in that extraordinary way.

She'd thought about the kiss a lot since it had happened. She knew people didn't usually kiss like that, with their tongue inside your mouth, and wondered if that was how a man put a baby inside a woman. Amanda Forrest had said her mother said it happened when a man put himself inside a woman, and he had certainly put himself inside her then. She shivered deliciously, remembering the bold sweep of his tongue over hers.

Did she have a baby inside her yet? Probably not, after all that vomiting on the ship, so perhaps he was going to kiss her in that special way again. She wouldn't mind it at all. It had been quite wonderful... She hadn't felt the need to flinch or anything, as her cousin had said she would.

The dressing room door opened and Magnus emerged, dressed in a heavily embroidered dark silk dressing gown, tied at the waist with a sash. He walked over to the bed and smiled. 'Move over,' he said softly, and with a small, nervous smile Tallie wriggled over to her side of the bed. He sat down on the edge of the bed and slowly undid the sash, watching her all the time. He peeled off the dressing gown and Tallie gasped and averted her eyes.

He was naked! Completely naked. No nightshirt at all!

He stood and, naked, walked a few steps to a chair, over which he neatly draped his dressing gown. Tallie shot a quick, furtive glance at him. She had never seen a naked man before. Aside from the powerful muscles across his shoulders and back, and the long, hairy limbs, men weren't all that different from women, she decided. They were just bigger and stronger and hairier. Then he turned, and Tallie's eyes almost popped out of her head. There was something *very* different about men...and her husband looked *nothing* like little Georgie in the bath!

Tallie suddenly realised he'd caught her peeking, and she hurriedly turned her head away, closing her eyes for good measure. He laughed, and said, 'It's all right to look, you know.'

Tallie didn't reply. She lay down in the bed, her eyes shut tight, and felt the bed sag as he climbed into it. His body was very close to hers—she could feel the warmth radiating from him, even though he was naked and should be cold.

'Will you blow out the candle, please?' she said after a moment.

'Not yet,' said a deep voice beside her ear. 'I think it's my turn to look, don't you?'

Tallie's eyes flew open and she clutched the comforter to her chin. 'Y...your turn?' she quavered.

'My turn,' he confirmed. 'It's what married people do.' He reached out, gently tugged the comforter from her nerveless grasp and pushed it down to her lap. Slowly he began to unbutton her nightgown...one button...two...three...until it was undone almost to her waist. She was shaking by the time he'd finished and her eyes were screwed shut.

'Don't be frightened,' he said softly, and began to stroke her cheek. He moved closer, and she could feel the solid heat of his body lying all along hers. He bent over her and kissed her lightly on the mouth, then kissed her again, moving his lips softly over her, small, tiny kisses, feathering them over her mouth, her eyelids, her cheeks. Tallie relaxed a little.

His hands caressed her, stroking her cheek, her throat, down her arms, then back up to her throat. He touched her breasts through the cotton of her nightgown, moving back and forth in the softest, lightest touch. Tallie felt a faint quiver pass through her every time he did so. He kissed her deeply, then touched his tongue to the hollow at the base of her throat and kissed her again. Slowly, slowly the kisses moved lower, and she felt the faint abrasion of his chin as he nudged her nightgown apart.

She felt the moist, warm trail of his kisses down in the valley between her breasts, then his hand slipped in and eased her gown aside. He sat up on one elbow for a moment, staring.

'Beautiful.'

Tallie's eyes opened for a fleeting, stunned glance. Beautiful? He thought her beautiful?

He cupped first one breast then the other, in a warm, strong hand, then rubbed his thumbs gently back and forth across their tips. Tallie felt them harden, and shivers of pleasure coursed through her. She watched, trembling, as his dark head bent and he suddenly buried his face in her breasts and made a low, deep sound in his throat. She had never before felt so close to another human being. She wanted to put her arms around him, to cradle his head against her. Her hands rose, hovered, and then dropped uncertainly.

'Let's get rid of this thing,' he said, sitting up. He reached under the bedclothes, took the hem of her nightgown and began to pull it upwards, over her legs.

Tallie tried to stop him. 'I...no... But it's cold...and this comforter is extremely light.'

'I'll keep you warm.' He tugged at the hem. 'Lift your bottom.'

Mindful of her wedding vows, Tallie obeyed, and in seconds she was lying in bed with her husband, not a stitch of clothing between them. He pulled the comforter down and gazed at her body with possessive, heavy-lidded grey eyes which seemed to burn into her skin. Tallie tried to shield herself from his stare, but he lifted her hands away, saying, 'I am your husband, Tallie. You don't have to hide yourself from me.'

He lowered his mouth to her breast again, and Tallie almost leapt out of her skin as red-hot spears of pleasure pierced her. He muttered inaudibly, caressing her with hands, mouth and tongue. Sensations spiralled through her and she found herself shuddering convulsively. What magic was he performing to make her feel this way? She wanted to take his head in her hands and press him tighter against her breasts, wanted to touch him as he was touching her. She pressed a small, shy kiss on his hair instead.

He caressed her softly, tenderly, and so slowly... It was... lovely... At one point he slowed, and seemed to hesitate, and Tallie opened her eyes. He, too, had his eyes closed. He was breathing heavily and gritting his teeth. She wondered for a fleeting second if he was in pain. But she soon forgot that thought because—ohhh... The feeling of his warm strong hands caressing, smoothing, shaping her body, learning it. She knew now why some people called this possessing—Magnus was possessing her. And it was wonderful.

She tentatively laid her hands on his shoulders and, light as thistledown, stroked his skin. He felt warm, slightly damp with sweat, and very, very good. His skin smelt of the cologne water he usually wore, and some darker, musky scent that she knew was him. He didn't react, didn't tell her to stop. Feeling braver, Tallie stroked the wide muscular shoulders and the crisp dark hair on his arms, exulting in the feel of his strength. Such a powerful man, and yet so tender with it.

He rubbed his hands down over her stomach and hips, and the slightly roughened skin of his palms set up a delicious friction on her soft skin, then dipped between her thighs. Quivers ran through her, and without conscious volition her legs fell open. He cupped her between her legs and began small circular motions that soon had her gasping with excitement. She felt his fingers moving intimately in the folds of her flesh, and she parted her legs further, writhing in pleasure at the sensations coursing through her body.

Groaning, he pushed her legs wider and settled himself between them, his hands stroking, caressing, probing and teasing, his mouth hot and hard on hers. She felt something hard and blunt nudging her between her legs, and she stiffened.

He paused, looking deep into her eyes. 'I don't want to hurt you, but the first time, I fear, it is inevitable.'

Suddenly Tallie recalled her cousin's instructions. She closed her eyes and grabbed the bottom sheet tight in her fists. He pushed, and she wanted to wriggle away, but she remembered the bit about not flinching and braced herself instead. He pushed harder, groaning, and Tallie gasped. She wondered if it was hurting him as much as it was hurting her, and then she stopped wondering as a sharp pain lanced through her and she forced herself to remain motionless.

He hesitated. 'It's done now,' he murmured, and caressed her cheek for a second. Tallie, panting, was relieved, and waited for him to remove himself, and the thing that was stretching her and stinging so dreadfully. Instead he started to move inside her, moving back and forth, slowly at first and then faster and faster. His mouth came back over hers, and she realised his tongue was moving at the same pace, creating those amazing sensations in her again.

She was not hurting so much now, but still an unbearable feeling of tightness was growing inside her, until she thought she must burst. She wanted to writhe and squirm and scratch, but she knew she could not move, nor flinch or cry out or otherwise disgrace herself. Or him.

This was her husband, and she was now truly his wife, and this was what husbands did to get their wives with child. But, oh—she wanted to take hold of him and hold herself hard against him while he was doing this to her. But she couldn't.

She loved him, she realised suddenly. Against all her expectations she'd fallen in love with this cold, kind, abrupt, gentle man. She wanted to cry out and cover his face with kisses, but she owed it to him to lie here without flinching, without crying out.

He mightn't love her, but she wanted him to be proud of her...

His movements built to a rapid crescendo, and she found herself panting shallowly in time with them, feeling as though something was about to happen...as though she was being swept away by some tide... She forced herself to lie still. Finally, with a loud, unintelligible groan, her husband gave one last heavy thrust, arching his body over her, his head thrown back in pain—or exultation—she wasn't sure which—and subsided heavily on top of her. They lay, unmoving, panting, their bodies beginning to cool.

He was still inside her, she could feel him, though it was not so uncomfortable now. He lay heavily on top of her and she could hardly breathe, but Tallie decided she liked the feeling of being surrounded by his strength and his warmth. His head was buried in the hollow of her throat. Tentatively she lifted her hand and stroked the short crisp curls on his head. They were damp. She trailed her fingers down the side of his neck and across his shoulders. His skin was moist and warm. He sighed and shuddered under her hand, and then moved away from her. She felt his withdrawal and felt a momentary sense of loss. The candle was still burning, and she felt him watching her in the flickering golden light.

He smoothed back a damp curl from her face. 'Are you all right?' he asked softly.

She couldn't look at him, felt too full of emotion, so she just nodded.

He slipped out of bed and disappeared into the dressing room. She watched him leave and felt like bursting into tears. He was going to dress and return to his own room.

He came back, still naked, carrying a cloth. She wanted to look at him properly, to see exactly how he was made and how it all worked now that she knew how he felt. But she was too shy to do more than cast a quick flicker in his direction, then look away.

He came back to the bed and reached for her thighs.

'Again?' Tallie jumped, disconcerted.

He smiled ruefully. 'No, not tonight.'

She sat back, relieved, then stiffened in shock as he parted her thighs and began to wipe her with a damp cloth. She was sticky and sore there, but for him to be doing such a thing! Her face burned with embarrassment and she tried to stop him, but he took no notice. Finally he finished, and stood up. She glanced at the cloth and saw to her amazement that there were streaks of red on it.

Emmaline Pearce had been right, thought Tallie as her husband moved around inside the dressing room. All those punishments from Miss Fisher for telling lies—and Emmaline had been right all along. There *was* blood, and there certainly could have been screaming had Laetitia not warned her it was not allowed.

Magnus returned and slipped into bed beside her, pulling the cover up around them both. 'And now we sleep,' he said, blowing out the candle and turning on his side. He pulled her against him, holding her around the waist.

Despite her recent experience, and the knowledge that she loved him, Tallie still felt odd, being naked in bed with him—with all that bare skin. 'Shouldn't I put on my nightgown?'

He pulled her tighter against him and stroked a hand up over her hip, briefly cupping her breast. 'You won't get cold,' he murmured, his breath warm against her ear. 'Now hush, and try to sleep.'

Tallie closed her eyes, and soon she heard the slow, deep breathing that told her Magnus was asleep. She sighed, feeling unaccountably miserable all of a sudden. A slow, solitary tear slipped down her cheek, then another.

Chapter Nine

'Six months?' Tallie's voice rose with surprise. 'In Paris?'

Magnus nodded. 'Unless, of course, you find yourself in a delicate condition before then.'

Tallie blushed. She knew now what he meant by 'a delicate condition'. The possibility she might be carrying his child made her heart beat faster. But it also made things even more urgent. She *had* to get to Italy before she became *enceinte*.

'I don't want to spend six months in Paris.'

Magnus pokered up and looked down his nose, the way he usually did when she questioned his decisions. 'I think you'll find six months is not long enough—or is that what you mean?'

'No, not at all,' Tallie said. 'Six months is far too long. If we stay in Paris for such a long time, it will be near winter, and we shan't be able to cross the Alps into Italy until next year.'

'Cross the Alps?' His dark brows rose.

She nodded vigorously. 'Yes. I have heard so many tales of crossing the Alps. It sounds monstrous exciting and I am most eager to do it. And to reach Italy...' Her voice tailed off and she diffidently twirled the wine glass in front of her. 'My parents' graves are in Italy,' she said, not looking at him.

Magnus stared at her for a moment. It was the first time she'd mentioned her parents.

'How old were you when they died?'

'Eleven, almost twelve.'

'And how did they die?'

She hesitated for a long moment, toying with the apricot pastry in front of her. 'I am not entirely sure,' she said at last. 'I think there was a coach accident.'

He frowned. 'You think?'

She nodded, pressed a crumb of sweet pastry onto her finger and transferred it to her mouth. 'The stories conflict. The official notification said their coach overturned and both my parents died immediately, but then I received a letter from someone who knew Mama which suggested that Mama died before Papa...and not from her injuries in the accident...' Tallie licked the grains of sugar which clung to her fingertips.

'What do you mean?' Magnus frowned, watching her.

She shrugged. 'I know no more than that. But it is why I wish so much to go to Italy. I would like to see their graves.' There was a lot more to it, but she did not wish to explain it to him. Not with him being so cool, and frowning as he was. As he had been since they had left Boulogne. Tallie sighed.

It had been almost a sennight since that momentous night, and he had been so cold and distant and abrupt with her that she could almost believe it had been a dream. Except that her body told her it wasn't. Despite the initial soreness and stiffness, her body still sang with the memory of how it had felt to have him hold her and caress her and possess her. She knew the difference now between dreams and reality...

But he had not shared her bed since. Nor had he so much as touched her, except to help her into the coach and such things, and even then he drew back his hand afterwards, as if she was hot metal... And when he spoke to her it was in such a formal manner he might well have been addressing the House of Lords, she thought despairingly.

She had, indeed, married an Icicle.

Magnus watched the changing expressions flit over her countenance and frowned again. It was not going at all as he had planned. His desire for his wife's body had not been slaked by that one night in Boulogne—it had only whetted his appetite for more. He'd watched her licking the sugar off her small pink fingers and felt more than ever like a rampant green youth.

But it was not to be thought of, he told himself sternly. She'd been an untried innocent and was not yet healed—he could tell by the way she tensed up when he came close to her. He would wait until they reached Paris before he shared her bed again. It was the only decent thing to do.

And besides, he had no intention of allowing himself to fall in thrall to a woman's charms. Down that path lay disaster. He'd seen it before—his father and a dozen others, dancing to a woman's tune, helpless in the face of feminine betrayal...

A few sparkling grains of sugar clung to her lips. Magnus refused to notice them.

'We shall reach Paris on the morrow,' he announced, rising from the table. 'We shall depart this inn at first light, so you had best retire early. I bid you goodnight, madam.' He bowed.

Madam. Tallie rose, a lump in her throat at his cool indifference. In a husky voice she murmured goodnight and left the private parlour.

'Tallie.'

She turned on the stairs, a tiny surge of hope rising in her at his voice.

'You will like Paris, I know,' said Magnus from the doorway. 'For a start, you will have a great many fine new gowns and hats and so on. Neither the Terror nor the war has managed to extinguish Paris's reputation for modishness.'

'Oh. Yes,' she murmured dully. 'I suppose not.'

'Think of it—gowns of silk, satin and lace—day gowns, evening gowns—the finest that money can buy.'

She stared down at him in silence.

'And gloves, slippers, French perfume. And balls and routs and glittering assemblies—you will enjoy it very much,' he insisted, frowning.

'Yes, my lord, if you say so.' She turned and mounted the stairs to her chamber.

Curse the woman! What was the matter with her? Magnus watched her go, watched the sway of her hips under the dreary gown she wore. She was dressed like the veriest drab and he had promised her the finest gowns money could buy. So why could she not offer him at least a smile? Any one of the mistresses he had kept in the past would have shrieked with delight and flung her arms around his neck at such an offer. She—his wife—had responded with a dutiful murmur of obedience!

Damn it! He would never understand women! Here he was, allowing himself to be dragged off to foreign parts for her benefit, enduring bad roads, poor accommodation and hard-mouthed horses for her benefit, opening his purse for her benefit and—not least of all—restraining his desires for her benefit!

And was she grateful? Not in the least! Swearing, Magnus took himself off to his cold, empty chamber and his cold, empty bed. He brooded on his wife's unnatural behaviour as he disrobed. He'd wanted a plain, convenient, grateful wife! Hah! He shrugged himself out of his tight coat and tossed it on the bed. She was none of those.

Plain! Even the dowdy gowns she wore hadn't been able to disguise her attractions—not since his so-called wedding night, when he'd put her to bed. He ripped off his cravat and shirt and flung them on a chair.

And as for convenient—why, that was sheer bloody fustian! He sat down on the bed. She was putting him to a vast deal of blasted inconvenience, he thought, tugging furiously at his long boots. He'd even had to do without his valet because of her passion to go to France—the fool had been too frightened to return to his native country, having escaped Madame Guillotine once already! With some difficulty Magnus managed to drag his boots off. And all the time, he thought, in spite of his own desires and frustrations, he had treated her with unfailing politeness and consideration.

But did she show the slightest bit of gratitude for her husband's generosity and forbearance? No! Not she! Magnus hurled his boots across the room. She had taken herself off to bed without a murmur, completely unmoved by the delights he had offered her! Even now she was disrobing, preparing herself for bed, only too happy to snuggle into bed alone. She would have removed that dull stuff gown, rolled her stockings down over those smooth calves and dainty ankles, discarded her petticoat and chemise and was probably—even now—standing naked, warm and pink and glowing, preparing to don that hideous voluminous monstrosity she called a nightgown!

Well, he would not stand for it! She was his wife. A husband had rights! She had no business making him wait until Paris! He snatched his dressing gown from the end of the bed, threw it on, and in bare feet crossed the hall from his chamber to hers, barely remembering to knock as he flung open her door.

'Oh! Magnus! Is there something wrong?'

'Why is your door not locked?' he snapped, staring at her, outraged. She was bent over a dish of water, up to her elbows in soap, clad in that dreadful nightgown and an even worse dressing gown. With not an inch of skin to be seen.

'Oh, I must have forgotten it.'

'See you do not forget it in future. Anyone could have just walked in.'

She looked at him for a long moment and a tiny smile appeared on her face. 'Someone just did.'

'Who the *devil* was it?' he thundered, glaring round the room.

Tallie giggled and bit her lip. 'You, my lord.'

Magnus stared at her for a moment. The tips of his ears turned faintly pink. 'Ah, yes...well...hrmph,' he said, and strolled around her chamber, glaring at the neat, untouched bed, her clothes hanging tidily on the hooks behind the door.

Tallie resumed her washing. The motion drew his attention.

'What are you doing?'

She blushed. 'Just rinsing out a few things.'

He strode over and stared at the basin. 'What the deuce are you doing that for? There are maids for that sort of thing. My wife does not wash clothes!'

'It's nothing, just a few bits and pieces,' she said, trying unsuccessfully to hide them from his sight. They were her underclothes, he realised—he recognised the patches. He had a set just like them in his valise, with the tapes cut.

'I don't care what they are—get the maid to do it.'

'But I don't want the maid to see—' She broke off, her cheeks rosy with embarrassment.

'See what?' he said, puzzled. A thought occurred to him. 'You're not...is it your time of month?'

Tallie's face flamed. 'No!' she gasped, horrified. She had not known men even knew of such things.

Magnus indulgently observed her flaming cheeks. His innocent little wife was easily flustered. He rather enjoyed it, found it surprisingly arousing, though he did not intend she should realise it. He shrugged. 'Then what do you not wish the maid to see?'

Tallie was infuriated by the cool enquiry. 'It is nothing to do with you. I will do as I like in my own bedchamber. There is no one to see me—you need not worry about what people will think!'

'You will do as I tell—'

'I am your wife, not a slave—'

'Exactly! And I will *not* have my countess washing clothes!'

Magnus stared at her, baffled by her intransigence over such a trivial matter. What the devil was wrong with the wench? Most women who'd had a life like hers would lap up the luxury of having unpleasant little tasks done by a servant. Why would she want to wash her own underclothes? And what did she not wish the maids to see? As if the maids had not seen underclothes before—and a damned sight better—

The truth suddenly hit him with the force of a blow to the midriff. She was embarrassed. Not because her unmentionables needed washing, but because they were in such appalling condition—patched and darned and ill-fitting. She had pride, his little wife, too much pride to have a maid pity her for her lack of adequate clothing. Again he called down silent curses on his cousin's head for her lack of care for Tallie. He vowed his wife would never again have cause to be embarrassed by her clothing. The moment they arrived in Paris he would procure her the finest garments that money could buy. From the skin out.

He shrugged nonchalantly. 'Very well, then, I will tolerate it this time. But once we reach Paris, mind, you shall leave all tasks of that nature to the servants.' He strolled over and sat on the bed.

Tallie stared at him a moment, stunned by his abrupt *volte face*. Then a fresh thought hit her. He had come to her bedchamber. He was sitting on her bed. In his dressing gown.

He was going to lie with her again.

With shaking hands she hurriedly finished rinsing out her petticoat and chemise, anticipation and excitement rising within her. She darted quick little glances at him as she worked. His large, strong hands fiddled with items on the bedside table. Tallie shivered with pleasure, imagining the way those hands would soon move across her skin, knowing her, possessing her.

He wanted her again. The thought thrilled her. Quickly she wrung out the clothes and laid them over the back of a wooden chair, out of his sight, then moved shyly towards the bed.

Blushing, she slipped out of her dressing gown and climbed into the high bed beside him. 'M...Magnus...' she whispered.

He turned towards her, cupped her chin in his hand and gazed deep into her eyes.

'It is not too soon? You do not mind?' His breath caressed her skin. His voice was low and deep and resonated through her bones like music.

She blushed, shook her head, and raised her face for his kiss.

Tallie learnt two new things about the marriage act that night. First, that it didn't hurt the second time—not one little bit. And, second, that it was very much more difficult for her to remain still and dignified while her husband's ministrations evoked all sorts of wondrous and thrilling feelings. It took all her will-power, every bit of concentration and determination she possessed, to lie passively under him, making no sound or movement, as her cousin had warned her to.

But she managed it.

The very most she allowed herself was to press several soft, moist kisses on his chest and jaw—and that was only after he had fallen asleep. He could not be disgusted by what he did not know she did. And he could not know the intense pleasure she gained from snuggling up to his warm, relaxed, naked body while he slept.

She was very proud of her efforts, too. She wanted so much to be a good wife to Magnus, wanted so much for him to be proud of her, to respect her—even, perhaps, to learn to love her, just a little. He wanted a child, that much she knew...perhaps he would come to care for her if she gave him one.

She lay in the dark, enjoying the feel of her husband's arm draped heavily across her, his chest and torso pressed against her back, one long, hairy leg thrust between hers. Sleepily she wondered whether she was increasing, and, if so, how she would know.

The princess gazed out through her prison bars, straining for a sight, a sound to indicate that someone was coming to rescue her. But all she could see or hear were the happy celebrations of the townspeople far below her. There would be no rescue today for the princess. She would have to remain here, in the highest turret of the Callous Count's castle. But wait, what was that scraping sound? She turned again to the high, barred window. A muscular hand reached out and effortlessly plucked the bars, one, two, three, from the window. 'Tallie, my love,' a thrillingly deep masculine voice called. She ran to the window and looked out. There, clinging to a rope, was her handsome outlaw prince, his dark hair blowing in the breeze, his grey eyes glinting... No! Not grey! Blue eyes, perhaps, or brown or green—anything except grey! People with grey eyes were selfish. And disobliging. And horrid!

Tallie sat fuming in a chair by the window of her *hôtel* room, glaring out. Outside were people and noise and activity such as she'd never seen or heard before in her life. She shifted restlessly in her seat and punched a cushion into a more comfortable shape.

Outside was a thrilling concoction of smells and sights and sounds that shrieked *Paris!* She bounced up and paced angrily around the room.

Outside was a huge, exotic city, and she'd never in her life been in a city. And where was she? Stuck inside a stuffy parlour, that was where, under orders from her stuffy husband not to venture out until he gave her leave! And where was *he*?

Outside, that was where! Exploring this wondrously exciting city. For the last four hours! While *she* was forced to wait.

It wasn't fair. He'd muttered something about preparations to make before she was ready for Paris and gone out into the city himself, needing, apparently, no preparations for his magnificent self! Leaving her with nothing better to do than study Sinderby. A guidebook. When the real thing was just outside her door! She snatched up the cushion and hurled it at the door in frustration.

'Oops! Sorry,' she gasped as the object of her fury ducked, regarded her with a raised eyebrow and then closed the door carefully behind him. His face was utterly impassive and Tallie's spirits sank. He was The Icicle once more. Ignoring the cushion at his feet, Magnus came forward and presented her with a large brown paper parcel, tied with string.

'A modiste will be here within the hour to fit you out with some decent clothes. You will need to don these before she arrives.' He strolled over to the window, glanced out into the street, then opened up a news sheet and began reading it, quite as if he had nothing more to say to her.

Tallie, clutching the parcel to her bosom, stared at him, suddenly confused. Part of her wanted to rail at him for leaving her for such a long time with nothing to do, but the large, squashy parcel in her arms intrigued her. A gift? She could not remember the last time anyone had given her a gift. Only her wedding pearls. And now, a gift for no reason... With trembling fingers she unknotted the string and spread open the wrapping. Soft, silken things dripped from her fingers and slithered to the floor.

'Ohhh,' she gasped, enchanted. She bent and lifted them. A chemise—no, six, in soft, silky material. And petticoats, in fine lawn and muslin, trimmed with lace. Silk stockings, dozens of them—*silk*! And six finely embroidered nightgowns, so thin and fine and delicate you could almost see through them. She had never seen the like, except once, on a friend of her cousin's. And...good gracious!

She picked the last few items up and frowned in confusion. These were surely not for her... But they, too, were made of the finest, most delicate lawn...pink lawn. Tallie fingered the garments, stunned. They could not possibly be for her husband, for they had lace on them, and besides, they were too small for him. But she had never worn such things...never heard of such things, except in a scandalised whisper. Not even Laetitia wore garments like these.

'I cannot wear these,' she whispered.

Magnus did not turn his head. 'Of course you can. You will oblige me by retiring to your chamber and donning them immediately, madam. The modiste is coming.'

Madam. Tallie gathered up the clothing and left the room, feeling mutinous. The first true gift she had received in years and was she allowed to be excited about it? No, she must be silent and obedient and don them 'immediately, *madam*,' for we would not wish to inconvenience an unknown French modiste, would we? *Madam.*

In her chamber, she stripped off her clothes and quickly slipped into one of the new chemises and a petticoat, savouring the cool, silken feel of them against her skin. The chemise was close-fitting, with gussets under the arms and side gussets to accommodate the flare of her hips. The neckline was extremely low and edged with a tiny frill of lace. The petticoat was long and straight, made of fine, sheer muslin. It was almost like wearing nothing at all. She felt very daring and sophisticated.

She glanced at the other garments on the bed. Drawers! For a woman! Pink ones, with fine French lace around each knee. She had never seen anything so scandalous in her life. Drawers were male attire. For a female to wear them would be truly shocking. Miss Fisher would have fainted at the very notion. Tallie picked up the drawers and held them against her. She ought not to...but her husband had instructed her to wear them.

Quickly she bent, and with some difficulty she pulled on the drawers. They felt very peculiar. She had never felt her bottom and legs so enclosed, so restricted... It was indeed very shocking. Tallie rather liked the feeling.

But however would she manage when she had to...? She pulled the drawers away from her body and peered down inside them. Good heavens! There was a slit. How very shocking! But practical, she supposed.

A knock on the door made her dart behind the screen in a panic. *'Qui est-ce-que—?'*

The door opened. It was her husband.

'I came to see whether the...er...things fitted.'

Tallie, blushing, nodded from behind the safety of her screen. 'Yes, thank you. They do.'

'Well, let me see them,' he said a little impatiently.

Blushing furiously, Tallie took a deep breath and stepped out from behind the screen.

Magnus's eyes narrowed as he took in the picture of his bride dressed in nothing but fine undergarments. His mouth dried as he noted the way the fine silk of the chemise did nothing to hide the creamy swell of her breasts or the faint dark pink of her small thrusting nipples. He dropped his gaze to her hips and frowned in surprise, as he saw what appeared to be pink drawers under her petticoat.

He had not actually selected the garments himself, had simply given the manageress of the establishment an order for the finest, most fashionable underclothes Paris could provide. So the drawers were a shock. He had heard that some women were wearing them, not just women of the *demi-mondaine*—ladies, too, but these were the first he had seen.

'Take off your petticoat,' he said in a deep, husky voice.

Tallie undid the tapes, took a deep breath, closed her eyes and dropped the petticoat. It pooled in a whisper around her feet.

Magnus felt all the breath leave his body at the sight of his wife dressed in intimate male attire. A feminised version of male attire, to be sure, but...no male had ever looked like that... He had never seen anything so erotic in his life. The drawers were gathered at her knees and he wondered how far he could run his hands up inside them. The delicate material hugged her thighs and her skin glowed beneath the fine weave. The drawers bunched slightly at the apex of her thighs over a shadowy, unmistakably feminine vee shape, and then pulled tighter against the slight swell of her stomach.

'Turn around,' he said huskily.

Slowly she turned, her eyes still clenched shut.

Magnus stared. The drawers hugged her rounded bottom and hips and suddenly he longed to see her bending over. 'You have dropped your new petticoat on the floor,' he said hoarsely, and she bent to gather it up. The material pulled tight across her bottom and Magnus could stand no more. He embraced her from behind, running caressing hands up over her body, cupping her breasts, moulding them, seeking out the hardening nipples.

'Magnus!' Tallie squeaked in surprise. 'It is the daytime.'

Ignoring that, he turned her in his arms and lifted her onto the bed, his hands feverishly exploring her scandalously clothed body. He ran his palms up under the knees and gloried in the smooth, satiny feel of her thighs. He bent down and suckled her hard pink nipples through the silk of the chemise and felt her shudder beneath him. He ran his hands down over her backside and up between her legs. 'Aha!' he exclaimed triumphantly as he found the slit. His hands caressed her and he frowned as he felt her stiffen.

'But you said the modiste was coming soon,' said his wife through gritted teeth.

'Damn the modiste!' He caressed her more gently, determined she would, this time, participate in his passion.

'But—'

'The modiste can wait!' he growled, annoyed with her hesitation. He continued to stroke and caress her with one hand, fumbling with his own clothes until he was free of their restraint, and then passion overcame his control and he surged into her and was lost.

Tallie clenched her teeth and hung on, determined she would not disgrace him by moving or calling out. It was getting harder and harder for her to behave as she knew she should. Her husband's desire for her thrilled her, and she probably would have wept with joy—if only she didn't have to concentrate so hard on controlling her own recalcitrant body. But it was so very exciting...

Tallie locked her legs into a stiff line and repeated the usual words over and over in her head. It was the only way she could concentrate on her duty to him.

* * *

The rest of the day passed in a whirl. The modiste, Mademoiselle Célestine, arrived—luckily a little late—with an entourage of assistants who draped, pinned, snipped and pulled as they discussed, with much hand-waving and Gallic imprecation, exactly how milady should be attired. Tallie was utterly scandalised by the new French fashions. They seemed to her to consist of nothing but a few wisps of gauze or muslin, and she felt almost naked wearing them. But the modiste and her assistants laughed and assured her everything was perfectly *comme il faut*, and milady didn't wish to appear dowdy, did she?

Tallie looked doubtfully down at her almost naked chest and the transparent veil of embroidered muslin covering the rest of her and thought that milady might indeed prefer to be dowdy if that was the only alternative. It was one thing to appear almost naked in front of her husband—she was becoming accustomed to that—but she could not imagine wearing these...these little wispy things out in public. But she was assured she must, *absolument*, and she supposed when in Rome...or Paris...

However, at that point Magnus entered the room. 'Just thought I'd see how—' He came to an abrupt halt, took one long, burning look at Tallie's flimsy new gown and snapped, 'No! It will not do. Not at all.'

'Oh, but, milor—' began Mademoiselle Célestine.

He strode forward and felt the fine embroidered muslin in long, disdainful fingers. 'Too thin, too flimsy. Shoddy goods.'

'Mais, non, milor',' gasped Mademoiselle Célestine, horrified. 'It is of the very finest—'

'No matter.' He brushed off her explanations. 'I should have made my requirements clearer. My wife requires much thicker clothing than this.' He flicked the material scornfully. 'You would not think it to look at her, but she has a very delicate constitution—'

Tallie gasped in indignation.

'She catches cold at the slightest draught and I will not allow her to risk her health for the sake of mere *à la modalité*. No, *mademoiselle* I wish Lady d'Arenville to be warmly and decently clothed, with high-necked gowns in thick, warm fabric.'

And he marched out, leaving Tallie fuming. A sickly constitution indeed! This from the man who'd called her sturdy! And how dared he criticise all her old clothes and then give the modiste orders to ensure she looked just as dowdy in her new ones? Suddenly Tallie felt perfectly comfortable with the new French fashions, flimsy or not.

'You will ignore my husband, if you please, Mademoiselle Célestine. Men do not have the least idea of fashion,' she said firmly. 'The gowns will be as we agreed.'

Mademoiselle Célestine smiled knowingly. 'Ah, but you play with fire, milady. *Alors.* Perhaps we make the necklines a little higher, *hein*? And then we take a slip, like so.' She took out an opaque underdress and held it up. 'Many women wear flesh-coloured stockings also. And of course there are your beautiful pink drawers, quite warm enough for the most fragile constitution, and yet, when the gentlemen look, they see only the colour of flesh...and they wonder...ah, *oui*, they wonder...' She laughed and pulled a very expressive face. '*Très chic* and yet *très respectable*, so your so-jealous husband is almost—but not quite—happy. Husbands must be taught their place, *non*?' She and her assistants laughed again.

Tallie smiled vaguely, distracted by the modiste's words. Her *jealous* husband? That could not be right, surely... Still, he had told all those dreadful lies about her delicate constitution. She felt a small glow in the region of her heart. It was a start, perhaps...

By the time the modiste and her chattering assistants finally left, promising to have a beautiful gown ready for her by the morning, and many more *au plus tôt*, Tallie felt exhausted.

However, her husband had not simply arranged a modiste but also a hairdresser, Monsieur Raymondo, a small, dapper man with an elegant waxed moustache. He prowled around her shrinking form a dozen times, muttering under his breath, bunching her hair this way and that and exclaiming in raptures over its texture and natural curl. Magnus ventured into the room just as the hairdresser picked up his scissors. 'Don't you dare shear off all that beautiful hair!' he roared, and Monsieur Raymondo dropped his scissors in fright. A long discussion ensued over exactly how much Magnus would tolerate being cut off.

Tallie took no part in it; she was in a small, happy daze of her own. *Beautiful hair!* He had lied about her fragility, now this, about her very ordinary hair.

In the end Magnus and Monsieur Raymondo reached a compromise. Short, feathery curls would cluster around her face, while the rest remained quite long. It would please her husband, yet still have the required classical look about it—the new fashions, like the new French Republic, paid homage to the Ancient Greek and Roman ideals.

Tallie could hardly believe the reflection which stared back at her from the mirror when Monsieur Raymondo had finished. Her face seemed quite a different shape; she looked elegant...almost pretty. Her eyes seemed larger, her horrid nose not so pointy, and curly wisps of hair caressed her cheeks and highlighted her cheek-bones.

Monsieur Raymondo showed Tallie several ways to arrange her hair. She could put it up and hold it with a crescent, like the goddess Diana. She could wind a spangled scarf around her head, wear it in long, snaky ringlets *à la Sappho* or in the unique style Monsieur Raymondo had invented for her. Milady was now completely *à la mode*. Tallie expressed some concern that she would not be able to manage the new hairstyles, but her husband called a smartly attired young woman into the room and introduced her as Monique, Tallie's new maidservant and dresser. Tallie's mouth fell open. She had never in her life had someone dress her.

But she didn't have time to question anything, for then a shoemaker arrived. He measured her feet, produced a pair of jean half-boots and two pairs of smart kid slippers for immediate wear, and promised to send a dozen new pairs within the week.

Finally, Magnus announced that if the dressmaker delivered as she had promised, Monique could take Tallie shopping on the morrow, so that she could be fitted out with all the other falderals women found so indispensable. Tallie's head was aching by this time and she took umbrage at his tone.

'I do not wish to go shopping tomorrow,' she announced. 'I have done without falderals quite happily—well, almost happily,' she amended honestly, 'for all my life.' She took a deep breath and faced him, her hands clasped to her chest. 'I do not wish to sound ungrateful, indeed I am truly very grateful for all these beautiful things you have bought for me—'

Magnus stiffened uncomfortably. So much for wishing for a grateful wife. He found he did not want gratitude from her at all.

'It must have cost you a tremendous—' She flushed suddenly and muttered, 'I am sorry. I know it is vulgar to refer to money. But I *do* thank you for all the purchases you have made on my behalf...I cannot remember when anyone gave me...' She broke off and scuffed her foot against the Turkish rug on the floor. Her eyes were bright with unshed tears, Magnus noticed, before she ducked her head down to hide them from him. There was a short pause before she resumed.

'It is only...I do not want to waste any more time in shopping for...for *things*. I want...I want so much to see Paris. Already I have been here a full day and a night, and I have seen nothing except this room. Could we not...?' Her eyes fixed on his, wide with entreaty. 'If I wore a cloak, no one could see my clothes and you need not mind...'

Magnus stood up, affronted. She thought he was ashamed of her clothes, ashamed to be seen in her company. She thought he had hidden her away until she was fit to be seen. To his chagrin, he found there was an element of truth in the unspoken accusation. Though he was *not* ashamed of her—he just wished her to feel equal to those clothed in the very finest.

'It is too warm to wear a cloak,' he said, 'but if you wish it, there is still time for us to see something of the city.'

'Now?' she blurted, surprised.

'Yes, immediately. If you are not too tired.'

'Oh, no, I am not,' she said, her eyes shining. 'Oh, Magnus, thank you. I will just fetch my hat.' She hurried from the room and returned in a moment, fitting an old-fashioned bonnet to her head. He watched her tie its strings.

'I wished only to please you,' he said stiffly. 'I did not think of how you must feel, cooped up in here all day, when you have looked forward so eagerly to our arrival.'

Her face fell. 'Oh, no, I did not mean to criticise—'

He interrupted her. 'Shall we?' he said, presenting his arm.

Tallie was enchanted with Paris. She loved the narrow streets and the incredibly tall stone houses—some as many as seven storeys high. She admired the public buildings with the slogans of *Liberté*, *Egalité*, *Fraternité* and *Indivisibilité* written on every one. She especially loved the wide, elegant boulevards, so thickly planted with trees the branches almost met in a cool green arch. And under those branches there seemed to be a constant scene of festivity. Parisians did much of their socialising out of doors, and Tallie adored the outdoor cafés, where it seemed a thousand happy people sat, quaffing lemonade, wine, cider, beer or coffee. They strolled through parks where she was delighted by the 'Theatres for the People' as they were called—outdoor booths with conjurers, puppet shows, menageries and music, always music playing somewhere, on an organ, fiddle, harmonica, tambourine or flute.

And when, finally, night fell, and she thought they must return to the *hôtel*, Magnus took her to a place where a thousand lamps sparkled like fireflies in the branches of the trees, and a hundred flickering candles lit tiny intimate tables. There he ordered champagne and a meal, and Tallie ate her first dinner in Paris out of doors, totally enraptured. The food was delicious, but she could not recall afterwards what it was, for she was entranced by the sights and sounds of Paris all around her, and by the sight of her handsome, silent, considerate husband, who had so splendidly made amends for his earlier ineptitude.

And afterwards they strolled back to their hotel.

And Magnus came to her room.

Chapter Ten

Tallie braced herself and gritted her teeth. The tension was unbearable. She couldn't stand much more. Her body was sheened in sweat. She clutched the sheets on either side of her stiffened body and imagined them shredding under the pressure. She knew exactly how they felt—if sheets could feel, that was.

'Oh, for heaven's sake get it over with,' she gasped. 'I can't take much more of this!'

Magnus, naked and sweating from his labours, froze. He stared at his bride of two weeks, outraged. Never, *never* had any female dared to suggest he was less than adequate in the bedchamber! And this chit, barely out of her virginity, was daring to criticise! He swung himself away from her body, and she gathered the sheet against her to cover her nakedness.

Tallie stared at his furious face, appalled at her own lack of tact. She hadn't meant to say it—it had just slipped out.

'I'm sorr—' she began.

'So I should think!' he rapped. 'I've never been so insulted in my life.'

'Well, but—'

'Do you think it is easy for me, making love every night to a bride as cold and unmoving as a corpse?'

'I have no idea, never having considered the matter, although it seems to me you do not exactly dislike the procedure. In any case, it is very difficult for me, too!' Tallie was incensed by his criticism. 'You have no idea how difficult. It is pure torture!'

'Torture?' Magnus's grey eyes glittered with rage. 'Torture, is it?' He was mortified. Furious. He had half a mind to storm out of the bedchamber and abandon her then and there. He glared down at her. It would serve her right if he throttled her where she lay, clutching that sheet so inadequately, provoking a response from his body despite his fury. He wanted to rip the sheet away and tumble her until she cried for mercy!

Except that she already had!

He was her husband, for God's sake! And she was his wife! His wife! He had every right to take her when and how he liked! And besides, she owed him children.

'Well, madam wife,' he said stiffly, 'I am afraid you must endure more of that torture until you are with child.'

'I know it!' she retorted. 'And if you care to recall, I did not tell you to stop. I said to hurry up and get it over with. The sooner I am with child, the better, I say.'

'Very well, then,' he muttered grimly, and, ripping the sheet from her clutches, he returned to his labours. By God, he would wring a response out of her if it killed him!

He used every skill and technique in his repertoire, stroking, caressing, teasing, his hands and mouth fully occupied.

'Enough!' she shrieked, pushing him off her at last. 'I can do it no more.'

'Do what?' he snarled, frustrated. 'You're doing nothing.'

'Well, of course I am doing nothing—what else would I do? And it takes every bit of concentration I have. Why can you not simply get on with it? Why must it take so much time?'

Concentration? Magnus swore. And was she complaining about the amount of time he took? If so, she was the first woman in his experience ever to complain of *that*. He started to pull on his clothes. He had no intention of staying in a room with her any longer, otherwise he might find himself strangling her. And it was simply not done to murder brides on their bride trip. Not in his family, at any rate.

'I understand now what my cousin meant. It is inhuman to expect women to endure that night after night,' said Tallie rebelliously, wrapping the sheet tightly around her.

Magnus paused, one leg sliding into his trousers. 'What do you mean—what your cousin meant?'

'My cousin warned me that my marital duties would prove to be difficult and painful.'

He frowned. 'Painful? I am causing you pain?'

'No...not pain, precisely. It...it is just...unbearable.'

She continued muttering angrily into the pillow while he finished dressing. Magnus attempted to block out her ugly words. So his lovemaking was unbearable to her, was it? Then his ears picked up one sentence and he was riveted.

'...to be forced to lie there night after night, not moving or uttering a sound, while a husband creates wondrously pleasurable sensations...'

Wondrously pleasurable sensations? Magnus dropped his shirt. 'What did you say just now?' he demanded, his voice harsh.

She blinked up at him. There were tears in her eyes.

'You said, "wondrously pleasurable sensations".'

Tallie sniffed and dropped her head. 'Yes, well...' She turned a deep, fiery pink.

Magnus stared down at her with narrowed eyes. Part of him wanted to storm out and give vent to his injured masculine pride. The rest of him wanted to solve the mystery. It seemed to hinge on one point—*my cousin warned me.*

He sat down on the bed. 'Tell me, Tallie. What exactly did our dear cousin Laetitia tell you about your marital duties?'

With much blushing and hesitation Tallie attempted to explain what her cousin had told her concerning her marital duties. 'And I have tried to remain still and dignified, truly I have...' She hung her head. 'I am sorry I have found it so difficult, but the...the things you do to me...well...'

Wide amber eyes, awash with tears, met his in a quick, fugitive glance, and she dashed a small hand across her wet cheeks. Her nails were chewed to the quick. Magnus felt as if someone had reached into his chest and squeezed his heart until it hurt.

'Please, my lor—Magnus, let us try again. I promise I will behave better this time. I have found that saying my multiplication tables can be helpful...'

Magnus could not believe his ears. 'Saying *what* is helpful?'

She hung her head lower. Tawny locks tumbled around her face, hiding it from him and exposing her delicate, creamy nape. He longed to plant a kiss on it, but was too distracted by her incredible words.

'You have been saying your multiplication tables while I make love to you?'

'Yes,' she whispered.

'So that you will not be distracted by my lovemaking?'

A tiny sob came from beneath the mop of hair as she nodded.

'And you think that this will please me?'

She nodded again.

'Because my cousin told you I would have no respect for you if you responded? And that you would shame your family and mine if you did anything other than lie as still as a corpse?'

'Yes,' she snuffled.

Magnus did not know whether to laugh or explode with rage. Rage won.

'Bitch!' he swore violently.

Tallie flinched. Magnus saw it and swore again. 'I didn't mean you, my dear.' He reached out and laid his hand on her shoulder. He felt her tense, and his heart clenched in his chest again. So small and naive and vulnerable...and his—all his—despite his bitch of a cousin and her malicious attempt to ruin his marriage.

'Come here, sweetheart,' he murmured. 'I'm not angry. Not with you. Come, there is no need to be upset anymore.' Gently he slid an arm around her resisting body and pulled her against his side. She still wouldn't look at him. He could feel repressed sobs convulsing through her.

'My cousin is a spiteful, malicious bitch,' he said softly, 'and the advice she gave you was completely and utterly wrong.'

The sobs suddenly stopped on a long, shuddering gasp.

Magnus continued, stroking her soft, smooth skin as he spoke. 'She did it to cause trouble between us.' He paused, and tightened his arm around her. 'But she hasn't succeeded, has she? Because I'm not angry with you; I'm angry with her.'

Tallie let out a long, quavery sigh and at last he felt her relax against him. Something unwound inside Magnus.

'Come, Tallie, look at me,' he murmured, putting a gentle finger under her chin. Slowly she looked up at him, her woebegone, tear-drowned face pale, her uptilted nose damp and rosy.

'You're not angry with me?' she whispered.

He shook his head. 'No. Are you angry with me?'

She stared at him, surprised, and suddenly tears began to well up in her eyes again. 'No, of course not,' she muttered, and with a tiny choke of relief fell into his arms. 'I love you, Magnus,' she wailed, and, completely overwrought, she burst into tears against his bare chest. Magnus gathered her close and held her tight, feeling as if the very foundations of his life had just been shattered.

I love you, Magnus.

Her head was tucked into the curve between his shoulder and his throat and he could feel the warmth and dampness of her tears as she sobbed, clutching him as if she'd never let him go. His cheek rested against her hair and he closed his eyes and held her and wondered what had become of him. Never in his life had he felt like this—so attached, so linked, so committed to another soul—and with absolutely no idea of what to do about it.

He was all at sea in a storm, with no anchor and no rudder and no one and nothing to guide him...except his heart...a heart which, in all his twenty-nine years, had neither given nor received love...

I love you, Magnus.

Oh, God. He groaned in despair and tightened his hold on her.

He did not know how much time passed, but eventually she left his arms and went behind the screen to wash her face. He lay on the bed, listening to the sounds of splashing water, imagining her movements. He felt exhausted, and for one cowardly moment thought of sneaking off to his own chamber before she returned. That way he could take the night to decide how best to deal with the situation. He had just eased himself upright and was preparing to slip off the bed when she returned, clad in a fresh nightgown. The look of soft expectancy in her eyes sent his spirits plummeting. She climbed onto the high bed and settled herself beside him.

'So...' She blushed rosily, unable to meet his eyes. 'If Laetitia was wrong...' She ran her finger back and forth along the hem of the sheet. 'How...? I mean, what should I...? How do you wish me to behave when we...you know?'

Magnus felt his throat tighten. He felt trapped, panic-stricken. What the devil should he say? Visions of the various women he had known flitted through his mind. Courtesans, sophisticated married women, widows—with painted faces, vulgar minds and quick, clever fingers. World-weary women, skilled in pleasing a man, who could calculate a man's needs and desires as quickly and efficiently as they calculated his income.

He did not want to teach his wife the tricks of their trade. He could not bear to imagine his innocent little Tallie earnestly and diligently learning how best to please him in bed as those women had. But he had to say something, offer her some guidance to replace Laetitia's poisonous advice... Only what? How? His mind was a complete blank.

'Magnus?' she prompted.

'Just...' He wiped a hand over his suddenly damp brow. Lord, who'd have thought marriage would be such a quagmire? It had seemed so simple and straightforward just a few weeks ago.

'Just be yourself,' he heard himself saying.

'But...'

'All I want from you are your honest reactions.'

She looked back at him, clear-eyed and doubtful, waiting for him to explain further.

'Don't hide anything,' he said, feeling suddenly as though he had stepped onto even more dangerous ground. 'Do and say exactly what you wish to. Honesty. That's all I require.'

'Honesty?' she said hesitantly. 'That's all you want from me?'

He nodded.

She beamed at him, and it was like the sun breaking through the morning mist. 'Then that will be easy.'

He stared back at her, uneasy at her apparent confidence. If she could be honest with him, then she would do more than any other woman in his life had done, his mother included.

'Easy?' He raised his eyebrows in doubt.

'Very easy,' she said, smiling radiantly and wriggling her fingers into his warm grip. 'A great deal easier than the multiplication tables, I can tell you. I am always making mistakes—especially with the eights.'

Magnus blinked for a moment, then from somewhere deep inside him he felt laughter begin to well up. 'The eights?' he gasped, grabbing her around the waist and pulling her down to the bed with him. His laughter echoed around the room and she rolled with him, clutching him and laughing with him. After a few minutes the deep chuckles slowed. He lifted his head and looked at her again, shaking his head. 'The eights?' he repeated.

'Utterly impossible,' she giggled.

His eyes darkened and became intent. 'Then from now on,' he said in a deep, slow voice, 'I suggest you concentrate on nothing but addition, starting from one plus one.' And he lowered his mouth to hers.

Tallie awoke very late next morning. Sunlight streamed through the open curtains and lay in slabs of gold across the floor of her chamber. She stretched and watched the dancing dust motes, feeling dreamy, pleasantly lazy and filled with contentment. She was alone in bed, but she did not feel lonely. Her husband had woken her at dawn and made love to her again. And then he'd kissed her and told her to go back to sleep and he'd gone out.

She had learnt many more things about the marriage act that night. The most important by far was that once she stopped fighting her own reactions it was utterly, thrillingly, splendid. She knew now why the vicar had said marriage was a holy estate, for there had been times, when her husband was making love to her, Tallie had known there could be no more wonderful feeling in heaven or on earth. And afterwards, when she had lain silently in her husband's warm strong arms, his hand caressing her hair while she listened to the beat of his heart slowly returning to normal, it had felt as if she was floating on a cloud, like the angels did.

She had been a little frightened at first about the extremity of her reactions, but Magnus had reassured her and encouraged her and continued that marvellous caressing and stroking. And then he had become rather extreme himself, she reflected, smiling a secret feminine smile. It was very exciting to think that a magnificent being like Magnus could be brought to such a state by ordinary little Tallie Robinson, she thought, snuggling into the pillows. She could still smell his scent on them, and if she shut her eyes she could imagine he was still here in bed with her.

'Milady?'

Tallie opened her eyes. Her new maid, Monique, stood there.

'Milady, your breakfast awaits you.' Monique indicated a tray containing Tallie's favourite French breakfast—sweet, flaky pastries and a large pot of hot milky chocolate. Reluctantly she sat up, then, blushing, clutched the sheet to her, recalling her nakedness. Monique showed no surprise, but came forward with a wrapper. '*Votre peignoir*, Milady.'

Tallie supposed that a dresser was used to seeing people without a stitch of clothing; it was she who had to get used to being seen. She was a long way now from Miss Fisher's establishment, where pupils had dressed and undressed beneath their voluminous nightgowns behind curtained screens. Married women had no privacy at all.

'Milor' d'Arenville said you are to go shopping after breakfast,

Milady. I have ordered the bath, and laid out a gown for you. I thought per'aps we go first to the milliner, and then later to the glover, and after that...'

'After that we shall see,' said Tallie, deciding she needed to be firm about this shopping business. It was all very well to shop, but she wanted to see more of Paris, too. She wanted to experience as much as she could before they left for Italy.

'Where is my husband, do you know?' she asked, picking up a pastry.

''E 'as gone out, milady. 'E say to tell you 'e will back in time to escort you to dinner.'

Dinner? She was to wait until dinner to see him? Tallie was crushed. She did so want to see him now, after all they had shared during the night.

'Oh, but—'

We 'ave Claude, the footman, to escort us, milady,' Monique assured her. 'Milor' d'Arenville 'as left instructions that you are always to 'ave 'im as your escort, so you need not worry. All 'as been arranged by milor'.'

So it seems, thought Tallie, disappointed. Escort indeed! A paltry footman instead of her magnificent husband. She did not want to explore Paris with a maid and a footman—she wanted Magnus.

'Very well, then, I suppose we will have to waste the whole day shopping,' she said dolefully. 'Perhaps if we hurry we can get it all finished and out of the way today.'

Monique gave her an odd look, which Tallie ignored. She finished her pastries and the chocolate, had her bath, got dressed and went downstairs. Her new personal footman, Claude, awaited her in the hall. She blinked in surprise.

Claude was a most unlikely-looking footman. He was short, with a barrel chest and long arms which hung down like a gorilla. His face, too, had a simian quality; most of his teeth were missing and his skin was badly pitted with the pox. He was quite the ugliest man Tallie had ever seen in her life.

Wondering what on earth had possessed her husband to hire such an odd-looking footman, Tallie allowed herself to be escorted off in search of feminine falderals, Monique tripping beside her, Claude trudging heavily in the rear.

Hoofbeats pounded over the cold ground, echoing in the dim silence of the Bois de Boulogne. The hooves of the sweating horse tossed up clumps of grass and damp earth. Branches swatted its sides. But the rider held his mount with a firm hand and pressed on, faster, harder, as if to outride the devil himself.

But it was not possible to outride one's own thoughts and fears, thought Magnus, even as he spurred his horse to greater speed. He was on the brink. She'd driven him to it. He rode onwards, oblivious of his surroundings.

Was this how it had started with his father, too? With a declaration of love from an innocent bride? A lifetime of control, shattered in an instant...

He pulled up his sweating horse, dismounted and led it to a stream. The horse drank thirstily. Magnus leaned against the warm, heaving flank and stared into the fast-flowing water, listening to the burble of clear water over smooth round stones. Her eyes were like that, he thought—dappled with colour, clear and bright and glowing with life.

He groaned. Had his father also felt this aching chasm open up in him? This void, this abyss...of need. Was this how it had begun for him?

He knew how it had ended—a slow, inevitable descent into hell... A strong man of honour and dignity reduced to...what? A beggar at his wife's gate. A slavish worshipper, whose happiness, well-being and position—whose very honour—depended, in the end, entirely on his wife. A wife who cared for nothing but riches and the pleasures of the flesh—with whomever her roving eye descended on.

Magnus could not remember a time when his parents had not fought, lavishly and long. The bitter recriminations and violent rages. And each time ending with his mother giving his father that sultry come-hither smile, the smile which had invited him to her bed once again. And his father gratefully accepting—honour, dignity and self-respect forgotten—until the next time he discovered her with a handsome footman, a good-looking stableboy, one of his friends or even a passing gypsy.

Magnus had grown up swearing he would never let a woman make a fool of him that way. He'd resolved never to marry, never to allow a woman close enough to cause such damage. He'd thought it no hardship...until he'd held a sleeping toddler in his arms and realised he was depriving himself of children... And so he'd married. Thinking he could handle it. Believing he could keep his wife in her proper place—at arm's length.

But he'd chosen Tallie, naive, innocent Tallie, who needed a protector more than any female he knew. Who'd undermined his defences from the moment he married her. No, from even before that—he would never forget the sound of her sobbing in the maze that day. He should have walked away then...only he hadn't been able to leave her alone and unprotected, to fend for herself in the world.

Bedraggled little orphan that she was then, he'd never suspected how much he would come to desire her. Magnus closed his eyes in despair. He had never desired a woman so much in his life. And that had been prior to last night...last night, when she'd accepted his embrace with a joy and a sweet, loving passion that had left him shaking inside. And even now, hours later...

He'd thought he could slake his desire for her...he only craved her more...

Man of the world that he was, thinking he'd experienced everything a man and woman could do together—he'd never known it could be like that, two coming together as one, an explosion of sensation and emotion filling a void inside him he had never known existed.

When one blurted, tearful declaration of love had shattered a lifetime's resolution and sent him spinning towards the abyss.

I love you, Magnus.

Magnus remounted his horse and spurred it onwards.

He returned in the evening. Tallie was overjoyed to see him, and hurried forward for his kiss, but he turned away to remove his coat and hat. When he turned back to face her his visage was impassive and coolly polite. 'Did you have a good day?' he said, walking past her to a sideboard and pouring himself a drink.

'I...all right,' she faltered, a little thrown by his coolness.

'Enjoy the shopping?'

'N... I...er, yes, I suppose so. We did a lot of it. Monique insisted.'

'Very good. It is almost time for dinner, so I suggest you make yourself ready. We have been invited to dine with friends of Laetitia who are also visiting Paris—Lady Pamela Horton and her husband Lord Jasper. Shall we say one hour?' And with that he laid his glass aside, stood up and left the room, leaving Tallie staring after him.

What had happened? Was he angry with her for some reason? Why was he treating her as a polite stranger would? Where was her husband of last night? The man who'd called her sweetheart—twice—and held her tenderly in his arms while she wept? And then made magnificent, glorious love to her—not once, but three times in one night. Four, if you counted the wondrous morning episode.

Hurt and confused, Tallie allowed herself to be dressed in her new finery. As Monique added the final touches to her hair Tallie stared at herself in the mirror and ordered herself to stop moping. She should be thrilled—she was going to dine out with her husband and his friends. In Paris—the most romantic and exciting city in the world. And she was wearing the finest and most fashionable clothes she had ever worn in her life.

But she didn't feel thrilled at all... All she could do was wonder what had gone wrong, why Magnus was acting so distant and cold towards her when only that morning he had made love to her and kissed her goodbye so tenderly...

Oh! It was foolish to repine, Tallie told herself sternly.

It wasn't his fault if he did not love her—it was a marriage of convenience, after all. He hadn't been cruel—not even cross or irritable. Only reserved and distant. And very polite. It would be foolish in the extreme if she allowed herself to fall into a fit of the dismals merely because her husband was *polite* to her.

On that bracing thought Tallie left her chamber and joined her husband in the entrance hall.

'Lord and Lady d'Arenville.' The footman's announcement caused a small stir in the spacious and elegant salon. Lady Pamela, a tall, elegant woman dressed in a ravishing green dress, came forward and greeted Magnus warmly.

'Magnus, you wicked man, you're late. And this is your little wife. How do you do, my dear?' She cast a quick, indifferent glance over Tallie, who at once felt small and plain, despite her fashionable dress.

'Now, Magnus, there are a dozen people who wish to renew acquaintance with you. Oh, and here is Jasper. Take care of Lady d'Arenville, my dear.' And, slipping her arm through Magnus's, she led him away to join the throng.

Tallie watched with dismay, then recalled it was not *comme il faut* for a wife to dwell in her husband's pocket. She didn't wish to embarrass him, particularly on this, their first social engagement as a married couple. She turned to smile at Lord Jasper.

'Champagne, Lady d'Arenville?' he said, and without waiting for her reply he beckoned a footman over and handed her a glass. 'That'll do the trick, my dear. Now, who do you wish to meet? Anyone you know?'

Tallie shook her head.

'Ah, well,' said Lord Jasper and shepherded her over to a small knot of people. He quickly introduced her and a moment later left. Tallie gripped her glass and did her best to join in the conversation, much of which concerned people she didn't know and places she hadn't been to. It was very difficult when one had spent most of one's life in Miss Fisher's, where pupils had been expected to be silent except when laboriously practising *conversazione* once a month over weak tea and stale cakes. Miss Fisher's *conversazione* had been nothing like this.

It seemed an age before dinner was finally announced. Tallie was heartily glad of it—Magnus would come to take her in to dinner and she could relax for a time. And besides, she was ravenously hungry.

Tallie dipped her spoon in the lemon sorbet and tried not to stare down the long table to where her husband was sitting. With Lady Pamela. Talking and smiling and showing every sign of enjoying himself. Sighing, she turned her head and shouted once more at her neighbour. He was an elderly general, and deaf as a post. His deafness, however, did not prevent him from firing question after question at her, obliging her to shout responses into his ear trumpet. She glanced at her other neighbour, a tall, thin, depressed-looking Polish man, who spoke no English, very bad French and had the appetite—and the table manners—of a starved gannet. His dinner was the only company he required.

On the other side of the table a lively middle-aged Frenchwoman flirted light-heartedly with her neighbours. She caught Tallie's eye several times and smiled in a friendly fashion. Tallie smiled back shyly, wishing it was possible to join in, but it would be dreadfully bad manners if she tried to talk across the table. No, she was stuck with the General and the Gannet.

She glanced up to the head of the table. Lady Pamela had her hand on Magnus's sleeve, whispering in his ear. Tallie sighed, and shouted once more into the general's ear trumpet.

At long last the ladies retired, to leave the gentlemen to their port, but by that time Tallie's throat was quite sore from all her shouting. In any case, almost nobody spoke to her. The friendly Frenchwoman had left early and everybody else seemed to have known each other almost from the cradle.

She might as well be a Hottentot for all she had in common with these people, she thought, sipping her tea. Lady Pamela was just like Laetitia—all she did was talk about people who weren't there, and the nastier the story the more everybody laughed. Tallie sat with a teacup on her lap and smiled and tried to look interested and smiled some more, feeling as if her jaw would crack if she had to go on smiling much longer.

The Hottentot princess sat chained to the chair of the foreign invaders. She was hostage for the good behaviour of her husband, the Prince of all the Hottentots, but her spirit was not daunted and she did not feel betrayed by her husband's absence. These were her enemies, these foolish, arrogant people who spoke so freely in front of her. The Hottentot princess smiled at her enemies, but it was the smile of a sleeping tiger. Little did they realise she understood every word they said.

Very soon her dashing husband would come to rescue her. 'Tallie, my dearest love,' he would say. 'Let me rescue you from these evil ones whose tongues wag like chattering monkeys. You mean more to me than any kingdom or throne. I will take you to a place far away from here, where we can be alone.' The beautiful grey eyes of the Prince of all the Hottentots would darken, and he would bend and add, in that wonderfully deep voice which never failed to send shivers of delight through her, 'And then, my beloved Tallie, we will make love all night long, and again in the morning, too...'

But at the end of a very long evening, Magnus brought her home, wished her goodnight, perfectly politely, and went to his own chamber.

Miserably, Tallie curled up into a small huddle in the middle of the large bed. It had become plain during the course of the evening that Magnus *was* angry with her. She had displeased him in some way. Some dreadfully significant way. Several times during the evening she had caught him staring at her, and the expression in his eyes had sent an icy chill down her spine.

It was if she had betrayed him in some way...almost as if he hated her. Tallie had obviously failed him...but she could not imagine how. True, she hadn't been very successful at the dinner, but she had tried...and he knew she'd mixed little in society. And besides, he'd been cold and distant to her before that.

But how could a man spend all night making passionate, tender love to his wife, and in the morning kiss her and call her sweetheart, and then return in the afternoon acting as if she had tried to destroy him?

When all she had done was love him?

Over and over in her brain, Tallie's thoughts churned, until she felt quite sick with misery.

The next day, when she awoke, Monique brought her the news that her husband had gone to stay with friends near Versailles. He would return in a week. Or two.

The first night Magnus was away Tallie cried herself to sleep. She had visited an art gallery during the day. The second night he was away she cried herself to sleep again. But during the day she had attended an outdoor puppet show, and gone for a promenade with Monique and Claude in the park. She might be unhappy, and upset with her husband, but she didn't want the world to know it.

The next morning Tallie had a visitor: the French lady she'd seen at Lady Pamela's—Madame Girodoux. Tallie was feeling utterly blue-devilled, but didn't have the heart to say she was not at home. Besides, she was lonely. Company might cheer her up.

Madame Girodoux swept into the room. She was a widow in her forties, very thin, very fashionable and very sophisticated, but there was kindness in her narrow, sloe-dark eyes. She seated herself beside Tallie on the chaise longue and chatted for a short time, but in the middle of a story she suddenly broke off, took Tallie's hand in hers and said, 'You must forgive my forwardness, my dear, but I was an unhappy young bride once, and I recognise the symptoms.'

At her words Tallie burst into tears.

'Now, *chérie*,' said Madame Girodoux some time later, 'it

seems to me as though your young man 'as bitten off more than 'e can chew.'

Tallie blinked. 'What do you mean?'

'It was a *mariage de convenance, n'est-ce-pas*?'

Tallie nodded.

'But you 'ave fallen in love, *oui*?'

Tallie nodded again. Madame Girodoux smiled. 'I think per'aps you are not the only one.'

Tallie blinked again.

'I have noticed your 'usband watching you—it is not the look of a man who is indifferent.'

'No, he... I think he dislikes—'

'Nonsense! I have 'eard of your 'usband before this. They call him The Icicle, *non*?'

Tallie nodded.

'Well, I see no ice in 'im when 'e looks at you, my dear. I see fire.'

'Fire?'

'*Oui*. Fire, to be sure. *Absolument*. And when ice meets fire, something must crack—and it is not the fire, believe me. Your 'usband is afraid, but 'e will return and the ice will disappear.' She patted Tallie's hand. ''E will not be able to stay away from you for long, *petite*—'e will be back soon. That will make you 'appy, *non*?' She eyed Tallie shrewdly. 'Your bed is lonely, *non*?'

Tallie felt a fiery blush flood her face.

Madame Girodoux chuckled. 'Yes, I thought so. The bed has a way of melting ice. May I give you some advice? I 'ave been married twice, you know, both times very 'appily—though the first one started badly.'

Tallie nodded, a little embarrassed at the other woman's frankness, but eager to hear her advice.

'No doubt when your 'usband returns you will be ready to do anything to please him. Per'aps entice 'im to your bed again.'

Tallie blushed rosily once more.

Madame Girodoux chuckled. 'No shame in that, *chérie*, but women need to use their brains as well as their bodies when it comes to marriage. It does an 'usband no harm to be kept a little uncertain at times—remember that when your man comes back to you. Men respond to the uncertainty of the chase.'

Tallie blinked. Magnus was not chasing her—on the contrary; he was running away. But she nodded, pretending to understand.

Madame Girodoux stood up. 'Now, my dear, run upstairs and wash your face. My nephew, Fabrice, will be 'ere in thirty minutes to take us to a concert. When your 'usband returns to Paris you will not wish him to know you 'ave been pining for 'im. I 'ave many social engagements planned for you—and it will do you good to go about more in society, *non*?'

Tallie's head was spinning, but she knew a lifeline when she saw it. She blinked back tears. 'You have been so very kind to me, *madame*, and I am no one—a stranger. How can I thank—?'

'Ah, non.' Madame Girodoux brushed Tallie's thanks aside gruffly. 'We are all strangers at first—*oui*—but 'ow else can we make new friends, eh? Now, run upstairs, child, and wash your face. Fabrice will be here any moment.'

True to her word, Madame Girodoux arranged all of Tallie's entertainment over the next ten days. With the willing escort of her nephew Fabrice, an elegant young fop, she showed Tallie a new side of Paris. Tallie made morning calls, attended concerts, routs and soirées. She still missed Magnus desperately, still felt as though she had failed him in some indefinable way, but now, with Madame Girodoux's assistance, she was learning to cope with the public aspects of her new life, at least.

But after a week had passed without a single word from Magnus, Tallie had begun to feel aggrieved. It was not right that he had left her to sink or swim in a foreign city. He was careless and thoughtless and cold-hearted. Obviously their night of passion meant absolutely nothing to him. The most wonderful night of her entire life and the very next day he'd gone off to some horrid hunting lodge. He didn't even seem to care whether she loved him or not, for how could he abandon her like this if he did?

And the worst thing was she still loved him—cold-hearted Icicle that he was!

Chapter Eleven

Two days later, in the evening, Magnus returned. Tallie was in the hall, about to leave for a concert. Mindful of Madame Girodoux's advice, Tallie greeted him coolly. He responded with equal politeness, quite as if he'd been away for an hour or two instead of abandoning her for days on end. He offered no word of explanation for his absence. That omission gave Tallie the courage she needed. She wished him a polite 'Good evening,' and sailed out of the *hôtel* to attend the concert.

Stunned, furious, Magnus watched her blithely step into a strange carriage. He'd spent the last two weeks missing her, fighting his desire to return to Paris immediately and take her straight to bed. He'd told himself he could handle it, handle her, that he would not fall in thrall to her like his father had to his mother. He'd kept himself busy during the day, riding, hunting, playing cards and drinking. But at night all he'd been able to think of was the sweet, loving way she'd responded to his caresses, and her words—*I love you, Magnus*.

The abyss had beckoned blackly. But the craving to hear those words again had grown within him until he'd been well-nigh unable to think of anything else, and so, with distracted words of thanks and farewell to his hosts, he'd ridden back, all the way to Paris, imagining her falling into his arms the moment he walked in the door.

He'd pictured it a thousand times, her start of surprise, pleasure and welcome. He would carefully remove his hat and coat, careful not to show her how much power she had over him. She would be waiting anxiously, that sweet look of anticipation and desire in her clear amber eyes, her tender body swaying gently towards him. He'd force himself to wait...and dinner would be spiced with anticipation and desire.

And at the end of dinner she would look at him, that wide-eyed look which never failed to move him, and he would wait no more. He would lay his table napkin down, push back his chair, walk around the table and hold out his hand. She would place her small, trembling hand in his and he'd raise her to her feet and escort her to his bedchamber. And then...

Instead, damn it, she'd greeted him politely, chatted for five minutes about how busy she had been while he was away and gone out to a concert with some damned French female! And an elegant blasted French fop!

'Where the *devil* have you been, madam?' demanded Magnus as he followed her into the breakfast parlour next morning. 'And who was that puppy who handed you out of his carriage just now?' It was the same fellow who'd escorted her last night. The fellow who'd be dead by now had Magnus not heard her return the previous night at about eleven. He'd also heard her lock her door, which had infuriated him, but he'd decided to deal with that in the morning. But when he'd awoken this morning, and found a spare key, he'd entered her chamber only to find her gone. And his rage had grown.

Tallie pulled up short at his accusatory tone. Where the devil had *she* been? *Madam!* When *he* had been absent for two long weeks! 'I told you about it last night,' she said indignantly.

He glared. 'I don't remember any arrangement about you leaving here at some ungodly hour of the morning. Where in Hades did you get to? And with whom?'

Tallie remembered Madame Girodoux's advice about quarrels and tried to quell her shaking insides. She carefully removed her hat and laid it on the side-table. Glancing in a gilt-framed looking glass, she took her time tidying her still-damp hair, well aware that her husband was glowering at her back.

He would have to learn she did not care to be spoken to in this tone before breakfast, particularly when she knew perfectly well she had done nothing wrong. He might well have forgotten where she'd said she was going, but he should know she never took a step outside without Claude, his tame gorilla, in tow. And *he* was the one who'd taught her that husbands and wives did not live in each other's pockets. Sauce for the gander and all that.

Finding her hair sufficiently tidy, she went to the sideboard and selected warm rolls, scrambled eggs and kedgeree, then seated herself at the table.

'Mmm, this kedgeree smells delicious. Have you tried it, my lord?' If I am to be 'madam' then he can be 'my lord', she thought rebelliously.

He slammed his fist down on the table. 'Damn it, Tallie, where the devil did you get to? You weren't in your bed when I woke.'

Tallie's annoyance dissipated in a rush of warmth. He had wanted her when he woke. He had missed her. Frustration—that was why he was so cross. Good. She hid a tiny smile and took a bite of eggs.

'Do you not recall, my lord?' she said when she had swallowed. 'I had an engagement to visit a bathing establishment with Madame Girodoux.'

'At half past seven in the morning?'

Tallie nodded, her mouth full of kedgeree. 'Yes,' she said eventually, 'but it was worth it. Do you know? They scent the bath water with any perfume you wish—eau de cologne, rosewater, lavender—even salt water if you want, which I believe is frightfully healthful. The *parfumier* even offered to create a scent especially for me.' Tallie blushed, remembering how the dapper *parfumier* had kissed her hand and called her *la belle Milady Anglaise*.

Magnus watched the pretty colour rising in her cheeks. He frowned. His desire for her was well-nigh unbearable.

'But I asked for lily-of-the-valley instead.' She raised her wrist to her nose and sniffed. 'Mmm, lovely, don't you think? It was the most wonderful place. Each bath is large, and so deep you can have hot water almost to your neck, and you just sit there in this deliciously scented water and look out onto an exquisite little garden simply filled with red roses—quite private, of course. I've never seen anything so lovely or exotic.' She blushed again, recalling how she had wallowed for over an hour in the deepest bath, dreaming of how Magnus would take one whiff of her, sweep her into his arms and make violent, passionate love to her.

Magnus's frown darkened. Her words painted a very vivid picture—one he could imagine only too well. His wife, pink and naked in her bath, her skin slick with water and scented oils, fragrant clouds of steam swirling around her, and outside a flower garden, giving the illusion of being out in the open. It sounded as if the bath would have been large enough for two. He swallowed, his mouth suddenly dry, his body throbbing, painfully aroused.

'And that damned French puppy?' he growled.

She made a moue of irritation. 'He is not a puppy, but a very pleasant and gentlemanly young man, my lord. Fabrice Dubout—Madame Girodoux's nephew. I...I took a little longer than expected in the bath, and Madame Girodoux had another engagement, so she asked Fabrice to escort me home.' Tallie bit into a roll.

'And on the strength of this brief acquaintance you call him Fabrice?' he grated.

Tallie glared across the table at her husband and set down her cup with a snap. 'Yes!'

Oh! He was infuriating. He could go off to who knew where, doing who knew what, leaving her behind, hurt, confused and lonely, and then return, growling and snarling like a suspicious wolf! Pretending to believe she would behave immorally. As if she would.

He knew perfectly well that she loved him—she'd told him so. And even if she hadn't fallen in love with a horrid, suspicious man, she had taken vows of fidelity and she would *never* break them, no matter how fashionable it was. And even if she *did* wish to betray him, how could she, when she was accompanied everywhere by the ubiquitous Claude?

No, Magnus was just being disagreeable because when he had returned she hadn't behaved as he'd expected her to, and when he'd awoken she hadn't been where he'd expected her to be. Madame Girodoux was right—a little uncertainty *was* good for a husband.

'I am invited to a *thé* this morning, my lord. Do you care to accompany me?'

'A what?' The frown had not left his face, but she refused to give in and explain herself.

'A *thé*.' Tallie smiled. 'Being English, we are known to adore tea—'

'Can't stand the stuff, myself.'

'I know, and though the French firmly believe their *thés* are

English through and through, any resemblance to an English tea party is purely coincidental, I promise you.' Tallie smiled reminiscently, recalling her first *thé*.

It was not the consumption of alcohol as well as tea, and the combination of children's games and gambling which had surprised Tallie at first—it was the French ladies' tea gowns.

Parisian women seemed to cover themselves more with cosmetics than clothing. To English eyes, their gowns left the ladies almost in a state of nature, being so light and almost transparent, and having *no* sleeves and baring the *whole* of the neck. It was a little disconcerting to address oneself to an elderly dowager attired as flimsily and inadequately as one of the statues in the Louvre—Tallie hadn't known where to look. She smiled again, imagining her husband's face when she appeared in her own French tea gown, only half as daring.

'And I suppose if I do not escort you to this blasted *thé*, that damned puppy will.' His voice bristled with dark suspicion.

'Yes, Fabrice will escort me...if I ask him.' She met her husband's gaze in a direct challenge.

'Hrmph!' Magnus fiddled with his coffee cup for a moment. 'It might be interesting to see how the French botch a simple tea party,' he said at last.

Tallie hid a smile. 'In that case, I must rush and change, for we leave at ten.'

Magnus watched her hurry from the room, noting the enticing sway of her hips and the damp wispy curls that tumbled around the nape of her neck. A faint trace of lily-of-the-valley hung in the air. It took all his resolution not to follow her up to her bedchamber.

Damn and blast it all. He was getting deeper and deeper into her toils. It had shocked him to realise how bereft he had felt when he'd looked for her that morning and found her gone. For one wild moment he'd thought she'd left him, and the feeling of abandonment and devastation still haunted him. He'd imagined all sorts of things, and when he'd seen her being handed down from a strange carriage by a mincing, hand-kissing Frenchman he'd been filled with a mixture of relief and rage.

She was picking up female tricks, he realised. Getting herself a damned Froggy *cicisbeo*. And when he'd challenged her about it, had she acted guilty or distressed? No! She had stared at him with those big amber eyes and got him all hot and bothered talking about a bath big enough for two.

It had been a mistake to leave her in Paris on her own. And perhaps she was a little annoyed with him—yes, that was it. She *wasn't* like his mother—not really. He was a fool even to consider it...

Dark uncertainty gnawed at him.

Damn it! If tea was what it took to keep his wife where she belonged, then he would drink gallons of the filthy stuff.

'Madame Girodoux has invited me to go vagabondising this evening,' said Tallie as they returned home. Her husband glowered silently from the corner of the carriage. He had not said a word since she had removed her cloak on arrival at the *thé*. Revealing her new pale gold French tea gown.

It was perfectly respectable—compared with most of the other ladies' gowns. But after his first stunned glance his eyes had narrowed to icy chips, and an even blacker frown had descended on his face.

He'd said not a word to a soul all afternoon. And to think she had once thought his manners were beautiful. He hadn't taken his eyes off her for an instant. Tallie had found that dark, icy glare decidedly unnerving, but her courage had been bolstered by Madame Girodoux's smiles and nods of approval.

And so Tallie had mentioned the vagabondising excursion, knowing full well Magnus would disapprove.

Magnus snorted wrathfully. 'Madame Girodoux and her simpering blasted nephew, I suppose.'

Tallie shrugged. '*Madame* did not mention who else was in the party, but it would not surprise me if Fabrice were included. She is very fond of him.'

Magnus grunted. 'What exactly does "vagabondising" mean?'

'I'm not entirely certain, but I think it means exploring the less respectable parts of Paris by night. It sounds utterly thrilling, does it not?' Still a little nervous about these tactics, Tallie forced herself to smile sunnily at him. She wished she had not to resort to stratagems to gain his attention... It would be wonderful if he craved her company as much as she craved his...but she was learning to cut her coat to suit her cloth. And if stratagems were what it took, then so be it. And he *had* responded to her gown in a wonderfully jealous manner.

Magnus glowered at her. 'I think I know as much about the night life of Paris as *madame* or her precious nephew. Would you object if I escorted you on my own private tour?'

'Oh, Magnus, it would be utterly splendid!' Tallie exclaimed and, jumping up, she flung her arms around him and pressed a fervent kiss on his mouth.

Taken by surprise, Magnus hesitated for a moment. Tallie started to draw back, but before she could he gathered her into a hungry embrace and was kissing her with unrestrained passion. He drew her onto his lap, kissing her hard, his mouth devouring her, one large, warm hand cupping her head in a firm, tender hold, the other possessively roaming her body, caressing, seeking, bringing her to the brink of pleasure.

'Oh, Magnus,' she gasped, overwhelmed by his unexpected move. She kissed him back with all the love in her heart, her anger forgotten. She slipped her hand into his shirt and rubbed the palm of her hand over his chest in a way she knew he liked. She felt a glow of feminine satisfaction, feeling him shudder beneath her fingers.

The carriage rumbled to a halt and they fell apart as the door was pulled open by a footman. Magnus stepped out and held out his hand to help her down, his eyes burning into hers. Blushing, she descended the steps and entered the house with her hand still clasped firmly in his.

As the front door closed behind them he swung her into his arms and took the stairs, two at a time, seeming not even to notice her weight. She clung to his neck, delighted with his passionate impetuosity, so unlike her Icicle. He kicked open the door of his bedchamber, stepped inside, kicked it shut and laid her carefully on his bed.

He took the neckline of her gown in his long, strong fingers, saying, 'You'll not wear this blasted thing in public again,' and ripped it open in one dramatic move. Tallie was utterly thrilled. His eyes darkened as they moved over her partially revealed body. He wrenched off his beautifully arranged neckcloth and flung his shirt away. 'I think, madam wife, any engagements you have made for this afternoon will have to remain unfulfilled.'

Tallie smiled naughtily up at him. 'Yes, but I doubt whether I will.'

He looked startled for a moment, and then eyed her hungrily. 'Nor will I, my dear. Nor will I,' he muttered hoarsely, and lowered his mouth to hers.

That night, Magnus took her out vagabondising—after ensuring she was muffled to the ears and buttoned to the neck. He directed the carriage to a part of the city Tallie had never seen, where the streets were narrow and dark and vaguely threatening. They were, nonetheless, full of people dressed in all sorts of costumes: gaudy women with painted faces, beggars and cripples, elegantly dressed gentlemen, shopkeepers, soldiers... Tallie almost slipped on the oily cobblestones, and Magnus held her clamped tight to his side. Claude loomed in the gloom several paces behind them, and for once Tallie was glad of his fearsome visage.

'After you, my dear,' said Magnus, stopping at a doorway lit by painted lanterns. He ushered her down the stairs into a dark and mysterious place called a cabaret. They found a table and called for drinks. Tallie's was bright green. She eyed it with suspicion.

'Does it not meet with my lady's favour?' Magnus said, quirking an eyebrow.

On her mettle, Tallie sipped it cautiously, then smiled. 'It tastes of peppermint.'

Magnus's white teeth glinted in the candlelight.

Setting down her glass, Tallie looked around her. All sorts of people of all walks of life rubbed elbows and mingled in the smoky gloom. Grimy crimson curtains hung across a small stage.

'What do the curtains conceal?' she asked.

'Wait and see.'

After a few moments a dwarf came forward, dressed as a Turk, with a red fez. With a shout of something unintelligible, he pulled aside the curtains and scattered applause filled the room as a sultry, exotic-looking woman came forward. She was dressed, quite indecently, in red satin and black lace. She sang several songs which had all the gentlemen chuckling, including Magnus.

'She has a lovely voice,' whispered Tallie, 'but I can hardly understand a word. Will you tell me what the songs are about?'

Magnus looked at her, a faint smile on his face, then shook his head. Tallie opened her mouth to argue, but suddenly a group of scantily clad dancers whooped onto the dance floor, twirling glittering scarves and performing some exotic dance to the rhythm of drums and wailing music. Their movements left Tallie in no doubt of what the dance, at least, was about. She stared, wide-eyed, feeling her cheeks warming. Magnus stood up, frowning, and said brusquely, 'It's time we moved on, I think.'

Tallie's face fell. 'Oh, no, it cannot be time to go home already, can it?'

He looked down at her and his frown softened. 'No, there's plenty more to see, little vagabond. Only not here, I think.'

'Oh, I suppose you are right,' said Tallie reluctantly. 'Those dances are vastly improper, aren't they?'

Her husband gave a choke of laughter and took her arm. 'Outside,' he said. 'Now.'

They took a carriage to a place beside the Seine, where a crowd of people were gathered in a large circle, watching. Magnus, keeping Tallie safe in the circle of his arm, shouldered his way to a place where she could see. Tallie felt as if there were just herself and Magnus in the world, as if everything else was just a magical many-splendoured rhapsody whirling around then, binding them together in a spell of enchantment.

Acrobats dressed in glittering finery leapt and tumbled on a tattered cloth of red and gold, while a one-legged man played merry tunes on an organ. Then a pair of young girls came out, looking as innocent as schoolgirls. They twirled and tossed burning brands, leaving trails of fire hanging in the dark night air. And finally, to the gasps of the crowd, they swallowed the fire, then spat out whooshing bursts of flame, bowing and smiling afterwards, apparently quite unhurt. Tallie clapped her hands until they hurt.

Then there was a puppet show about a young girl lost in the forest, and a dragon and a brave bold knight, and Tallie's heart was in her mouth. She knew they were just puppets, but she clasped Magnus tight even so and was glad of his warmth.

They watched until there was no more to see, then strolled on beside the silently flowing Seine. They ate hot nuts cooked on a brazier before their eyes, and Magnus had to lend Tallie his handkerchief to wipe her greasy fingers. And he kissed her in the darkness and tasted salt on her lips.

Later, following the sound of music down a dark lane, they came to a small, open courtyard, where gypsies sang and leapt and gyrated under flaming torches, their heels tapping out a frenzied tattoo, their guitars and throats sobbing with tragic passion. Tallie found them very moving, even though she could understand none of the words, and she clutched her husband's arm and watched the gypsies with tears in her eyes.

And Magnus dried Tallie's eyes and took her home and made love to her, first with an urgency and passion that left her gasping with ecstasy, then later with such tenderness she found herself weeping again. Only this time he did not dry her tears, but kissed them away, and held her in his arms until they both fell asleep.

The next evening they went to the Théâtre Français to see Fleury, the most famous actor in all France. It was Tallie's first visit to a theatre, and though it was hot, stuffy and crowded, she found it quite wondrous and fantastical. Her husband found he could barely take his eyes off her enraptured face, and when he brought her home that night he made slow, sensual love to her, marvelling at her passionate response, fearing and hungering for her to say it again. *I love you, Magnus.*

But she didn't say it.

Magnus accompanied her everywhere. He took her to the new Palais Royale, which contained libraries, gambling houses, coffee houses, pawnbrokers, jewellers, ice shops, exhibition rooms, theatres and even a chess club. They attended balls and masquerades. And each night they made magical, tender love.

And she seemed happy, Magnus thought. She told him once in sweet exhaustion that she imagined two people could feel no closer than when making love. He wanted to tell her it could also be the loneliest feeling in the world, that it had been for him—until her. But he couldn't.

And she never again said the words he both craved and dreaded. *I love you, Magnus.*

'Milady,' said Monique one morning while she was arranging Tallie's hair. 'When do you think your baby will be born?'

Tallie stared in surprise at the reflection of her maid in the looking glass. 'Baby? What do you mean, Monique?'

'*Oui*, you are *enceinte*, are you not, milady?'

'*Enceinte?* I have no idea.'

The maid frowned. 'But, milady, I 'ave been with you more than seven weeks now.'

'Yes, it would be about that. But what does that signify?'

'In all that time you 'ave not 'ad your monthly courses.'

Tallie's eyes widened. 'No, that's right,' she said slowly. 'How clever of you to notice. But what has that to do with a baby?'

Monique explained.

'Really?' exclaimed Tallie. 'So that's how one knows... And you really think I am increasing?'

'*Oui*, milady. Unless your courses are always irregular?'

Tallie shook her head. 'No, never. I just thought I had missed them because of being married or travelling or something.' She felt a quiver of excitement ripple through her. A baby. How wonderful.

Monique smiled at her mistress. 'Lord d'Arenville will be very pleased, yes?'

Tallie froze. Once her husband discovered she was increasing, he would want to take her home to England and d'Arenville Hall. He had said so in no uncertain terms.

And then she'd never get to Italy.

And getting to Italy was almost as important to Tallie as her baby was. She had delayed too long in Paris as it was. There was something much more important at stake here than mere pleasure. She had been selfish and thoughtless and had allowed herself to be seduced by pleasures and entertainments.

'No, Monique,' she slowly. 'I will not tell my husband just yet. It will be our little secret, agreed?'

Monique looked troubled. 'If you say so, milady.'

'I do,' said Tallie firmly. 'And now, if you please, we must make preparations to leave Paris.'

'Leave Paris?' gasped Monique.

'Yes, in three days, I think,' said Tallie firmly. 'You will come with us, will you not? To Italy?'

Marie shrugged. 'Of course, milady. Why not? I 'ave never been to Italy. But milor'—will 'e wish to go so suddenly?'

Tallie smiled. 'You may leave milor' to me.'

Chapter Twelve

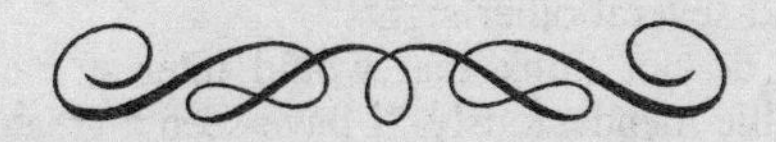

'Oh,' said Tallie, stretching luxuriously in her canvas seat and gazing contentedly at the passing scenery. They had left Paris three days before by coach, but had transferred to a barge that morning. 'This is indeed much more agreeable than I had expected it to be. How pretty those fields and vineyards are. And how smooth the water slipping by.'

Magnus smiled. The barge trip had been suggested by Luigi Maguire, the major-domo hired to make arrangements for the journey, a Frenchman with an Italian mother and an Irish father. Maguire was already proving his worth.

'I did tell you it would be easier on the bones than a carriage, but you wouldn't have it, would you? Now confess—you thought you would get seasick, didn't you?'

Tallie nodded. 'You are right, as usual. Oh, the Rhone is such a pretty river. How long do you think it will take before we reach Italy?'

Magnus frowned. There was something peculiar about her sudden rush to get to Italy. Of course, she had told him once that she wished to go there—to visit her parents' graves, or some such thing—but he'd thought she'd forgotten about it. Certainly one would have thought the delights of Paris would more than compensate for what could only be a duty visit, after all. But she was adamant, and he was finding it more and more difficult to refuse his wife anything these days. He pushed aside the unwelcome thought...

But if they wanted to get to Italy, they had to cross over the

Mount Cenis Pass. Magnus repressed a shudder. He hated heights, and would infinitely have preferred to go by ship, but with his wife's tendency to seasickness there was no question of it. It had been difficult enough to persuade her to travel down the Rhone in a flat-bottomed boat. Besides, there was always the danger of pirates in the Mediterranean.

'According to Maguire, we will remain on this barge for at least five days,' he said. 'Until we reach Avignon. And I thought we could rest there for a week or so. You will want to visit the Palais des Papes, and several other sights.'

'Oh, no, I do not think that would interest me very much,' responded Tallie mendaciously. 'I have seen a great many palaces now, and one more, even if it belonged to a pope, is no great thing. I am not greatly interested in popes.'

Magnus regarded her thoughtfully. 'I did hear,' he said casually, 'that some people prefer to view the Palace des Papes by moonlight...'

'Moonlight?' Her eyes lit up, as he had known they would. Tallie thought for a moment. 'Perhaps if we stay in Avignon for just a day or two, then.'

Magnus repressed a smile. It was becoming easier to calculate his wife's tastes. He watched her as she turned her head back towards the riverbanks. He had found so much of his life dull and tedious before his marriage. But Tallie's open fascination with all sorts of things had opened his eyes to a host of small pleasures and interests and he was beginning to see the world differently. It was probably a sign of weakness, he knew, but there seemed nothing he could do about it.

After Avignon, they returned to their coach, which had also been transported on the barge. The roads were a little rough, and Magnus had been worried his wife would be sickened by the incessant jolting. Instead, she spent most of the journey peering out of the window and deriving great enjoyment from the way the postilions leaped out of their enormous jackboots at every stop, leaving the boots in the stirrups until a new man came out and leapt into the same boots.

Finally the roads narrowed and their pace slowed as they climbed higher into the foothills of the Alps. Tallie called to Magnus, who was riding. 'Magnus, I don't think these poor horses can pull us any more. It's getting terribly steep. Whatever shall we do?' She stared up into the mountains. 'They cannot possibly pull us over those mountains.'

'We stop at the next village,' he called back. 'The coach will be dismantled and mules and men will carry it, and us, over the pass.'

'Carry the coach?' she squeaked in amazement. 'Are you hoaxing me?'

He grinned. 'Wait and see.'

They stopped for the night at the next village, and in the morning Tallie saw the coach had been dismantled and bound with rope into a number of huge packages. A dozen men and as many mules were assembled outside the tiny inn. There was much shouting and discussion as the packages was strapped to the mules under the supervision of Maguire. John Black, Magnus's coachman, watched with phlegmatic English disapproval.

'Oh, the poor things,' Tallie said, clutching Magnus's sleeve in distress. 'Those bundles are far too big and heavy for such dear little animals.'

'The porters know what they are about, my dear. Do not concern yourself, they've all—men and mules—done this trip many a time before today.'

Tallie looked around. 'And how do we travel?'

'By mule, I believe,' he replied.

Tallie looked aghast. 'I cannot ride a mule.'

Magnus frowned. 'You have no choice. There are no horses.'

'It would make no difference if there were. I cannot ride. I have never been on the back of an animal in my life.'

Magnus was stumped. He had never heard of such a thing. Everyone he knew rode; even the females. 'What, never?'

She shook her head and bit her lip worriedly.

Magnus walked over to Maguire and the head porter and a brief discussion ensued. Maguire called out an order and a young boy emerged from a nearby barn, carrying a large, odd-shaped wicker basket. He began to strap it to the back of a mule.

Tallie observed the preparations with deep mistrust.

Magnus's lips twitched.

'I am not going over the Alps in that!' she muttered mutinously.

'Then there is no point in continuing. We shall return to Paris at once,' responded Magnus.

She flung him a black look, then stalked over to the mule and waited to be helped into the basket. One of the porters reached towards her to do it, but Magnus was there before him. He swung his wife into his arms and set her sideways in the basket. 'There you are,' he said, tucking a thick bearskin around her to protect her from the cold. It emitted a pungent odour uncomfortably reminiscent of its original unfortunate inhabitant. Tallie wrinkled her nose. Magnus bent forward and kissed her lightly on it. 'As snug as a bug in a rug.'

She gave him a baleful look. 'I feel very silly. Why can I not walk, like those men?'

He didn't respond, but glanced over to where Monique, with shrieks and giggles, was being installed likewise on another mule.

'Oh, very well,' said Tallie crossly. 'I shall behave myself—but I feel ridiculous.'

'Sometimes we must sacrifice dignity for expediency,' said Magnus austerely, and walked away.

The ascent was slow and tortuous, the pathway narrowing visibly until it seemed to Tallie's eyes no more than a few inches wide. It was amazing how the porters even knew which was the path, for there were goat tracks leading off it at almost every turn. The men took it in turns to carry the huge packs of their belongings. Tallie thought of all the shopping she had done and felt guilty.

However, she soon cheered up, because the scenery was magnificent: enormous jagged peaks and rough crags, the occasional twisted tree, gnarled and bent by the harsh weather. And the higher they climbed the colder it became, even though it was summer.

The track was narrow and tortuous, but Tallie had no time to be concerned. The most splendid, awe-inspiring vistas lay all around her, and fresh delights were revealed with each turn of the track and each minor peak accomplished. She had never seen anything like it in her life—only imagined it from books like Mrs Radcliffe's.

And silence seemed to hang in the air all around them. She could see some bird of prey, a falcon or a hawk, perhaps, circling with grim patience over a crag in the distance. She watched it bank and soar effortlessly, then suddenly dive out of sight, and she shivered, imagining some poor tiny creature caught in its talons. The air was cold and crisp and so pure that she felt almost dizzy breathing it. All she could hear was the stomping of the heavy boots of the men walking close to her and the occasional musical ringing of a mule's horseshoes on a stone. The sound carried in the still, crystal air, rebounding and repeating from the jagged peaks.

Tallie had never heard such a superb echo. She could not resist it.

'Helloooo,' she called. The echo came back to her from a dozen distant crags. Ahead of her Magnus turned on his mule and looked back, as if concerned. She waved. 'Hellooo, echo,' she called again and, 'Echo-echo-echo,' her words came back to her.

One of the porters grinned at her delighted face and began to sing. In seconds others joined in, strong male voices, deep and true, ringing through the mountains with the joy of being young and strong and alive. Someone up ahead began a harmony and another man joined him, then another. An older man with a thick white beard began a third line of harmony, a deep bass, and more voices joined him. The mountains threw back the sound, magnifying it and leaving a trail of echoes to mingle with the harmonies. It was better by far than any choir Tallie had heard. It had none of the solemnity and restraint of a choir. There was something special about a score or more lusty male voices, ringing in the open air, echoing with the confidence of strength and vigour as their heavy boots pounded out the rhythm. Music rolled and swirled and echoed around the mountains.

Tallie was enchanted. She sat spellbound, drinking in the wonder of what was happening. Here was plain, ordinary Tallie Robinson—who had once thought she would never go anywhere—and now look at her! Almost at the very top of the world, gazing at what was surely one of the most utterly splendiferous sights imaginable. And listening to the most glorious music in the world. And up ahead rode her handsome, magnificent husband. And she was almost in Italy, where she should be able to discover the truth about her mother's death. And she was going to have a baby. The cold mountain air prickled at her eyes and she had to grope for a handkerchief to wipe her eyes. It was odd how easily she cried these days, she reflected, when really she had nothing to cry about.

She finished wiping her eyes, then, noticing one of the porters watching her, began to clap her cold hands in time to the music, humming along to the tune. With the singing, the time passed more quickly, until at last the porters stopped and Magnus came to lift her out of the basket.

'Could you hear the singing from up ahead? Wasn't it utterly wonderful?' she said, stretching her cramped limbs.

'Very nice,' he responded. 'Are you warm enough?' He took her small cold hands in his and began to chafe them gently. His hands were not exactly warm themselves, and she became concerned when she saw he looked rather heavy-eyed and preoccupied.

'Are you all right?' she asked.

He shrugged. 'Picked up a bit of a chill, I suspect. Nothing to worry about. Now, I think those fellows have brandy, or some such local brew. I want you to have a little—keep the cold out.'

She looked around. 'Magnus, what are they doing?'

The porters were unloading the mules. Magnus went to discuss it with them. He came back, a faint grin on his face.

'This is as far as the mules go. And now, my dear, you will have to resign yourself to being carried.'

Sure enough, the men had brought out some rough-looking woven wicker litters attached to crude poles. They gestured to Magnus, and Tallie went forward reluctantly.

In minutes she was installed in a litter, tied down—for safety, they said—and packed in straw, as well as bearskins, for warmth. 'I feel ridiculous,' she said. Magnus chuckled and wound a thick woollen shawl around her face.

'You look quite delightful, my dear.'

Tallie could hardly move, so she directed an almost invisible glare at him.

'Monsieur?' said a porter. Magnus turned. The porter gestured to another litter, sitting beside Tallie's. 'Please, *monsieur*, we must hurry.'

'What? I don't need a blasted litter!' said Magnus, outraged.

The porter shrugged. 'It is the only way, *monsieur*. The way we move, no one who was not born in these mountains can keep up with us. You must go in the chair.'

A muffled giggle came from the bundle that was Tallie. Magnus hesitated, stiff with annoyance.

'An inexperienced person will slow us down. And there are wolves, *monsieur*, and bears.'

Magnus didn't budge.

'And *madame*, she is getting cold, *monsieur*.'

'Oh, very well—damn your eyes!' said Magnus, and allowed himself to be strapped into the litter. Tallie watched in glee as her immaculate, elegant husband was bundled into a litter and wrapped until he looked like a pile of old washing. Two porters hoisted his litter onto their shoulders with a jolt. They moved forward.

'Oh, Magnus?' called Tallie as he came alongside her. The porters paused.

Magnus glared across at her. 'What?' he snapped.

'Sometimes we must sacrifice dignity for expediency, my dear,' she said solemnly.

Magnus swore and ordered the porters to move on.

'Don't worry, my dear,' she called. 'You look delightful in your litter, too.'

He swore again, and her laughter followed him up the steep pathway.

The porters must be part mountain goat, Tallie decided breathlessly after an hour of climbing. There were four for each litter and they leaped up impossibly steep slopes at a pace which Tallie doubted she could maintain on flat ground for more than a minute.

On one side, the narrow, winding path dropped away to a bottomless precipice, on the other were violently soaring peaks and huge vertical slabs of rock. There was no room to manoeuvre; the slightest misstep would have them plunging hundreds of feet over the precipice, to perish on the ragged rocks below. The porters didn't even pause or blink when Tallie heard what she was sure were wolves howling in the not very far distance. She hardly dared to breathe.

Tallie heaved a sigh of relief when they came to the top of the pass and stopped for a break of perhaps a minute or two. The view was superb. In every direction lay mountain peaks—some glittering with snow—sharp against the crisp vivid blue of the sky. On one side of them was France, down there somewhere below was Italy, and across in the distance were the peaks of Switzerland. It was a moment to remember, she thought excitedly, a moment to tell her children. She laid her hand on her flat stomach, marvelling, still unable to believe that there was a baby growing inside her.

With a sudden jolt, she found herself on the move again, this time at a breathtaking pace. The bearers ran, rather than walked, taking tiny little steps where the path was most perilous and great bounding strides when it levelled out or widened. Tallie clung on like grim death, bouncing and swaying.

Finally they came to a tiny village, which clung to the side of the mountains in apparent impossibility. The panting porters set down the litters and one of them came forward to lift her out. She looked for her husband. He was still in his litter. She hurried over on stiff legs.

'Magnus was that not the most terrifyingly thril—? Magnus, are you all right?'

His face was death-pale, his eyes closed. He did not move.

She pulled her gloves off and felt his forehead with her hand. Despite the chill in the air, his forehead was hot and clammy. 'Magnus!'

Slowly he opened his eyes. 'Oh, there you are,' he said, and fumbled to get out of the litter. She helped him out, but when he tried to stand he reeled, and would have fallen if one of the porters had not grabbed him. Tallie was greatly alarmed.

'He's ill! Is there a physician nearby? Maguire!'

Maguire and the head porter came over and there was a brief discussion.

'He's ill,' Tallie repeated. 'He needs a physician. Can we take him to an inn or somewhere?'

The porter shook his head and glanced significantly around. Tallie followed his gaze. The village consisted of a half-dozen tiny cottages. Certainly there would be no doctor here. Anxiety gripped her throat.

'I must get him to the nearest physician,' she insisted.

'I'm all right,' muttered Magnus thickly. 'Just a bit woozy, that's all.'

Tallie ignored him and fixed the head porter with a determined stare. 'Please transport us with all haste to the nearest place where I can get help for my husband,' she said firmly. 'At once, if you please!'

The porter nodded, then smiled and patted her on the shoulder, saying something in a dialect that Tallie could not understand. He called out to the others, and to her relief they soon had a vaguely protesting Magnus safely stowed back in his litter and were moving off down the mountain. This time Tallie saw nothing amusing in the sight. 'Hurry,' she urged the bearers.

The trip down the mountainside was a nightmare to Tallie. She wished she could see how her husband was faring, but the path was still too steep and narrow for them to go in anything except single file.

They passed several more tiny hamlets, but Tallie didn't even consider them. She had to get to the nearest town big enough to support a proper physician. Whenever they slowed, even for a moment, she urged them on. 'Hurry, oh, please hurry!'

Finally one of the porters pointed and mumbled something. Tallie followed the direction of his arm. Far, far below, she could see a town, a tiny sea of terracotta rooftops and the spire of a church. Her heart leapt. It was still a long distance away. She nodded. 'Doctor?'

The man nodded back. *'Dottore.'*

Tallie caught her breath. 'Oh, thank the Lord. Now, please hurry.'

The men jogged onwards. Tallie noticed nothing of the scenery; her eyes went from the bundle that was her husband, then down to the town, then back again.

Suddenly shots rang out. Tallie was jerked to a sudden halt. She blinked, and was almost thrown out of her litter as her bearers dropped it. They had stopped on a corner. Above them on both sides were steep rocks. She could see nothing ahead, nothing behind. All around her was sudden silence.

'What is it?' she called. 'Pray, what is the matter? And why have we stopped?'

'No questions,' an unfamiliar voice shouted in rough Italian above her. She looked up and saw a tall, dark-haired man with a large moustache pointing a gleaming silver pistol in her direction. He was thin, but broad-shouldered, and dressed in a ragged uniform; there were battered traces of dull yellow embroidery on his jacket, which she supposed might once have looked gold. Was he a soldier? But the war was over, surely.

There was a sudden flurry ahead and a single shot rang out. Tallie's heart almost stopped. Magnus! But she could hear or see nothing. The man above called something to someone unseen and then nimbly leaped down onto the path ahead, bringing a scattering of small rocks down with him. Immediately a dozen more men appeared, all dressed in some sort of uniform, one in braided trousers, another in a waistcoat, all ragged, none of them matching. Each one of them brandished a knife or a pistol or both.

'What is it? Who are they?' Tallie whispered to the porter standing nearest her.

He turned to look at her, his eyes sombre. *'Banditti,'* he said.

Chapter Thirteen

'*Banditti?*' gasped Tallie.

The porter jerked his head significantly up to the left. 'Bad men. Live up there.' His lip curled and he spat in scorn. 'Not our people.'

More orders rang out in dialect and the porters moved slowly forward. The ragged collection of armed *banditti* watched every move from their lofty positions on the rocks above. The party reached a small clearing, bordered on three sides by rock walls and on the fourth by a plunging precipice along which the narrow track passed. It would be impossible to escape; only one person at a time could move along that path. This was obviously a well-planned ambush.

The bandits had already disarmed the guards and Tallie could see that two porters were injured, although it didn't seem as if they were badly hurt; they could still walk, though with some difficulty. The hired guards, luckily, seemed untouched.

The tall dark man in the ragged gold braid uttered a sharp order and two bandits with pistols shepherded the porters and guards to a shallow cave in the rock, and forced them to sit, hands on heads. Tallie breathed a sigh of relief. The bandits did not mean to kill anyone—yet.

Several ruffians hovered over the prisoners still in their litters, a variety of firearms and gleaming knives and stilettos pointed menacingly, while the rest fell upon the bundles of baggage, emptying their belongings onto the mountainside with careless greed.

They removed everything of value, even Magnus's fine leather boots.

Bundled in her litter, Tallie waited helplessly. The bindings that had been for her security now kept her imprisoned. She wondered how Magnus was faring, and struggled inconspicuously to escape her bonds.

The bandit leader thrust his silver duelling pistol through his belt and swaggered towards them. 'Aha, what have we here?' he said in oddly accented but surprisingly urbane Italian. 'A lady—no, two ladies,' he added, lifting a rug to discover Monique cowering underneath. 'And four gentlemen.' He glanced at the litters containing Magnus, Maguire, John Black, and Guillaume, Magnus's valet. 'Which one is the English milord?' His vivid green eyes examined each man narrowly.

The English milord? How did he know one of the travellers was an English milord? wondered Tallie anxiously. Their major-domo, Luigi Maguire, had stressed that they should appear as ordinary travellers. 'Naturally, while no foreign traveller is precisely poor,' he had said in his unique accent, 'it is not a good idea to advertise wealth, so if you will accept my advice, Lord d'Arenville, you will travel as plain Mr d'Arenville. Or even Mr Smith, if you like. And in your plainest coat and boots. Your good lady, too, in her plainest, most serviceable gown and cloak.'

And they *had* taken his eminently sensible advice. So how did this bandit know there was an English lord in the party?

'Come, gentlemen, I know one of you is an English milord, and a fine fat pigeon for my plucking.'

No one said a word.

The bandit leader strode forward, and with a rough oath he dragged first Maguire, then Guillaume, then John Black from their litters. He examined each man briefly, then thrust them towards his men, who stripped them of any valuables they found.

Behind her Tallie heard Monique shrieking as she was robbed of her finery. A slap rang out and a bandit laughed. John Black swore in a litany of solid English curses and surged forward. A scuffle broke out. There was a loud crack and John Black fell to the ground, groaning and clutching his head. Guillaume and Maguire did not stir. Guillaume looked terrified. Maguire seemed unmoved. After a moment, to Tallie's relief, John Black struggled to his feet, shaken but apparently still in one piece. A bandit tied his hands.

The bandit leader turned and dragged Magnus from his litter.

'Leggo of me, damn y'r eyes!' muttered Magnus, swaying as he stood, trying to fend off the bandit.

'Aha, our arrogant English milord, I presume,' said the bandit leader in excellent French, and he bowed mockingly as he drew the money belt from Magnus's waist.

Tallie's eyes widened. This ragged villain was no simple peasant.

Magnus swayed again, and the bandit grabbed him by the coat, laughing. 'Is it drunk you are, my fine English milord? Or are you a coward, like the rest of your kind?'

'He's nothing of the sort! He's ill,' shouted Tallie furiously, struggling to clamber out of her litter. She freed herself, scrambled out and rushed over to her husband, thrusting her body between him and the bandit. 'Leave him alone. He's ill. Can't you see?'

The bandit snorted. His green eyes narrowed.

'He is, otherwise he would have shot you dead, you villain!' Tallie said fiercely, wedging her shoulder under Magnus's to support his swaying form.

The bandit looked at Magnus again and spat on the ground. 'Pah, look at him! He's shaking with fright!'

'He's shaking with *fever*,' Tallie retorted angrily, wiping her husband's brow with her handkerchief.

The bandit leader snorted disbelievingly. He reached out a surprisingly clean hand and took her ear between his fingers. Tallie froze as he carefully removed her gold studs. Then he reached for her neck, slipping his fingers inside the neck of her gown, and she recoiled.

'Take y'r filthy hands off my wife, you ruffian!' Magnus lurched forward, his arm shooting out in a clumsy, but well-aimed punch. The bandit reeled back and stood clutching his chin, while Tallie struggled to help Magnus regain his balance. Her gold necklace lay broken on the ground.

The bandit stood silently for a moment, then shrugged. 'We'll take him anyway.' He bent and scooped up Tallie's necklace.

'What do you mean, take him? Take who? My husband?'

'*Si*,' said the bandit, reverting to Italian. He called two of his henchmen over. They grabbed Magnus by the arms and started to march him away.

'No, stop!' cried Tallie. 'What are you going to do with him?'

The bandit leader turned back and regarded her impassively for a moment, then shrugged again. 'He is a fine English milord. Someone will pay gold for his safe return, *si*?'

'Ransom?' gasped Tallie. 'But you can't take him. He's too ill! He needs a physician immediately.'

The bandit shrugged and turned away.

'No!' shouted Tallie angrily. 'I will not allow it!'

The bandit turned and regarded her in faint surprise. He grinned, and a gold tooth glinted in the sunlight. '*You* will not allow it?'

'No, I won't,' she retorted defiantly, and moved to rejoin her husband. 'You will have to kill me before I allow you to kidnap my husband!'

'Be quiet, woman. Stay out of this,' Magnus mumbled angrily. His skin looked white and papery, but there was a hectic flush across his cheekbones.

'I will do no such thing. You are in no condition to be dragged off to some horrid bandit lair in the mountains, and even if you were, I still wouldn't allow it!'

Magnus staggered and swore, dashing his hand impatiently across his brow, as if wiping off sweat. 'Hold your tongue and wait with John Black and Maguire.'

'I have no wish to wait with John Black and Maguire. My place is beside my husband.' And, with that, Tallie pushed one of the bandits aside and took Magnus's arm. She glared defiantly, first at her husband, who was ineffectively trying to detach her from his arm, and then at the bandit leader, who watched them both in amusement. He chuckled, then, sobering, reached out and effortlessly hauled Tallie to his side. Magnus lunged out to save her, but missed. Another ragged robber came and held him back.

'R'lease my wife, damn you,' slurred Magnus, swaying. 'Harm a hair on her head and I'll kill you.'

The bandit leader's brilliant green eyes narrowed, and his grip tightened on Tallie.

'Oho, so the English milord cares for his wife, does he? And she for him? Good. A loving wife will ensure her husband's ransom is paid quickly and without fuss.'

'You shall *not* take—'

The bandit clapped a hand over Tallie's mouth. 'Take him,' he ordered.

Tallie wrenched herself free with a cry. 'No! He is sick! He will *die* if you take him,' she said desperately. 'Then how would you get your precious ransom?'

The bandit shrugged indifferently. 'It is a risk we will take.'

'It is not your risk! I will not allow it!'

The bandit grinned. 'How will you prevent us, little English milady?'

Tallie fumed impotently. She could not stop them; she knew it. But Magnus was swaying and shivering in the cold, and unless she did something, he would die. And that she could not bear. She had to do something!

'Take me instead,' she said.

'Damn it woman, hold your—' Magnus's angry bellow was cut short as a rag was stuffed in his mouth. Another man came to assist the two who were already holding him.

'Take you?' said the leader, surprised. His green eyes narrowed. 'What game are you playing now?' He glanced at Maguire, who said nothing.

'No game,' said Tallie. 'You clearly will not leave without a hostage. My husband is too ill to go with you, but I am not. It is a perfectly sensible arrangement.'

A muffled roar came from Magnus. His eyes glared at her over the gag, charcoal pools of rage and frantic worry in an unnaturally pale face.

'Take a woman hostage?' The bandit regarded her suspiciously, smoothing a finger over his thick, dark moustache. 'Is this one of your immoral English games, milady? You think it will be romantic to dally with a handsome bandit in the mountains, eh?'

Tallie was outraged. 'No, of course not!' she spluttered indignantly. 'How dare you suggest such a wicked thing? I wouldn't walk two steps with you if I had any choice in the matter, but I will *not* let you take my husband when he is ill!'

'But if he was well...?'

'Hah!' Tallie snorted. 'If he was well you would never have taken us prisoner in the first place!' She cast a look of magnificent scorn at Maguire, and the silent gaggle of guards he had hired to protect them. 'My husband would never have surrendered without a proper fight!'

To her astonishment the bandit leader winked at Maguire.

'All right, then,' the bandit said, 'we take you with us and leave your loving husband to arrange the ransom.'

Magnus surged furiously, but was held down by his captors.

Tallie swallowed, her mouth suddenly dry. She had not truly thought the bandits would agree to take her, and she was suddenly terrified. But she had offered herself, and there was really no choice after all, she told herself. And the sooner they left, the sooner the others could get Magnus to a physician. She squared her shoulders and stepped forward to speak with her husband, whose eyes glowered over his gag, angry, desperate and fevered.

'It's all right, Magnus. I am happy to do this.' She swallowed again. There seemed to be a large dry lump in her throat. 'Please try not be angry with me. I could see no other way... And if...if I...' She swallowed again. 'If I should not see you again—'

Magnus shook his head, furiously chafing at his bindings.

'Please, my love, I...I do not want what may be our last moments... Oh, please, do not be angry with me.' Tears filled her eyes as she laid her hand on his cheek. He stilled, his eyes boring into hers in a silent, frustrated message. She tried to tug his gag away, but it would not budge, and the bandit beside him growled an incoherent warning, so with trembling lips she reached up and kissed him fervently on an ice-cold cheek. 'I love you, Magnus,' she whispered, and clung tightly to his body, as if she would never let him go.

'Enough,' said the bandit, and with another kiss Tallie released Magnus, tears spilling down her cheek.

The bandit regarded Magnus for a brief, solemn moment. 'She will not be harmed,' he said at last. 'We are bandits, *si*, but we do not harm women.' He took Tallie by the arm and led her away.

'*Mais, non, non.* You cannot take milady into the mountains,' cried Monique, suddenly aware of what was happening.

The bandit ignored her and kept walking.

'*Elle est enceinte!*' shrieked Monique in desperation.

The bandit froze. He glanced at Tallie's face, down at her stomach, then at her face again. She was gazing at her husband, her eyes filled with a mixture of joy, anxiety and entreaty. The bandit did not need to ask; her stomach might be flat, but confirmation of her maid's story was there in her eyes, for all the world to see.

He swore long and violently, released Tallie's arm in disgust and stamped across to Maguire. An argument ensued, in a language Tallie had heard somewhere before. She stared at the arguing men and the truth suddenly dawned. It was Gaelic. A maidservant at Miss Fisher's had been Irish, and had taught Tallie a few words.

'*You* betrayed us, Maguire,' she cried.

Maguire started, looked across the small rocky clearing at her, and shrugged in a manner which uncannily echoed the bandit's.

Tallie noted the way the two men were standing and her eyes widened in sudden suspicion. 'He...he's your *brother*,' she accused. 'He has the same long, thin face and the same nose...and your eyes are green, too, only not so...' Her voice tailed off.

The bandit turned and grinned, his gold tooth glinting in the light. 'Correct, milady,' he said in perfect lilting English. 'The Maguire brothers at your service. I am Antonio.' He bowed. 'And my little brother, Luigi.'

Tallie ignored him. She turned to the erstwhile major-domo. 'Why, Maguire? Why did you do it?'

Maguire sneered and shrugged. 'The wars are over and a man must earn his living somehow. And we have no love for English lords. It was an English lord who hanged our father and grandfather, an English lord who drove us from our homeland—'

His bandit brother interrupted, 'And English lords who have provided us with a steady income since we took to living in the mountains like our mother's people.' He glanced from Tallie back to Magnus. 'But it seems we will get only the pickings of the baggage this time, for it is one thing to hold a man to ransom, but if an English lord died on us we would have the authorities hounding our every footstep. And I do not kidnap pregnant women.'

He turned and shouted orders, and the clearing suddenly became a hive of activity as the bandits packed up every portable item that could possibly be of any value.

'*Adieu*, milord,' said Maguire the bandit. 'I envy you your wife—she is your real treasure. *Au revoir, bella donna.*' He took Tallie's hand and kissed it lingeringly, quite as if he was a gentleman born and not a ragged mountain robber. In moments the *banditti* were gone, Maguire the younger and his false guards with them. The others watched them go until no echo of their leaving remained in the cold mountain air.

Tallie rushed to relieve Magnus of his dirty gag and bindings.

He spat the gag out, gasping for breath, and tried to say something, but his knees buckled beneath him and he sank to the ground, clutching at Tallie as he did so.

'Oh, help me, please,' she cried to the porters. 'Let us be gone from this dreadful place immediately. I must get my husband to a physician at once. Quickly, we must go!' She turned to beckon to one of the men but found her wrist caught in a hard, feverish grip.

'Don't...leave...me,' Magnus grated hoarsely, fixing her with a wild, agonised stare. 'Not...leave... Not—' He collapsed, insensible.

'*Signora*, the fever has broken.' The dapper silver-haired physician bent over Tallie, speaking in a gentle voice.

Tallie stared up at him dazed, blank incomprehension in her face.

'It means your husband is over the worst,' the physician explained. 'He will be well soon. A week, perhaps, before he can get up. He needs to rest.' He looked at her and his face softened. 'And so do you, *signora*. You are exhausted.'

Tallie blinked at him as his words slowly sank into her tired brain. Magnus was going to get better. He would live. Tears flooded her eyes as she turned back to the still figure on the bed beside her. Magnus was breathing more easily now, and his skin was drenched with sweat. Beautiful, healing sweat. A sob escaped her.

'Come now,' said the doctor. 'Carlotta and the good John Black will stay here with your husband and your maid will put you to bed. You must sleep. You have slept little the last three days, *si*?'

Tallie nodded. Was it really only three days since they had arrived in the town of Susa? It seemed so much longer... A nightmare journey down from the mountains with Magnus strapped onto a mule, unconscious, his head swaying and bouncing with every bump so that she was terrified he would break his neck. But he hadn't. And then the fruitless, interminable search for a place which would house a stranger with no money and a fever.

Thank God for Carlotta, who was some sort of relative by marriage to one of the porters. She had glanced indifferently at Magnus bundled on his mule and begun to argue with the porter in a thick dialect Tallie hadn't been able to follow. Tallie had been terrified that Carlotta, like all the others, would shut the door in their faces. She'd pushed past the porter and, summoning up her best schoolgirl Italian, had begged Carlotta to help her husband. Carlotta, a large, flamboyant-looking woman with improbably brilliant rust-coloured hair, had taken one look at Tallie's youthful, tear-stained face and flung the door wide.

Within moments she'd sent a boy running to fetch the *dottore*, called for wine and refreshments for Tallie and the others, and loudly supervised the men carrying Magnus up to a bedroom. She had stripped Magnus's shivering body with firm, motherly hands and had him sponged down and in her dead husband's best linen nightshirt by the time the physician had arrived.

He'd examined the patient carefully. To Tallie's relief he had announced that the patient was unfit for cupping—she hated seeing people being bled. But then, to her horror, he had produced from his bag a small box containing a half-dozen leeches, which he had applied to Magnus's skin with deft fingers. She'd watched, appalled, as the leeches swelled and grew fatter, until at last, shiny and bloated, they'd fallen off, leaving a trickle of blood behind them. Tallie had felt ill just watching, but she hadn't been able to leave.

The doctor had carefully collected the gross leeches and replaced them in the box. He'd then shaken out a mysterious-looking powder, mixed it with wine, added several drops from a thick greenish bottle and administered the mixture through a funnel forced between Magnus's clenched teeth. 'Laudanum. He will sleep now,' he had said to Tallie in careful French. He'd given Carlotta more instructions in rapid Italian and left.

And that had only been three days ago, Tallie thought incredulously. It was all a blur to her now...days and nights spent at Magnus's bedside, watching him toss and turn and mutter unintelligibly, sponging him down when he was hot, rugging him up when he was cold...and all the time praying that he would live.

'Come, *signora*, it is time you slept. Your husband is safe now,' the doctor said again.

Tallie nodded, and winced as she gently prised her husband's fingers apart. She stood up stiffly, tried to flex her fingers and winced again.

The doctor made a low exclamation and, frowning, bent to look closer. Tallie hurriedly thrust her hand in a fold of her skirts.

'*Signora*, you permit?' Tallie shook her head and moved to step back, but the doctor ignored her. He reached down, gently brought her hand from its hiding place, and examined it. He swore softly in Italian. 'Why did you not say something?' he said in a low, angry voice.

Tallie shook her head, embarrassed. 'It's nothing—a bit stiff, that's all.'

Carlotta came up behind him and peered curiously over his shoulder. She gasped. Tallie's left hand was black and blue with bruises, where her husband had gripped it in his fever. Several fingers were swollen. She could hardly move them.

'Ice for the *signora's* hand, immediately,' the doctor snapped. Carlotta ushered Tallie from the room in a tender rush, scolding her gently in Italian, interspersing her comments with shrill calls to the servant to hurry up with the ice.

Tallie had no choice but to be swept away in the motherly embrace. It was strange, but oddly comforting to have someone fussing over her, even for such a trivial matter. No one had ever done it before, not even when she had been ill at school. She couldn't recall her mother very well, but perhaps her mother had fussed over her like this when she was a baby. Tallie laid her good hand on her belly, feeling the faint swelling beneath it. One day she, too, would fuss over this child the way that Carlotta was fussing over her. It was a wonderful thought. A tear trickled down her cheeks. Oh, heavens, she was more tired than she realised.

Her hand was plunged into a bowl of ice-water, and after the first excruciating pain there was a blessed numbness. After a while the feeling started to come back. It throbbed, but not as badly as before. Carlotta smoothed on some foul-smelling ointment and wrapped the hand lightly in a cloth, then bustled her into a huge warm nightgown and tucked her into bed.

'*Signora*...Carlotta, I must thank you—' Tallie began, but Carlotta shushed her and pressed her gently back on the pillows, smoothing her hair with a gentle rhythmic touch. She started humming—a lullaby, Tallie supposed—and a faint smile crossed her lips as she recognised that she was indeed being mothered like a small child. It was foolish, for she was a grown, married woman, and not a child at all...but it was very comforting... She closed her eyes and slept.

'Magnus, you must stay in bed! The physician said—'

'Damn that blasted leech. I have no intention of idling—'

'But you are not yet strong enou—'

Magnus flung back the covers and swung his legs to the edge of the bed. He sat there a moment, then shakily stood up, gripping the carved wooden bedhead for support.

Tallie, despite her anxiety, found herself smiling. Carlotta's late husband had evidently been much shorter than Magnus, for his nightshirt dangled well above Magnus's knees. The length of hard, hairy leg looked incongruous beneath the embroidered linen. She bit her lip and tried to look cross. 'You are not supposed to be up this soon,' she said severely.

'Nonsense. I feel perfectly well. And besides I am bored—'

'But—'

'And damnably lonely,' he finished, giving her a heated look.

Tallie blushed. This time she could not stop the smile which quivered on her lips. She, too, had been lonely in the bed next door. It was amazing how quickly one could become accustomed to sharing a bed. Only a few months ago she had been unable to imagine it as anything but an intrusion, an inconvenience, an invasion of her privacy...but now she would not wish to fall asleep anywhere except in her husband's warm, strong arms. She'd missed his warmth, missed the wonderful feeling of belonging, the feeling of safety she felt when she fell asleep in his embrace. She loved waking up in the night and finding his long hairy leg wrapped around hers, loved resting her cheek on his smooth, hard chest and hearing his heart thudding steadily under her ear, loved the way he sometimes woke her in the morning... *'Morning, sweetheart...'* knowing that it was the prelude to a splendid bout of lovemaking.

She loved those mornings best, watching his sleepy eyes focus, then darken into that brooding, storm-cloud grey that meant he wanted to make love to her. The look never failed to thrill her... And the feel of his unshaven jaw scraping sensuously against the softness of her skin... A pleasurable shudder passed through her. Yes, she had been lonely in her bed, too.

'Fetch me that robe, would you?' Magnus said. 'It's chilly.'

The man was impossibly stubborn! She didn't want to assist him, but he was clearly going to get up whether or not she agreed, and it *was* cold. Reluctantly she went to do his bidding, but before she reached the hook where the robe was hanging he took a few steps and wavered dangerously. She raced back to his swaying form.

'I told you it was too early to venture out of bed,' she scolded. 'The physician said you must rest for another few days and regain your strength before you try to move. If you try too soon, you could have a relapse.'

'Damned quack!'

'He saved your life.'

'What would a blasted village leech know?'

Tallie, incensed by his stubbornness, abruptly let him go and stood back. Magnus swayed. His knees started to buckle. She gave him a tiny push and he collapsed onto the bed, swearing.

Hiding a triumphant smile, she bent to lift his legs back into the bed, but with a jerk Magnus pulled her on top of him. 'That's more like it,' he growled in soft satisfaction, and planted his mouth on hers.

Tallie gave up the struggle. It was bliss to be back in his arms again, and a kiss wouldn't tax his strength too much, surely. She kissed him back with all the fervour in her heart. Oh, she loved this stubborn man so much. His kiss deepened, and hazily she felt his hands seeking to undo the fastenings of her gown.

'*Madonna mia!* Stop that at once! It is not the time!' It was Carlotta in the doorway.

Magnus swore. Tallie tried to pull back from his embrace, but he refused to let her go. Trust his strength to come back now, she thought, embarrassed.

'Signora Thalia, Signor Magnus, you must stop it now! *Basta!* Enough!'

'Out, damn it, *signora*! Now!' snapped Magnus. 'A man and his wife are entitled to...to— Confound it, Tallie, what's the Italian for privacy?'

Carlotta ignored him. She hurried over to the bed, scolding in an undervoice, and tugged Tallie off. 'Quick!' she whispered. 'Fasten your gown. And as for you, Signor Magnus—' She broke off and began to smooth the covers over him.

'Blast you, woman—'

'Hush!' Carlotta snapped. 'It is the Father.'

'What father? I haven't got a father,' retorted Magnus angrily. 'Damn it, woman, what the devil do you think you are doing?'

He tried to fend off the hands that were busily buttoning his nightshirt to the neck, but Carlotta would have none of it.

'It is *the Father*!' she hissed. Footsteps sounded on the landing outside and she turned, smoothed her dress with quick, anxious hands and waited, a deferential smile on her lips.

'Hell and the devil confound you, woman, I told you I haven't got a fath—'

The door opened and an elderly priest in a long black robe entered. He paused on the threshold, took out a small vial and sprinkled a few drops of liquid around the room, murmuring in Latin.

'Holy water,' whispered Carlotta, crossing herself.

Magnus closed his eyes in resignation and Tallie stifled a giggle. What if the priest had just walked in on them? Thank heavens Carlotta had come in first. But what was he doing here anyway?

'How do you do?' the priest said in slow, rusty English. 'I am Father Astuto. Carlotta tell me you make the difficult...' he frowned, then his brow cleared '...convalescence.' He bowed, clearly delighted at having remembered such a complicated word. 'I come to entertain you with English conversation. I speak the English well, no? So we shall converse.'

He placed his vial of holy water on the bedside stand, pulled up a chair and sat facing Magnus with such a look of pleased and proud expectancy that Tallie was hard put to it to maintain a straight face. Magnus groaned and rolled his eyes.

'You are in pain, my son.' Father Astuto laid a thin, veined hand on Magnus's brow. 'Do not try to talk. Repose yourself and I will talk to you of my life and my travels. It will be of great interest to an Englishman. I was born in the small village of—'

A smothered choke of laughter escaped Tallie. Magnus opened one eye and glared balefully at her. Clapping a hand over her mouth, she hurried from the room. Behind her, Father Astuto's voice droned on.

'Coffee, Signora Thalia?' said Carlotta, following her down the stairs. 'The Father, he will stay at least three hours.'

'Th...three hours?' quavered Tallie.

Carlotta nodded. 'Three, possibly four.' She gave Tallie a sly glance. 'That will keep your husband quiet, no?'

Tallie's jaw dropped. She stared at her hostess incredulously. 'You mean—?'

'*Il Dottore* said he must stay in bed, yes? And who better to keep him there than Father Astuto? He loves to practise his English. He will come every morning for the rest of the week.' Carlotta winked. 'And if your husband doesn't sleep for the rest of the afternoon, then Father Astuto is losing his touch.'

'Carlotta, you are brilliant!' Tallie exclaimed. 'I couldn't keep him from over-exerting himself, but Magnus is too polite to argue with a priest...especially such a sweet old man. How splendidly devious!' And she laughed until tears ran down her cheeks.

Finally she sat drinking Carlotta's strong, milky coffee. Magnus was recuperating safely and she had no need to worry about him anymore. And with Carlotta and Father Astuto's help he would be out of the way for at least a week. This was the opportunity she hoped she might get. A chance to trace the last footsteps of her mother.

'Signora Carlotta,' she said slowly. 'My parents are both dead.'

'Ahh, you poor child—' Carlotta began, her broad face crumpling in sympathy.

'They died in Italy,' Tallie interrupted the flow.

'What? In Italia? No.'

'Yes, somewhere between Turin and the mountains.'

'Eh? Near Torino, you say?'

Tallie nodded. 'Yes, but I'm not sure where, exactly. Near some small village. There was a coach accident. It was about seven years ago. Did you hear of anything like that happening around here?'

Carlotta frowned. 'You say your *mamma* and your *papà* died in this accident?' She shook her head slowly. 'I do remember something about an Englishman's coach... It was near the village where my husband's sister-in-law's uncle lives, but I do not remember anything about an English lady in the coach. And I would know, yes, for English ladies are not common in these hills.' She patted Tallie's hand sympathetically. 'I am sorry, child.'

Tallie felt the excitement inside her grow. It was as the letter had said. Her mother had not died in the coach accident with her father. 'But you do remember a coach accident where an Englishman was killed? About seven years ago?'

Carlotta nodded.

Tallie took a deep breath. 'Carlotta, can I trust you?'

Carlotta frowned, and drew herself up as if insulted. 'But of course—'

'No one, not even my husband, knows this secret,' Tallie said hastily. 'Especially not my husband.'

Carlotta's eyes gleamed. 'I swear by the robe of the Holy Virgin, I keep your secret to the grave,' she said, crossing her breast quickly. She spat into her palm and offered it to Tallie, who shook it gingerly.

'I thought my parents died together in the coach accident, but a few years ago I received a letter which said that my father was killed but my mother died a week before, in a small village.'

Carlotta frowned. 'I have not heard of this.'

Tallie continued in a rush. 'The letter said she died giving birth...to a little boy. It said that my father believed my mother had been unfaithful and that he would have no foreigner's bastard foisted onto him.' She fixed her eyes on Carlotta. 'The letter said he left the baby behind in the village where my mother was buried.'

Carlotta looked stunned. She shook her head in disbelief at such goings-on.

'Carlotta, don't you realise? All my life I have been without a family, with no one in the world who belongs to me. No one who loves me.'

'But your husb—'

Tallie waved that aside. She didn't need to burden Carlotta with the knowledge that while Magnus might act possessively towards his wife he did not love her. 'It's not the same. But perhaps, in some small village not far from here, there is a small boy who also believes he belongs to no one. But if the letter is right, and there is such a boy, he has a sister—a sister who wants him, who will love him.' Her eyes sheened with tears. 'I want to search for him, Carlotta, and I need your help.'

'But why not wait until your husband is well?'

'He mustn't know.'

'But why, *cara*?'

'I know we told you that we were Signor and Signora d'Arenville, but the truth is, in England, my husband is a great lord, from a proud and ancient family. It was bad enough that he chose a nobody for his wife, but what do you think his feelings would be if the nobody wanted to search for her bastard half brother?' Tallie shook her head. She loved her husband, but she was not blind. He had chosen a nobody because she would cause him the least amount of bother.

And the only child Magnus was interested in was an heir to carry on his family name. Certainly he would have no interest in a bastard child of unknown parentage, possibly half-foreign and raised in a small and probably dirty peasant village. She could just imagine what he—and everybody else—would say. But if she found her brother first... Magnus was not the only one who could be stubborn.

'Do you honestly think my husband would help me? Or would he hurry me back to England and thus prevent a scandal?'

Carlotta's eyes were sombre. She nodded. 'I will help you, *cara*. I know of these great proud lords. If we can, we will find your little brother. But are you sure Signor Magnus would deny him shelter?'

'Shelter, no,' said Tallie with feeling. 'In an orphanage or school, perhaps. Or he might pay a tenant to keep him. But if I do have a little brother, I want more for him. I never had a home of my own, but I will do everything in my power to ensure my brother has one. And if my husband doesn't like it...' Her eyes filled with tears. 'I do not know what I will do—but I will *not* give up on my brother—bastard or not.'

Chapter Fourteen

'So, John Black and Monique and Carlotta's nephews and I will travel to Turin with your letters of credit and introduction, and you'll stay here with Carlotta.' Tallie patted the reticule containing the letters. She was dressed for immediate travel.

'But—' Magnus glowered at her from the bed. He was not at all happy about her travelling without him. But Tallie was determined.

'Magnus, you know it is the only possible thing to do. We cannot all go, for then Carlotta will think we mean to run out on her, when she has already been to so much trouble and expense on our behalf. And besides, I'll be perfectly safe with Carlotta's nephews and John Black—and if you cannot trust him, who can you trust?'

'Yes, but—'

'Would you prefer I stay behind, then—by myself? While you risk your health and possibly your life? Or perhaps it suits you to continue to allow a lone widow to support us and our servants. To be sure, she has not yet begun to dun us, so perhaps—'

Magnus looked frustrated. 'No, of course I do not wish it. It galls me past bearing, but—'

'Very well, it is agreed,' Tallie said decisively. 'You need not worry, Magnus. I am not at all tempted to take your purse and continue my journey. I have no intention of abandoning you.'

The look of blank shock on his face told her he had not even considered such a thing. But now he was, if the black frown was any indicator. Tallie hid a smile.

'And you could not possibly be lonely, with dear Father Astuto visiting you so often. I wonder if he could visit more frequently while I am away?'

A low growl erupted from the bed. 'Saddle me with any more of that blasted priest, madam, and you will rue the day you wed me.'

'Will I? And are you so sure I do not do so already?' she said lightly, and, planting a quick kiss on his mouth, she hurried from the room, leaving Magnus frustrated and uneasy.

Curse it, but there was a vast deal of decision about his wife these days. What the devil had happened to the dependent little creature he had married? He missed her. She was fast turning into an impertinent baggage. He swung his legs out of bed and tried to rise. Blast—he was still as weak as a kitten. He had to get his strength back quickly, or the way things were going his wife would consider it was she who wore the pantaloons in this family... She was already wearing the drawers.

He felt his body stir as he recalled the sight of her in those damned alluring pink drawers. He settled back into bed, prepared to indulge himself in a fantasy where his wife was standing over him, clad in nothing but her pink drawers, her hair tumbled around her pert, naked breasts...

'Ah, Signor d'Arenville, you are awake, I see.'

'Father Astuto,' groaned Magnus.

'Repose yourself, my son, and I will tell you of the Holy City and my audience with His Eminence,' said the priest with a gentle, reminiscent smile. 'It was a cold, wet day...'

Magnus closed his eyes and tried to recapture his fantasy about his wife in the pink drawers with their very erotic slit...

'I was wearing a new cassock—that is the correct term, yes?—which I had purchased especially for the audience...'

It was no good. It was simply not possible to indulge oneself with an erotic fantasy when one was entrapped by an elderly, unworldly, celibate, stupefyingly dull priest.

Magnus closed his eyes and prayed that sleep would come soon.

'And of course I had prepared a small speech to make to the Holy Father. To this day, I still remember—it went like this...'

Magnus hunched down in his bed, trying to block out the priest's rambling. But sleep eluded him. He was kept awake by his wife's last comment.

Did she rue the day she had wed him? It was an unsettling thought. She seemed to him to be quite happy...but you never could tell with women. Women were natural actresses, in his experience. They never said what they meant... Although his wife was not like most women... She was different...but how different? Could she feign happiness so consistently? He pondered the notion. Now he thought about it, there were times he had caught her looking at him as if... Damn it, what was that look she got sometimes? Sad? Wistful? Pensive?

This wretched weakness of his—he *hated* the idea of her heading off to Turin alone, with none but John Black and a gaggle of Carlotta's nephews to protect her. What if there were more *banditti* on the road? They would not be so gallant as that blasted Irishman. Magnus snorted... A bandit who kissed women's hands! And who did that fellow think he was—rot him—to compliment Magnus on his wife? None of his business what sort of wife Magnus had. Shouldn't even be looking at another fellow's wife, blasted bandit. Blasted green-eyed bandit.

Magnus closed his eyes, reliving the moment when he had realised that the bandit was taking Tallie up into the mountains to hold her hostage. It still haunted him. He had never in his life felt so furious...or so terrified...or so helpless.

If he lived to be a hundred years old he would never forget that brave little smile she'd given him as she kissed him goodbye. *I love you, Magnus.* And then she'd hugged him as if he was the most precious thing in the world.

She'd *offered* to go. To take his place as hostage. Like a heroine in a Greek drama. Because she'd thought if they took him he would die of his fever in the mountains. And she would have gone, too, quite happily...if that maid of hers hadn't said what she'd said.

Pregnant. Every time he thought of it, he felt... He didn't know what he felt. Breathless? Joyful? Proud? Obviously. Then why did it feel so much like terror? Lord, what was the matter with him these days? He should be over the moon—after all, a child of his own was the reason he'd decided to take a wife. He tried to envisage a child, a child of Tallie's. A little girl with glossy honey-coloured curls and big amber eyes. A miniature tip-tilted nose and teeth like tiny pearls, one of them endearingly crooked... But all he could think of was that women died in childbirth all the time...

He broke out in a cold sweat just thinking about it. *Pregnant.* Oh, Lord.

He thought of her playful threat to abandon him. After the first shock, he hadn't actually believed it for a moment. Of course she wouldn't leave him. He knew it as well as he knew himself. She'd do exactly what she'd said she would—go straight to Turin, get the money and return to him immediately. With a start, it occurred to Magnus that he trusted her; he actually trusted a woman.

No—he didn't just trust a woman—he trusted Tallie.

Good God! When had that happened? When she had offered to take his place? No. He thought back. He couldn't pin a time on it, but it had started well before then... *He trusted her.* The realisation was shattering. His heart thudded faster in his chest and he shivered, feeling suddenly exposed and vulnerable. What if she—? No, he wouldn't think about that. There was no point in dredging up the past—she was different; his wife was different. Somehow, by some incredible, wonderful stroke of luck, he'd got himself a wife who was different from any other woman he had known... And he was overwhelmingly grateful for it.

He trusted his wife.

And she was increasing. But, oh, Lord...what if he lost her?

The priest's voice droned on in the background. Magnus wrestled with his demons, plunging from exhilaration, to doubt, to despair, then back to exhilaration, until at last, in the middle of a description of the vestments worn by a bishop at a mass Father Astuto had attended forty years before, Magnus finally dozed off.

'What the *devil* do you mean, the mistress isn't with you? Where the hell is she, then? Don't tell me you left her on her own in Turin—you know better than that, John!' Magnus stared at his coachman, baffled and not a little worried. Of course he didn't believe for a moment that his wife had gone off and left him...but where the hell was she?

John Black shifted uncomfortably. For the first time in twelve years he failed to look his master in the eye. Magnus felt a cold hand steal around his heart. She couldn't possibly have left him. She couldn't. She wouldn't. But where was she? He braced himself.

'Out with it, man, where is she?'

'The mistress never went to Turin,' said John Black at last.

'Never went to Turin? What do you mean? I saw her leave.'

John Black nodded. 'Went with me a dozen miles or so, then turned up into the mountains.'

Magnus felt as if he'd been hit in the chest with a hammer. That damned green-eyed, hand-kissing bastard!

'And you just let her go? By herself?' It was more than a week ago. He'd never be able to catch her now. His insides felt hollow.

'No, my lord, of course not,' said John Black indignantly. 'I hope I know better than that. She had that French wench with her, and a half-dozen of the Italian widder-woman's relatives, including one old woman.'

'What?' Magnus stared at his coachman. Something eased slightly in his chest. It was one thing to suspect his wife had run off with some damned good-looking bandit, but quite another to imagine her taking her maid, an old Italian lady and half a dozen relatives of the eminently respectable Carlotta with her. It was not the usual way of elopements. But then his wife was not the usual sort of wife.

'If she was escorted by the widow's relatives, the widow will no doubt be able to cast some light on the matter.' Magnus strode to the door and flung it open. 'Carlotta,' he roared.

She came immediately.

'What the devil have you done with my wife?'

Carlotta looked at him for a moment and smiled. 'Do not worry Signor d'Arenville, your wife is perfectly safe. She has gone on a visit with the wife of my husband's oldest brother. She wished to visit her uncle, you understand.'

'Her uncle?' Magnus was dumbfounded. 'She never she told me she had an uncle living in Italy.'

Carlotta laughed. 'Not your wife's uncle, *signor*. The uncle of my husband's sister-in-law.'

'The uncle of your sister-in-law's husband? But why on earth—?'

Carlotta laughed again. 'No, not the uncle of my sister-in-law's husband—he lives in Chiomonte—he is the stonemason, you understand? No, your wife has gone to visit the uncle of my husband's sister-in-law. The uncle of my sister-in-law's husband is a very unpleasant man. The uncle of my husband's sister-in-law is—'

'I don't give a hell's bloody damn about your blasted relatives, madam. *I want my wife.*'

Carlotta drew herself up and gave him a look of magnificent Italian scorn. 'I do not care for cursing in my house, *signor*. No matter if you are a great lord in England.' She sniffed, turned her back, and with immense dignity began to depart.

Magnus groaned. 'Carlotta.' He laid a hand on her shoulder. It remained stiff and averted. Magnus took a deep breath and counted to ten. '*Signora*—Carlotta.' He forced himself to use a much softer voice. 'I apologise for cursing in your house.'

The shoulder twitched huffily.

'And I apologise for any offence I may have made concerning your relatives. I am sure they are very worthy and respectable people.' He would have them all hanged if harm came to Tallie.

The shoulder twitched again.

'Please forgive me. I did not mean to upset you, *signora*, but I am extremely worried about my wife.'

Carlotta turned and said stiffly, 'She is with my relatives, *signor*. No harm will come to her, I assure you.'

Blast the woman's touchy Italian soul. He should give up this soft-soaping and just choke the truth out of her. Magnus made one more effort. 'I know,' he said. 'It is just that I am very anxious about her. She...she is increasing, you know.'

Carlotta frowned in puzzlement. 'Increasing?' Then her face lit up. 'You mean a baby?'

Magnus nodded, wishing he knew whether he was telling the truth or not.

'Oh, *signor*, that is wonderful. No wonder you are anxious about the *signora*. But how happy you must be. A baby.'

Magnus nodded, and managed what he hoped looked like a joyful smile. But he was too damned worried to waste much more time grinning at some woman whose blasted relatives had carted Tallie off into some godforsaken mountain village. 'So, would you tell me now, please, where is my wife?' He managed a reasonably polite tone.

'But I told you, *signor*, she is in the village of my sister-in—'

Magnus held up his hand. 'No more relatives, I beg of you.'

Carlotta sighed and said simply, 'She has gone to find the place where her mother died.'

The breath left Magnus in a great gush. So that green-eyed

scoundrel hadn't got her after all. He closed his eyes in relief. The place where her mother died. Of course. She'd mentioned it before. It was very important to her, he remembered. The main reason she'd wanted to come to Italy.

But why had she not waited until he was well enough to escort her? He would have gone with her. No question about it. In fact, now he came to think of it, he damn well *wanted* to go with her. She needed him—not just as an escort, but to support her in her grief. She would need support; his wife was a very emotional little creature.

So why the deuce had she not waited? And why sneak off as she had, pretending she was going to Turin? As if there was something havey-cavey about visiting her mother's grave. There was no need for secrecy and deception for such a visit. So what was she about, creeping off behind his back? He frowned. Carlotta shifted uncomfortably under his stare. She averted her eyes and gazed with sudden interest at the ornately carved settee beneath the window.

His suspicion deepened. There was funny business going on, or Magnus was a Dutchman. And he wasn't. He was English to the core, as far back as the Conqueror. And beyond.

So what was his wife up to, the deceitful little baggage?

Tallie stood and stared desolated at the tumbledown cottage. The whitewash was ancient, dirty, and falling off in great flakes. The uneven shingled roof had holes visible from the narrow track below. A door swung drunkenly on one leather hinge and the wind rattled broken-slatted shutters and whipped at tattered remnants of oilcloth. It was a ruin. Nobody could possibly live here.

Her heart sank. She turned to their guide. 'I thought you said a man and woman lived here. With a little boy.'

The man shrugged and mumbled something in an incomprehensible dialect. One of Carlotta's nephews translated. 'He says they used to live up here but he hasn't visited for a year or so. He doesn't know what's happened to them. He's been living in Torino.'

'Well, what about one of the people in the village down there? Would any of them know?' Tallie said.

'Perhaps.'

They retraced their steps down to the village, about five

minutes' walk from the ruined house. They knocked at door after door, but no one wished to answer questions posed by a strange young female, a foreign English female at that. But Tallie insisted they try every house in the village. She had not come this far to give up merely because people were suspicious of foreigners. Finally they came to a house where, after some dialogue between a nephew and the householder, a connection was established; it seemed to involve a great many cousins and in-laws.

Tallie was ushered into a small, neat room which seemed to fulfil the function of kitchen, sitting room and bedroom. A fire crackled and a pot of something pungent and aromatic was bubbling over it. Fat brown sausages, flitches of ham and plaited strings of garlic, onions and herbs hung in the rafters. The room was warm and cosy, with colourful hand-woven rugs on the floor and the bed. Tallie sat on a crude wooden bench. The woman of the house offered her an earthenware bowl filled to the brim with creamy milk. She drank it thirstily.

'Thank you very much, *signora*, that was delicious,' she said gratefully, wiping a rim of cream from her upper lip. The woman smiled and bobbed her head in shy acknowledgement. Then, with the nephews translating, Tallie began her questioning.

'*Si*, Marta, who lived in the cottage up the hill, is dead.'

'No, he was not her husband; he was her brother. Her husband died a long time ago—four years, maybe five. Her brother? He went away. Nobody knows for certain. Maybe he went to be a soldier.'

'A little boy? *Si*, there was a little boy. Her *miracolo bambino*, she called him. She was nine years barren, then, *presto*, one day she comes home from church with a little baby.'

'*Si*, it would be about seven years ago.'

'No, the baby had blond hair. Marta was dark.'

'No, the little boy did not die. Where? Who knows, *signora*? Not anyone around here.'

'With the brother? No, he did not like the child. Called him little foreign bastard. Said he was no relative of his.'

'God only knows, *signora*. In times like these, many children lose their parents. Some run wild in the hills—those who have no relatives, of course. *Si*, it is a tragedy, but what can one do? One has enough trouble feeding one's own without looking for more.'

'What sort of boy, *signora*? A bad boy, to be sure. Bad? Eh, steal my apples, ride my goats—*Madonna mia*! But always merry, you understand—whistling, laughing. *Si, signora*—a bad, merry little boy.'

'*Si*, of course. If I hear anything... It has been a long time now...but, *si*, I will ask.'

'No, no, you are welcome, *signora*. God go with you.'

'They come, *signor*. Your wife and my nephews, they come—see?' Carlotta gestured triumphantly.

Magnus strode to the window and stared out, breathing heavily. It had been four days since he had discovered Tallie had not gone to Turin. Four days of ever-increasing anxiety. Four days in which he had discovered that his wife was indeed a liar.

'Yes, I can see her,' he growled. He had barely slept the past few nights, and now, to see her coming down the street unharmed and apparently perfectly content... He'd begun to believe he would never see her again, and now...

Relief, after days and nights of the most intense anxiety, turned to rage. How dared she arrive as if nothing in the world were wrong? As if she hadn't just run off, willy-nilly, with a bunch of foreigners, leaving her sick husband with a demented old priest? Pretending she'd gone to visit her mother's grave. Then just to bounce casually in, for all the world as if she'd been off on a picnic! He'd teach her a lesson. One she'd never forget.

He stalked to a window facing the opposite side of the house and glowered out of it, at the mountains in the distance. She wasn't going to think he'd be waiting for her, arms outstretched. Behind him the door opened. Magnus didn't move; he gazed out of the window. There was a short silence.

'M...Magnus?' she said tremulously.

'Madam?' he said coldly, turning at last to face her. 'Did you find what you were looking for?'

She opened her mouth to answer him, but not a sound came out. Her lower lip quivered, then suddenly her face crumpled. 'Oh, Magnus,' she wailed, and ran across the room and hurled herself into his open arms.

He gathered her to him—hard—a dry lump working in his throat. She clung to him—hard—as she had when she'd been about to be taken away by the bandits, as if she would never let him go. Her head was buried in the hollow between his shoulder and his jaw. He could feel the chill on her skin from the biting wind outside, smell the faint tang of woodsmoke in her hair and the lingering fragrance of the lavender soap that Carlotta had given her. He laid his face against her hair and inhaled deeply, tightening his hold around her quivering body. She was weeping; he could feel the damp warmth of her tears on his skin. After a moment he became aware of Carlotta beaming benevolently upon them, and with a silent oath he swung his wife into his arms and carried her up to the bedroom.

He wanted to drop her onto the bed and fling himself down beside her and tumble her until she knew where she belonged, who she belonged with. He forced himself to set her carefully on her feet, then released her and stepped back. Her face was awash with tears.

Magnus groped in his pocket and handed her a handkerchief. He wanted to dry her tears himself or, better still, kiss them away, but he could not let himself move a single step towards her. If he did, he would be lost for ever, that much he knew. As it was, he was in the grip of an emotional turmoil he had never dreamt was possible. He could not believe how weak and irresolute he felt, how strong was the impulse just to take her in his arms and forget the past week. Forgive and forget. Like his father. Forgive the fact that she had lied to him. Forget that she had gone off into the mountains without his knowledge or permission. No, he was weak, but he would make himself strong. He would neither forgive nor forget.

He paced over to the window and stood, coolly looking out, staring at the mountains into which she had disappeared, forcing down the overwhelming feelings of hurt, humiliation and betrayal, replacing them with cold anger. He waited until the sobbing had stopped, then turned and repeated his question in a bitter, icy voice.

'Well, madam, I asked you before and I will repeat the question. Did you find what you were looking for? Did you find your mother's grave?'

She looked up at him with drenched, bewildered eyes and nodded. 'Yes,' she whispered.

'And once you found it, you came straight back here?'

She hesitated, paled, scrubbed at her face, dropped her lashes and nodded.

'Liar!' he roared, slamming his fist against the wall.

She flinched, and regarded him with huge, wary eyes.

'You found your mother's grave eight days ago! I saw her grave myself and spoke to the priest about you. Eight days, madam! Eight days! And what did you do in those eight days, eh?'

She opened her mouth, then shut it again, biting nervously on her lower lip in a manner that drove him wild. He slammed his fist against the wall again and swore. 'Shall I tell you what you did in those eight days—shall I? You betrayed me, madam. Betrayed the name you took on the day we were wed. Broke the vows you made before God and man.'

She flinched again. 'B...betrayed your name? So...so you know? Carlotta told you?'

He snorted. 'No, to be sure she did not. You women stick together in your deceptions.'

'So how—?'

'Do you think I am a fool, madam? I worked it out for myself.'

She frowned, puzzled. 'But how could you?'

He snorted again. 'Betrayal is something I have been acquainted with all my life. I believe I am an expert on it.'

'Betrayal...I was worried you might see it in those terms.' She sighed, and sat on the bed.

'Worried I might see it in those terms?' he repeated incredulously. 'Pray, how else would I see it?' He paced furiously around the room.

'I thought...hoped you might be different...only—'

'And I hoped...believed you were different, madam,' he said bitterly. 'But now I see you are just like all the rest.'

'All the rest of whom?' She stared at him, apparently bewildered.

And he had convinced himself she was no actress! Hah! 'Well, I hope you learnt your lesson. So, did he weary of your charms after only a week?'

'Weary of my charms? What charms? Who are you talking about?'

Her wide-eyed look of confusion and innocence enraged him. He strode to the bed, grabbed her by the shoulders, yanked her upright and shook her in fury. 'That blasted green-eyed Irishman, of course! Do you take me for a complete fool?' He glared down at her, his rage compounded by the knowledge that he still desired her.

There was a long pause as they stared at each other, then suddenly her face flooded with dawning comprehension. Her mouth dropped open.

'You think I betrayed you...with that bandit?' she gasped.

'I know it,' he responded coldly.

They stared into each other's eyes for a long moment. Abruptly she flung her arms up, breaking his grip on her shoulders. She thrust at his chest—hard—pushing him away, and stepped back, panting, hurt, shock and anger in her eyes.

'You think I betrayed you!' She side-stepped him and marched to the other side of the room. Her hands shaking, she picked up an ornament on the shelf and stared blankly at it for a moment, her mouth working. Setting the ornament down with a snap, she turned. 'How dare you? Oh, how *dare* you say such a thing!' Her chest was heaving as she fought to control herself. 'As if I would ever, ever betray you with another man!'

She took several deep, shuddery breaths. 'Oh! I cannot believe you could think such a thing of me!' She began to pace around the room.

Magnus watched suspiciously. Was this another very good act? It didn't feel like it.

She continued her pacing, then suddenly whirled on him. 'And with that...that *bandit*! Ooh!' she raged.

'So you deny it?' he said coldly.

'Deny it? Deny it?' She snatched the ornament off the shelf and hurled it at him. He ducked, and it shattered against the wall behind him. 'No, I don't deny it—I don't have to deny anything—there is nothing to deny!' she stormed. 'I cannot believe you would even *think* such a thing.'

His eyes narrowed. 'So you did not go to meet that bandit?'

He ducked as another ornament was hurled at his head.

Magnus suddenly felt very uncertain of his ground. He'd never seen her like this before. He could not believe it was an act. The cold knot that had lodged in his chest slowly started to loosen.

'So where did you get to in those eight days?' he said slowly.

'None of your business,' she snapped.

'It is my business. I am your husband. Where you go concerns me.'

'Oh, does it indeed? And you wish me to account for every moment, do you? Well, I am sorry to disoblige you, but I will not explain my every movement to a horrid, suspicious beast who believes I am...I am...' She sniffed, and blew her nose defiantly into his handkerchief. 'Well, from now on, if you cannot find me you will just have to assume I am off cavorting with a lover, preferably some unshaven criminal.' Her voice quivered with hurt and outrage.

Magnus stared at her. He could not bring himself to believe that she was not completely and utterly genuine. She had not betrayed him. No one could be that skilled an actress. Relief swamped him. He took several steps towards her. She snatched another ornament off the shelf and held it up in an unmistakable threat.

'I believe Carlotta's late husband gave that to her on their last wedding anniversary,' he murmured mendaciously.

She glanced at it in sudden shock and guiltily bit her lip. Hesitantly she put the ornament down. He took another step towards her and she moved instantly away.

'Don't come near me, Magnus,' she warned. She was like a wary woodland creature, mistrustful, poised to run.

Magnus took a deep breath. There was no alternative. He would have to do what he had sworn he would never do. Break the rule of a lifetime.

'I thought... I was—' He dashed his hand through his hair and took another deep breath. 'I was worried about you, and then when I went to that church and found you had been there days before...' He found it hard to meet her eyes and had to force himself to look at her. 'I didn't know where you were. I only knew you weren't with me—where you belong.'

He walked over to the window and stood there, fiddling with a fringed curtain. He turned and met her eyes, his face sombre and vulnerable. 'I was...I was jealous. I was wrong. I'm sorry. Please forgive me.'

Tallie's lip quivered. Her eyes fixed him with painful intensity, searching for the truth in his face.

The moment stretched, interminably. Magnus could hear nothing but the thudding of the heart in his chest and the thin, high cry of some far-off bird soaring on the wind. He had accused her of the vilest conduct. Would she, could she forgive him? Or forget? He thought he might be able to forgive her, in similar circumstances, but doubted whether he could ever forget. Trust, once shattered, was not easily mended. Who understood that better than he?

'You were jealous?' she whispered at last.

He nodded.

'Oh, Magnus,' she cried, and flung herself into his arms.

Chapter Fifteen

After a time Magnus woke. The late afternoon sun streamed through the open shutters, spreading golden oblongs of warmth over the walls and the bed. He lay there, savouring the moment. His wife lay warm and relaxed against his chest, her body curled against him like a small, sensuous cat. He reached down and gently lifted one of her hands and examined it. Four smooth ovals, just one slightly ragged end—her little finger. He laid the ragged nail gently against his mouth.

She stirred. 'Magnus?' she said sleepily, and smiled. 'Love you.' Still with her eyes closed she turned her cheek and began planting small sleepy kisses over his chest. Magnus closed his eyes, as if in pain. It all came so easily to her. It was these times when he felt the most vulnerable and uncertain. Bed sports he understood—he was experienced, in control; he knew what to do, how to give pleasure and how to gain it.

But this...this intimacy...when affection simply poured from her, and small clumsy kisses filled him with a piercing sweetness... He felt on the edge of...what? The abyss?

It terrified him, yet filled him with a ravenous hunger.

She'd said it again. *I love you, Magnus.*

They were only words, he told himself. Women used them all the time. It seemed to come easily to them, too easily. He recalled the times she'd said it; the first time, when she'd still hardly known him, after their marriage had been consummated.

And though he'd waited for her to say it again every night since, dreading it, but waiting for the words with a hunger that had frightened him, she hadn't.

Not until she'd been about to be taken from him, by that bandit. When he'd been furious, and terrified for her safety. She had whispered it then, as she'd kissed him goodbye. *I love you, Magnus.*

And now, a third time.

Again, after a quarrel...

He still didn't know where she'd been for those eight days. The question burned into him...but he didn't want to ask. He'd become a coward, too, just like his father. But as long as she was here, with him, he could tell himself it didn't matter.

Her hands caressed him and he felt his body stir in response. Yes, he could find oblivion there, sweet oblivion. He rolled over, taking her with him, and raised himself over her pliant body. She smiled and stroked his cheek, then lifted her head and kissed him. He tasted the tender passion in her and groaned. She wriggled under him, smiling into his eyes, and thrust her body eagerly against him. Magnus needed no further prompting. He surged into her, and found his sweet oblivion.

'Signor d'Arenville, Signora Thalia, wake up!' Carlotta banged furiously on the door.

Magnus swore. 'Wait, I will be with you in a few moments.'

'No, it is urgent, *signor*, very urgent! Please, *signor*, open the door!'

Cursing, Magnus threw on a robe, stalked to the door and flung it open. 'What the devil is all this noise about, Carlotta?'

Carlotta glanced past him to where Tallie sat in bed, the downy quilt tucked around her naked body. '*Signor*, *signora*, I am so sorry to disturb you but there is news, terrible news.'

Tallie sat up straighter. 'You mean about—?'

'No, no, *signora.* Sorry, but no news about him yet.'

Magnus frowned. *Him?*

Carlotta continued. 'No, this is important news just arrived from Torino. I heard it from my—'

Magnus held up a hand. 'Let me guess. Your cousin's uncle's brother-in-law's niece's great-aunt's nephew.'

Carlotta shot him a look of blank surprise. 'No, *signor*, I heard it from my neighbour who just got back from Torino.'

Magnus rolled his eyes. Tallie giggled.

'It is war, *signor*,' Carlotta said.

'*What?*' Magnus was dumbfounded. 'War? Are you certain.'

'Very certain, *signor*. My neighbour said in Torino the streets are full of soldiers. England and France are once again at war. And we are at war, too. Napoleon's troops are all over the Piedmonte.' She glanced from him to Tallie and back again. 'You must flee at once, *signor*. The soldiers are taking foreigners for questioning.'

Magnus swore again.

'He said he passed a troop of soldiers on the road. They will be here in two hours. They are searching houses on the way. They will most certainly come here.' Carlotta added, a little shamefacedly, 'All of Susa knows of my English visitors.'

'We will leave at once,' Magnus assured her. 'You have been exceedingly good to us, Carlotta. We would not wish to cause you trouble.'

Carlotta laid an anxious hand on his arm. 'Oh, no, Signor Magnus, it is not myself I am concerned for. I would not like to see you and Signora Thalia taken by soldiers.' She glanced at Tallie, who had already slipped out of bed and was dressing quietly. 'Especially with the baby coming. You must hide in the hills until dusk. It is too dangerous to try for the coast from here—Napoleon has soldiers all over Piedmonte. And you cannot go back through France. My nephews will take you into Switzerland. It is arranged.'

She turned to leave. Magnus stopped her with a hand on her arm. '*Signora*...Carlotta,' he said. 'You are a...a queen among women.' He took her hand and, bowing, kissed it lightly.

'Oh, *signor*.' She blushed, flustered. 'One does what one can. Now, I make food for you to take. Pack only what you can carry. My nephews will you meet after dark, so that no one will see you leave.' She shrugged apologetically. 'Some of my neighbours have no honour. If they do not see, they cannot tell which way you went. Most will expect you to go south, to the coast—there are too many soldiers that way, but they do not know it.'

'We will be ready within the hour,' Magnus said.

Carlotta turned to leave, then hesitated and turned back, a tiny smile on her face. 'My neighbour said in Torino all is confusion. English ladies are fainting; the men are in panic.' She regarded Magnus and Tallie proudly. 'Not *my* English visitors.'

* * *

Less than two hours later, Magnus and Tallie were sitting on a bundle of straw in a small shed a mile or so out of town. It belonged to Carlotta's uncle. They were waiting for John Black, Monique and the nephews to meet them in the shed after dark. Then they would make their way to Switzerland. Tallie had bidden Carlotta a tearful farewell. The two women had embraced, Carlotta whispering assurances in Tallie's ear that she would keep an ear out for news of her little brother.

Tallie sat chewing a piece of straw. Magnus glanced down at her worriedly. She had said very little since they left. 'Don't worry. I won't let any harm come to you,' he said softly.

She smiled up at him. 'I know,' she said simply. 'I was not worrying about that.'

The heavy feeling came into his chest again. She was so trusting and certain... He wished he could be as certain.

'You never did find out what I was doing when I didn't come back for those eight days, did you?' she said at last.

Magnus felt as if a fist had slammed him in the chest. He didn't want to know—what the hell was she doing, deciding to confess now? He wanted to get up, to pace around the tiny shed, to change the subject. He knew from her face it was something dreadful—it had clearly been weighing on her conscience since she'd arrived back from her mysterious journey. But he'd already decided he could live with whatever she'd done—as long as she stayed with him from now on. 'No, but it doesn't matt—'

'I was looking for my brother.'

'Your brother?' he said, stunned. *Brother?* It was the last thing he'd expected. 'I never knew you had a brother.'

'Neither did I, until some years ago—well, actually, I wasn't absolutely sure of it until a few days ago.' She leaned against him and sighed, and without conscious volition he put his arm around her. Quietly, without looking at him, she told her story.

'...and I wasn't sure whether to believe the letter or not—it was so incredible—but I couldn't get it out of my mind, and so when we came here....' She told how she had found her mother's grave, and met a young priest who had not known her mother but who had recalled the story. He believed the orphan child had been given to a woman who was childless—a good woman, a true daughter of the church.

'But the woman's husband died and she went to live with her

brother, who hated the little boy. And then she died and the brother just went away and left him.' Tears sparkled on the ends of Tallie's lashes. 'Left a little boy of only seven years to fend for himself.'

Magnus pulled her into his arms and held her tight against his heart. 'The boy died?' he asked gently.

She shook her head. 'No, not that anyone knows of.' She looked at him in distress. 'Oh, Magnus, apparently there are children living wild in the mountains since the war, because no one will take them in. People are too poor to worry about somebody else's child.' She hugged him convulsively. 'It is so utterly dreadful. I wish I could do something, but now here we are, fleeing from the French and in no position to do anything. I did so much want to stay and search for my brother.' Tears ran down her cheeks and he kissed them softly away.

'We have to leave, my dear. You know that.'

She was silent.

'If not for our own safety, then for this child.' He laid his hand on her stomach and felt the now familiar surge of joy—and of terror. As far back as he could remember, from the time he was a little boy, he had always felt alone. Alone in a bleak, cold world. With only a bleak, cold future ahead of him.

But now there were two people who belonged to him, two people to care for—and to protect. He had never dreamed it could happen to him, never dreamed he would be so fortunate. And so grateful. He would protect her and her unborn child with his life. He drew her head down, laid his cheek against her hair and simply held her. His throat was full.

Half an hour later they were joined by John Black, and a few moments afterwards Monique arrived, a handsome young nephew with her. Then the rest of the nephews slipped in under cover of darkness, carrying baggage and bringing mules.

They set off in the moonlight, towards the far mountains glistening with snow.

'The captain says we shall reach England tomorrow,' announced Magnus joining his wife at the ship's rail. 'He plans to land at the nearest port—some problem with the mast, I gather.'

Tallie nodded but did not reply.

'It is a glorious night, is it not?' he said, looking out at the moon-tossed waves.

'Mmm.' His wife nodded. Magnus's arm closed protectively around her, bracing her against the slight rolling of the ship. They had made it. He had brought them to safety. But it seemed that was not enough.

'Look, there are traces of fire glittering in the water.' He pointed as he spoke.

'Yes.'

'It's caused by the movement of the ship.'

Tallie nodded again.

'Can you see the luminescent bubbles trailing in our wake?'

'Yes,' she murmured. 'Very pretty.'

Magnus tried again. 'And all the stars are out, so clear and bright. Nearly as clear as they were in the mountains...but not as close. I do not think we have ever been as close to the stars as we were in the mountains. Do you remember when you said it was as if you could truly just reach out and touch them?'

Tallie did not reply. Magnus tightened his grip around her, silently willing the return of his eager, excited bride. It was the sort of night which would have had her in raptures just a short time ago...

Tallie sighed. 'It is difficult to believe so much time has passed... Sometimes it feels like it was just a week or so, and at others...a lifetime.'

'It's just over two months,' murmured Magnus.

'But it feels like less, doesn't it?'

Magnus slipped his free hand under her cloak, laying it on the rounded curve of her belly. 'It feels like more to me.'

Tallie smiled and leaned her head against him.

'You've coped magnificently, my dear.' Magnus pulled her closer. There had been times he'd thought he'd never get her home safely.

The journey had taken much longer than anticipated, and had been much more arduous. For when they had reached the Swiss border they had discovered that Napoleon had invaded Switzerland as well. There had been no alternative but to head into Lombardy, and then east, towards the Austrian border. Numerous times they'd had to scramble off the road and hide from French soldiers.

Once over the border, they'd made their way towards Vienna. From there they had travelled to Prague, on to Dresden, and thence to Berlin. From Berlin they had headed towards the coast, and finally, at Husum, in Schleswig-Holstein, they'd managed to secure passage on the packet *Lark*, which was crowded with other fugitives—not only Englishmen and women, but others hostile to Napoleon's conquests.

They had boarded the boat with great relief, only to spend the next two anxious weeks at anchor, waiting for a favourable wind. Magnus had chafed at the delay. But now, finally, after six days and nights of sailing, England lay ahead.

'You have become a much better sailor, have you not?' Magnus was determined to cheer her. He hated to see her so low in spirits.

She shrugged. 'I suppose it has something to do with my condition.'

Magnus trailed his knuckles down her cool cheek in a gentle caress. 'Are you not enjoying this beautiful night, my dear? You are cold, perhaps? Would you like to return to your cabin?'

'No, not at all. You are right, my love—it is a lovely night,' said Tallie sadly. 'On such a night one finds it almost impossible to imagine that there is such ugliness in this world as war...'

But she knew there was, because lashed to the deck in front of her, secured in oilskin bags, were all the important papers on board—passports, regimentals, letters and dispatches. The captain of the *Lark* had ordered them secured out in the open—ready to be tossed overboard should the ship be boarded by the French. It was no idle threat, because for two days their ship had been pursued by French cruisers. On the third night the *Lark* had managed to slip away.

And so she was safe...but her little brother was still in danger. Her unknown little brother, so much more real to her now than he had been when first she had decided to search for him. *A bad, merry little boy*...alone in the mountains. She hoped there were plenty of apples for him to steal...but winter was drawing nearer.

'Oh, I do hope he will be all right.'

Magnus frowned. He knew full well who *he* was. She'd spoken of him almost every day since they had left Carlotta's, just like this—out of the blue—indicating how constantly he was in her thoughts.

He wished there was something he could do about it, but there was nothing. He'd racked his brains, over and over. It was his unexpressed opinion that the boy was probably dead, but he would rather cut off his hand than say so and distress her further. But he could not bear to see his vivacious little bride so wan, and his inability to do anything about it chafed him unbearably.

'No doubt one of Carlotta's relatives will find him,' he said bracingly. 'They do turn up in the most unexpected places.'

He inclined his head towards the couple standing at the rail near the bow of the ship. Monique and Gino—the handsome young nephew who had followed them to Switzerland and then Austria. Finally, in Berlin, he had convinced Monique to marry him.

'I hope I won't be obliged to provide homes and jobs for all of Carlotta's relatives,' Magnus murmured jokingly in her ear. 'I doubt even d'Arenville Hall is big enough for them all.'

Tallie smiled, but it was still a trifle too wistful for his liking. Damn it, he wished he could do *something*.

It was almost an anticlimax to land at the placid English town of Southwold, with its small fleet of sailing boats and its line of little bathing boxes arrayed along the beach.

They found an inn, and Magnus and Tallie entered while John Black went to hire a coach and horses. The smell of new-baked bread and roasting beef informed them dinner was almost ready. Tallie's stomach rumbled as they sat down to table in a private dining room. Magnus smiled. 'It smells very good, does it not, my dear? At last—fresh bread and good honest English beef with no fancy sauces. And plain baked potatoes and boiled vegetables.' He rubbed his hands. 'A real pleasure after all that foreign food and our recent rations of pickled pork and ship's biscuits.'

Tallie cast him a look of burning reproach. 'At least *we* always had plenty to eat. *We* were never in danger of starving.'

Magnus gritted his teeth. It was not his fault they had not been able to stay and search for her brother, blast it! And he was getting fed up with feeling guilty about it. He had his wife to protect—and her unborn child! What did she expect him to do? Take a pregnant wife on a wild-goose chase, searching for a child who'd been abandoned in the mountains God only knew how long ago! No child would have survived that. Even without the added danger of the war, it would have been an exercise in heartbreak—and he knew whose heart would break. And he was *damned* if he'd allow it!

'You cannot prevent your brother starving by starving yourself,' he said bluntly. 'And besides, you have another child to consider.'

'Oh, yes, I am well aware of that!' she retorted, suddenly angry with the way he kept trying to divert her from speaking of her brother. 'A more important child—*your* child, the heir to the great d'Arenville name. Not some poor little lost, half-foreign bastard—' She stopped, clapping her hand to her mouth, horrified by what she'd suddenly blurted out.

'A bastard?' said Magnus, frowning. 'Your brother is a bastard? He is only a half brother, then?'

'No, he is *my brother*!' she insisted angrily. 'I do not care what Mama may have done, or who his father may have been. I do not care a rush for what anyone may say—he is my brother!'

'But—'

She pushed her chair back from the table and said bitterly. 'I planned never to tell you. I knew how it would be. The noble family of d'Arenville must never be tainted with such as he.'

She glared at him. 'Oh, do not bother to deny it, Magnus, I can see from the look on your face what you think. That is why I never told you why it was so important to me to find my mother's grave, why I went off into the mountains to search for him without your permission. I knew what you would say, knew you would find some way to prevent me finding him.'

'I was not responsible for the blasted war breaking out again!'

She waved his objection away. 'I know that! But even without it you would not have taken me into the hills to search, would you?'

He met her level gaze. 'No, I probably would not have allowed my pregnant wife to drag herself around the mountains on some wild-goose chase—'

'Exactly! And if I had found him, what then?'

Magnus hesitated.

'You would have considered him an embarrassment, wouldn't you?' She nodded, as if she had read confirmation in his eyes. 'I thought as much. You would have sent him away to be hidden from the eyes of the world, wouldn't you? Farmed him out with a tenant—the more obscure and distant the better, no doubt.' She sniffed. 'And you wonder why I did not tell you.'

She seemed to have it all worked out, he thought dully.

She thumped her fist on the table. 'Well, I won't have it. Do you hear me, Magnus? As soon as this frightful war is over I will go back there myself and search until I have found him. Do you understand? And I will bring him home and we will be a family. I do love you, Magnus, but if you do not like it, you can...you can *disown* me!' She burst into tears and fled the room.

Magnus sat there, unmoving, his face stiff and hard. So that was what she thought of him, was it? That he would be so shocked by a bastard half brother...an unknown bastard half brother who meant more to her than...and that he valued his family name more than...

You can disown me. The choice she expected him to make.

Yes, her news had come as a surprise to him. What man would not be shocked? But he had said nothing...nothing to make her think...

She certainly seemed to feel she understood him well enough to predict his reaction... She'd been judge, jury and executioner.

Would he have predicted her reaction with such complete and utter certainty? Yes, he realised ruefully. His wife was nothing if not predictable. She was loyal...and loving. It was not in her to turn her back on anyone who needed her—not a bastard half brother. Not even a cold-hearted earl...

She still claimed to love him. He still found the notion terrifying...even though he had come to depend on it utterly for his happiness. Happiness. Six months ago happiness had been a foreign concept to Lord d'Arenville of d'Arenville Hall. As had love...

He loved his wife. He recognised the truth of it now. He loved her, loved Tallie, with an intensity that rocked him to his soul. And he had no way, no words with which to tell her.

The words sounded easy enough, simple enough to say.

The words came to others so easily—a lie to smooth a path, to get a diamond necklace, to flatter, to deceive. He had never been able to utter the lie before. Had never expected to wish to.

But now he loved her.

And he could not say the words.

She wouldn't believe him anyway, he decided. Not after what she had just revealed. She thought him a cold, proud man, who cared only for his family name. Her reading of his character had shocked him, hurt him... Because there was an element of truth...

She expected him to disown her bastard half brother and to force her to do the same. And six months ago, before he had met her, he might have. Six months ago he would have had every expec ation that a wife of his would no more acknowledge a foreign-born bastard half brother than walk naked down St James's Street. But that was six months ago.

A great deal had changed in six months—not the least Lord d'Arenville. Magnus drained the tankard of ale at his elbow and called for another. He knew what he had to do.

'That is d'Arenville Hall?' Tallie peered out of the coach window, looking up at the imposing edifice with some trepidation. It was enormous. A great grey building, heavy with carved, ancient stonework, glittering mullioned windows the only sign of life.

'Your future home, my lady,' murmured Magnus behind her.

Tallie blinked. She could not imagine herself as mistress of such an impressive establishment. And as for a small boy who'd been raised by Italian peasants...

'It...it's very grand,' she said at last, casting him a quick glance. He still had that...that stony look on his face. He hadn't forgiven her for her outburst yet.

He seemed deeply offended by her desire to provide a home for her brother. It upset Tallie to think of it, and she was distressed by his coldness towards her, but she had resolved not to give in to him on this. Her husband would have to learn to accept that at times she could be just as stubborn as he.

And if she couldn't go into raptures about his home she was sorry. It was very difficult to manufacture delight she didn't feel, especially difficult when he kept looking at her like that.

It was her fault, she knew. She had annoyed him with her defiance, and he was punishing her with his stiff and starchy manner. But now that they'd finally arrived at her husband's home she would have the opportunity to mend their differences. Hopefully they would share a bed once more. Their differences had a better chance of being sorted out there, in her experience...

Tallie sighed. It had been a long time... She'd had to share her ship's cabin with three other ladies. She missed him in her bed most dreadfully...missed the comfort of waking in the night, feeling his warm body beside hers, hearing his deep, even breathing. It was lonely in bed without him. And since their quarrel she felt lonelier than ever.

The coach drew up on the curved, immaculately raked gravel drive and a string of servants poured from the house and lined up.

'The butler's name is Harris and Mrs Cobb is the housekeepe
They will take their instructions from you,' said Magnus gravel
He moved solemnly forward, introducing this servant or that.
was all horribly formal, Tallie thought, as she received yet anoth
bow and curtsy. She walked into the huge marble entry hall. H
steps echoed and she shivered.

'Are you cold?' Magnus enquired with cool solicitude. 'Harri
please show Lady d'Arenville into the Brown Room. I presum
you've lit a fire?'

Harris bowed. 'Yes, of course, my lord. This way, my lady.'

Tallie was ushered to the Brown Room. It was enormous an
gloomy, for the windows were shrouded with heavy brown velv
curtains. The room was stuffed with large, ornate, heavy items
furniture. Tallie wrinkled her nose. Everything upholstered in th
same horrid dark brown. She wandered over to the fire, having
step around no fewer than three occasional tables, two embro
dered firescreens and a settee. The room was immaculately clea
but she felt stifled. She thought instantly of the little peasant co
tage in the mountains of Piedmonte and its cosy simplicity. Sh
pushed the thought out of her mind with a pang of regret. The
was no use in her worrying about her brother just now. This w
her new home and she needed to accustom herself to the fac
Besides, she had fences to mend with her husband.

A few minutes later Magnus entered, followed by Mrs Cob
the housekeeper. 'Are you warm now?' he asked. Tallie nodde

'Then Mrs Cobb will show you to your room. You will wis
to rest. I've ordered a tray sent up for your dinner,' he informe
her.

No, Tallie wanted to cry, I do not wish to rest. I want you
show me your home and introduce me to all your favourite haun
I want you to tell me stories of when you were a little boy growi
up here, so that I may learn to love this hideous mausoleum.
want things to be normal between us again.

But she could not bring herself to say it. This Magnus was n
her beloved Magnus; this was Lord d'Arenville of d'Arenvil
Hall, very cold and formal, and she did not yet know how to de
with him. Tallie followed the housekeeper dolefully. She did n
like the sound of *your room*. She hoped she had misheard Magnu
she hoped she was being taken to *our* room.

But she was not. It was clearly a woman's room, fussy ar

expensive and elegant. The chairs were tiny, dainty, with delicate twisted flutes for legs. They matched the dressing table. The windowframes and bed were painted white and draped with gold silk. Large gilt looking-glasses were on every wall and Tallie could see herself reflected no matter where she stood in the room. White fur rugs lay scattered on the floor. Tallie hated the room on sight. It had an atmosphere, a hardness she did not like. She could not feel comfortable sleeping in here.

'Whose was this room?' she asked Mrs Cobb tentatively.

'His lordship's mother's, my lady.'

'Oh,' said Tallie. Magnus had never spoken to her of his mother. Perhaps he found it too painful to talk of her. It was hard, losing someone you truly loved, and a mother was special. 'What was she like?'

Mrs Cobb pursed her lips oddly, then shook her head. 'More'n my job's worth to say, my lady, begging your pardon.'

Tallie stared at her, astonished. 'I didn't mean you to *gossip* about M—Lord d'Arenville's mother. Just to tell me what sort of a person she was.'

Mrs Cobb shrugged. 'Can't do one without doing t'other,' she said. 'Best not enquire too closely about the past. Only one Lady d'Arenville is important now—best you forget about what's gone and get on with your life, begging your pardon, my lady.' She eyed Tallie's waist shrewdly. 'I hope you don't think me impertinent, my lady, but would you be expecting an interesting event in the not too distant future?'

Tallie blushed and laid her hand on her belly. 'You mean the baby?'

Mrs Cobb beamed and nodded. 'Thought as much. Good news for d'Arenville, my lady. His lordship's pleased, I expect. May I tell the other servants?'

Tallie nodded. 'I do not see why not. They will all be able to see for themselves before too long. I am getting so fat!'

'Fat? What nonsense! Bloom about you. A joy to behold.' Mrs Cobb nodded again. 'Good news you bring us, to be sure. 'Tis too long since there was a child at d'Arenville.'

'Were you here when Magn—his lordship was a boy?' Tallie asked eagerly.

'Not really,' Mrs Cobb said. 'I've been here just over a score of years, come Michaelmas.'

Tallie frowned in puzzlement. 'Twenty years? But my husband is only nine and twenty. You must have known him as a boy.'

Mrs Cobb looked at her a moment, then shook her head. 'He were off at school years before I started here.'

Sent to school at the age of six or seven, poor little boy, Tallie thought. She touched her stomach protectively. If this child was a boy he wasn't going to be parcelled off to school at a young age like his father. 'But in the holidays—'

Mrs Cobb shook her head sorrowfully. 'He weren't often asked home in the holidays.'

Asked home? As if he were a *guest*? 'Not asked home in the holidays?' repeated Tallie, appalled. 'But why not?'

Mrs Cobb pursed her lips, shook her head, opened her mouth then closed it. After a moment she said, 'You never heard this from me, mind, but word was in servants' hall his ma couldn't abide him. And his ma's word was law to his old lordship. Despite her immoral ways.'

Tallie could hardly believe her ears. His mother hadn't been able to abide him? And so Magnus hadn't often been asked home in the holidays? She had never heard of anything so shockingly selfish and callous in her life. Oh, to be sure Tallie had spent her own childhood in a school, but that had been because her parents had been forever travelling, not because they hadn't been able to abide her. She had a packet of letters from her mother, tied with a ribbon, to prove it. But poor Magnus. Poor little boy. What sort of a woman would do that to her own child?

A horrid, cruel woman, and Tallie knew she would sleep not a wink under her vile gold silk canopies. 'I won't sleep here,' she said decisively. 'Please find me another bedchamber.'

'But his lordship said—'

'You may inform his lordship that I did not wish to sleep in his mother's old room and that I chose another.'

'But—'

'That will be all, Mrs Cobb,' said Tallie firmly, feeling bold and autocratic. She had learned a thing or two since she was insignificant Tallie Robinson, and one was how to avoid an argument—with servants, at any rate. Her husband was a different matter.

Chapter Sixteen

Tallie looked around the breakfast room in surprise. She turned to the butler. 'Has his lordship not yet come down?'

'Yes, m'lady, he broke his fast early.' Harris pulled a chair back and waited.

Tallie sat, feeling quite despondent. It was her own fault—she had stayed awake late last night, hoping he would come to her, and then overslept this morning. 'I suppose I shall see him later, then.'

Harris, in the process of serving her with scrambled eggs, hesitated. 'He had urgent business to attend to, m'lady.'

Tallie ate her eggs slowly. She had no idea what to do with herself. The previous day Magnus had made it plain that he wished her to take up the reins as mistress of this establishment. Thanks to Laetitia's habit of delegation, Tallie was not without some experience in running a household. But this house was at once bigger and much grander than anything she had ever seen before. At Manningham she'd been her cousin's dogsbody, an errand-runner rather than mistress. Here she'd be expected to know everything.

Tallie glanced around the breakfast room with a critical eye. The room had a pleasant prospect, facing east, receiving morning sunlight. And the windows would have let in plenty of sunlight, had not they, like every other window here, been shrouded in heavy drapery. It was all so gloomy.

She wondered how Magnus would respond if she asked his permission to make a few changes. In her admittedly limited experience, men didn't like changes to their homes. Her cousin's husband George had complained incessantly when Laetitia redec-orated their country home. He hadn't minded her turning the Lon-don house upside down with 'fancified nonsense', but his boyhoo home had been another matter. On the other hand, according t Mrs Cobb, Magnus had not spent much of his boyhood here a all, so...

No, Tallie decided, she'd speak to him about it at dinner. An in the meantime she'd ask Mrs Cobb for a tour of the Hall.

By the end of the day Tallie was tired and dusty, but faintl satisfied. She'd been through the pantries, the linen presses an the storerooms, and examined the house from attic to basemen Many of her tentatively offered suggestions had been roundly ap-proved by Mrs Cobb, and she now felt more confident about dis-cussing changes to the house with Magnus. It was barely half a hour until dinner, so she hurried upstairs to bathe and to chang her gown. Magnus had seen her rumpled and untidy enough times and hadn't seemed to mind, but that had been when they wer travelling. This was different. Tonight they dined at home togethe for the first time in their married life and she wanted to look he best. She had a quarrel to mend.

She hurried through her preparations and sat impatiently in fron of the looking-glass while Monique did her hair, scanning he reflection intently, hoping her looks would please Magnus.

The gown she had finally chosen was one he'd bought her i Vienna. It had become a little limp during their travels, but now in a big house with skilled laundrywomen, it looked almost a good as new. The fabric was fine and delicate. It clung to he breasts and swirled around her hips. It looked a lot like her golde Paris tea gown that Magnus had ruined so dramatically.

Her eyes misted reminiscently as she recalled how he'd swep her into his arms and ascended the stairs two by two. Could thi gown, too, cause a wondrous, utterly splendid night of passion And put an end to a distressing period of coldness.

Tallie gazed at the gown in the looking-glass. She was countin on that reaction tonight. It was the only way she could think of t break down the icy barrier that had arisen between them. Talkin would do no good, for she was determined not to give in to hin and she could not imagine him giving in to her. No, this was th only way. And maybe then he would be able to forgive her in transigence.

She fastened a string of pearls around her neck. Her breasts, lightly enlarged with pregnancy, swelled above the low-cut gown nost satisfactorily. Her skin, with a light dusting of rice-powder o disguise the dozen or so freckles, looked pale and smooth. Tallie rowned critically at her image, then tugged the neckline a little ower. She had no intention of being sent to her room tonight, lone with a supper tray, like a naughty child to contemplate her ins. No, her husband might be displeased with her defiance on he matter of her brother, but she had every intention of seducing im back into her bed. Tonight.

His urgent business, whatever it was, had kept him away from he house all day. She had imagined her first day at d'Arenville Iall—Magnus would show her around, telling her tales of this and hat as he introduced her to her new home, her arm on his, or, etter still, his arm around her. Today Mrs Cobb had shown her he house, not Magnus, but Tallie was determined Magnus would how her the rest. And then, perhaps, she would come to under-tand the man she loved—to discover the boy and learn what had nade him the man he was.

Urgent business or not. She could wait for urgent business, but he would wait *with* him, not for him. And when it was finished, he had urgent business of her own... Tugging her gown a little ower, Tallie stood up, took a deep breath and left her chamber.

The pale young princess descended the curving marble stairway lowly. Her enchanted silken gown clung to her figure, whispering oftly with every movement. Below her, a statue of a handsome, lark-haired prince awaited her, his marble features cold and un-noving, his eyes blind and unforgiving, trapped in a spell by an vil Ice-Witch. Candlelight gleamed on his frozen features.

The princess came closer. With each whisper of the magic gown, ach flicker of golden candle-flame the statue seemed to warm. he eyes flickered and darkened from a pale ice-grey to a stormy ea-dark colour. The blindness lifted from him and marble melted nto flesh. Slowly he moved towards her, first one step then an-ther, then he was leaping up the stairs towards her, two, three teps at a time. He swept the princess into his arms. 'Tallie, my learest love, forgive me my coldness. I need your warmth, your ove.' And his mouth descended on hers and the evil spell was roken...

But there was no Magnus waiting for her at the foot of the stairs. There was only Harris, the butler. Magnus must already be in the dining room. She was a little late from fussing about her appearance. He must have become impatient.

'Good evening, Harris.' Tallie smiled. 'I am looking forward to dinner. The aromas coming from the kitchen earlier were delicious and I must confess I am extremely hungry.' She hurried towards the dining room.

But when she entered, she came to a sudden, shocked halt. The long, gleaming table was set for only one person. He could not surely, still be attending to his business?

'M'lady,' murmured Harris. Hiding her anxiety, Tallie allowed him to seat her.

'Is my husband not joining me?'

A footman entered with soup, and Harris waited until she had been served and the footman had gone before answering. 'I told you this morning, m'lady. He left on urgent business.'

'But his business surely cannot last all night,' she said. 'Lord d'Arenville must eat, must he not?'

Harris looked awkward. 'M'lord left d'Arenville this morning. He did not say when he would return.'

Left d'Arenville? Tallie stared at the butler in confusion, a cold thread of dread winding around her heart. 'I assumed you meant he'd left the house.'

'No, m'lady. He left.' The butler looked at her in concern.

Left? Left for where? Tallie tried to keep her features even.

'Did you not know about it, m'lady?'

Tallie attempted a smile. 'Yes...yes, of course I did, but I did not realise he meant to leave today. I thought he was going to...to...' She felt her lips quivering and hastily touched a starched linen napkin to them to hide her distress. 'A foolish misunderstanding, that is all,' she mumbled, and lowered her head as if to say a silent grace.

Where had he gone? And for how long? All day and night, obviously. But without a word to her? She spooned up some steaming substance and conveyed it to her mouth. Her hands were shaking. She laid the spoon down with a clatter, hoping the butler hadn't noticed.

There was a short silence. She wondered whether Harris could hear her heart pounding. It sounded terribly loud to her.

After a time he cleared his throat and said, 'Lord d'Arenville left a letter for you, m'lady. Did you not receive it?'

Tallie stared. 'A letter?'

'Yes, m'lady. I shall fetch it immediately,' said Harris, sweeping from the room. He returned in a moment, bearing a sealed letter on a silver salver. He placed it beside her, hesitated, then bowed and left the room.

Heart pounding, Tallie watched him leave. Her first letter from Magnus. She broke open the wafer and began to read.

My dear Lady d'Arenville,

Lady d'Arenville. Not Tallie. Her heart sank.

You were sound asleep when I came to your room and I did not wish to disturb your rest. I know how much you need it.

Not as much as she needed him. Why could he not have woken her?

I have important business to transact and must leave for London first thing this morning. I am unsure of when I shall return, but be assured I will do so as soon as my business allows it.

London? The letter dropped from Tallie's nerveless fingers and fluttered onto the table. *Gone to London?* He had just gone off to London? Without explaining or saying goodbye? With shaking fingers she picked up the letter and continued to read, her numb brain hardly able to take it in.

You will have plenty to occupy you in settling in to the Hall and making preparations for the nursery. I noticed you did not sleep in the chamber allotted you. You have my full permission to make any changes you wish and draw on any sums you think necessary. My man of business, Jefferies, has been informed thus.

Full permission to make any changes she wanted? Draw on any sums she thought necessary? How long was he expecting to be gone to make arrangements like that? Informing his man of business?

In addition, you will need to order a new wardrobe.

Tallie glanced down at her golden tea gown. It probably was a little shabby, she reflected sadly. Despite the miracle wrought by the maids. And it was growing a trifle tight. Yes, she supposed she would need a new wardrobe...

You will not lack for either advice or masculine support during my absence, for I offered my oldest friend, Freddie Winstanley, the living at d'Arenville and he moved into the vicarage last month. You may repose complete confidence in both Freddie and his wife, ~~Joan~~ ~~Janet~~ Jenny. You will like them.

Was that an opinion of her taste in people or an order to like his friends? It was hard to know. But why was he not here to introduce her to them? How long did he plan to stay away? Tallie read the last lines with great trepidation.

I will make every effort to return before you are brought to bed of a child, but if not my thoughts will be with you. Take care, my dear.

Yr affectionate husband,

She could just make out the scrawl at the bottom—*d'Arenville.*

Tallie crushed the letter slowly to her breast and stared blankly out of the window. She had no idea how long she sat there staring, but she was vaguely aware of Harris coming in at some stage and silently removing the dish of cold soup.

He brought a plate of roast beef, fresh and hot, but she took one look at it and pushed it away. She felt sick.

I will make every effort to return before you are brought to bed of a child, but if not my thoughts will be with you.

She could think of nothing, no business, however important that ould keep him away for such a long time...

Harris took away the second untouched plate and returned with Mrs Cobb and Monique. Tallie was vaguely aware of some whisering behind her, but she could take in nothing...nothing but the act that Magnus had brought her here to d'Arenville Hall and left er the very next morning. Leaving a coldly formal letter explainng he might possibly find the time to return after his heir had een born.

He had abandoned her. The truth pounded in her brain like a ammer against an anvil, but she could not take it in...

It was as she had heard him say to Laetitia all those months go... He wanted a plain, convenient wife whom he would get with child and live in the country...

But he *couldn't* have just left her. Not Magnus. Surely he wouldn't...not without even saying goodbye...

Unless he really *had* abandoned her... He would have found it ifficult to face her, knowing what he planned...maybe too diffiult...

A new thought occurred to her. Perhaps his coldness towards er after their difference of opinion about her little brother had een feigned...or at least exaggerated. Perhaps even then he had een preparing to leave her here...alone...

She shivered, suddenly feeling very cold.

'Milady,' said Monique at her elbow. 'Are you all right?'

Tallie did not answer.

'Feeling a bit poorly, the wee mite,' said Mrs Cobb gruffly. She icked up the linen napkin and gently blotted Tallie's face with . The napkin came away damp, and Tallie stared at it, dimly uzzled. She lifted a trembling hand to her cheeks and found tears. he'd been crying without knowing it.

Shakily she stood up.

'I want to go to bed, please. I don't feel very well.'

On trembling legs Tallie approached the staircase she had oated down so hopefully only a short time before. It loomed efore her now, an almost impossible climb. Doggedly she took ne step, then another, then another.

'Tallie, my dear, forgive me for calling unannounced—'

Hurriedly Tallie sat up, surreptitiously wiping her eyes before turning to face the minister's wife, Janey Winstanley, who ha become a good friend over the last few months.

Janey stopped in midsentence. Her face crumpled with concer as she took in Tallie's woebegone face and reddened eyelids. 'Ol my dear—' she began.

Tallie interrupted. 'All these dratted changes to the house hav stirred up so much dust and I am forever catching it in my eye She rubbed her handkerchief over it, blinked carefully, and the said with a bright, false smile, 'See, it is out now. Shall I ring fc tea?'

Janey looked at her in dismay. 'My dear, you don't have t pretend with me. It is monstrous crue—'

Tallie cut her off. 'Yes, tea, I think, and shall we take it in th new Blue Room? I am anxious for your opinion.' She took he friend by the arm and led her towards the new blue salon.

Janey allowed herself to be taken, a troubled frown on her face She stood in the doorway, admiring the newly refurbished roor 'I cannot believe what a change you have wrought in this hous Tallie,' she said. 'I never did like— I mean, this house was alway very grand and impressive, but—'

Tallie smiled. 'I didn't like it much either.'

Janey smiled back. 'Forgive me, I didn't mean to be rude. Bu you've made such a difference. It is so light and...so pleasant an welcoming. How did you manage, in your condition?'

Tallie shrugged. 'It was not difficult. My husband gave me *cart blanche* to do as I wished with the house, and all I had to do wa decide what changes to make.'

Tallie made light of her achievements, a little embarrassed t receive praise for something done in a surge of anger. During th first shock of Magnus's abandonment she'd blamed the house itsel for her predicament—the house where the boy Magnus had nc been welcome, where the man Magnus could dump his unwante bride.

If he'd had a home instead of an ancient showplace Magnu might have been a different man, a man who could let himsel care, even a little, for his wife. So she'd attacked it with a ven geance, changing everything she could, forcing the past into ob scurity, removing all reminders, all echoes of his forebears. I might not ever be a home for Magnus, but she was determined i would become a home for her children. And for herself.

'I cannot believe what you have done,' added Janey.

Tallie looked at her new friend with faint trepidation. She had done what she'd set out to do—made Magnus's boyhood home unrecognisable. Men hated change. He would probably be furious with her. Good. She was utterly furious with him—she told herself so a hundred times a day so she would not forget.

'You have turned a mausoleum into a home.'

Tallie smiled politely, but she knew Janey's words were not true. The house was more pleasant, but it was not yet a home. A home needed love to warm it...and children. She felt her eyes mist and laid her hand on her stomach.

Janey's eyes followed her movement. 'It won't be long now, my dear. Do...have you had any word from your husband?'

Tallie rubbed a hand over her swollen belly and gazed out into the garden. She turned to her companion and smiled brightly, but without a great deal of conviction. 'Oh, no. But then he is extremely busy. Urgent business, you know.'

Janey snorted. 'In all these months?'

'Well, men do not enjoy writing letters, I believe. In any case, they say no news is good news,' said Tallie with a pathetic attempt at cheeriness. The two women fell silent for a while.

'I cannot believe he—' began Janey.

Tallie laid a hand on her friend's knee. 'Don't, please.' She bit her lip and Janey subsided.

'I am sorry to distress you. It is just I cannot bear to see you so unhappy.'

'Unhappy?' said Tallie tremulously. 'How could I be unhappy? I have a lovely house, a secure home, wealth to spend as I like... You forget I was little better than a pauper before I married.'

'As if that—'

'But I explained it to you before, Janey. I knew what I was doing when I married Magnus. I knew then he planned this, planned to leave me here as soon as I began increasing.'

'It is just so cruelly unjust—'

'No! It is all my own fault. It is just... I have a foolish tendency to indulge in silly, childish daydreams, and in my foolishness I read something more into Magnus's behaviour towards me, that is all. But he never said anything to make me believe he...he lo— He never lied to me. It is just...I misunderstood...he has...he has beautiful manners...that is the trouble.' Tallie pulled out a damp and crumpled handkerchief and blew noisily into it. 'This dust is shocking, is it not?' she added, blinking her lashes furiously.

There was a long pause as Tallie dabbed at her eyes. At last Janey spoke. 'You know you do not need to face this alone, my dear. I will—'

'It is very good of you, but I will not be alone, thank you, Janey. My husband said he will come, if he can. This child means a great deal to him, you know.' Tallie added wistfully, 'He needs an heir. The d'Arenvilles are a frightfully ancient family.'

Janey patted her hand. 'Well, just in case, be sure to send for me the minute you experience the slightest twinge.'

'There is plenty of time. Monique says it will be several weeks yet,' said Tallie. Poor Monique, Tallie thought. She, too, had been unlucky in love.

'Um...Freddie wrote to Magnus, you know.'

'Does *Freddie* know where he is?' Tallie turned a look of painful intensity on her friend.

Janey shook her head, regretting her impulse. 'No, he sent it to Magnus's lawyers to pass on. It was just about...about parish matters,' she lied.

'Oh.' Tallie nodded dully. 'Parish matters. Of course.'

'I must go now,' said Janey. 'Sorry I cannot spend more time—'

Tallie forced herself to brighten. 'No, no, of course you must go. I cannot keep you from your dear husband and your two lovely children. It must be wonderf— It was very good of you to visit me, Janey. I find it hard to walk far these days; my ankles swell so if I overdo it.' She levered herself out of the chair.

Janey bent to kiss her on the cheek. 'Take care, my dear,' she said, and left.

Take care, my dear. Magnus's last words; his last written instructions to her. Tallie closed her eyes. It was dreadful how shockingly weepy her condition caused her to be. It would pass soon, she told herself. That and the dull aching pain of knowing she was not loved, not valued at all, except as a brood mare.

It was her own fault, she told herself firmly. She had deceived herself. He had *never* said he loved her.

And it wasn't as if she had anything to cry about. Others had much more serious problems—her little brother, for instan— No

The thought of a small boy facing the winter alone was too distressing even to contemplate.

It was just her condition that made her feel a touch melancholy. And it wasn't as if she didn't have *hundreds* of moments of happiness to look back on...

Tallie gasped suddenly as a tiny fist or foot thumped her from within. It was a timely reminder... She should stop fretting over the past and think only of the future, for soon she would have a dear little baby to love.

The pain would pass.

Everybody said it would.

Although they were only talking about the pain of childbirth.

Chapter Seventeen

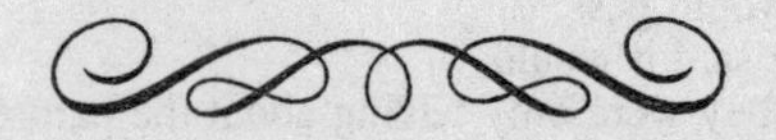

Tallie sat on the terrace enjoying the winter sunshine. She had several shawls tucked about her, for it was very cold. It would have been sensible to go inside, but she did not feel inclined to be sensible. She felt both lethargic and oddly restless.

Idly she watched a coach bowling along the road bordering the estate. She knew most of her neighbours' conveyances and she did not recognise this one. A passing stranger?

She sat up straight as it turned in at the gateway. Miles Fairbrother, the gatekeeper, came out to speak to the driver. Then he opened the gate and the coach drove through. Whoever it was must have legitimate business, for Miles did not grant entry lightly.

For one terrifying, ecstatic moment it occurred to Tallie that it might be Magnus, returning for the birth of the child, but this coach was plainly not her husband's. It was small, outmoded and shabby, and the horses were not at all the sort of cattle her husband would own. The horses seemed tired. Whoever it was had travelled a long way.

Tallie pushed herself out of her chair and walked around the house towards the front. Harris had also seen the visitors, for the front door was wide open and he stood there, waiting.

'Do you know who it can be?' she asked him.

'No, m'lady. I've never seen that coach before. I hope Fairbrother knows what he's doing. Would you care to wait inside the house, m'lady?'

'No. I know it is not the thing for me to wait here like this, but I'm curious,' answered Tallie. 'I'm sure it will be all right.'

The coach came rapidly up the drive and halted. The driver, an unshaven ruffian in a frieze coat and red muffler, climbed down. Tallie frowned. He reminded her of Gino, but he turned to let down the coach steps and she could see his face no longer.

Tallie stood watching. A frisson of tension passed through her and a hand crept to her throat. A tall man stepped down from the shabby coach, a tall, weary-looking man, with overlong dark hair and—she knew without seeing them—grey eyes.

'Magnus!' She hurried down the steps and ran awkwardly towards him, then recalled herself and stopped short, hesitating, suddenly afraid. By the very manner of his leaving he had made it abundantly clear he did not want her love. So how was she to respond to his return? All she wanted was to be in his arms. But what did he want?

He took several steps towards her, then stopped and stared.

Tallie ran a hand self-consciously over her stomach, but she did not take her eyes off Magnus. His skin was uncharacteristically bronzed, but under that he looked exhausted. He had not shaved in several days and his eyes had dark shadows beneath them. His face was thinner, too, almost gaunt. A tattered greatcoat was draped around his shoulders. He lifted a hand in an awkward, half-hearted greeting, and the coat slipped from his shoulders. His arm was in some sort of sling, she realised.

'Magnus, you are hurt,' she cried, and hurried across the gravel towards him, her misgivings forgotten in her concern. But just as she was about to reach him he turned away from her. She stopped, unbearably wounded.

He said something she didn't catch to a person inside the coach. Tallie waited, struggling for composure. He had brought a guest.

A small figure scrambled out of the coach and stood behind Magnus, as if hiding. The coach rumbled away, leaving the three of them standing on the gravel drive. Magnus reached behind him to pull the small person out, but he or she resisted.

Magnus said something. In Italian.

Italian? Tallie's heart was in her mouth.

A thin, sharp, not very clean little face peered out at her, frowning, then ducked back behind Magnus. Tallie could hardly breathe. The face peered out at her again, examining her intently. Tallie didn't move. After a moment he stepped out, a skinny little boy, dressed in clothes too big for him. A boy with ragged, curly, light brown hair, streaked with sun. A boy with a scattering of freckles over the bridge of his nose. A boy about seven years old.

'My dear,' said Magnus, 'I have brought you your brother. Richard, this is your sister.'

'No Richard—*Ricardo*,' the little boy muttered fiercely, but he did not take his wary brown eyes off Tallie.

'Of course, Ricardo,' said Tallie, smiling through her tears. She held out her arms. The boy looked up at Magnus, who nodded. The child shrank back a little. Magnus gave him a gentle push towards Tallie. The little boy came towards her slowly, suspiciously, glancing frequently back at Magnus, as if fearing he would disappear. Magnus nodded encouragingly. The child allowed himself to be embraced, standing rigid in her arms for a moment or two, like a small, stiff block of wood. It seemed to Tallie she could feel almost every bone in his body, even through the layers of ill-fitting clothing. Poor little lad. As soon as she loosened her hold he wriggled out of it and scurried back towards Magnus, gripping Magnus's sleeve firmly in his grubby little hand. It was plain her little brother trusted only one person.

Magnus laid a gentle hand on the child's shoulder. 'He has had a hard time of it, my dear,' he said softly. 'You must not take it to heart.'

Tallie shook her head, smiling, her heart too full to speak. Tears streamed down her cheeks, but they were tears of joy, not sorrow.

Magnus, his intense gaze boring into her, stepped forward, took out a large handkerchief and carefully dried her face, cupping her chin in a large warm hand. She stood motionless, drinking in the beloved Magnus smell of him, the tender motion of his hands on her skin, his warm, ragged breath on her face. She had yearned for this so often during the last months she was almost afraid it was yet another dream.

Shakily she lifted a hand to his thin, lined cheek and traced the long groove that bisected it. Whiskers rasped beneath her fingers. He was real. Magnus had come back to her.

'Oh, Magnus,' she whispered tremulously, and lifted her face blindly up to his. With a hoarse groan he drew her against him and lowered his mouth to hers.

He kissed her hungrily, as if unable to get enough of her, his tongue moving ravenously, possessively, slaking a desperate need, arousing desperate desires. He pressed burning kisses on her mouth, her nose, her throat, her wet eyelids, her mouth again, holding her hard against him, smoothing her body against his, remembering, reclaiming.

She kissed him back fervently, feverishly, with equal passion, burning away the lost months of loneliness, the anger, the distress and the fear. She only knew he was here, with her, and that the part of her that had wanted to die was vibrantly, joyously alive. Her arms clasped him around the neck, pulling him closer, and she pressed herself against him, hard. She ran one hand through his long thick hair, glorying in the cool texture of it and the bony, beloved shape of his skull. She slipped her other hand into the opening of his shirt, longing to feel his skin against hers once more. There was a sharp thud.

'What was that?' Magnus pulled back suddenly and looked at her, shocked.

Tallie smiled mistily. She took his hand and laid it gently on her stomach. 'That was your son.'

He stared at her, then jumped as he felt another little kick. His eyes fixed on the swell under his hand for a long moment, then his eyes met hers in a look of dazed wonder. The baby kicked again, and again Magnus started.

'Does it happen often?' he whispered.

Tallie nodded.

Magnus blinked. 'Does it hurt?'

She shook her head. 'Not at all.'

'Oh, Lord,' he groaned, and drew her into his arms again and buried his face in her hair. They stood there a long time in silence, feeling the baby kick occasionally.

After a few minutes Tallie felt a movement at her elbow. She glanced down. A small grubby face scowled up at her, then tentatively pushed closer to Magnus. Gently she reached down to draw him in to their embrace. His body was stiff and resistant, like a wild animal, and he gripped hold of Magnus's shirt possessively. Gently she touched his hair. She felt him flinch, but he didn't move away.

She started to stroke the tangled honey-coloured curls, so like her own, and he let her, still poised like a wary creature, to flee or to fight. She continued stroking his hair, lightly at first, then more confidently as she felt him start to relax. It was the last thing she would have expected to do with her brother, tame him like a little wildcat. Her heart bled at the thought of the life he must have led, the life which made him so wary and mistrustful.

After a time she felt him thrust himself between her and Magnus and she dropped her hand away in disappointment. It would take time for her to earn his trust, she told herself. He turned his head to glare at her again, then looked away. Slowly, without looking at her, he reached down and took her hand, then placed it back on his head. Tallie felt a surge of joy as she began stroking him again, and she felt him lean imperceptibly into her caress. He was hungry for love, she realised.

He was not the only one.

She looked up at her husband and saw with amazement a sheen of tears in his sea-grey eyes as he gazed at her.

'Shall we go inside?' he said huskily.

She nodded, her heart once again too full for words.

She moved to step away, but he pulled her back, his good arm holding her hard against his side. A small bony body burrowed defiantly between them and Magnus smiled and loosened his hold on her, making room for the little boy. 'I see I'm going to have to learn to share you,' he murmured.

Tallie smiled tremulously back. 'Me, too,' she said, and then, with not a sliver of the dying evening light showing between their bodies, the little family moved slowly towards the house.

'Gino and I took a shorter version of the route we left by,' said Magnus, sipping a glass of burgundy with pleasure. 'Into Holland, then Westphalia and so on, travelling overland, mainly by night.'

Tallie listened in silence, her eyes wide. Travelling across miles and miles of enemy territory in the middle of a war, and by night.

It sounded terribly dangerous, yet he spoke of his journey as if it were nothing. 'Have some more roast beef,' she urged him.

His eyes travelled to Tallie's brother, who was ploughing happily through a second plate heaped with food. He smiled. 'I think young Richard is proving himself the better trencherman here.'

The boy looked up frowning, his mouth full. 'No Richard—*Ricardo!*'

Magnus shook his head. 'He will soon accustom himself to his English name.'

'Ricardo,' came a mutter from the other side of the table.

Tallie intervened. 'And then where did you go?'

'Back through Venice and thence to Piedmonte. Carlotta sends her love, by the way.'

Tallie smiled and nodded, but she was not going to be sidetracked. 'Wasn't it terribly dangerous to travel all that way?'

Magnus shrugged. 'Oh, we ran into a French patrol here and there, but honestly, my dear, if you'd seen them—more than half of Napoleon's recruits are beardless boys, dragged off their farms. And the officers are not gentlemen, as ours are. I was in no great danger.'

He was lying, thought Tallie. She had heard Freddie discussing the war. There might be a lot of young lads in Napoleon's army, but there were also a lot of strong men. And if his officers were not gently born, it seemed to her they would be even rougher with an Englishman caught in the wrong place.

'It took some time, but in the end I found him—and half a dozen other young orphans.' He darted an odd look at her. 'You'll never believe who was keeping an eye on them, making sure the children didn't starve. That bandit fellow.'

'Maguire?' Tallie was astounded. And intrigued.

Magnus nodded. 'Hard to believe, but it's true. In fact he brought me to the little chap...after he'd bound my wound up.'

'*Maguire* bound your wound?' Tallie squeaked. Then she frowned in dire suspicion. 'He didn't cause it, did he?'

Magnus shook his head, smiling. 'No, it was a French bullet. The bandit dragged me to safety.'

'Oh, I knew he was a noble fellow!' Tallie clasped her hands in thankfulness.

'Odd you should say that,' Magnus drawled. 'He claims to be Irish nobility—well, they all say that, of course. But still, he's got a look about him. I sent him back to Ireland.'

Tallie sat up, alarmed. 'But won't they hang him? He said—'

Magnus snorted. 'I'd like to see them try! No, I've appointed him manager of my Irish properties—for his lifetime.'

Tallie's jaw dropped.

'Fellow might be a damned blackguard, but he's got a good heart,' said Magnus gruffly. 'Those children would have perished without him. And he did save my life.'

'Yes, of course, and I think it's a wonderful idea,' exclaimed Tallie warmly. 'And what did you do with the other children?'

Magnus regarded her oddly a moment. Naturally his wife would expect him to take care of any other orphans he came across. 'They are in the very best of care.'

'With whom? Maguire?'

Magnus grinned. It had been a tempting thought, to saddle the green-eyed rogue with a pack of children, but he hadn't done it. 'No, I thought they were better off in the care of a good woman.'

'What good woman?'

'Guess.'

Tallie thought for a moment. 'Carlotta! Of course! What a splendid idea, Magnus.'

He nodded. 'I left her with five hungry little urchins, cooking up an enormous batch of pasta and mothering them to her heart's content. I settled money on her, of course, to help with the cost, although she was damned stiff-necked about it.'

Tallie regarded her husband in amazement. She could still hardly believe it; not only had her husband *not* abandoned her, he had risked his life a hundred times over, so that she could be united with her brother. Her bastard, half-foreign brother... *And* he'd given a childless widow five needy children to care for. He'd even removed Maguire from his life of crime and given him a position of respect in his homeland.

The very contemplation of his noble deeds threatened to overwhelm her. She watched the small boy as he mopped up gravy with a piece of bread, then lifted the plate to lick it clean. Out of the corner of her eye she saw Magnus frown and open his mouth.

She laid her hand on his arm. 'There is plenty of time to teach him his manners.' Magnus relaxed.

The door flew open and Harris entered, carrying a trifle—a staggering confection of cake and cream and jelly that had young Richard-Ricardo's eyes popping. The very thing to appeal to a young boy, thought Tallie delightedly, making a mental note to thank Cook for her thoughtfulness later.

'M'lord's favourite,' Harris announced. 'Cook prepared it especially.'

Tallie glanced at her husband. He looked almost as pleased as Ricardo, though he was trying not to show it. She hid a smile. All these months and she hadn't realised he had a secret sweet tooth.

There was a long break in the conversation as the trifle was treated with the respect it deserved. Tallie, whose own sweet tooth had disappeared during her pregnancy, watched her husband and her brother attack the towering confection with gusto. She was hard put to it to decide which one of them enjoyed it the most, but she could see which of the two had never tasted trifle before.

Her little brother was still dressed in his ill-fitting clothes. There would be time enough tomorrow to find more suitable attire. But he looked a great deal cleaner in the face and the hands, at any rate. Tallie smiled as she observed the ecstatic expression that passed over the thin, vivid face with each sweet, gooey mouthful.

He looked so much like her, she mused. There could be no doubt in the world that they were brother and sister. It was an utterly wonderful thought—people would look at them and know they belonged to each other. But it was such a peculiar feeling, to be looking across a table at someone and seeing a miniature version of oneself. The same curly hair in a dozen tawny shades. The same freckled, pointy nose—only his didn't turn up, like hers. And the same eyes. *The same eyes!* The thought hit Tallie like a bombshell. *Ricardo and she had the same eyes.* And she had Papa's eyes. And Papa's curly streaky hair. And Papa's nose. And so did Ricardo.

Ricardo was Papa's son!

Papa had been wrong. Her brother was her true brother. He wasn't a bastard. Relief and joy poured into her. Bastardy would have made no difference to her, nor, apparently to Magnus, but it was a huge handicap in the eyes of the world. It would have affected his acceptance in society, his chance of making a good marriage, of making his way in the world. Her little brother had had a difficult enough beginning; she was glad, so very glad, the rest of his life would not be so hard.

She could not keep the wonderful news to herself. 'Magnus!' she said in a low, excited voice.

He turned to her.

'Ricardo looks exactly like me, does he not?'

Magnus glanced from the boy back to her, and nodded. 'But you are prettier.'

She blushed with pleasure. 'Thank you, but that is not the point. I am held to be the image of my father!'

He made the connection instantly. 'So your father was wrong. Delighted to hear it.' He reached out and lifted her hand to kiss it. 'Excellent news for all concern—' He broke off with an oath, staring at her hand.

'Why the devil have you been chewing at your nails again?'

Tallie flushed with embarrassment. She tried to tug her hand from his grip. 'I'm sorry.'

His eyes scanned her face intently. 'Has something been upsetting you? Or someone? Tell me instantly and I will see to the matter.'

Tallie blinked and stared at him in disbelief.

'Tell me at once, Tallie. There is no point in hiding it.' He brandished her ragged nails in her face and ran his thumb over them. 'These are testament enough. If someone has been upsetting you I intend to get the matter sorted out immediately. I do not like you to be upset. Did you not speak to Freddie about it—surely he could have sorted the matter out for you?'

Tallie tugged on her hand, feeling no small degree of irritation. Who did the stupid man *think* had upset her—the cook or the butler? Did he think he could just disappear from her life with a cold, horrid formal note and *not* upset her? She wrenched her hand from his and stood up.

'It is time to get that boy into a proper bath and then to bed,' she said.

'Do not change the subject, wife,' growled Magnus in a low voice.

'There is a time and place for everything,' she retorted, 'and this is neither. Now, Harris, could you arrange hot water for his lordship, and also for young Master Ricardo's bath?'

Ricardo looked up, grinning, recognising nothing in the speech except his name. *'Si, Ricardo.'* He gave Magnus a triumphant look. 'No Richard,' he repeated, and allowed Tallie to take him by the hand and lead him from the room.

'He is asleep.' Magnus stood at the doorway of Tallie's bedchamber.

Tallie nodded. 'Good,' she whispered. *And you?* she thought. *Where are you going to sleep?*

'You were right; the puppy did the trick. They're both tucked up in bed together.'

Tallie nodded again.

'Good idea that.' He stood in the doorway, staring at her, the burning heat of his gaze at odds with the casual diffidence of his voice. 'Um...I like what you've done to this room.'

Tallie nodded again. There was a lump in her throat, making it difficult to talk. Chit-chat, like one had with a guest or a stranger, not a husband.

'Like a garden in the bottom of the sea,' he said. 'Very light and airy, all that green...muslin, is it? Nice.' He gestured to the gauzy window drapes and then to the curtains surrounding her bed. He strode across the room and caught a bunch of the fine soft fabric in a fist. He stood there, running it through his fingers for a moment, and then said diffidently, 'I thought to sleep in here with you tonight. Do you mind?'

Tallie stared at her husband. *Did she mind?* Was the man totally blind to her feelings for him? She supposed she had not been as blatant as she'd thought. But how often did one need to tell a man you loved him before he took notice?

'I mean—' he said awkwardly. 'Er...I know we can't... You can't... Oh, Hell!' He dashed his hands through his hair and said in a rush, 'I know we cannot make love, but if you do not mind, I want very much to hold you tonight.'

If I do not mind? She couldn't answer, just shook her head dumbly and held out her arms to him. He reached her in two strides and pulled her into his arms. His mouth came down on hers...tenderness...leashed hunger...possession.

After a while he lifted her onto the bed and sat down. He sat there looking at her, devouring her with his eyes. He reached up to smooth her tumbled curls away from her face, delicately, clumsily, his big hands trembling slightly.

'There were times when I thought I would never do this again, never see—' His voice cracked and he pulled her tight against his chest.

'Me, too,' she whispered, rubbing her face against his freshly shaven chin.

He pulled his head back and stared at her in surprise. 'You thought *you'd* never see me again? But you didn't know where I was.'

'No, I didn't.'

'Then how—?' He frowned. 'Why on earth would you think I wouldn't return? You weren't to know I'd gone back to Italy, that I was behind enemy lines. I distinctly told you I'd gone to London on business.'

Tallie scanned his puzzled face in utter disbelief. 'I *know* what you told me,' she said, unable to disguise the edge in her voice. She knew his horrid letter off by heart.

'So then...?'

She stared at him. He seemed genuinely confused.

Magnus stared back at her. 'You sound upset.'

'Of course I am upset!' she snapped. 'How did you expect me to feel when I got that letter?'

'I didn't want to worry you, so—'

'Didn't want to worry me! Didn't want to *worry* me!' Her voice rose in indignation. 'You great mutton-headed man! You dumped me here like an unwanted cat and slipped away in the night like a criminal, leaving me a note that said you had important business elsewhere and that I was to get on with my life! How did you expect me to feel?'

Magnus's mouth gaped open. A frown furrowed his brow. 'But it wasn't like that at all,' he said slowly.

'It was *exactly* like that!' Tears quivered on her eyelashes and she groped for a handkerchief. 'Oh, drat it. This always happens,' she mumbled, and reached for one of the muslin bed curtains to dry her eyes.

He lifted her trembling hands from her face, holding them gently in his, and gazed into her swimming eyes. 'You thought I had abandoned you?' he said slowly.

Tallie nodded.

'That I didn't care?'

She nodded again.

His grip shifted and he lifted her hands, the ragged nails showing stark and ugly between his fingers. 'Then these...' he stroked them with his large tanned thumbs '...are all my fault.'

Tallie said nothing. She bit on her lip.

'Oh, God,' Magnus groaned. 'I never dreamed you would take it like that.'

'What did you expect?' she whispered. 'I told you I loved you.'

'But—'

'But what?

'Women say that sort of thing all the time,' Magnus said after a moment. 'I was not sure you really meant it.'

Tallie closed her eyes, unbearably hurt. After a time she managed to say, 'Well, I did. I'm sorry if you don't—'

'Hush!' he murmured, and drew her into his arms. A long silence passed with only the sound of two heartbeats to fill it.

'I have heard more "I love you"s than I care to remember. Starting with my mother,' he began in a low, roughened voice.

Tallie drew back a little, regarding him with heavy eyes. 'But I thought—'

Magnus gave a hard little laugh. 'Only in company, of course. Then she pretended to dote on me. As for the rest... She couldn't bear the sight of me.'

'But why?'

'God knows. I started by ruining her figure; I remember that accusation.' He shrugged carelessly, but Tallie could sense the ancient wounds in him. They had cut very deep. She stroked his cheek.

'Oh, it's all water under the bridge now,' he said, 'but I suppose it made me hesitate to...to trust a woman. I have known a numbe of women,' he continued. 'Birds of paradise, cyprians, that sort o thing. Each one told me they loved me.' He shrugged. 'Alway when they wanted something—a bauble of some sort, usually.. Although sometimes it was because they had betrayed me an were trying to placate me with their lies...'

Tallie continued stroking his cheek, loving the faint rasp o whiskers beneath her skin. He was telling her he could never lov her. She could deal with that, she thought sadly, as long as h continued to hold her, as long as he let her love him.

'And then I married you,' he said softly, and his voice changed 'I hadn't planned to. I'd planned to ask one of Laetitia's girls.'

'Why did you change your mind?' whispered Tallie, wonderin if he'd tell her the truth, as she'd overheard him tell Laetitia tha night in the library.

'I think it was the puppy.'

Tallie pulled away to stare at him. 'The *puppy*?' She fe vaguely offended.

He drew her back into his arms and tucked her head under hi chin. 'I saw a small boy whose puppy had got them both int trouble. The puppy was to be destroyed as a punishment for th child's disobedience.'

Tallie sighed, remembering.

'I knew exactly what it was like to be that little boy. My fathe destroyed a number of my own pets for the same reason—in ou family it is called "making a man of the boy",' he added bitterly 'I watched that boy, knowing grief was inevitable.'

He hugged her tighter and rubbed his jaw against her hair. 'An then out from nowhere sprang a young lioness to defend the cub a lioness who risked her own insecure position in the househol to save a boy-cub who was not even her own.' He planted a kis on her ear. 'She even saved the puppy...'

Tallie lay against his chest, her eyes wet once again at th thought of the boy Magnus and how little he had known of lov and joy.

'I wanted that young lioness for my own children,' he said a last. 'I knew it was too late for me, but my children would grov ıp knowing what it was like to be...to be...' His voice shattered nto dry splinters.

'To be loved, Magnus. *Loved.*'

He nodded, overcome.

'And they will be, I promise you,' Tallie whispered, placing oth their hands on her belly. 'This one already is.' She cupped is face with her hands. 'And so are you, Magnus. It isn't too late or you at all. I love you.'

She gazed into his tormented eyes and said softly, 'I love you o much, you have no idea. You are everything I've ever dreamed f, you know.' She smoothed his hair and said again, 'I *love* you, Magnus. Even when I was so hurt when you left, and so angry vith you, I still loved you. I think I will always love you. It doesn't natter if you don't love me back; I've enough love for both of s.'

'But—'

'Hush, it doesn't matter,' she said, and kissed him.

He kissed her back, ravenously, but after a moment he drew ack with a groan. 'But it does matter—'

'No—'

'Let me finish,' he said, kissing her again, a brief, hard kiss. ...I never expected marriage to be like this... I thought...I ought I could just pick a suitable woman and continue my life, lmost unchanged. It was the children I was thinking of.'

'An heir.' She nodded.

'No, *not* an heir. Children. If we only had one little girl, I would e happy. If we had a string of little girls I would be just as happy.'

'Do...do you not want a boy, then?' she asked worriedly.

'A boy would make me very happy, too,' he assured her. 'A oy, not an heir. I want a *child*. The sex is immaterial.'

She smiled, not entirely sure she understood, but reassured just e same.

'My father had me thrashed every morning from the age of five,' e said bluntly. 'It was the time-honoured way to ensure the heirs f d'Arenville became strong enough for the position.'

'But that is appalling,' she gasped. 'In that case I am glad you ere sent away to school so young. Such a thing is utterly bar-arous.'

He smiled, a smile of cold reminiscence that made Tallie shudder. 'Oh, he had me thrashed at school, too. Every morning at eight o'clock sharp, except for Sundays. Until my eighteenth birthday.'

'Oh, Magnus, that is...' Words failed her. She could only hug him tight and press kisses on whatever part of him she could find.

'You understand now why I do not want a d'Arenville heir?'

Tallie hugged him tighter and kissed his ear. 'I love you, Magnus, I love you,' was all she could think of to say.

He rolled her back on the bed and kissed her, covering her face, her neck, her breast with his kisses. He cupped her breasts gently. 'They are bigger,' he murmured, lavishing kisses on them. He ran a hand down to caress her swollen belly. 'I want to see you—all of you.'

Tallie blushed. 'But I look—'

'You look beautiful, and I want to see you,' he repeated, and reached for the hem of her nightgown. Slowly he drew it up, over the long slender legs, up to the thatch of tawny curls at their junction and up over the smooth, tight mound of her belly. He lifted it over the creamy swelling breasts and over the tumbled honey-streaked curls. He tossed the gown to the foot of the bed and knelt above her. And then he just stared, his eyes moving over her, absorbing every change, every nuance of her body.

Tallie's embarrassment died away.

His storm-dark eyes caressed her, bathing her in a warm radiance. She had never felt so beautiful in her life. Obscure little Tallie Robinson, plain and ordinary, swollen and ungainly with pregnancy, feeling so utterly beautiful when this man looked at her.

'I love you, Magnus,' she said softly, reaching for him.

'I wish I had been here to see all these changes,' he murmured, stroking her body, learning it anew.

'Thank you for bringing me my brother.' She arched against his hand like a cat. 'I don't think I said it before. I don't understand why you wanted to, but it has made me very happy.'

His hand stilled. 'I had to.' His voice was husky and deep.

'Had to? But why?' She reached up and began to undo his shirt.

'To...to show you.'

'Show me what?' Her hands finally undid his shirt and she eached for the buttons on his pantaloons. His hand stopped her.

'Don't you see?' He gripped her hands tightly. 'I couldn't *say* t—the words mean...meant nothing to me. I couldn't say it, so I ad to...to show you.'

'Show me what?' she said softly.

'That I—' He stopped. 'Damn it, you know what I am trying o tell you.'

She shook her head gently. 'No, Magnus, I don't know.'

'That I... I... Oh, curse it, that I love you, of course!' he said ruffly.

Tallie scrambled up on the bed and knelt facing him. 'Oh, Magus! Oh, Magnus!' And she flung herself into his arms.

After some time he said, 'I know we cannot make love at this tage of your confinement, but...do you think...? I want to touch ou here.' His hand cupped the curly thatch at the base of her tomach.

Tallie blushed and shook her head happily. 'I'm sure it will be ll right...if you want to.'

His eyes darkened into the brooding sea-grey darkness she had ever thought to see again. 'I do want to.' He lowered his head o the curls.

Tallie's jaw dropped. 'Magnus, what are you—?' She gasped. hen she gasped again. Then she gave a little wriggle, an ecstatic ttle wriggle. 'Ohhh...Magnus...'

Epilogue

A lady sits gazing out over the rolling fields of green to the dee dark woods beyond. Her smooth, pale unfreckled brow is wrinkle with worry...nay, more than worry; it is fear she feels, fear f her loved ones. For in that dark and dangerous forest lurk a hu dred unknown hazards—raging torrents, fierce beasts and dreadf monsters. And her loved ones are there, on a Quest. All for th sake of her unworthy self. The Lady hangs her head.

A faint, plaintive cry causes her to raise her head like a startle doe. She lays a hand on the innocent babe slumb'ring at her elbo and whispers, 'Fear not, my darling. Our brave and galla knights will return unharmed from their Quest, I am sure of it.

'My Knight has been on a Quest before, you know—a terribl long, dangerous Quest—with danger at every turn—bold, gree eyed banditti, *ungentlemanly enemy soldiers and slavering wolve But my Knight returned, triumphant and unharmed, or only a litt harmed—just a flesh wound which healed very quickly. And h was most dreadfully thin and gaunt...but still, he was unharme so, you see, you need not fear for him, my precious, for he strong and brave.'*

The baby gurgles again and the Lady bends to her. 'It was th most wonderful Quest in the world, you see, for he did it to w his Lady. Only the Lady was already his, heart and soul.

'But his Quest was for you as well, my darling, did you kno that? For do you know what my Brave and Gallant Knight broug back from the wilds of the terrible Alps? He brought our own litt

night, your uncle Ricardo, rescued him from Durance Vile. ʼasn't that a wonderful Quest to make—better than finding a silly ld Grail, don't you agree?'

The Lady turns her head and stares at the darkening woods. It getting very late and she wishes her Knight would return from is latest Quest soon. And when he does he will stride up to her n his long, handsome legs and bend over her and kiss her, saying, Oh, my beloved one, I have returned to you. Tallie, my dearest ve...'

'Tallie, we're back, sweetheart,' said Magnus. 'Were you sleep?'

'No, I—'

'Look, Tallie, I catch you three enormous fish—three!' Ricardo outed excitedly. 'And this one on the very first cast. Magnus ever catch not even one. Me—I catch everything! All by myself. ook!' He brandished three large, glistening, very dead fish in her ce. Their eyes stared glassily at her, their innards gaped hol-wly.

Tallie shuddered. 'How absolutely clever of you, Ricardo. Now ke them around to Cook at once.'

'Cook!' exclaimed Ricardo scornfully. 'Cook does not know ow to cook Carlotta's fish stew! Cook just boil fish in salt water d call it cooking.' He snorted with fine Italian contempt. 'Gino, has garlic and herbs and oil and wine—Gino will make it just ow you remember it—only better, he says.'

Tallie nodded, wishing she had never mentioned how she would ve to taste Carlotta's fish stew just once more. 'Then take it vay to Gino at once, my love, I beg of you, or you will be ipping water on your little niece.'

'She doesn't mind, do you, *cara*?' said Ricardo, pushing aside agnus, who was tickling the baby's chin. 'You named her after e water, no? Little Marina, the water baby.' He bent over the by and whispered to her in Italian, then announced, 'I will teach r to fish and swim next year, when she is older.'

'Oh, but—' began Tallie.

'Whatever you like, Richard, but take those fish to Gino now!' terrupted Magnus.

'Not Richard—Ricardo,' retorted Ricardo automatically, and

grinned at Magnus cheekily. But he took the fish off, whistlin
In the six months since he had been in England he had become
new boy, filling out and shooting up like a healthy young wee
And without a trace of the fear and suspicion he had brought wi
him. Tallie watched him go, her heart full. His adoptive moth
must have loved him, too, or he would not have recovered s
quickly from his ordeals. He was her bad, merry boy again.

'I should have fed that boy to the wolves when I had th
chance,' said Magnus gruffly.

'Oh, no, how can you say it?' said Tallie reproachfully. 'Wh
has he done to annoy you now? Oh, I cannot like his plan to tea
Marina how to swim—it is not at all proper for a little girl—but—

Magnus covered her mouth with his own. 'He kept me fro
doing this,' he said, and kissed her again. He lifted her out of h
seat and sat down again, with her resting in his lap. 'I come hon
from a day's fishing with a chattering bagpipe of a boy and fi
my beautiful wife dreaming in the sunshine. What were yo
dreaming of, my love?'

Tallie smiled blissfully at him. 'Of my brave and gallant Knigh
of course.'

Magnus sat up straight, almost tipping her from his lap. 'Wh
knight?' he said ominously. 'I didn't know you knew any knigh
Who the devil is this blasted knight?'

'My very own Sir Galahad,' she said softly, caressing his chee
'A dear, brave, wonderful, occasionally mutton-headed Knight
sometimes call him Magnus.' She lifted her mouth and he d
voured it in a way that sent shivers of delight through her bod
The hunger was never far away for either of them.

'I've got news for you, my love,' said Magnus after a time.
may come as a shock to you.' His voice was deadly serious.

'What is it?' She scanned his face anxiously.

'I'm not your Knight, you know.'

'Yes, you are my Knight,' she reassured him.

'I am not,' he growled, his grey eyes dancing wickedly. 'I'
your Earl.' And he planted his mouth on hers.

* * * * *